DESTINATION HOPE

SEPARATION

DESTINATION HOPE

SEPARATION

Charles J. Patricoff

CHARLES J. PATRICOFF

A Division of WINEPRESS PUBLISHING

TABLE OF CONTENTS

ACKNOWLEDGMENTS

To complete a project of this scope requires the help of a team. I must thank many faithful friends, prayer partners, and family members who sacrificed their time, talents, and energy to help bring this story to life.

I want to thank: Nettie and Todd Groat, Kathy Henry, Patrisa McHone, Kelley O'Brian, Mike and Linda McCracken, Jan Fallon, Kathryn Mackel, Kathleen Schulz, and Jim and Joyce Beckett. These wonderful people believed in the project; provided comments, feedback, and recommendations; helped craft the story and develop characters; uncovered inconsistencies and over used words or phrases; challenged word choice and usage; breathed new life into the story; improved its pace and flow; and made it easier to read before I turned this work over to the professionals at WinePress Publishing.

I give a special thanks to my wife, Mary, who believed in me and stuck by my side as I dragged her from battlefield to battlefield and populated our home with one Civil War text after another. She caught the vision for this story and helped me put a voice to my personal cry for liberty.

And finally, I am eternally grateful to Jesus. He accomplished a great revival affecting both sides of the bloody Civil War to create a new nation under God. I am thankful that the evidence of His divine intervention was recorded for our inspiration today.

I dedicate this work to my dad, Jack H. Patricoff, who gave me *The American Heritage Picture History of The Civil War* (American Heritage Publishing Co. Inc., 1960) for my tenth birthday and imparted to me his admiration for Abraham Lincoln. His gifts started my forty-year journey to find an answer to the question—why must so many die to set the captive free?

PLAYERS IN THIS NATIONAL TRAGEDY

Northern Soldiers: They represent the United States of America (USA). They wore blue uniforms and marched under the "Stars and Stripes," or "Old Glory!" They fight to preserve the New World's unique form of self-government, a democratic-republic. They abound in government provided resources. They are called, "Yankees," "Federals," "Unionists," "Billy-Yanks," "Blue Bellies," "Bluecoats," and "Those People."

Two Northern Historical Characters:

- **Lt. Colonel Edward Ellis**, USA, of Rockford, Illinois. Killed at the battle of Shiloh, April 6, 1862
- **Major General George B. McClellan**, (✶✶) USA, of Chicago, Illinois. Commander of the Union Army of the Potomac.

Five Northern Fictional Characters:

- **Catherine Ellis of Rockford**, Illinois. Wife to Lt. Colonel Edward Ellis. Mother to Paul, Eleanor, and John Ellis.
- **Eleanor Ellis**, daughter of Lt. Colonel Edward Ellis, USA, and Catherine Ellis. She wants the war to end and to bring her brothers home.

- **Paul and John Ellis** enlisted USA Soldiers.
- **Jason Merritt**, Esquire of Rockford, Illinois. Young attorney with strong political ambitions.

Southern Soldiers: They represent the Confederate States of America (CSA). They wore gray and butternut colored uniforms and marched under the "Stars and Bars," – The new symbol of the peoples' second revolution for independence. They are mostly volunteers and self equipped. They fight to be separate and free from a despotic, oppressive government. They want to be left to pursue and preserve their aristocratic way of life. They are called, "Rebels," "Confederates," "Johnnies," "Gray Backs," "Secessionists," and "Slavers."

Three Southern Historical Characters:

- **Lt. General Robert E. Lee** (✳✳✳) CSA, of Alexandria, Virginia. Commander of the Army of Northern Virginia. Survived the war.
- **Lt. General Thomas ("Stonewall") Jackson** (✳✳✳) CSA, of Lexington, Virginia. Second Corps Commander of the Army of Northern Virginia. Died from medical complications May 10, 1863.
- **Brigadier General John C. Breckinridge** (✳) CSA, of Lexington, Kentucky. Former Vice President of USA. Survived the war.

Two Southern Fictional Characters:

- **Captain Nathaniel Thomas Graham**, CSA, of Franklin, Tennessee, Chaplain and Company "G" Commander of 19th Tennessee Volunteers.
- **Lt. Marvin Jenkins**, CSA, of Nashville, Tennessee. College friend of Nathaniel's, Company "H" Second-in-Command of 19th Tennessee Volunteers.

Chapter 1

ONE BULLET

Eye-burning, smoky haze filled the air. The smell of spent
gunpowder mixed with an increasing stench of death.
Thunderous cannon bursts, popping musket fire, screeching
yells, and an occasional cheer filled the air in the near distance to
the north. Chaplain Nathaniel Graham only heard the sound of
pain and suffering, only smelled torn flesh. Faced with the panic
of the dying, he struggled to know what to do.

"Pray for me, Parson," panted the wounded Confederate soldier
lying on the bloodstained ground. "Pray, oh God, pray, oh it hurts,
God."

What's your name, Private? What unit you with?"

A twelve-pound shell exploded not more than twenty yards
away and shook the earth. Writhing in pain, the soldier choked
on blood. "Tell my Mamma that I was brave, tell her, Parson, tell
her."

"You can tell her yourself. You're going to be fine."

"I don't want to go to hell. Oh, God, don't let me go. Tell
Mamma," he began to shake. He grabbed at his stomach, his skin
swelling with blood.

"The surgeon is close by, working his way over. I hear he is General Johnston's personal physician."

"Oh, God." The dying Rebel's voice was not much stronger than a whisper. "Pa, can you hear me?"

"I'm here, son, I'm here. I'm very proud of you."

"Tell Mamma," he drifted off, barely breathing. Nathaniel looked over to the doctor tending to a fallen Yankee. The surgeon stood up, said something to the stretcher-bearers, waved his right arm and pointed toward the woods behind Nathaniel. The bearers picked up the wounded Bluecoat and started walking in the direction the medical officer indicated. Then, the surgeon walked directly toward Nathaniel.

"He's coming, the surgeon is coming. You'll be just fine. You're gonna make it." Nathaniel looked down at the ashen face of what once was a strong, tall lad. Gone, his eyes stared into the sunshine that broke through the haze, but he did not blink. The pain the boy suffered was fixed on his face and etched into Nathaniel's mind forever.

Suddenly, a rider galloped toward the medical party. The messenger yelled something about General Johnston to the doctor. He jumped down from his horse, gave a rough half salute to the medical officer, and quickly began his report. A corporal walked toward Nathaniel.

"Nothing more you can do for that one, Padre," the corporal nearly yelled above the thundering cannon and popping muskets a short mile away. "I'm sure if you look around, you'll find others you can help." Nathaniel just stared at the boy's face. He looked to be about seventeen. "He wasn't going to make it no matter no how, even if we got here to examine him and carry him to the field hospital," the corporal announced in his deep woods, Alabama-twang accent.

"Why is that," Nathaniel asked.

"Look at where he's hit," the corporal lifted his head and pointed with his eyes at the dead soldier's stomach. "See there; see how he's pulled at his belly. Gut shot's the worst, slow and painful. Ain't it something what one bullet can do? Nothing we coulda done. If we saw him, we'd just have the slaves pick him up for burial, even if he was still breathing. Come on Padre, there are more needing care."

Nathaniel lifted the boy's head out of his left hand and carefully laid it back down on the ground. He looked up through the tall trees at the brown, hazy sunlight that beamed through the clearing smoke. He pleaded silently. Then, Nathaniel dropped his head and sighed, "Let's go, Corporal." As Nathaniel stood up, he could see the excited messenger helping the doctor onto his horse. Once seated, the rider spurred his horse to a gallop. They rode toward the northeast where the sounds of war were most intense. Again, Nathaniel just stared.

"What's the matter with you, Padre? You look a little green around your gills. Ain't never seen a man die before?"

Nathaniel closed his eyes and breathed out, "Not like this," shaking his head side-to-side. "No, not like this."

"You're gonna see plenty, more Blue Bellies than our boys."

Nathaniel dropped his head again and said, "He asked me to pray for him and I didn't have time."

"Don't fuss yourself, Pastor, there'll be plenty more souls to save."

"I didn't even catch his name. He died before I could get his name and pray with him."

"I'm sorry, Pastor, but there are other men all around that need our help." Just then, another member of the surgeon's team, a sergeant, came up to both the corporal and Nathaniel. The corporal asked, "Hey, Sarge, what's the big rush about? Why'd he take Doc with him?"

"General Johnston has been hit. He's down over in that peach orchard over yonder. Corporal, take Chaplain Graham over yonder—with your permission, of course, sir."

Nathaniel replied, "Is the general hurt badly?"

"I don't think so. That lieutenant said he'd been hit in the leg. He might lose it, but he'll live. I suggest you move out, sir. The general's a busy fella."

Nathaniel shook himself back to the moment and said, "Okay Sergeant. Corporal, show me the way." They both jogged across the field. Earlier that Sunday morning, it had been a Yankee tent city for nearly 39,000 troops. The Federal soldiers encamped around a little log-cabin church called "Shiloh," named for an Old Testament place where the Ark of the Covenant was once kept and considered a special place of worship. Nathaniel did not think about worship this Sunday. His mind fixed on one thing, those few words uttered by his guide, *"Ain't it something what one bullet can do?"*

As they ran, the sounds of battle increased. They heard vicious, staccato musket fire to their left. Now and then miniballs would thud the earth around them or buzz bee-like through the air above them. The loud bark of Union cannon fire opened up huge holes in the ground and the ranks of Confederates that pressed toward an unseen but clearly heard and deadly enemy. More pain-filled screams added to the intense horror. Nathaniel saw Rebel artillery batteries forming for a barrage of the Federal defenses. The Southerners had to do something to break up the small pocket of Union defenders dug-in along a sunken road. The Yankees had repulsed four hours of repeated Rebel attacks against this natural defense and slowed the Confederate advance to the Tennessee River. The barrage would be devastating. Sixty-two guns prepared to shell an area a quarter mile in length not more than one hundred yards away.

The Rebel gunners opened fire with a roaring thunder. The ground beneath Nathaniel and the corporal shuddered. They lost their footing and tumbled. Nathaniel fell on top of a dead Yankee. He pushed himself off the corpse. He looked at a tormented expression fixed in the dead man's eyes. Captain Nathaniel Thomas Graham, a chaplain in the Confederate Army of the Mississippi's Reserve Corps, Third Brigade, Nineteenth Tennessee Infantry Volunteers, met the horror of war face-to-face.

The two men quickly got back on their feet. Nathaniel yelled, "Let's go." They ran as fast as they could toward the trees. Another shell hit the ground close to them peppering them with debris. Both fell. Nathaniel shook off the effects of the blast. He wanted to crawl into the smoking shell crater and wait out this firestorm, but his strong sense of duty kept the paralyzing fear at bay. He refused to let his own desire to run and hide overtake his spirit.

Spitting, the corporal said, "Looks like them Blue Bellies knows how to fight after all. If'n they keep this up, you'n me is both likely to end up like your'n friend back there a ways."

"You didn't really believed that stuff about one Reb could whip any ten Yankees, now did you?"

"Yes Sir. I sure did. They'z sure ain't never whipped us'n at anything serious yet. We about pushed 'em into the river. I could just see it from that small hill we just passed over."

"It ain't gonna be that easy. We tend to forget that some of them boys are our relatives. My own general has kin on the other side somewhere. He might be right in those woods getting blasted by our cannons right now." Nathaniel pushed himself up a bit to try to see through the smoke, and then he commanded, "We better keep moving."

"Yes, sir. We just need to reach that large oak tree over yonder," the corporal pointed and yelled. "Can you see it, Sir? Do you see the men gathered 'round the tree, away from the fighting? That's where we're headed."

Seconds later, Nathaniel and his guide were close enough to walk the ten yards more to the large oak tree. They seemed to be just beyond the range of buzzing stray shots and destructive shells. Nathaniel could make out the figure of a man on the ground with his back propped up against the tree. As they came near, one of the officers standing over the fallen one pulled his hat off his head and held it over his chest. Another followed and then the others. Something was terribly wrong. *Where is the General's surgeon?*

Nathaniel looked into the circle of officers and then to the man on the ground. Lieutenant General Albert Sydney Johnston, Commanding General of the Confederate Army of the Mississippi, the military leader with the most combat experience, the best strategist, and the most aggressive commanding officer of the Confederate States of America, lay dead before him.

Chapter 2

SUNDAY WALK

W asn't that a lovely service, Ellen dear?"

"Yes, Mother. I am glad you enjoyed it."

"Whatever do you mean, dear?"

Eleanor stopped in front of Pickering's Dry Goods Store and stared at the attractively arranged furnishings. Sighing, she replied, "Mother, don't you think it's presumptuous to make comments on the war's progress from the pulpit?"

"I'm sure Reverend Kelley meant no harm. After all, he simply confirmed the things your father stated in his last letter. I'm sure he's just as anxious to have his son home as we are to have our family back again. Frankly, I appreciate the fact that Pastor Kelley gives us insight into the information reported in the newspapers and he certainly gives us more details then I get from your father's notes."

"Yes, but Mother, I'm afraid he's giving us false hope."

Catherine was puzzled by her daughter's concern and asked, "Eleanor, what's really troubling you?"

Eleanor turned away from the store window and looked into her mother's eyes. "What if he's wrong about the war?" She began to walk slowly down the quite street. Catherine followed. "How can he be so certain that God is giving us victories? Just because Confederate General Johnston appears to be in full retreat and our forces are massing strong attacks in the east and the west doesn't mean the war will be over soon. How can he be so bold to declare that God is on our side?"

"I can't answer that for you, dear, and I wouldn't want to speak for Reverend Kelley. I can tell you how I feel." The two women reached the edge of town and started the gradual incline that would lead them home.

"I'd like to know," Eleanor pressed.

"Well, dear, the way I see it is this. We need all the hope and strength God can give us right now. With your father fighting with his regiment in the west, and Paul and John training to fight, I appreciate news that tells me we could all be together again soon."

"I don't know, Mother. Everything I read tells me that General Johnston is a great military leader. Father could be in great danger. And President Lincoln keeps calling for more volunteers. I think it angers everyone, especially our Southern neighbors."

"Saving the Union is very important to him, and your father respects him immensely. Your father told me before he left that Lincoln is the only man with the conviction to see this war to a successful end."

"I just want this war to be over. It doesn't seem worth the loss of life," Eleanor brooded.

Catherine attempted to cheer her daughter, "If Reverend Kelley is right, the war will be over very soon. Your father will be home and hopefully the boys won't see any fighting at all."

"Yes, you're right. Father should be home next month. His military commitment is just about over."

"All the men in his unit will come home together. Many of the ladies from church are planning a big, town-wide welcome home party. I pledged my support. They told me that Mayor Ramsey will declare a holiday when they return."

"That will be wonderful. You can count on me to help. For Father's homecoming, we should decorate the house, too."

"Yes, dear, it will be nice to have all the men home again. Our town seems so empty since they left to fight the Rebels."

"I just wish the war ended today."

"I do too, dear. I do too."

Eleanor hated talking about the war and wished to change the subject. "Mother, what are you planning to make for Easter dinner?"

Catherine had given it some thought and even desired to invite a few guests. As she began to share her ideas, a gentle spring rain began to fall.

The corporal said quietly to Nathaniel, "What you make of that, Captain?"

"I don't know. This can't be true. We better just stay here and wait for orders."

"Yes, sir."

Nathaniel and the corporal stood respectfully just outside the ring of officers.

One colonel said, "I didn't think he was hurt badly. The bullet hit his thigh. He said he was tired and wanted to rest a minute, and then he wanted to press the attack on Pittsburg Landing. He ordered his doctor to go back and help others worse wounded. I can't believe he's gone."

A member of General Johnston's staff asked, "When did he get hit?"

The colonel turned to the staff officer and replied, "A little while ago. He just led another charge against that hotbed of Yankee fire.

He turned and rode away from the main fight to call up General Breckinridge and his reserves. When the ball hit him, he just shook it off. He didn't stop for a minute. He kept pushing the men and himself forward. He gave me an order to find you and help him press the far right of the Federal line. I was only gone a few minutes."

Johnston's staffer added, "When I got here, I found him slumped in his saddle just over there. I asked him if he was wounded and he answered, 'Yes, and I fear seriously.' He passed out and started to fall off his horse. I caught him and eased him to the ground. Then, I placed him here. When he woke up, I told him that I sent for his surgeon. He seemed to get mad at that and slowly shook his head as if to tell me he didn't need any help, or maybe—," he paused. He furrowed his brow thoughtfully and then continued, "Maybe he was trying to tell me it was too late. Then—," Johnston's staffer sighed heavily, "I watched him die. I couldn't help him. He was the best military leader in the entire Confederate Army. With him gone, do we even have a chance to win this thing?"

No one answered. Another shock wave hit Nathaniel. He went numb with a total sense of helplessness and uselessness. The sounds of intense fighting just a half-mile away did not penetrate his confused mind. *Ain't it something what one bullet can do? What purpose did I serve this day? I am no help to anyone.*

Not a single member of Johnston's staff knew that the stray bullet struck Johnston's right femoral artery. A simple tourniquet could have saved him, but no one knew how to apply one. They watched Johnston slowly bleed to death. Their very aggressive, decisive and determined leader was gone. With him went the best chance the Confederacy had to destroy Union General Grant's army, force a quick end to the war and gain their country's independence. The ever-cautious Beauregard would have to take over.

Suddenly, they heard the pounding of hooves. A general officer and his staff rode up quickly. Nathaniel turned and recognized his corps commander. General Breckinridge asked, "Where's General Johnston?"

"He's dead, Sir," the colonel reported. The officers parted, revealing Johnston's body propped against the tree.

"Oh, God, no, it can't be," General Breckinridge looked down at his fallen commander. "He died from that little leg wound?"

"Yes, sir, General Breckinridge, it appears so," Johnston's staff officer answered.

"I just spoke to General Johnston minutes ago. We just took that pesky Yankee defensive pocket. My boys are calling it the 'Hornet's Nest.' Their general finally surrendered. I told Johnston his leg was bleeding, and he said it was just a nick. Then he ordered me to press on to the river and Pittsburg Landing. I came back to let him know my men are in position to move forward against the next Yankee defense up that hill through those woods. I believe Johnston would order me to advance."

"Sir, you better check with General Beauregard," cautioned the colonel.

"Where can I find him?"

The colonel answered, "He's made his headquarters in that little church. He's sick, down with a fever."

Breckinridge shot back, "Tarnation! Doesn't anyone know what to do?" All the men kept silent. Breckinridge tried to steady his horse, looked back to the southwest, up the hill, and continued, "Yes, I remember. Unless General Bragg sends other orders, you men hold here until I return."

Almost in unison, the officers said, "Yes, sir," and saluted.

General Breckinridge quickly returned their salute, wheeled his horse around and spurred him into a run toward the little church called Shiloh.

Chapter 3

ORDERS

An hour passed. Nathaniel still waited for his corps commander's return. Terrible, intense Yankee shelling continued to fall from the Union position on the bluffs just a half-mile away. Nathaniel didn't know that Yankee gunboats on the Tennessee River came to Grant's rescue and fired at any Confederate movement south of Grant's last defensive position near Pittsburg Landing. Nathaniel wondered just how long this day's fighting would continue. Exhausted, he knew he should return to his main assignment. *I will do better this time. I'll record each man's name and unit in my journal. I am not going to let another unknown soldier die.*

One came crawling out of the underbrush. He looked exhausted. He dragged his left leg leaving a trail of blood behind him. It looked like bone was sticking out through his ripped pants. As soon as he saw Nathaniel, he cried for help.

"My leg's shot." He reached back to show Nathaniel and continued, "It's broke too. I've been crawling for near a mile. Can't go no further."

I'm not going to correct him. We're only a hundred yards or so from that "Hornet's Nest." I guess to a crawling man it must feel like a mile. Nathaniel calmly asked, "What's your name and unit, Private?"

"My name's Oliver Sir, Private Zachary Taylor Oliver, like the president," he announced proudly. Then he reported efficiently, "I am with Bragg's Second Corps, Ruggles First Division, Anderson's Second Brigade, Major McDonnell's First Florida Battalion. We sure beat those Yankees today, didn't we Sir? This war is gonna be over tonight. Too bad for Major McDonnell. I saw him go down in our last charge. There ain't many Yankees left from what I could see. They turned tail and ran for the river. I think I killed one of their officers before one of them got lucky and shot my leg. It don't hurt too bad, but I am tired."

Nathaniel remembered. *That's what the colonel reported General Johnston said before he died.* Nathaniel's mind couldn't, or wouldn't, let go of that peculiar declaration, *"Ain't it something what one bullet can do?"* "Stretcher!" Nathaniel yelled. He looked around, and saw two slaves turn to the sound of his voice. Nathaniel stood and waved both his arms above his head. They started toward Nathaniel. He bent down to minister to the man lying at his feet. "Private Oliver, I need to ask you a question, son, straight out."

"I know what you gonna ask, Captain, you being a chaplain and all. You want to know if I know Jesus. Yes, sir, I do. I suspect He's the reason I ain't dead yet."

Nathaniel winked at the young man and replied, "I suspect you're right about that Zachary. He must still have work for you to do. What do you think?"

"I think it will be slow work since I'm only gonna have one leg."

The bearers arrived and prepared to place Private Oliver on the stretcher. Nathaniel didn't want to lie to him, so he quickly answered, "God can use you even if you have no legs. Just trust Him and He will do His work through you."

As the men lifted Private Oliver, he said, "I do trust Him, Pastor. This," pointing to his leg, "is nothing. I just wish I could have seen the war end today."

Nathaniel said to the wounded soldier, "I do too, Zachary. I do too." The slaves carried him away quickly.

"Why did we stop? It ain't dark yet," asked the commander of the Tenth Arkansas Infantry. "We nearly pushed old Grant and his invaders off the bank and into the river. It looked to me that the few of them left were less than one hundred yards from the water's edge."

"General Beauregard issued the order," General Breckinridge replied. "I guess he didn't like Bragg and me attacking without assessing the situation further." Breckinridge spoke to his staff, "Now, he wants us to rest, enjoy some captured Yankee food, and get ready to destroy Grant and Sherman in the morning. Had we taken that ridge on our first attempt, we'd be chasing the Yankees across the river, but they held. Those gunboats saved them. General Beauregard thinks we've done all we can do today. He also wants us to tend to our wounded before it gets too dark. By the way, how's that coming along, Captain Graham?"

"Sir, between ours and theirs, we've picked up thousands. I've never seen so many injured men. The field hospital can't handle the numbers. The wounded are scattered everywhere. There are a few thousand dead too, both sides. We haven't had a chance to do anything with them. Many of our boys, we don't know. They must be from other outfits."

"I know you're doing the best you can, Nate. I hope that all this mess will be over tomorrow. Then, we can give our boys a proper burial."

"Yes, sir," Nathaniel replied. He didn't share his general's confidence and his face showed it.

"Is there anything else you wish to report, Captain?"

"Yes, sir, there is one matter that does cause me concern."

"You may speak freely, Captain."

"Well, sir, our men keep stripping the dead and dying Yankees of their clothes and shoes. Sir, if the situation were reversed, would we want their men rummaging through our men's belongings?"

Breckinridge understood. He must do something to curb this barbaric behavior. He may not be able to stop the actions of the entire army, but his men would not rob the dead. With one word, "Gentlemen," Breckinridge forcefully commanded his staff. "Make sure this order gets through to every man in this command. It came from General Johnston himself. General Beauregard reissued it, and gentlemen, I wholeheartedly agree with it. No member of this Army is authorized to strip the Yankee dead. Gentlemen, tell your men if I catch any man in this outfit stripping a Yankee, I will shoot him on sight. Is that clear?"

"Yes, sir," they all replied.

"Good. You have your orders. Tell your commanders to feed and rest their men. Then prepare to continue the assault in the morning. We must push the Yankees into the river before their reinforcements arrive. Any questions?"

Again, they gave a near-unanimous, firm response, "No, sir!"

"Then, gentlemen, you are dismissed." As the commanders filed out of Breckinridge's tent, the general added, "Nate, thanks for bringing that to my attention. You can always speak freely with me, son."

Surprised by General Breckinridge's informality, Nathaniel replied gratefully, "Thank you, sir. I'll try to remember that."

General Breckinridge nodded affirmatively and pursed his lips thoughtfully. Then he said, "Go on, son, you have work to do tonight."

Encouraged, Nathaniel quickly brought himself to attention, saluted, and said, "Thank you, sir!"

Breckinridge returned the salute, gave his chaplain a wink and directed Nathaniel to the tent flap. Nathaniel dropped his salute, did an about-face, bent down, exited the tent and disappeared into the cloudy night's thick darkness.

Chapter 4

TENNESSEE RAIN

The Yankee shelling continued through the night. A cold spring rain fell. At times, it came down heavily making it impossible to see. The showers cleansed the bloodstained ground. It seemed God, the Holy Father of all life, wept over the murderous destruction wrought by the hands of His sons against each other. It was a miserable night. No one could sleep between the constant bombardment and the moans of the wounded.

Nathaniel crawled from one body to another, checking for any sign of life. A Yankee shell struck a very old, large oak tree near its midsection. Fire and branches came crashing down all around him. As soon as the debris hit, he heard a loud, painful moan just to his right. The flames gave him enough light to see the poor soldier trapped under a large fallen limb. The rain was quickly dousing the flames and any useful light. Nathaniel had to move fast if he was going to help this man.

As soon as Nathaniel rose to his feet, Yankee musket fire burst out. Hot lead flew through the brush whistling and slapping into the surrounding trees. Fortunately, Nathaniel reached the injured soldier unharmed. As soon as he crouched low, the musket fire ceased. Painfully, the soldier spoke to Nathaniel, "You trying to get yourself killed, son?"

"I wasn't planning on it. I'm hoping to get you out of here before you get burned alive," Nathaniel said as he lifted the burning branch off the legs of the soldier revealing the truth of the man's condition.

"You can't help me, son," the injured soldier stated. With his eyes barely open, he looked to his left and then to his right at the smoldering branches being doused by the steady rain. He labored to add, "This rain is taking care of the fire." The splintered wood sizzled and smoked. Gradually, darkness returned. The man coughed and strained as he asked, "What makes you think you can do anything for me, anyway? I can't move."

"Where are you hurt, soldier?"

The man moaned and choked, "Where aren't I hurt is a better question, son. I don't remember much. A cannon blast knocked me down. It must have been grapeshot. When I came to, both legs, my right shoulder and this." With his one good arm the soldier pulled his shirt to expose his left side.

A dime-sized hole surrounded by pockmarked flesh, muscle tissue, and blood mixed with the rain. Nathaniel almost vomited when he smelled the odor and saw the wound. Nathaniel closed his eyes, furrowed his brow and turned his head down to his right side. He swallowed hard, turned to face the wounded man and said, "I'm not going to leave you here to die."

"I'm dead already; my body just hasn't caught up yet." The man coughed. Then he pleaded, "Kill me now, please."

"I don't have a gun. I'm a chaplain, and I'm going to get you to the hospital."

The soldier almost choked as he responded, "I don't think that's a good idea, Padre. You will be killed trying to carry me out of here."

The dreadful screech-like whistle of another incoming shell flew over their heads. Nathaniel ducked. The explosion erupted a good twenty-five yards from them. Nathaniel looked up at the noticeably older man propped up against the tree. Smoldering embers surrounded them. Nathaniel knew the soldier was right. Too large to carry, Nathaniel couldn't drag him out of these thick, rain-soaked woods. Nathaniel just stared at him.

The soldier returned Nathaniel's gaze and replied, "My time's up, Parson. Nobody can help me."

Nathaniel was determined, "Jesus can." he stated confidently.

"I never put much stock in any of that religion stuff, Padre." The man struggled to breathe, "It didn't seem to make much sense."

"Do you mind if we talk about Him now? It sure can't hurt you any more than this war did."

The soldier rolled his eyes, and with labored breath answered, "Why not?"

Nathaniel crawled closer to the soldier, turned around and sat next to his wounded side. Nathaniel quickly and silently prayed, *Lord Jesus, please give me the right words for this man.* Nathaniel sensed that he had to be truthful with this man and that time would not permit idle conversation. He started, "I think you are right, you're dying. Have you thought about life after this one?"

"Yes, Padre, but what's the point?"

"Have you considered the fact that life is impossible without a creator? Something can never come from nothing, correct?"

Coughing, the soldier answered, "I suppose so."

Nathaniel continued, "If that is so, and if life is a miracle brought into existence by a creator, do you think The Creator might care about His creation?"

"I guess it's possible, but maybe He doesn't."

"Do you have any children?"

"I have two grown sons, Paul and John, and a daughter, Eleanor. She's our middle child." Again, straining with his one good but weakening arm, the soldier reached into his shirt to an inside pocket and pulled out an opened envelope. "I just got this letter from her yesterday. She hopes I'll come home soon, since my commitment is almost over. I guess she's going to be really hurt and disappointed. Why doesn't your Creator care about that?"

"He does." Nathaniel swallowed hard. He wasn't expecting this. A Yankee shell hit a few yards behind Nathaniel shattering another tree and causing the ground to shake just as he shook inside. He silently petitioned for help and wisdom. "Our Heavenly Father does care about her more than you do, and He wants you to be able to see her again. He's provided a way for you and her to do just that."

This seemed to help ease the tension. The soldier relaxed, breathed easier, and asked, "How's that?"

Nathaniel silently thanked Jesus and continued, "God sent His only Son, to die a very cruel death. He suffered, not too much differently from what you're going through now, to pay the sin penalty for all of us so that we can live with Him, a Holy God. The Bible says, *'For He made Him who knew no sin to be sin for us, that we might become the righteousness of God in Him.'* So, acknowledge your sin to God, receive Jesus right now as your Savior, and when you die, you will pass from this life into God's Holy Kingdom. If your daughter makes this choice, if she hasn't already, she will join you there."

Coughing, the soldier struggled to breathe again. Painfully, he turned his head slowly toward Nathaniel and said softly, "It sounds too good to be true. But what can I do, shot up like this?"

"Just believe that it is true. Believe in your heart and confess with your mouth that Jesus Christ is God's Son, that He died for your sins and that God raised Him from the dead for you." Nathaniel paused. He took a breath, and quickly finished, "Then, you will be saved. You don't have to do anything more."

"That doesn't seem right. It seems too simple."

"God meant it to be that way. Do you remember any stories about how Jesus died?"

The soldier's strength faded as he replied softly, "Yeah, on a cross."

"Do you remember that two thieves hung on crosses on each side of Him?"

Wincing, the soldier coughed out, "Yes."

"When one thief ridiculed Jesus, the other spoke and defended Jesus saying that Jesus had done nothing wrong, but they deserved their punishment. He simply recognized that he was a sinner, that Jesus was God's sinless Son, and then He asked Jesus to remember him, when Jesus came into His Kingdom. Jesus responded and promised that they would be together in paradise. The thief couldn't do anything else but hang on the cross next to Jesus, believe the Lord's promise, and accept the truth that Jesus is the Savior. So, that is all that God is asking of you now."

Nathaniel stopped talking and let the information settle. The soldier said nothing for a minute. Nathaniel was about to speak when the soldier said, "I think I understand. I am a sinner. God knows I almost enjoyed killing those fellas today. I deserve to die." He choked and coughed again. He didn't have much strength left.

Nathaniel watched this man run a long race and stumble before reaching the finish line. He wasn't going to let this man slip away. He asked, "Can I pray for you?"

The soldier just nodded slowly. Nathaniel asked again, "Do you think you can repeat for yourself what I pray?" Again, he nodded affirmatively. Nathaniel took a deep breath. He began, "Try this." The soldier nodded agreement. Nathaniel prayed, "Heavenly Father," and paused.

"Heavenly Father," the soldier spoke in little more than a whisper.

Greatly encouraged, Nathaniel continued until the man's fate was sealed eternally.

The rain continued to fall. The light from what was once a raging fire had gone out like the life that passed from this man. Just moments before, he became Nathaniel's brother in Christ. Nathaniel sat quietly as this large man, known only to God, walked into the very presence of his Savior and Lord, Jesus Christ. More shells fell and exploded, but it was as if they fell silent so as not to interrupt this precious moment.

Nathaniel wiped tears from his eyes. It was a good night after all. Nathaniel did not care who won the battle or who would win the war because a much more important eternal conflict had been victoriously resolved. *I forgot to ask his name and unit. It's all right. He's safe in the arms of Jesus.* Nathaniel examined the peace on his face, so different from the expressions he saw earlier that day. Nathaniel caught out of the corner of his eye the letter still grasped in the soldier's hand. He pulled it free and looked at the name on the envelope. Because of the mixture of blood, mud, rain and darkness, he could barely make out the man's name, Lieutenant Colonel Ellis, Edward.

Turning from the envelope back to the man's face, Nathaniel made another promise, "I'll find your daughter, and I will tell her how you gave your life to Jesus so you could see her again in His Kingdom. I'll find a way to convince her that she should follow in her dad's footsteps." *I wonder if General Breckinridge can help me. He knows more people than I'll ever meet.* In the blackness of this night, Nathaniel introduced the man to the true light. It did not matter to Nathaniel that Edward Ellis was a Yankee.

Chapter 5

THE CAUSE

On Sunday morning, the Rebels caught Grant and his army completely by surprise as they tried to enjoy breakfast. They almost destroyed the stronger Union force. It puzzled General Grant that the Rebels stopped their advance before dusk. He considered the possibility that the Confederates lacked reinforcements for their decimated ranks. He believed that the Rebels were disorganized and scattered across the Shiloh battlefield. Grant guessed they were too weak to mount another attack. He guessed right.

Suddenly, the steady nightlong bombardment turned into an explosive, massively destructive daybreak barrage. Union shells rained down as heavily as the showers during the night. Throughout that long fateful night of April 6 and morning of April 7, 1862, General Grant regrouped and reinforced his troops. He added thirty-two thousand to his tired, but still capable, fifteen thousand men. Grant's combined strength was now greater than the total Confederate force that had attacked the Federals the previous morning. He released a full-scale counteroffensive at dawn.

Grant caught the Rebels by an even greater surprise. Grant's men were ready to redeem themselves and the ground they lost. They met little resistance as they moved away from Pittsburg Landing toward their encampment around the Shiloh church. Many Rebels simply surrendered as they saw the advancing horde. They quickly realized that all they'd fought for had been in vain. Others just ran. If not for the dead and wounded littered all around, the Union troops would have been able to chase the Confederates from the battlefield. Obstacles of men, horses, mules, and broken or abandoned military equipment slowed their hot pursuit. The Yankee advance became deliberate and steady. The Confederate officers took full advantage of the additional time. They regrouped and prepared a defensive stand near the church.

"General Beauregard will pay for this disaster," General Breckinridge complained aloud to himself. "He should not have sent that message to President Davis that we had won a great victory and that we would destroy Grant today. Look who is destroying whom? We'll be lucky if we are not all killed or captured." Breckinridge tried desperately to rally his men. He followed General Johnston's example. He waved his sword, shouted encouragement, and rode back and forth along a line of fire that continued to fall back away from the unexpected Yankee masses. He faced the enemy. If he died, he would die with honor. He would not allow his men to run away as cowards. Considering the overall situation, he concluded, *even if we lose this field, we must be able to escape in force so that we can fight again.* He could not help but ask the question that he was sure his men asked too, *where did all these Yankees come from?*

Just south of a peach orchard, Breckinridge organized a defensive line along the Hamburg-Purdey road. Strengthened by Captain Rutledge's Tennessee Battery and concealed by the thick woods on the south side of the road, they would have clear shots at the Yankee advance. The Union infantry would have to circle a bloody pond, and then they would be in the open field. Breckinridge knew his men had to hold this line long enough to allow time for the rest of the Confederate Army to escape.

Fortunately for the reorganizing Southerners, the Union forces made the same mistake as the Confederates. They advanced faster than their artilleries' ability to keep pace. They marched headlong into Breckinridge's position without cannon support. Breckinridge gave the order, "Open fire!" From Breckinridge's position, it looked like a great invisible scythe cut them down to ground level. The Union soldiers fell en masse. Breckinridge commanded, "Reload and fire at will." The one-time contender for the presidency of the United States of America ordered the destruction of men he once would have happily served and who would have called him, "Commander in Chief." He had held high hopes of continuing the great American compromise of slave and free States, but not this day. He wanted those invaders of the South stopped.

"Keep firing, boys," Breckinridge shouted. He checked his timepiece, *nearly noon. I wonder how long we can hold here.* Breckinridge gazed through his field glasses. "The Yankees are bringing cannon support forward," he said to the staff officer. "We have a few minutes before they hit us with solid shot and canister shells." Breckinridge ordered, "Tell the men to fire one last volley. Orderly, find the commander of our artillery. Tell him to move south to the Peabody Road and prepare another defensive stand there."

His orderly saluted smartly and galloped to the right end of Breckinridge's defensive line. Moments later, Yankee shelling began. Breckinridge ordered, "Pull back, men! Withdraw through the woods." *Withdraw before we are all butchered!*

The Rebels passed the Federal camps they had advanced through the previous day. By midday, Breckinridge regrouped his corps along the Peabody Road. A light afternoon shower began to fall. A courier from Beauregard's headquarters rode up the Eastern Corinth Road. "Where can I find General Breckinridge?" Nathaniel pointed to his commander. Once introduced, the courier saluted and announced, "With General Beauregard's compliments, sir. You orders are to withdraw. General Beauregard plans to reform on the grounds of our Saturday encampment."

"He can't be serious," Breckinridge fumed. "I prepared a solid line of defense here. We can hold this position."

"General Beauregard disagrees," the courier responded as if prepared for this resistance. "General Beauregard has observed the Yankee advance along our entire line. If we do not pull back now, we suffer the loss of this army. We must defend Corinth. Your corps will fight as our rear guard and protect our retreat. Withdraw and reform along the Corinth Road. You have your orders, General." The courier saluted Breckinridge but he did not wait for the general's. Instead, he wheeled his horse and road due east to find Third Corps Commander, Major General William J. Hardee.

Reluctantly, General Breckinridge complied. As he gave the order to withdraw, he thought, *Withdraw? Beauregard has not the stomach to fight. We followed his battle plan yesterday and I think we damaged ourselves more than we hurt the Yankees. This retreat will demoralize my men. We fled Kentucky for this? If we are not fighting this war to win, then what are we fighting for, exactly?* Breckinridge looked around at the carnage that surrounded him as his men moved south. The Confederate attempt to destroy the Federal forces at Shiloh was a terrible and complete failure.

Chapter 6

DECISION

The evening of April 10, 1862 fell silent. General Breckinridge's infantry combined with Colonel Nathan Bedford Forrest's Tennessee Cavalry Regiment turned and stopped General Sherman's advance south toward Corinth. It cost Forrest a bullet in his back, but he would survive the wound. Finally, the Battle of Shiloh was over. Breckinridge issued orders to his Division Commanders and hoped that he would be able to get a good night's sleep, something he'd sorely missed the past ten evenings. It seemed as though it had been a year since this army left Corinth, Mississippi, for the Shiloh campaign.

Breckinridge allowed his mind to drift. *I can't believe two weeks ago we entered the gates of hell. The weeks before the fight, soft spring rain fell almost every day around Corinth. Each morning as we prepared for battle, a still mist would shroud the land covering every tree, shrub and blade of grass with droplets of water. It covered the tents too. Many of my men slept on the open ground. They'd wake up damp, with a mood that matched. But by mid-morning, the fog would lift and sunshine would pour through the budding forest of flowering dogwood, and leafy oak and maple trees. I can smell the fir, pine and spruce trees too. Oh, how the sun's rays warmed us as we marched and drilled.*

Dreamily, he closed his eyes and let his thoughts drift to a time just six months earlier, when he, the then Honorable John C. Breckinridge, prominent Kentucky Senator, fled arrest. "Yes my fellow Kentuckians, that grand fool Lincoln and his minions charged me with high treason against the Government of the United States."

The crowd condemned the president abusively. A few choice words echoed through the evening air.

Breckinridge raised his hands to quiet his constituents, "I come before you tonight to say farewell to my beloved home and my many friends here in Kentucky. Since I cannot stay, I will ride south. Tonight I exchange my congressional seat for the musket of a soldier." Breckinridge drifted off to sleep to the memory of a cheering crowd.

Suddenly, he stood before his very good friend, Confederate President Jefferson Davis, who granted him a commission as a Confederate Brigadier General. Davis immediately assigned Breckinridge to Lieutenant General Albert Sydney Johnston, Commanding General of the Confederate Army of the Mississippi. In turn, Johnston placed Breckinridge in command of the Army's Reserve Corps.

Tossing and turning on his cot, Breckinridge watched his men break their encampment around Corinth, Mississippi, that first day in April. They marched twenty-five miles to Pittsburg Landing, Tennessee. "Keep moving men. I know the roads are muddy, but we must keep this army moving forward. Remember your homes and families. Do you want those Yankees to take away our way of life?" *Who am I fooling? Most of my men don't have any combat experience. I don't have any. But Johnston says this coming battle could decide the war. We're going to spring a trap that will destroy the Yankees encamped near a place called Shiloh.*

Those days were filled with excitement by the entire army and his men from Kentucky. The thrill of glory passed away along with General Johnston and his hope for a quick end to this war. He saw his commander's face—dead. Startled, Breckinridge woke up. *Where am I? Steady John. It's April 10, 1862. You have unpleasant, unfinished business. You can't avoid it any longer.* Casualty reports and letters to family members had to be written. He summoned his Corps Chaplain, Captain Graham, to his tent.

"Orderly," Breckinridge shouted. Sergeant Moore entered the tent.

"Yes, General," he responded saluting and standing at a sharp attention. Breckinridge failed to return the salute.

"Send for Captain Graham. I need to speak with him right away."

"Yes, Sir," the orderly maintained his salute and stature.

Several labored seconds passed before Breckinridge realized that nothing further would happen until he returned the sergeant's salute, which he did awkwardly. Responding with a crisp salute, the orderly left the tent and repeated the orders to another soldier on duty and ready.

Moments later, Nathaniel entered Breckinridge's tent, snapped himself to attention, saluted and announced, "Captain Graham reporting as ordered, sir."

Breckinridge did not turn from his desk. He just asked, "What are our losses, Nate?"

Nathaniel dropped his salute but remained at attention and answered, "Sir, we're still counting, but I would guess that we are close to official numbers. Now the real problem is to identify how many wounded, missing, and killed we left behind. So the best I can do—," Nathaniel paused, "Well, sir, I can give you a total casualty count. It's not good, sir."

Breckinridge turned and faced Nathaniel. He looked him squarely in the eye and continued his inquiry, "What is it?"

Nathaniel swallowed hard. He was very unsure how to present this information. He closed his eyes and simply remembered that bad news is not like a fine wine, it will never improve with age. Then he spoke up, "Around thirteen thousand, sir."

Breckinridge put his right hand to his face and covered his eyes as if in disbelief. "Are you sure?" he asked. "How many do you estimate from our divisions?"

"Yes Sir, we're sure. The roll calls support this count. Our division loss is around fifteen hundred. General Bragg's divisions suffered the heaviest, more than twice our numbers." Nathaniel sensed that the past week's horrors weighed heavily on his commander. He decided to continue carefully, "General, we could do a better job of verifying just who is missing, wounded or dead if we requested permission from the Federals to care for our men back on the battlefield."

Breckinridge seemed to appreciate a sound suggestion for a change and quickly responded, "That's a good idea, Nate. I'll send it to General Beauregard. Maybe he'll push it forward to Grant." Just then, he noticed Nathaniel's posture. Breckinridge commanded, "At ease, Captain. Stand at ease." Nathaniel thanked his general and continued with more details. While Nathaniel was speaking, Breckinridge performed the rough calculations in his head and sighed, "Nearly thirty percent of our strength gone in two days. It was a mistake, it was a terrible mistake. How am I supposed to write to mothers and wives if I don't know what happened to their sons and husbands?"

"What, sir?" Nathaniel was not sure if his general was talking about the numbers or the battle.

"Nate, I've been a senator of the United States, vice president of the United States, I even ran against John Bell, that fool Lincoln, and Stephen Douglas in the 1860 presidential campaign. I've been a public servant my entire professional life. Since you are my chaplain, can we talk confidentially?"

"Of course, sir."

"Okay, man-to-man, not general-to-captain, and please call me John tonight. I need a friend."

"Yes, sir, of course, sir," Nathaniel stuttered. Again, he instantly became uncomfortable with his general's informality. Nathaniel had to force himself to accept General Breckinridge as a man—a man just like any other man in need of the Lord's counsel. Nathaniel corrected himself and responded, "Of course," paused, and then finished with, "Of course, John."

"Nate, take a seat. This could take awhile because I have many things on my mind." As Nathaniel sat down in the other field chair in the tent, the oil lanterns flickered, creating an odd strobe effect of their shadows on the canvas wall. Breckinridge dropped his quill, turned away from his field desk, and continued keeping his voice muffled so as not to be overheard by anyone outside. "As I said before, I've been a public servant most of my adult life. I never went to West Point, like Johnston or Beauregard and some of the others. Nate, I haven't had any military training whatsoever. I picked up General Hardee's book and I have this worn Federal army field manual, which I've read. But honestly, I do not know the first thing about waging warfare. With that said, I can't help but think this whole campaign was a huge series of mistakes. Johnston made the first mistake by assigning Beauregard the responsibility of planning the attack. Beauregard made a bigger mistake of calling off our advance after Johnston died. Now we are in full retreat and can't account for our own losses. I know my people from Kentucky and I think I understand the people of both sides better than most. Because of the mistakes we just witnessed, I am very afraid that this war is far from over."

"What do you mean, John?" Nathaniel asked. He still struggled to adjust to a nonmilitary role.

"When I left Washington, I was still debating the issues. I was trying to tell people that Lincoln was usurping his constitutional authority as president, and I tried to find a compromise to our regional differences. I believed that we could resolve the war without further bloodshed. But once people hear the casualties from this battle, I think we will hear two voices. One will cry loudly to stop the war now. The other will demand vengeance. Our Southern brethren will insist that we throw the Yankees out. Nate, you saw what happened. We threw everything we had at them. They absorbed our best blow and then came right back at us with more strength than we had when we started. The Yankees will sense that they can overpower us with the weight of their numbers. So the way that I see things tonight, we will hear a soft voice crying for mercy to stop the war, but a very loud, bitter voice shouting to fight till someone wins."

Nathaniel recognized that it was his turn to speak so he offered, "I know that the Bible teaches that the Lord said, '*Vengeance is Mine, I will repay.*' I also know that many of my neighbors believe that they represent the hand of the Lord, exacting the Lord's vengeance on those Yankees invading our land. I think you're right about us Southern people. We are very proud and we are very certain that God is on our side. But frankly, I'm not too sure."

Breckinridge was surprised at Nathaniel's last remark and stated, "Nate, if you're not sure, how do you expect to help any of us? You of all people should know why you are wearing the uniform of the Confederacy. I know I do."

"Well, General," Nathaniel had his prepared answer ready, "I believe God called me to minister to His soldiers fighting for freedom."

Breckinridge saw through the pat answer and challenged Nathaniel, "Nate, I told you I'm a politician. I earned my living lying to people and telling them what they wanted to hear. You will have to do better than that with me."

"Well, sir," Nathaniel slipped back into a submissive posture, "I think I got caught up in the emotions of the day. Everyone was joining to fight the Yankees. Because of my convictions and position as a pastor, I believed it would be wrong for me to fight, but I just couldn't sit back and do nothing."

"I can believe that answer," Breckinridge nodded. Their roles reversed, Breckinridge counseled Nathaniel. Maybe Breckinridge had that in mind all along. Breckinridge continued, "Son, I don't know how long this army will be kept together. I know Jeff Davis well. He will remove Beauregard from command as soon as possible. Bragg is another West Point graduate, like Davis. The president knows Bragg well. Everyone knows that the general is a hard-driving man. It's not surprising that his command suffered the most casualties. I think he has a strong chance of taking command. If that happens, I may ask Jeff to pull me back east to Richmond. Nate, you have to know why you are here and why we should be fighting this war if you are going to help my men. They think they fight for their rights, their freedom, or to create a separate nation. Those are pieces of the issue, but not one is the central point." Breckinridge stopped to let this information sink in and waited for some recognition from Nathaniel.

Nathaniel blinked his eyes, furrowed his brow and then looked at Breckinridge, uncertain of what he'd just heard. Then Nathaniel asked, "If we are not fighting for our independence, then what are we fighting for?"

"The real issue is power. Whoever has the power controls the nation. That will always be the contest. If we lose this war, we will lose the power to decide how we want to govern ourselves and we will become more dependent upon the central federal government. Over time, Washington will dictate every aspect of our daily lives and we will be powerless to stop it. Unfortunately, Richmond is starting to act the same way."

Nathaniel answered respectfully, "General, I disagree. The only real power is God. He is the one who raises up and puts down governing authorities."

Breckinridge stood up and began to pace as though he was giving a lecture. "Nate, I respect your view, but I don't think it is the only one. Simple Bible-verse quotations will not be enough to solve these problems we face. You must have answers for the hard questions. For example, the Yankees call us sinners for owning slaves. If my men begin to think of themselves as sinners, they will lose their resolve. I need an answer for what Fredrick Douglas claimed. He said that if a man calls himself a Christian and he keeps another man in bondage, his Christianity is false. I can't simply dismiss his statement by saying he's just a complaining Negro. I met him myself. He seems intelligent enough to be a man. In some ways, he's smarter than many of our proud Southern people. How do I argue and support the Supreme Court's decision that he's not a person, that he cannot then be a citizen, and that he is not entitled to any of the protections granted a citizen of the country?"

Breckinridge lowered his head and continued, "Frankly, I don't know what I'm going to do. All I know is that if Bragg takes command," Breckinridge sighed deeply, then continued, "he'll drive this army into the ground." Breckinridge looked back at Nathaniel and made sure they had solid eye contact, then continued, "Nate, you must understand why God-given self-government is the most important political and social concept. You wouldn't want the government telling you how to run your church, would you?"

"Certainly not," Nathaniel quickly replied.

"Well then," Breckinridge continued. "We don't want Lincoln and his 'Black Republicans' telling us how to run our towns, counties and states." Breckinridge paused and breathed deeply again, then said, "That's what this war is all about. Lincoln threw out the First Amendment, the Bill of Rights and the rest of the Constitution so that he could become a dictator. He wants total power over all of us, just like the kings of Europe. I don't expect you to grasp its importance tonight or any time soon, but promise me, you will think long and hard about what I am saying."

Nathaniel stared at his newly self-appointed political mentor and asked, "Why are you telling me this, John?"

"Because you have a better chance of surviving this war than I. Even if we win, and I survive, I can never go back North again. If I did, I would be arrested and then either hung or shot as a traitor. But you Nate, you don't have to be in the front. You don't have to face death head-on as do the troops."

"General, several times I just missed being killed during those two hard days at Shiloh," Nathaniel rebutted defensively.

"I know, and I realize you're taking chances too, but you don't have to, and, Nate, I don't want you to risk your life. You have important work to do. As I said, I need you to be able to encourage my men so that they can believe in something bigger then themselves. When you minister to the wounded and dying—of either side—you have to be able to bring comfort, so you have to be strong inside. Do you understand me, son?"

Nathaniel, startled by what his commander just said, thought *I wonder if he knows about that Yankee I helped, and his daughter's letter. Should I ask if he knows an Edward Ellis from Illinois?* He then responded almost mechanically, "I understand my duties to the men, sir." Then he stood up, came to attention and said, "I promise that I will try and understand what this war really means." As he left the tent, Nathaniel thought *how did we get ourselves in this terrible mess?*

Chapter 7

Simpler Times

The Confederate Army of the Mississippi camped outside the north edge of Corinth. Badly battered from the fighting at Shiloh one month ago, General Beauregard expected the reported outnumbering Federal forces to appear any day. A mix of tall lodge-pole pine, maple, oak and elm trees dripping with moss surrounded the various temporary shelters. Most of the enlisted men kept themselves busy reading or writing letters in their wedge-design canvas tents. The fit was snug, but four men could find protection from most outdoor nuisances. Some of the fortunate occupied the larger, more comfortable, Indian teepee-looking Sibley tents. Soldiers neatly staked their muskets in tripod fashion by their tents to retrieve them quickly. Some played cards or participated in cockroach races in a vain attempt to relieve their boredom. Smoke rose from hundreds of breakfast fires and mixed in the fresh spring air. Each billowing pillar represented a company of men attempting to receive a daily ration of food before the mindless marching and close-order drill began.

General Beauregard prepared the men under his command to protect the mighty Mississippi River, and preserve the main artery of the South's supply line. Thanks to the Confederate government's initiation of the military draft, his troop strength grew steadily. Unfortunately, the new men needed critical training—fast—and Beauregard lacked the resources to provide it. Worse, sickness ran rampant through the camp. Nearly forty percent suffer from "soldier's disease," typhoid fever, dysentery, and malaria. Acquiring and keeping soldiers healthy was Beauregard's number-one priority. It is the same concern throughout the Confederacy.

Along one of the muddy tent-city pathways, a lone junior officer walked, almost marched, toward one of the larger, wall-styled tents that served as his regiment's headquarters. As he neared the tent, Nathaniel returned the armed guard's salute. He removed his kepi cap as he entered the canvas structure. Once inside, he approached his commanding officer seated at a desk. Nathaniel came to attention, saluted and asked, "You wanted to see me, sir?"

Colonel David H. Cummings, Regiment Commander of the 19th Tennessee Infantry, replied, "Yes I did, Captain. I requested that all my staff officers and company commanders assemble for a briefing. You're the first to arrive. Stand at ease."

"How's your wound, sir?" Nathaniel inquired, attempting to stir a causal conversation while they awaited the arrival of the rest of the colonel's staff.

"Oh, I've been hurt worse back home on the family farm. The surgeon says I should be good as new in another month. I was lucky. If the bullet had hit me closer to my shoulder, I would have lost my right arm. If it were a hair lower, we wouldn't be talking right now. It passed right under my collarbone and out my back. It sure knocked me down, and made a mess of me for a few days, but I'm doing fine now."

"That's good to hear, sir," Nathaniel replied respectfully and sincerely.

Other officers began to arrive. Nathaniel's friend from college, now Lieutenant Marvin Jenkins, still deeply sad about something, stumbled and almost fell in the mud just outside the colonel's tent. Nathaniel's messmate, Major Patrick Duffy, always the prankster, marched right up to the tent and announced the reason why he called this meeting. "I'm going on a scouting mission to capture Yankee food supplies and General Grant. Anyone want the glory and honor of joining me? I sure could use some brave volunteers. How about you, Marvin? God knows you could use a little recreation." Several men laughed. Marvin looked for a place to hide.

Once all of his officers arrived, Colonel Cummings' second in command, Lieutenant Colonel Francis M. Walker, called everyone to attention. Colonel Cummings stood up from behind his field desk, walked a few steps toward the gathered officers and quickly put his men at ease.

"Gentlemen, contrary to what our dear Major Duffy has nobly suggested, the reason I called you here this morning is simply this: we have transfer orders prepared by General Breckinridge and approved by General Beauregard. We will move out today. Company commanders, have your men break camp and be ready to march in two hours. You staff officers will work with Lieutenant Colonel Walker to prepare our regimental headquarters for the march. Are there any questions?"

Lieutenant John B. Countiss spoke up quickly, which was his habit, "Sir, may I ask where we are going?"

Cummings replied whimsically, "You may ask, Lieutenant, and I may answer that you do not have a need to know that strategic military information at this time. You'll know where you are going once you get there."

The other officers chuckled, some quietly under their breath. They understood that the young lieutenant, who proved to be a fine Southern soldier at Shiloh, had impetuously stuck his foot in his mouth once again. Colonel Cummings did not make anything more of the matter. Discipline was never formal around camp, and no need to embarrass the boy further.

Cummings looked around at the rest of his officers and repeated his inquiry, "Now, are there any questions?"

This time he got the response he hoped for the first time. Nearly in unison, his officers replied emphatically, "No, sir!"

"Then gentlemen, you have your orders. Carry on. I expect the 19th Tennessee to be ready to march in two hours."

Lieutenant Colonel Walker ordered, "Regiment. Attention!" The officers came to attention instantly and all issued the proper salute. Colonel Cummings brought himself to attention, returned their salute, and looked at Walker. Walker uttered his commander's unspoken command, "Gentlemen, dismissed."

Minutes later, Nathaniel reported to Lieutenant Colonel Walker. Walker did not need to give specific instructions to the staff officers. Like the others, Nathaniel knew his responsibilities for striking the regiment's headquarters. Nathaniel would care for the personnel records. He hoped to overhear any information that would reveal the answer to Lieutenant Countiss' question. He knew from his brief military experience that it would be best to wait. Nathaniel would be told soon enough. After Shiloh, he wrote many letters to let loved ones know that their brothers, fathers, or sons would not return. Nathaniel was in no hurry to march into another battle.

As the troop train pulled out of Corinth, Mississippi, heading southeast, Nathaniel stared out of the window. *"Ain't it something what one bullet can do?" How did we get ourselves into this terrible mess? It's all about power. Who has it and what they will do to keep it from those who want it and will do anything to obtain it? Is slaveholding a sin? Am I a false Christian because I don't believe that it is a sin? Why, dear God, didn't You prevent this from happening?* Restlessly, he tried to remember a simpler and happier time.

It must have been six Aprils ago. The train settled into a thirty miles-per-hour monotonous pace. The constant sideways rocking and regimented clacking of steel wheels on steel rail joints put him into a dreamy state of mind as he watched the sun peek above the hilly horizon.

Life couldn't be better. Nathaniel stared across the campus grounds. *In a little more than six weeks, I will be a college graduate. These past years at the University of Eastern Tennessee seem like a dream. I can't believe how scared I was to leave home. Now, I'm scared to leave school. Lord, I wonder if anyone else feels this way. The one thing that could make this sunny day better would be to—"*

Samuel Cleburne rudely interrupted, "Mr. Graham, are you even listening to me? "You daydream far more than any man I know."

"What Sam? I'm sorry. I was thinking about what I'm going to do after I graduate."

"Mr. Graham, if you keep looking to the sky for answers, you may not have to worry about graduating. We still have classes to complete before we face our futures. I asked you a question about our government topic. What did you find out from the newspaper?"

"They're going to hear the case. Did you know that this whole thing started the same year you and I were born?"

"You're kidding me. Really, 1834?"

"Yep, 1834 and it isn't over yet."

"I can't believe they're going to allow the case to be heard," Sam said shaking his head. "Some judicial leadership we have appointed for this nation. A council of monkeys could do a better job. Don't you think that sends the wrong message?" Sam asked rhetorically. "I think I remember the lower Federal Circuit Court said that if they even entertained the case, it would appear to recognize his citizenship."

"I don't know why they took the case. I didn't finish reading the article," Nathaniel admitted. "Maybe if we read the whole piece, it will tell us or give us some insight into their reasoning."

Other fellow students began to gather around the two friends. They were curious about the story, most because they wanted a good grade, some because a negative judgment could dramatically effect their lives and livelihood, and still a few others genuinely cared about what might happen to one person, if he could be called that.

"It doesn't make any sense at all," said William Poole. His family owned a very large and wealthy cotton plantation. "He always was Doctor Emerson's property. If I take my dog or horse to New York City, or to old Boston town, they still belong to me. I should be able to take my property wherever I want to go." William became more forceful in his speech as he continued. "Just because I go some place where folks choose not to own a cow or a chicken, doesn't mean that my livestock—what's rightfully mine, remember—no longer belongs to me. It's a free country and I should be free to take my property where I please. That's the Constitution and the law of this great land. That's the way I see it, anyway."

"Yes, Sir, Mr. Poole," Joseph Webster affirmed. "Some folks think that just because a few darkies have learned to read, write, count and take care of themselves, they should be considered people. My horse can count and he's still a horse." Several students laughed. Webster paused and furrowed his brow contemplatively, and then he continued, "I can't believe anyone could reach that conclusion. I don't know anyone who even thinks that way. Have we not learned that the Negro is a higher form of animal? They are more closely related to the ape in the jungle from where they originated. Isn't that what we learned in our science class about Charles Darwin's theories of how we all got here? Even if Darwin is wrong, how can we prove that they have an immortal soul, like us?"

Thad Holt a handsome and dashing, medium built agriculture student, true to his immature and impulsive ways, interrupted and said, "I know several of ours pray and sing to the Lord all the time. That must prove something. Besides, how does anyone know that they have an immortal soul?"

"Oh, come now," the argumentative and always opinionated Webster rebutted. "I have a parrot that can sing. That's all Negroes are doing when they sing and pray. They've just seen what we do and imitate our actions. They really don't know what they are doing or why. They don't know the difference between God and a pile of rocks."

Sam had never liked Webster. He chided, "Excuse me, gentlemen. Mr. Webster, I'm not sure you know the difference either, but we have more important issues to grasp." Sam turned to Nathaniel and urged him to continue his summarization. "Mr. Graham, what does the newspaper have to say?"

Nathaniel started his paraphrased report of the newspaper account, "This is from an article originally published last week by that radical abolitionist newspaper the *Liberator*. You know the one owned and edited by William Lloyd Garrison. Now the *New York Tribune* has picked up the story and distributed it to newspapers around the country. It says here that neither party disputes the facts of the case. The petitioner is Dred Scott, a Negro slave belonging to Doctor Emerson, a United States Army surgeon. Dred Scott claims that in 1834 Doctor Emerson took him to Illinois. Slavery is forbidden there. Did you hear when all this mess started? This happened before some of you boys were born."

Webster interjected, "That was twenty-two years ago. Who cares what happened to some dumb Negro back then?"

"Yeah, this whole thing seems to be a plot by those abolitionists to stir up trouble," William Poole complained. "Seems like it's always a few trouble makers who want to make life difficult for everyone."

Sam came to his friend's rescue, saying, "Go on, Mr. Graham. Please tell us what else the paper says."

Nathaniel swallowed hard, shook the paper, looked around at all the faces fixed on him, and answered, "Okay, there is only a little more to read." Nathaniel found where he left off and continued, "Some years later, Doctor Emerson took Scott to Fort Snelling, in the Louisiana territory, north of the boundary where slavery was forbidden by the law passed by the United States Congress otherwise known as the Missouri Compromise. Subsequently, Doctor Emerson took Scott to Missouri, where the law of the land protects slavery. Scott brought suit in the Unites States Circuit Court in Missouri to recover his freedom. Scott bases his action on the claim that residence in a free territory, or Free State, conferred upon him the status of being a free person. The Circuit Court ruled that Scott's claim was in error and dismissed the case. Based on that ruling Scott filed his appeal to the United States Supreme Court."

"Where'd a slave get the money to file a case with the Supreme Court?" Webster challenged.

"I'll tell you, from the abolitionists," Poole nearly shouted. "Those Yankees can't seem to leave things alone."

"I agree, but I'd like to hear the rest of the story," Sam said calmly. "Nate, please."

"Very well. The Constitutional question that the United States Supreme Court should rule upon is simple. Can a Negro slave become a citizen of the United States by residing in a free territory or Free State? If so, is that Negro then entitled to all the rights and privileges guaranteed by the Constitution to a citizen of the United States? One of those rights is the privilege of suing in a court of the United States." Nathaniel suddenly stopped reading.

"What's the matter?" Sam asked, recognizing a look of uncertainty on Nathaniel's face.

Nathaniel hesitated and then responded anxiously, "The paper says that Garrison declared that if the court does not recognize Scott's petition, and renders its decision strictly upon constitutional grounds, then the Constitution of the United States should be burned."

Nathaniel lowered the newspaper and breathed deeply. He looked around at the faces again. Their expressions registered confusion, disbelief and shock.

Marvin Jenkins, a small skinny boy from Knoxville, broke the silence saying, "I wonder if the Supreme Court will grant citizenship to Negroes?"

"They can't do that," Poole said angrily. "The Court is not authorized by the Constitution to decide who or who is not a citizen. That authority rests with the Congress. Didn't you learn anything in class? Don't say you were absent that day because you're absent even when you're here."

Everyone laughed except Nathaniel. He looked at Marvin as his friend's face started to turn red. Marvin was just a sophomore and small for his age. His eyes always appeared dark, sad, and sunken. In some ways, he seemed frail. Nathaniel decided to come to his defense. "I guess the Court is choosing to use its self-proclaimed power of judicial review. We studied that subject last semester remember? But I think I agree with what Sam said earlier, that they shouldn't even hear this case."

"Well, someone needs to make a decision, and soon," blurted Poole. "My slaves are my property, and no one, and no government can just take my property from me. The Court must protect our rights as property owners. Isn't the whole purpose of government to serve the people? If the government starts taking away our property rights, before too long we will be a people serving the government, just like the countries of Europe."

Several of the students vocally agreed with Poole, but Nathaniel thought they were getting away from the real issue. Trying to re-direct the conversation, Nathaniel insisted, "I think the decision of who is or who is not a citizen is critical to our future. It's as if they are deciding who is or who is not human. It seems the stuff Charles Darwin promotes about the evolution of all creatures is behind this somehow. I think a biblical point of view should be examined. I've done some research into this matter for my religious studies and I think the Scriptures speak for themselves regarding the state of the Negro."

"Oh, Nate," Webster chimed, "You doomsday theologian types are always looking for a conspiracy. The Court is made up of the most intelligent men in this country. Don't you think they read the newspaper? The country is tired of waiting and debating. The Court saw that it had an opportunity to resolve a smoldering social issue and they decided to take a close look into the situation. The Bible has no relevance in our modern and enlightened times."

Samuel Cleburne's hot Irish temper could no longer stomach Webster's attitude. His anger surfaced. He came to the physical defense of his friend. Sam grabbed Webster by his shirt collar and pulled him close. They stood nose-to-nose. Then Samuel said, almost shouting, "Look here, Joe, I expect the Supreme Court to answer to the highest authority of all, and you should too if you know what is good for you. What are you Webster, some kind of Yankee abolitionist, trying to say darkies are something they ain't?"

Almost by instinct, the boys formed a circle and prepared for a fistfight. Webster knew better than to support the Yankee point of view, but he proudly defended himself as he pushed Cleburne away, "I'm no Yankee, and I could care less what a few extremists think. But I think we need to act as educated men who carefully consider all sides of an issue."

"Why you," Sam started to charge Webster, but Nathaniel and then Marvin grabbed Sam and held him back. Webster's words had rendered the desired effect. Sam failed to act as an educated and refined college man, and reverted to a backwoods brawler.

A new voice suddenly spoke up from the crowd. Howell Cobb, the president of the student body, attempted to bring calm and order before an affray erupted, "Well, I think Nate has a point." As more students gathered around the impromptu rally, he continued, "I'd like to hear Nate's theory based on biblical authority."

Marvin looked at Nathaniel and timidly spoke up trying to project encouragement in his voice, "Nate, I know you've been working on your thesis for some time. I think you are onto something and your point needs to be made. Go on, let us hear what you have to say."

Nathaniel released his hold on Sam and stepped away. He swallowed hard, looked around at the crowd, and quickly perceived that he better become accustomed to making public statements. Slowly he began, "When I first began my research, I never anticipated that this topic would attract anyone's attention like it has today."

"Please continue, Mr. Graham," Cobb requested.

Taking another deep breath, Nathaniel pressed forward. "I did not choose this subject. It is by no means exhaustive and it needs more work. However, my biblical studies professor, Dr. Jackson, believed I should try to expose objectively a pernicious fallacy. Under a strong sense of duty, I completed this study. I did not depend upon any reasoning of my own but by a statement of facts supported by the authority of Scripture. From this basis, any inferences that you may draw from this study are yours alone. Should these facts prove unpalatable to men of extreme opinions is naturally to be expected. However, a key fact remains and cannot be disputed—the texts of Scripture do not directly or indirectly denounce slaveholding as a sin. No one from the North or the South can quote such a text because it does not exist. So I examined upon what authority the question, whether slave holding is a sin before God, can be answered."

"My study concentrated on two parts: first, how far back in history can we trace the existence of slavery; and secondly, is slaveholding recognized as an acceptable social condition in Sacred Scripture?"

"It is generally accepted that slavery had its origin in war. The victor holds the power to take the life of his vanquished enemy. Instead of death, he chooses to let his captive live and reduces him to bondage. The life the conqueror has spared the body he might have mutilated or destroyed, becomes his absolute property. He may dispose of it in any way he pleases. Such was, and throughout a great part of the world still is, the brutal law of force. When bondage of this kind first began, it is next to impossible to determine."

"If we examine the Sacred Scripture, the original Hebrew records available, we find the Hebrew word 'evved' which has been translated into the word, 'slave.' The more recent English version renders the term, 'servant.' It is first used by Noah, who, in Genesis 9:25, curses the descendants of his son Ham by saying they should be 'Evved Avadim,' or the Hebrew phrase meaning the 'meanest of slaves.' Our English version now has it, 'servant of servants.' The question I think that naturally arises is how did Noah come to use the expression? When did he come to know anything of slavery? As best we can tell from Scripture, no other human beings existed on earth after the flood except Noah and his family of three sons, apparently by one mother, born free and equal, with their wives and children. When Noah and his family left the ark, he had no slaves. Further, the Bible does not indicate if Noah owned any slaves prior to or during the ark's construction. It therefore becomes evident that Noah's acquaintance with slaves and the nature of slavery must date from before the flood. It must have existed in his memory until the crime of Ham called it forth. It may be regrettable that Noah in his anger recalled the idea and practice of slavery, but that he did is a fact traced back to and rests on the authority of Scripture. From this antiquity evidence, I concluded that next to the domestic relations of husband and wife, and parents and children, another ancient social relationship existed—that of master and slave."

Angrily, Poole interrupted, "Okay, that's all well and good. I think you've made a great argument. I hope the Court knows this too. They have to protect our property and business interests."

"I still think you should send your thesis to someone in Washington," Marvin added.

Samuel Cleburne knew something about Nathaniel's work and insisted, "Gentlemen, please give Nathaniel a chance to finish. He's just getting started and the best is yet to come." Samuel turned to Nathaniel and said, "Go on Nate, but I think you need to get to heart of the matter quickly."

Nathaniel looked at the faces of his fellow students to see if they understood him or if his speech created more confusion. Satisfied that they were with him, he continued, "Okay, Sam, but let us move on from this curse by Noah and examine other instances from Scripture. Among the many prophecies contained in the Bible and having reference to particular times, peoples, and events, there are three singular predictions referring to three distinct races, which seem to be intended for all times, and accordingly remain in full force to this day. One of these speaks directly to the Negro as the descendants of Noah's son, Ham. Another is to the descendants of Israel, but for now; I only wish to talk about one. The Bible foretells nearly 4,000 years ago the character of the descendants of Ishmael, the Arabs."

Poole jumped in, "What do those camel herders have to do with anything?"

Nathaniel looked at Poole and replied, "It has been said that knowledge of a particular prophecy's existence helps to work out its fulfillment. I am quite willing to allow that this may be true. However, it may be doubted whether the fanatic Arab of the desert ever heard of the prophecy that he is to be as, the Holy Scripture says, a *'wild man; his hand will be against every man, and every man's hand against him.'* But you and I—" Nathaniel paused and looked directly at Poole. Then he turned and quickly scanned the others and continued "—and all men of ordinary education, know that this prediction at all times has been, and is now, literally fulfilled and that it has never been interrupted. The pronounced character of Ishmael on his descendants has never changed. History reported this wild nature when the followers of Mohammed rushed forth to spread his doctrines with the Koran in one hand and the sword in the other. We also know that later Arab conquests rendered the fairest portion of the Old World subject to the empire of their Caliph."

Samuel Cleburne broke his own urging to be silent and stated, "Remember the Barbary pirates?"

William Poole answered, "I sure do. If not for those crazy Muslims attacking our merchant ships, we might not have the navy right now. Those murderous barbarians sunk our ships and enslaved our sailors. White men forced into slavery. It's unnatural."

Joseph Webster added, "They had the nerve to demand ransom and tribute from our government to release our men and to stop the piracy."

The students' agitation grew and many began to grumble. They remembered these stories from their parents and grandparents. They also remember the heroes of this era and how President Thomas Jefferson, the United States Navy, and the United States Marines forcefully ended the menacing followers of Islam's repeated attacks on American shipping interests.

Howell Cobb seized the moment and stated, "That fine Southern gentleman, Virginia statesman, and principal author of our founding document, the Declaration of Independence, President Thomas Jefferson, understood that a strong nation uses its strength to bring about peaceful resolutions."

Several of the students acknowledged with, "Hear-hear!" and "That's right!"

Samuel Cleburne added, "There was that story about the young naval officer from Maryland, Stephen Decatur. He commanded the *Enterprise,* which was one of several navy ships that made up the Mediterranean squadron. On the night of February 16, 1804, he took a small vessel, the *Intrepid*, with a handpicked band of Americans, into the harbor of Tripoli. There he set fire to the frigate *Philadelphia*, previously captured by Barbary pirates. Under fierce fire from the enemy's batteries, he made his way back to the fleet stationed at Syracuse. One man was wounded, none killed. English Admiral Horatio Nelson called this assault the 'most bold and daring act of the age.' Later, at an awards ceremony, Decatur gave an enthusiastic toast saying, 'My country, right or wrong.'"

This brought louder cheers from the crowd of students and an even more enthusiastic, "Hear-hear!"

Nathaniel had lost control, not that he cared. However, there was so much more he had to offer from his thesis that he attempted to bring his peers back to the point, "Gentlemen, please, I do appreciate your enthusiasm for this debate and your solid grasp on our nation's history. It is helpful to this discussion—but do you want me to continue?"

Almost apologetically, the boys turned to Nathaniel, and Samuel Cleburne encouraged, "I'm sorry, Nate, please finish. I, for one, will try to be quiet."

Nathaniel nodded and started again, "As you gentlemen so clearly demonstrated, even in our enlightened civilization today coupled with frequent interchanges with Western travelers, the Arab is still a wild, very unpredictable creature. Has this prophecy ever been withdrawn? The Holy Scripture declared that his hand would be against everybody, and every man's hand against him, and this is still the case today. I think this is convincing and durable proof that the Word of God is true, and that the prophecies of the Bible were dictated by the Spirit of the Most High."

Simple and emotional Marvin couldn't help himself as he shouted out, "Amen!" Again, the crowd of students laughed. Nathaniel was not sure if they laughed at Marvin or at what he was saying.

Cobb looked right into Nathaniel's eyes and nodded in affirmation to continue. From Nathaniel's perspective, it was easy to see that Cobb was in control of this meeting. With this assurance, Nathaniel picked up with his second point.

"Having thus on the authority of Scripture traced slavery back to the remotest period of written history, I next request your attention to the second and more important concern, 'Is slaveholding condemned as a sin in Sacred Scripture?' Forgive my personal opinion here, but how this question can at all arise in the mind of any man who has received a religious education and is acquainted with the history of man and the Bible is a phenomenon I cannot explain to myself. Fifty years ago, no man would have dreamed of this notion. But we live in times when we must not be surprised by anything."

This brought more laughter from the students. However, it was an appropriate response for the moment. It let Nathaniel know they were paying attention.

"Now, Gentlemen, there are those who choose to accept moral instruction from such eloquent Yankee preachers as the one from Brooklyn, Henry Ward Beecher. However, I think you and I should continue to take our requirements for moral instruction from the Bible. Unfortunately, the Reverend Beecher takes a lead among those who most loudly and most vehemently denounce slaveholding as a sin. This prompted the assignment from my professor. He asked me to find whether any Scripture justified Reverend Beecher's argument that now incites the emotions of millions of our friends to the north. I objectively examined the various books of Scripture and found that they afford no authority for his declarations. The Testaments nowhere directly or indirectly condemn slaveholding, which indeed is proved by the universal practice of all Christian nations during many centuries. Acknowledging slavery as one of the conditions of society, the New Testament nowhere interferes with or contradicts the slave code of the Old; it even preserves a letter written by the Apostle Paul to a slave owner, Philemon, to receive back his runaway slave, Onesimus. Paul returns Onesimus as both slave and brother in Christ to Philemon."

"Finally, when I looked at that most solemn occasion when God gave the Ten Commandments on Mount Sinai, slaveholding is recognized and sanctioned as an integral part of the social structure. Regarding the Sabbath of the Lord in Exodus, chapter twenty, at verse ten, God commands that the Sabbath bring rest to *'Thy manservant and thy maidservant.'* Further, the scripture at verse seventeen places the right of property ownership of slaves under the same protection as any other species of lawful property. It states that, *'Thou shalt not covet thy neighbour's house; thou shalt not covet thy neighbour's wife, nor his manservant, nor his maidservant, nor his ox, nor his ass, nor anything that is thy neighbour's.'* Christians and Jews the world over recognize The Ten Commandments as the Word and Law of God. As such, they are considered the highest legal and religious authority. If slaveholding was lawful then, when and on what authority did it become sinful?"

Chapter 8

FUTURE LEADERS

Applause erupted with many cheers. Nathaniel blushed because he really was not used to this much attention. Clapping his hands, Cobb walked over to Nathaniel's side and patted him on his back. "Well stated, Nate," Cobb, the born statesman, said enthusiastically. "You are going to make a wonderful preacher someday. You should write your class essay in a more formal paper and send it to Washington."

"Yeah, Nate," Marvin affirmed. "Didn't I tell you? I think you really should."

Cobb looked around and decided to take complete control over the student gathering. "Gentlemen, I think we can approach this matter logically from all sides—theological, scientific, political and practical. First, I'd like to summarize a key point that Nate made. We recognized that slaves are and have always been private property. My family's Negroes belong to us. We breed them like we breed our other livestock. William, your family has horses, cattle and other farm animals too, right?"

The question caught William Poole by surprise, but he responded, "Huh, yes. We have several high-quality thoroughbreds."

Cobb continued his point, "Thanks, Will. I suspect many of you gentlemen, or your family members, own livestock. I would also wager that all of you do what you can to improve your stock by careful breeding practices when the opportunities arise." Cobb started to work the crowd like the master politician everyone knew was his destiny. Pacing, using his hands for emphasis, and looking into each man's eyes as he passed, Cobb captured his audience. "Practically speaking, we've brought this problem on ourselves. Many plantation owners have improved their Negroes through careful breeding practices. Clearly, we evolved our Negroes into a higher order than their African ancestors. I've even heard, and I don't know if it's true, that some owners father their own slaves as soon as young Negro females are old enough to bare offspring. My point is this: we have improved the animal to where they are almost human. Those uninformed and overzealous people from the North who really don't know the Negro animal like we Southerners do, have come to believe that Negroes are human beings. That's why I am glad to hear that the Supreme Court is going to make a decision. We can't have a few renegade abolitionists telling us that Negroes are human when we, who work with them, day in and day out, know that they are just smart farm animals."

From the gathering crowd, several voices affirmed Howell Cobb's last remarks. Many heads nodded agreement as encouraging phrases like, "That's right," and "Go on," rose from the attentive throng.

Cobb continued, "As we've learned here at this great educational institution, John C. Calhoun—considered to be the last, and maybe the greatest of our founding fathers—was very outspoken regarding these issues before he passed over the river to rest under the shady trees, just a few years ago." Howell Cobb mastered the use of the long, emotional pause.

Someone from the student group said, "God rest his soul."

Recognizing the desired affect, Cobb pressed, "You all should remember his service to this country. From 1810 to his death in 1850, he served as a member of Congress, secretary of war, vice president under presidents John Quincy Adams and Andrew Jackson, U.S. senator from South Carolina, and secretary of state under President John Tyler. In our government class, we studied his essay, 'A Disquisition on Government.' Gentlemen, in my humble opinion, his work is a masterpiece on politics and economics. He recognized the dangers we face today.

"Remember, he wrote that the right of citizenship, including the right of suffrage is 'the indispensable and primary principle in the foundation of a constitutional government.' But he warned that in order for the right of voting to serve this purpose the public must be sufficiently enlightened to understand their own rights under the Constitution and 'the interests of the community.' He also stated that citizens must be able 'to appreciate the motives and conduct of those appointed to make and execute the laws.' Knowledge of the United States Constitution is almost nonexistent in American society and does not exist among the Negroes. Because we failed to understand our Constitution, the new political party, the 'Black Republicans,' and the so-called 'cultural elite' have begun a full-scale assault on our individual liberty. The Northern city schools not only fail to teach about the Constitution but they also undermine it with abolitionist propaganda. Consequently, an incredible number of Americans remain unbelievably naive about what Calhoun referred to as the, 'motives and conduct of those appointed to make and execute the laws.' Our neighbors to the north have a childish mentality of trust when it comes to government. They believe that it is our government's responsibility to somehow take care of and provide for them. I believe this is why the average Yankee does not expend any disciplined effort to resolve our political and economical slavery issue. The Black Republicans understand this, which is why they bury us in an avalanche of abolitionist lies about slavery and how we treat our slaves. Public ignorance, combined with abolitionist rhetoric, will destroy our liberty. As Calhoun said, we must assure that 'government benefits primarily the ruled and not the rulers.'"

Several students surrounding Cobb muttered agreement. Now he would insert his own personal ideas for his future constituents to consider. "My friends, let's consider a bigger picture for a minute. Let us suppose that we free the slaves, grant them citizenship and the right to vote."

"Never!" someone shouted from the crowd.

Cobb smiled and continued, "I agree, but for argument's sake, let's keep an open mind to the possibility. Calhoun wrote and warned about what could happen if ignorant people had the right and power to vote. He anticipated a much worse problem, as I hope you will see. Calhoun stated that it is the tendency of democratic governments to divide the population into two groups: taxpayers and tax consumers, with the latter group employing the apparatus of the state through the power of the vote to plunder the former group. 'When once formed, the community will be divided into two great parties—a major and minor—between which, there will be incessant struggles on the one side to retain, and on the other to obtain, the majority.' Consequently, 'some portion of the community must pay in taxes more than it receives back in disbursements while another receives in disbursements more than it pays in taxes.' The community is economically unbalanced and thus divided into 'two great classes—one consisting of those who pay the taxes and the other consisting of those who are the recipients of the proceeds.'"

Cobb paused, stopped his pacing, and turned his head around to look at his listeners to let his doomsday message take hold. Then he continued, "Calhoun further warned that this could lead to 'one class or portion of the community,'—let's say the freed slaves—'elevated to wealth and power. The other—that would be us—reduced to 'depressed, abject poverty and dependence simply by the fiscal action of the government.' We would be controlled by the ignorant Negroes who will use the power to tax in our created democracy for the purpose of aggrandizing and building up their portion of the community at the expense of us. This will, Calhoun believed, 'give rise to violent conflicts and struggles between the two competing parties.' As you can see, over time we would be robbed of the very wealth our fathers and their fathers before them worked to create and fought to preserve.

"Calhoun also foresaw that the enemies of liberty, like the Black Republicans, would say anything—anything—to dilute the power of the Constitution. It is 'a great mistake,' Calhoun wrote, 'to suppose that a mere written Constitution would be sufficient to protect individual liberties because the party in power will never have need of its constitutional restrictions on governmental powers.'"

"My friends, unless we understand what is really at stake we could find ourselves being naive defenders of the Constitution. We, with childlike faith, will initially believe that it can be protected by, as Calhoun said, 'an appeal to reason, truth, justice, or the obligations imposed by the Constitution.' Unfortunately and conversely, the power-hungry Yankees will wage a perpetual political war against the Constitution. Calhoun told us that they would use 'cunning, falsehood, deception, slander, fraud, and gross appeals to the appetites of the lowest and most worthless portions of the community,' until 'the restrictions would be ultimately annulled, and the government converted into one of unlimited powers.' Does anyone here today deny that this is essentially the situation in which we citizens, charged with the responsibility to protect liberty, now find ourselves?"

"I'd rather die fighting to protect my rights then let some darkies rule over me," Poole yelled. Many agreed and tempers began to boil.

Now with the full weight of his argument delivered, Cobb determined to conclude it calmly, "Gentlemen, the Supreme Court understands these things and they will settle this matter for all time. I think it is safe to say that they will uphold the lower court's decision. I am sure they realize that citizenship can only be granted to human beings and that it would be silly to recognize, to even casually think, that God granted animals civil rights. Just think where poor logic like this would lead. Before long, we will want to extend equal protection status to our dogs, cats, sheep, goats, horses, mules, cattle, and pigs. The next thing you know someone will promote equal rights for the wild animals that roam the forests or the fish that swim in the seas."

Cobb's last remark came home to the crowd, which started to laugh at its obvious absurdity. Cobb ended his argument peacefully saying, "Friends, we don't have to worry about the outcome of this case. The High Court will make a sound decision. I am confident that they will decide to uphold the righteous law of this land and the Constitution will not be put to the torch. Negro slaves will remain slaves, no matter where their owners travel. The only way a Negro can become free is if its owner foolishly grants it freedom. In my experience, that is a very unwise thing to do. We all know that the Negro animal is taken care of better under the protection of an owner, not the government. Rest assured, the Supreme Court will define who is and who is not a citizen protected by the United States Constitution, and Negroes won't be included. The trouble-making abolitionists will just have to live with that decision."

Cobb heard more affirmations from the crowd as he finished, "I think we will safely see the end of this issue, so I suggest that we, who have classes to attend, move on about our business." Cobb started to walk toward the main classroom building. With his reminder and movement, the crowd dispersed in all directions.

A much cooler Samuel Cleburne said to Nathaniel, "I think he's right. This whole slavery issue will soon be a thing of the past."

"I hope so," Nathaniel said to his good friend. *But I'm afraid that is simply wishful thinking.* They walked to the university's library.

This last memory brought Nathaniel back to the present. Nathaniel looked around the rail car at the men who now fought to preserve and protect what once was the law of all the country. *Wishful thinking; what fools we were to believe that the Yankees would simply let the matter rest. We naively believed that the Supreme Court's ruling in favor of the Southern way of life would put an end to the matter. They confirmed that a Negro is an inferior being, not ever meant to be considered a citizen. The framers of the United States Constitution intended Negroes to be protected by their owners not its provisions. The Court upheld the law. Why couldn't the people of the North simply abide by the law of the land? And they call us "Rebels." I believe they are the real rebels because they do not obey the Constitution and the sound, God-given righteous judgment of the Supreme Court. That's why I know God is on our side and why I know we are going to win this war.*

Chapter 9

DEAR MISS ELLIS

A hint of smoke from burning wood invaded the cloudy summer sky. The lower Appalachian Mountains, east of Huntsville, Alabama, teemed with new life. A hawk called as she hunted small field rodents to feed her young. The trail of smoke grew blacker, thicker, and mixed with small burning cinders of wood as metallic noises became louder. Rabbits fled from the approaching menace, and a small herd of whitetail deer bounded deep into the thick protective covering of trees and brush. A pulsating cadence disturbed the peaceful valley surrounded by wooded peaks. The vaporous steam, thick choking smoke, and rhythmic chugging sounds, came from the manmade iron horse that made its way along a steel path. It pulled tens of odd looking, multi-colored, rocking boxes.

This Confederate troop train carried much-needed supplies and reinforcements. From Corinth, Mississippi, they followed a circuitous route that ran parallel to the Tennessee River, south of the greater-than-one-hundred-thousand-man Yankee force. They crossed the river at Decatur, Alabama, and headed northeast. The train stopped in Huntsville to pick up more men and supplies. The crew took on more wood and water for the engine. Travel-weary men crammed the boxcars. They hoped that their next stop would be long enough for them to sleep for the night before moving on to their unknown, but strongly rumored destination.

The train reached a switch junction at Stevenson, Alabama. It connected the rail line with Nashville, Tennessee, but this train curved north and further east toward Chattanooga. As Nathaniel gazed out the window, he remembered that not far from this very spot, over the east side of the mountains before him, a terrific locomotive chase had occurred a month earlier. In his mind, he saw the remnants of damaged railroad tracks and scorched bridges and telegraph poles. This covert Yankee operation left little doubt in the minds of Southern men and women that the Northern Federal government would allow any dishonorable act to justify its existence. The mere thought of sending a band of spies deep into enemy territory to destroy communication and supply lines was foreign to a Southerner's sense of honor and duty. This cowardly attack demonstrated how low the evil, power-hungry Yankee government was willing to stoop.

Early in the morning of April 12, just days after the heartbreaking losses from the Battle of Shiloh, James J. Andrews, a foul Yankee, led a sixteen-man raiding party south to Big Shanty Station, just north of Atlanta, Georgia. There, they hijacked a train, pulled by a locomotive named *General*. The saboteurs drove the commandeered train north toward Chattanooga stopping at remote points where they cut down telegraph poles and removed sections of track. They set fire to bridges after crossing them so they could not be pursued. Their main objective lay further down the line near Resaca, Georgia. Each act of destruction fueled their determination to reach their target—the very large covered bridge over the Oostanaula River—and burn it down. That immense trestle bridge would take months, or more, to rebuild. Once destroyed, Andrew's Raiders could cut off a main supply artery and greatly hinder the South's ability to wage war. But their plans failed, thanks to the heroic efforts of William A. Fuller, the conductor of the stolen train.

Fuller tenaciously pursued the cowardly Yankees on foot, next by handcar, and then by train, the *Yonah*. When he reached Kingston, Georgia, other rail traffic blocked his way. Fuller abandoned the *Yonah*, and commandeered the *William R. Smith*. Later that afternoon, Fuller and the men on the *William R. Smith* train nearly collided head-on into a southbound train, the *Texas*. Moments after both trains came to a stop, Fuller stood at the controls of the *Texas* feverishly explaining to the displaced engineer what was happening. Unfortunately, the only way he could continue to give chase was to run the *Texas* backwards. Fuller would not give up. Nothing would deter him from catching the Yankees. He even drove the *Texas* across a burning bridge.

By the time Andrews and his men reached Resaca, Fuller was close behind. The raiders tried to set the timbers of the rain-soaked covered bridge on fire. They abandoned their mission once they realized the closeness of the Confederates. Andrews and his men boarded the *General* in haste to avoid capture, or worse. Then the locomotive chase began. Finally, a short distance past Ringgold, with the *General* almost out of fuel, Andrews ordered his men to jump off the train and scatter. Within a week, diligent Southern soldiers and civilians caught the spies and quickly brought them to justice. They hung Andrews and seven of his men. The surviving raiders were sent to prison.

So ended another Yankee plot, which only served to strengthen Southern resolve to be free from a tyrannical government that would conceive of and carry out any dastardly deed to preserve and protect its interests. This resolve gave the Confederate army inner strength to fight anywhere they were needed. If this meant riding for days on a train to fight Yankee aggression, so be it.

While in transit, most of the enlisted soldiers concerned themselves with essential matters—such as when would they next eat?

The commanding officers enjoyed their roomy accommodations and an occasional sip of whiskey. Confederate junior officers sat in standard passenger cars. Most of these men tried to sleep. A few read newspaper reports about the Yankee capture of Yorktown, Virginia and their force buildup at Cumberland Landing on the Pamunkey River. Some engaged in idle, casual conversation.

"Where do you think we're going to end up, Nate?" Lieutenant Marvin Jenkins asked his friend and protector since their time together in college.

Nathaniel was lost within his own troubled mind. He had a distant stare that looked outside the window. His glazed-over eyes did not comprehend the beautiful forest scenery he passed as he road along in silent isolation even though his comrades-in-arms surrounded him. He didn't hear the question directed to him.

"Nate, didn't you hear me? What's the matter with you? I swear you seem to be hundreds of miles away."

Nathaniel snapped out of his self-absorbed condition and asked sincerely, "I'm sorry Marvin. What did you say?"

"You sure do day-dream. I couldn't tell if you were awake or sleeping with your eyes open."

Nathaniel blurted out rudely, "Marvin, what does that have anything to do with anything?'

"Well excuse me, Captain, sir," Marvin replied sarcastically. "I was just trying to talk to you about where you think we might be headed. It is obvious that we are heading north. Do you think we are going to hit the Yankees near Nashville?"

"Frankly, I don't know and I don't care."

"You don't care? Nate, what is the matter with you? This is not like you. I've known you for years. You always care about something."

"It's not that I don't care, Marvin. It's just I have something important on my mind right now. It's a matter that has bothered me for some time, and I still don't know what to do."

"Sounds serious."

"It is to me."

"I know I'm not the sharpest tool in the shed, but why don't you tell me about it. Who knows, maybe I can help."

"Marvin, I think this one I'm going to have to work through on my own. Thanks all the same."

"It must be a woman. That's it, isn't it? You got a woman in your life and you didn't tell your old friend. Who is she?"

Other officers turned to look at Nathaniel expecting to hear a new girlfriend story. Nathaniel quickly scanned their eyes knowing he would disappoint them all. He looked back at Marvin and replied, "I've never met her. I don't know anything about her, but I need to write her and tell her that her father died."

With that, everyone turned back to his respective private business. Nathaniel looked around once more. Then he turned his attention back to Marvin, who replied, "I guess I would be miles away too. I would hate to have your job." Marvin paused for a minute, then he continued with that old sadness in his voice, "I guess I don't care where we're headed anymore either." Marvin looked around the railroad car, stood up and said, "I need some air. You want to stretch your legs?"

"No thanks, Marvin. You go on. I'll be fine here."

Marvin turned and walked toward the rear of the passenger car. He swayed with the rocking motion of the train. Nathaniel was alone again and immediately became engrossed in his thoughts. *I know I should write, but what do I say. "Dear Miss Ellis, I watched your father die, and I am a member of the Rebel army that killed him?" I can't say that.*

Nathaniel knew that he should stop thinking and take time to pray. He began slowly and quietly, *"Lord Jesus, I need Your help if You want me to write her. I know I said I would find her and try to convince her to follow You, but how is that possible? I can't travel to Illinois. I would be shot or hung or thrown in prison by the Yankees.*

If my own people stop me, they may think I'm a spy for the North. They'd kill me for sure. That can't be Your plan." Nathaniel paused. His prayer collided with his thoughts. He furrowed his brow as if suddenly confronted with new information. Then he continued to pray. *"Although, millions who followed You in the past ended up the same way. Please, Father, grant me some insight and understanding of what it is You want me to do. In Jesus' name, Amen."*

With his prayer ended, Nathaniel stopped to listen for a second. Maybe God would answer if he sat quietly. He began to hear only the rhythm of the train as it passed over rail joints. He closed his eyes and relaxed. He listened to the train wheels' click-clank, almost as steady as a heartbeat. He drifted off to sleep.

Lieutenant Colonel Edward Ellis looked whole. He stood tall, erect. He appeared to be the picture of health and vigor. He had no wounds, no bloodstains, and no sign of disfigurement. He seemed to be as perfect as a man could possibly be, and he gazed upward. A unique, white light broke through the heavens and shone brightly upon his smiling, peaceful face. "Jesus, I know You are coming for me now. I know Catherine knows You. Please help, Eleanor, Paul, and John find this peace, the assurance that I now have. Send Nathaniel to tell them for me."

Nathaniel woke up suddenly. It was the same dream with the same ending. It always raised the same question, *why me?* Nathaniel stared out the window. It was another hot summer afternoon in northern Georgia. He watched the rolling hills pass in the distance as they sped by the famous red clay lining both sides of the railroad tracks. In a few more hours they would reach Chattanooga, Tennessee. Nathaniel thought about the enlisted soldiers in the freight cars. *Those men must be dying in this heat.* At least the open windows on the train let a breeze blow through the sweltering passenger cars filled to the bursting point with exhausted soldiers.

Soot and burning cinders from the engine's smoke stack carried on the wind through the train windows. Nathaniel watched the sleepy officers in his car. Occasionally, a hot cinder would land on a man. Most brushed them off as they would pesky insects in their sleep. Hot intruders awakened some, but once they dismissed the annoyance they would seek elusive sleep again. Suddenly, a screaming commotion erupted near the rear of his car. Nathaniel turned completely around in his seat to see what had happened.

Laughter from the surrounding observers exploded as one after another recognized Lieutenant Frank Nelms jumping and spinning trying to beat a fire out that quickly burned a large hole in his wool over-blouse.

"Modern railroads do have their drawbacks," Captain Terry Lamkin announced with his distinct lower-Mississippi accent so that most could hear. The comment generated the desired effect, more laughter. Other officers began to make more jester-like remarks to further the young Lieutenant's embarrassment. Nathaniel started to laugh too, and join in the comic relief, when suddenly the terror on Nelms' face impressed him. Captain Conrad Irvin sat down in the seat vacated by Lieutenant Jenkins and commented softly to Nathaniel, "I'd rather a bullet find me and take me home then to be burned up by fire. Yes sir, fire is the worst way to die."

Those words triggered Nathaniel's memory. People whose names are not found in the Lamb's Book of Life will be cast into the lake of fire that burns eternally. Nathaniel's focus returned to his repetitive dream. He thought to himself critically, *You cannot let them pass away without knowing about Colonel Ellis. He is saved for eternity. It is possible that his family members are not. The job is yours. You cannot wait until this war is over. You must do something. Anything you do will be a step in the right direction, but whatever you choose, you must do it now before another distraction prevents you from obeying His command.*

Nathaniel looked out the window. *What should I do? Where should I start?* Nathaniel reached into the inside pocket of his uniform and pulled out the letter Eleanor Ellis wrote her father. He looked at it wondering if he did the right thing. *Maybe, taking this out of Colonel Ellis' hand was wrong.* As Nathaniel considered the affection in the words from a loving daughter to her father, he became convinced in his heart that he was right to take the letter and write this young woman. *I promised I would find her. If nothing else, I will be a faithful. I will keep my word even if Colonel Ellis never heard my pledge, Jesus did.*

By late afternoon, a midsummer rain fell. It chilled the already-cooler mountain air as the troop train came to a slow, jerky stop. The engineer released the excess steam with a great sounding whoosh. Once the side doors were opened, companies of soldiers escaped the freight cars, stretched their weary bodies, and quickly assembled as junior officers shouted commands. At best, the scene was chaotic.

The Chattanooga rail yard was larger than southern legend alluded. It absorbed the twenty thousand man military force with room to spare. Officers gave the ranks instructions. Once dismissed, the men began to move about in good order. The soldier rumors flew as a new tent-city rose just outside the stable of steam engines and freight cars. Several men believed they would stay in Chattanooga to defend the city and vital rail line. Others believed that they were part of a large flanking maneuver so they could attack and regain Nashville from the Yankees. Only a few high-ranking officers knew the stay was just for two nights and one day. A hoped-for additional five thousand recently drafted troops were expected.

The Confederate army was learning how to best use the railroad system to move tens of thousands of men, weapons, horses, and other war materials. As always, the lowly foot soldier paid for this military education.

Later that night, in the quiet of his tent, Nathaniel sharpened his quill and began to write. After five rough drafts and nearly as many hours into the night, Nathaniel read his work aloud one more time to make sure Eleanor would understand his message.

Dear Miss Ellis,

I sincerely hope this letter finds you well. I am truly sorry to know of the deep loss of your father, Lieutenant Colonel Edward Ellis. Please accept my personal condolences. I did have the honor of meeting your father and he spoke lovingly about you. I felt compelled to write to you because I was with him the night he passed.

This is not intended to be an official letter to tell you that he died facing the enemy with honor and that he served his country with distinction. I am sure those things are true. What I alone know is how he entered God's eternal Kingdom.

He was severely wounded. He knew he did not have long to live, and he was thinking of you and your mother, not this terrible war or who is right or wrong. Your father showed me a letter he received from you. He was worried that you would be disappointed that he would not be coming home. The truth is, though it may be very hard to accept, he went to a better home, and that's why I believe it is important for you to know about his last moments.

As he lay on the ground, he talked about you. When I got the chance, I began to talk to him about Jesus. He asked some very good questions regarding God and eternity. I didn't have answers for every question, but he seemed satisfied with my inadequate responses. I finally asked him if we could pray together, and he consented. I can tell you that he made an intelligent choice to receive Jesus Christ as his personal Savior. I am an eyewitness to his salvation. It was not an emotional decision driven by the reality of the moment, but he thought the issues through for himself and concluded that it was the correct decision to make. He entered into a personal relationship with Jesus. He prayed on his own. He prayed for you and your mother. He was completely at peace and he was no longer in any pain as he crossed over the river and rested under the shade of heavenly trees. His last prayer was that Jesus would help you and your brothers find the same peace of heart and certainty of mind that he found that night.

So that is why I am writing this letter. I believe Jesus wants to reunite you with your father, and the Lord will not let me rest until I tell you. I humbly request your permission to write to you and your mother further. I would be happy to discuss any questions you may have regarding your father or about any matters I raised by this letter.

Very truly yours,
Nathaniel Thomas Graham, Captain
Chaplain, 19th Tennessee Volunteer Infantry
Army of the Mississippi
Confederate States of America

"That will do," Nathaniel said to himself. He hoped Major Patrick Duffy listened as he read the letter aloud but softly and that Major Duffy might provide useful criticism, since he claimed to have bountiful experience with women. Unfortunately, Major Duffy slept, breathing heavily and about to break into a resounding snore. This night, Nathaniel finished the letter to Miss Eleanor

Ellis. He exhaled a heavy sigh. He decided that he had said what he wanted to say. He addressed the envelope and inserted the letter. He would take it to the camp postmaster first thing in the morning, before breakfast. Finally he could sleep, because he believed that his current burden had been lifted.

"What do you mean you can't mail this letter to Illinois," Nathaniel demanded an answer.

"Captain, in case you need to be reminded, we are at war with those people," the postal worker proudly stated the obvious.

"I know we are at war, sir; however, I know letters are being transmitted between the South and the North. Men in my command receive and send them frequently."

"That may be, but just recently things changed," the postal worker replied hoping to be the bearer of news that he had the privilege to possess.

"How so?" Nathaniel suddenly felt desperate. He needed to know.

"Well, sir, it seems that one of those Yankee generals, I believe his name is McClellan. Yes, that's it, George McClellan. He is concerned that military information is being passed through simple letters to family members. I heard that this was his security officer's idea, some little angry man by the name of Pinkerton. So anyway, he's stopped the mail traffic. I haven't seen a letter postmarked north of the Mason-Dixon Line in weeks. I'm told that anything we send north ends up in dead letter piles in Richmond."

"You're telling me that if I leave this letter with you, it will only go to Richmond?" Nathaniel restated the message angrily.

"Captain, don't raise your voice at me. I'm just telling you that you can't expect this letter addressed to Rockford, Illinois, to ever reach your Miss Eleanor Ellis until maybe this war is over and lines of communication are reestablished."

"I am sorry, sir, for shouting," Nathaniel replied apologetically. "I am not angry with you, sir. I am frustrated with the situation."

"I too am sorry that there is nothing more that I can do for you."

Nathaniel thanked the postal worker and turned to walk away. He hung his head in despair and dropped his arm still carrying the letter. He nearly let it drop to the muddy road beneath him.

The postal worker watched him walk away. His face reflected empathy for this soldier. A thought came for him. He furrowed his brow and then, his countenance lifted. "Captain, come back here a minute," he yelled.

Nathaniel stopped, turned around and saw hope in the eyes of the postal worker. He hurried back to the teller's window.

"Listen carefully," he said. "I will help you."

Those words Nathaniel needed to hear.

Chapter 10

ON TO RICHMOND

Twelve hours passed since the train carrying desperately needed reinforcements, supplies, and equipment left Chattanooga. Nathaniel could not wait to reach their planned stop at Petersburg, Virginia. He would need a twenty-four hour pass to make all the postal arrangements briefly sketched for him by the post office worker he met in Chattanooga. Much depended on whether or not the telegram he sent from Chattanooga to his cousins got through to them. Soon he would know.

Nathaniel shifted his weight rhythmically to keep his balance. The train's rocking made it difficult to stand next to the seat that held his sleeping commanding officer. It was after five o'clock in the morning. The sun began to rise in the distant eastern sky. Nathaniel knew he should let his colonel rest, but he needed the authorized leave. Nathaniel wondered if the colonel would allow him to visit his cousins. Mailing one letter had become much more difficult than he imagined. But if God really wanted him to send it, then God would open the door for Nathaniel to have the time away from his outfit.

Nathaniel mustered his courage. The sleeping officer turned his body away from the window and toward the aisle in a vain effort to find a more comfortable position. As he briefly stretched, his eyes opened slightly, catching the image of a young officer standing by his side. Before he drifted back to sleep, Colonel David H. Cummings mumbled, "What is it, Captain? What do you want?"

The muffled words caught Nathaniel by complete surprise. He had rehearsed his request but he wasn't comfortable with his speech yet. He almost instinctively snapped himself to attention before responding. The train's rocking motion caused Nathaniel to stumble over the seat practically falling onto Colonel Cummings.

Pretending to be annoyed, Colonel Cummings chided, "Hurry up, Captain. Make your point before you fall down and hurt someone or yourself!"

Nathaniel tripped over his own words as he timidly replied, "Yes, sir. Excuse me, sir. I didn't mean to disturb you, sir. But, uh, Colonel, sir. I uh, wanted to uh, ask you, sir if I, uh—"

"Spit it out, Captain. We're all pretty busy here."

"I uh, could I have uh, day-pass when we reach Petersburg, sir."

Those few words got his commander's attention and that of a few others. "You want a what, Captain?" Colonel Cummings spoke forcefully as he shook himself to full consciousness.

"A, uh, day-pass, sir," Nathaniel repeated sheepishly.

"And why in God's name should I grant you a pass, Captain? We do not intend to remain in Petersburg. It is a scheduled stop on our way to Richmond, but we won't be there long." Several surrounding officers turned their attention to the conversation. Eyes peered resentfully at Nathaniel. He observed some of the glares with his peripheral vision. His anxiety increased. More perspiration appeared on his forehead as real or imagined ridicule slowly injected its poison to weaken his resolve. Fear of bringing dishonor to himself or his Lord gripped his heart. He began to shake, thankfully hidden by the continuous jerky train movements.

"Well, sir," Nathaniel continued finding it difficult to speak clearly. "I, um, may meet two of my kin at the train station. It would be very nice to visit with them while the train is being refitted, sir."

"Very nice indeed," Colonel Cummings emphasized for the hearing of all around. Several other officers snickered quietly under their breath but still loud enough so that Nathaniel and Colonel Cummings could hear their discontent with Nathaniel's request. "Well, Captain, I am not sure it would be wise to let you leave the station with your family. Nor do I think it is fair to my other officers to grant your request. I'm sure other men under my command have relatives in Petersburg, or Richmond for that matter, and no one else has made such a bold request. However, I will sleep on it. We won't reach Petersburg for another couple of hours or so. I'll let you know my decision before then."

Nathaniel breathed a sigh of relief that at least Colonel Cummings heard his petition and that this difficult moment was now history. Nathaniel replied happily, "Thank you, Colonel. I do appreciate your consideration. My family will, too."

As Colonel Cummings turned away from Nathaniel he muttered, "Now don't go counting your chickens, Captain. There is no guarantee that I will grant you leave. Is that understood?"

"Yes, sir, perfectly."

Colonel Cummings smiled to himself so that no one, especially Nathaniel, could see and then said, "Good. Now Captain, go get some rest."

"Yes, Sir," Nathaniel almost saluted. He returned to his seat quickly. Several jealous eyes followed him, particularly those of Captain James Nash from one of the new Georgia outfits. Others who overheard Nathaniel's conversation wished that they had thought of a similar plan. At least in Petersburg they might receive a good meal and maybe some female entertainment.

The Petersburg, Virginia, railroad station was larger and busier than the one in Chattanooga. Multiple tracks converged from nearly every point on the compass to this strategically important transportation hub. Hundreds of people and thousands more soldiers crowded the station's wooden platforms. A southbound train swallowed men smartly dressed in traveling suits and women dressed in flowing hoop skirts of every color and pattern that mixed with the warm colors of spring. Slaves loaded cargo boxes; mostly goods from Europe smuggled passed the Yankee blockade that patrolled the ocean outside the mouth of the James River. Most of the people seemed to be very busy or in a hurry to go somewhere or do something. Some awaited the arrival of Nathaniel's train. Nathaniel looked out the window beside him. *I wonder if my cousins are in this crowd. Will I recognize them? Well, if they didn't receive my wire from Chattanooga, or if for some reason we miss each other here at the station, I'll just have to find a way to City Point and find the special Postmaster on my own.*

The train slowed to a stop. The engineer released the excess steam creating a huge moist cloud, which added to the morning's increasing humidity. The whooshing noise coupled with the engine's steam whistle announced to the passengers that it was time to get off the train. Porters shouted the arrival in Petersburg. The tired soldiers wished that they would be able to stretch their legs without standing in formation. It would be wonderful to enjoy the cool Virginia spring-morning air. That hope was unlikely to come to fruition. Officers began shouting orders to the enlisted men. It was time for the men to eat breakfast. In the rail yard, the officers could maintain control of the men and provide them a place to rest.

When it was time for the men to report to the train for their final leg into Richmond, they could assemble the troops efficiently.

With Colonel Cummings' hand-scribed pass in hand, Nathaniel eagerly desired to make his escape from the train. He knew he had little time to travel from Petersburg to City Point and return. Fortunately, Colonel Cummings gave him the full twenty-four hour pass. If he missed the late afternoon Richmond-bound train, he could catch another tomorrow morning. He would have fewer questions to answer if he simply made the round trip quickly. He stepped from the passenger coach and gazed both directions, hoping to spot a familiar face. Fortunately, one of Nathaniel's cousins, Miss Margaret Nisbet, spotted the young Confederate captain first.

"Captain Graham," a clear southern female voice shouted above the crowd noise.

Nathaniel turned his head in the general direction of Margaret's voice, but still he did not see her.

Margaret waved her white-cotton kerchief and raised her pink-and-white-laced parasol. Margaret yelled, "Nathaniel Graham, over here!"

This time Nathaniel spotted Margaret. She wore a solid pale rose dress with vanilla-white lace bordering her neck and wrists. He returned a strong wave to acknowledge her presence. As he stepped off the train onto the station platform, he breathed a slight sigh of relief and quickly thanked his Lord for taking care of another detail. He worked his way across the crowded station platform. *I am so grateful that You, Lord, provided the inspiration to write the letter, the information from where I can send it, the much-needed day-pass, and You obviously delivered the telegram to my cousins. I am confident You will see me finish this unusual mission.*

A small one-horse carriage left the Petersburg, Virginia, railroad station and headed northeast along the Petersburg–City Point Turnpike. This well-worn two-lane sandy road followed a near ten-mile footpath that ran parallel to the railroad line. All three connected the two towns. They passed over terrain mixed with rolling hills, thick woods and open—but obviously neglected—farm fields. A few smaller fields appeared plowed and ready to receive a late spring planting. This coastal region of Virginia was sketched with many small streams and creeks, which contributed to the thick foliage making natural boundaries between the many large farms that dotted the landscape. In this peaceful, picturesque setting, it would be difficult for anyone to imagine that a vicious struggle for the survival of a nation took place less than fifty miles to the northeast.

Under the clear blue late-May sky, the all black, canopy-styled four-wheeled wagon carried three occupants. Fortunately, the thickening, humid coastal air kept the dust stirred by the very large chestnut-colored stallion from flying into the faces of the travelers. The two women were extremely curious about why this trip was so important.

"Cousin, why do you need to go to City Point?" asked Margaret's older sister, the refined Mrs. Louise LeConte. "You know it's not a place for proper ladies."

"Yes, tell us," Margaret gleefully interrupted. "You did not give us any real information in your cabled message. I must say, it certainly made us wonder what could be so important. I think it must have something to do with a young lady."

Nathaniel blushed. "Uh—"

Louise interrupted in her hurt southern girl's-pouting tone, "And to send us a telegram. Do you have any idea how much fear and worry you created when we saw the telegram carrier bring the notice up to our house? We thought that our little brother, Clinton, was wounded—or worse—in the fighting outside of Richmond. Mother nearly fainted."

What do I do? Should I answer Louise's first question or respond to the second? I think the second is more important. I should apologize for the telegram. He took a deep breath. "Um—"

Margaret spun another length into the tangled communication web. "I am certain that this whole trip is about a woman. What other possibility could hold his interest and cause him to rush away from his regiment? Sister, did you see the way he blushed when I suggested the possibility? I bet she lives in City Point. Only God knows why and what sort of girl she is. How did you meet her? Is she a sister of a friend of yours from college or the army? Does she come from a respected family? I doubt it, if she lives in City Point."

"Is this true Nathaniel?" Louise pressed the feminine inquisition deeper. "Are you courting this girl, and just when were you going to tell us of your intentions toward her? Does she know you're coming? Is this a surprise visit? Why didn't you ask her to meet you at the train station? I'm sure she would have met you if you asked."

Nathaniel's head was now swimming in bewilderment. He didn't know how or where to begin an answer. He completely fell back on his instincts. He pulled the reins back on the strong Morgan and yelled loud and long, "Whoa!"

The horse quickly brought the carriage to a jerky stop. Margaret, surprised by this sudden change, asked, "Why are we stopping?"

Nathaniel realized that Margaret did not get his not-so-subtle hint and he seriously doubted that Louise grasped what he just said and did either. Before either woman spoke again, Nathaniel started, "Ladies, please. I will be happy to explain everything to you, but first you must give me a chance to breathe. We haven't seen each other since before the war started. I would like to know how you and the rest of your family members are holding up since the Yankees now occupy so much of this part of Virginia."

Margaret instantly offered, "Oh, we're doing just fine. Pa says the Yankees will find themselves too deep to get out of Virginia alive if they come any further. Pa says we got 'em right where we want them. Two weeks ago, there was some fighting near here along the James River, a place called Drewry's Bluff. It's just seven miles or so from Richmond?"

Margaret's tone sounded like she was asking a question, so Nathaniel responded, "I'm not sure how far from Richmond it is. I never heard of the place. I had no idea the Yankees controlled this much of the river. Maybe I should take you both back to Petersburg and go to City Point alone."

"I wasn't asking you if you knew where Drewry's Bluff is, silly," Margaret giggled. "I'm just telling you this story to show how foolish the Yankees have been." Margaret laughed some more, then continued, "Our boys beat them so badly that they've quit trying to use the James River as an approach to Richmond. Their gunboats try to come up river now and then, but for the most part, they stay down by the ocean near Norfolk. City Point is dangerous enough all on its own, but not because of the Yankees.

"But the fighting worries many people. I'll tell you the truth, Natty, many of my friends don't share Daddy's faith. They were scared after we heard the news. I even read in the *Richmond Enquirer* that President Jefferson Davis sent his family to North Carolina and that he was thinking about abandoning the capital city. I know that's a lie. Daddy says our army is going to drive the Yankees right back to the sea. Just you wait and see. Daddy says…"

As Margaret rambled, Nathaniel just smiled. He had diverted Margaret's attention. If Louise followed, then he had successfully changed the direction and subject matter of the conversation. But Louise would not take the bait. She pulled everyone back to the real issue.

"Yes, we are doing well. However cousin," Louise interjected firmly. "I still would like to know why it is so important that we take you to City Point."

Realizing that his diversion had failed, Nathaniel turned first to Louise, then around to Margaret on his right side, and said, "Fine, I will explain. But can you both promise me that you will let me speak without further questions? I can only address one subject at a time."

Nathaniel looked again at the older, matronly Louise. She answered, "Of course I will let you speak."

He turned around to Margaret and looked squarely into her flighty countenance until she responded, "I'll try not to interrupt," she said sheepishly. But she added, "I still think this whole thing is about a girl."

Satisfied that he had gained control of the conversation, Nathaniel snapped the reins. The stately Morgan pulled the carriage forward. Nathaniel began, "Well, in part, Margaret, you are right. This trip is about a girl."

"I knew it!" Margaret shouted.

Both Nathaniel and Louise looked sternly at Margaret. They let her know that they were both disappointed with how quickly she broke her promise.

Cowering, and scooting further to the right of Nathaniel, Margaret said quietly, "I'm sorry. I will try to be quiet."

As the horse settled into a steady trot, Nathaniel replied, "Your apology is accepted. Now, where should I begin? I guess it was about eight weeks ago," Nathaniel paused and shook his head. He continued, "It seems like a lifetime has passed since those early days in April. My regiment was heavily engaged at the battle of Shiloh in Tennessee. I'm sure you heard about it?"

Louise answered, "It was horrifying; so many good men died."

"I'm glad you were not hurt, cousin," Margaret added.

"Thanks Margaret," Nathaniel acknowledged her kindness. "Louise, this trip is about one of those good men who died and his daughter. I made a promise to him and to God, and now, God willing, I'll be able to fulfill that promise. That's why this is so important."

Nathaniel told his story to his cousins. It was ten miles to City Point. Normally, every minute of an hour trip feels like ten as a carriage negotiates the dips and bumps. But this day the time passed quickly for Nathaniel's cousins. They hardly noticed being bounced around on the uneven road. Louise and Margaret were enraptured by the details of the battle: the rain-filled night, the conversation with the Yankee colonel, the letter from his daughter, and finally, Nathaniel's promise to write Eleanor Ellis. He spared few details. Compassion and purpose filled the hearts of both women. For Louise, she now understood and joined Nathaniel's sense of mission. For Margaret, she now saw the trip as a romantic fantasy, and the sense of adventure thrilled her completely. Regardless, both women were, in their own way, committed to help Nathaniel mail his letter.

Chapter 11

BLACKMAIL

City Point is a typical harbor town. Now it is vital to the life of the Confederacy. Settlers chose to develop this land where the Appomattox River flows into the James. She rose approximately fifty feet above the south bank of the James River deep inside the protection of Virginia. Periodically, Yankee gunboats harass her. But City Point is easy to defend, and she is too far from Yankee blockade ships to prevent loading goods for Europe used in trade for essential European manufactured war materials.

The wharf just below the town stretched for nearly a mile. It contained four docks to service large ocean vessels. Maritime engineers worked daily to dredge another channel to accommodate one more ship. Several smaller vessels were scattered about. One of the docks appeared to wait the arrival of a ship. Cotton bales were stacked six deep and three high. These days the cotton often rotted before it could be loaded onto a ship, let alone reach England or France.

Just three years before, cotton had been the economic sovereign that for generations fueled and grew the aristocratic Southern lifestyle. England and France demanded more cotton than the South could produce. Shortly after the war began, the South needed war supplies from Europe but, more importantly, she needed national recognition for her claimed independence. Several political leaders and state governors unwisely decided to impose an embargo on cotton exports to Europe. They erroneously believed that England and France would need cotton to such an extent that they would intervene on the South's behalf and demand that the North remove its blockade of the Southern seaports. This proud miscalculation did not yield the desired results, and with the current Confederate military setbacks, may never achieve the intended goal. Now raw cotton sat on docks throughout the South—like this one at City Point—aging, waiting, and slowly turning worthless.

Three visitors walked along the pedestrian-congested wooden plank sidewalk raised above the mixed earth and gravel thoroughfare. Louise and Margaret were both shocked and wide-eyed as they witnessed war up close for the first time.

"Oh my, Louise, those buildings must have been hit by Yankee cannon fire."

"Do you see the pockmarked road that leads down to the docks?"

"There must have been a terrible fight here. Why didn't we hear about this?"

"I don't know, but do you see the faces on the people. They look distressed and downtrodden. What do you make of all this Nathaniel?"

He didn't know how to answer. This sight of overwhelming misery was new to his cousins, but all too familiar to him. He simply offered, "We should hurry."

Louise agreed, "Yes, we should find the post office, and quickly."

Margaret added, "I don't like this place, Natty. What if the Yankees come back?"

Nathaniel fixed his attention on their objective and shared, "The post office is at or near the city's government building. I was told it is the largest building in the center of town."

Margaret asked, "The post office?"

Louise interpreted for Nathaniel, "No sister, the government building."

"That's right. It must be just up that way." Nathaniel quickened his step.

On their right side, down by the docks, two large ships and a small boat were a flurry of activity. Seagulls screamed overhead, horses whinnied below, and the voices of ship crewmembers, dockworkers, and wagon masters filled the sea air. Occasionally, the crack of a whip mixed with the noise of supplying this Southern war for independence.

Nathaniel and his cousins barely noticed the slaves unloading the heavily guarded *Nashville*. They hauled the desperately needed munitions from the ship to ten covered wagons that circled one of the two main warehouses. They carefully arranged into the wagons crates filled with French-manufactured muskets, barrels of gunpowder, and boxes of miniball cartridges. One heavily loaded wagon pulled by a team of six horses gradually crept up the sloping, shell-cratered road that traversed the face of the bluff, which separated the town from the wharf. Eventually the wagon would reach the waiting-to-be-filled cargo train that was building steam in its boilers at the town's south-side station.

Nathaniel took a long, studious look at the *Nashville. I wonder if that's the ship that will carry my letter to England. It looks weathered. I hope it's seaworthy. What do I know? If the captain and crew were willing to sail her, I suppose that should be good enough for me.*

Nathaniel, Margaret, and Louise continued through the town. On the left side of the hard-packed street, one wood-framed shop after another serviced this vital supply artery. Flags of Southern independence flew from every business establishment. Craftsmen made repairs to the damaged buildings, and new warehouses were under construction. The staccato pounding of hammers declared the building progress. The three family members passed a saloon where the caretaker swept out trash from the festivities of the night before. They walked by one of the town's newest hotels. It appeared to be damage-free, very clean, and comfortably inviting. Next they passed a dry-goods store, but when they reached a small dressmaker's boutique, Margaret became distracted.

Margaret stopped and stared into the store's window. Louise quickly realized that she and Nathaniel had left her sister behind. Louise turned and angrily marched back to retrieve Margaret. She grabbed Margaret's right arm and scolded, "We don't have time for this, sister. Our cousin must catch the train from Petersburg to Richmond later this afternoon. We can't hold him up."

Pouting, Margaret responded, "I know. I only wanted to stop and look. It would only take a few minutes. I meant no harm."

Louise shook her head and closed her eyes for a second to let Margaret know her disapproval. She tugged on Margaret's sleeve and commanded, "Let's go!" The two sisters picked up their pace to catch up with Nathaniel.

Suddenly, Margaret shouted, "There it is!"

Nathaniel turned around to see where Margaret pointed. He turned around again and spotted it. Without question, the city government building was the largest in town. Its red brick was a stark contrast to the other wood framed buildings, which made it the perfect artillery target. It stood a story taller than the tallest two-story buildings surrounding the center of City Point, Virginia. They were close. All three instinctively quickened their pace. Nathaniel gently patted his over-blouse where he kept the letter safely in his inside pocket. *It won't be long now.*

Nathaniel stepped up to the postal worker's window and asked, "Are you Macalister, Norman Macalister?"

The postman responded, "No. He's off today. Is there anything I can do to help you, Captain?"

Nathaniel's heart sunk. Up until this very moment he had little doubt that he would be able to deliver himself of this now overwhelming burden. *Without the right contact, how can I mail the letter? If I ask this man for help, would he turn him in for attempting to collaborate with the enemy?* Louise noticed his hesitation to speak. She nudged Nathaniel over, looked at the postal worker intently, and interrupted on Nathaniel's behalf.

"Sir, we have a matter of personal importance. May I speak freely without fear of retribution?"

The post office employee looked at Louise, but his attention was clearly focused on Margaret. The astute Louise noticed his stare and quickly realized that her sister could be a much-needed distraction. She proceeded to present her case.

"Sir, my cousin, Captain Nathaniel Graham, has a letter he wishes to send to a young lady. This is a discrete matter. Being a gentleman, surely you understand why it is important for this soldier of the glorious South to be able to communicate with a young lady who holds his interest?"

The romantically minded Margaret also recognized the man's repeated inspection. His gaze went from her eyes to her shoes, making noticeable pauses in between. She pressed herself close to him and pushed Nathaniel further away. Margaret boldly took the man's left hand into both of hers. Nathaniel stepped aside. He watched his two cousins work their feminine magic. In seconds, Margaret captured this dutiful steward of the Confederacy's mail service with her charms. Nathaniel marveled. *Are we men that easy?*

Making sure his eyes were fixed on Margaret's, Louise continued, "Kind sir, our dear cousin needs to dispatch a letter to his betrothed. Unfortunately, she lives in the North. We have been instructed by a loyal postman that this office is authorized to send letters to our loved ones who have the misfortune of living on the other side."

This bit of information snapped the postal worker out of Margaret's trance. He quickly pulled his hand away from Margaret's and stood stiffly erect on his side of the iron-barred counter. Defensively, he responded, "Ladies, I am sorry, but you heard wrong. Neither this office, nor any other post office of the Confederacy is permitted to send correspondence of any kind into enemy country. I should have you all arrested." With those words, a Negro letter sorter exited the Post Office through a rear door that led to the ally behind the strip of shops and offices next to the government building.

Nathaniel recognized the need for mediation and stepped forward. Respectfully he asked, "If you will please pardon me, ladies," waving his hand to have both women step aside. Turning back to the postal worker, Nathaniel continued his plea, "Please excuse my cousins, sir. They mean no harm to the cause of the Confederacy. Further, they are both slightly misinformed about the purpose and destination of my letter." Both Louise and Margaret looked shocked at Nathaniel's last comment. Louise gasped, and Margaret made a more indignant comment under her breath. Regardless of the side comment, Nathaniel continued, "Sir, if I may, you see I intend to send this letter to England. I was told by another post office that your office could still send letters to England. Is that not true?"

The postal worker relaxed his posture and breathed easier. He responded thoughtfully, "Well, Captain, it is true; however, it is going to cost you and we do not guarantee that your letter will reach England."

"Why is that?" Nathaniel questioned.

"What is it you don't understand, the cost or the lack of assurance?"

Nathaniel paused thoughtfully before he responded. Then he answered, "Both, I guess."

"I'm surprised that I have to explain this to you, Captain. Have you not heard that the Yankees have a naval blockade surrounding our seaports? They control the mouth of our James River. Just two weeks ago, Yankee gunboats shelled us. Rumor has it McClellan is moving this way to cut us off and occupy our town. It is impossible to know if a ship that leaves here will slip past the Yankee army or naval ships. The best time to run the river is at night in bad weather. If the ship is lucky enough to escape the Yankees, and if it doesn't sink in the stormy sea, it just might reach England. It costs a lot of money to cover the risks of transit."

Nathaniel knew these details but he wanted to give the postal worker an opportunity to regain control of the conversation, as well as his dignity. Nathaniel responded, "I see." He reached into his over-blouse and pulled the envelope from his pocket and continued, "Well, then, exactly how much money will it cost to send this letter to England?"

The postal worker looked at the envelope and said, "Wait a minute. The address here says Rockford, Illinois. I can't send this. If you want to send this to England, it must be addressed to someone in England." He handed the letter back to Nathaniel.

With both hands extended, Nathaniel stopped the letter on the countertop and replied, "That is a minor detail, which I am sure we can work out together. It seems to me, all I need is another envelope with the London address. I was told this office keeps it. Then I place this letter inside that envelope, seal it, pay the postage, pray for safe passage and say, 'Bon voyage.'"

Nathaniel failed to notice that other people had entered the post office. The line behind him grew both in length and impatience. The postal worker, however, noticed several angry faces and decided to dismiss the situation immediately. "I am sorry, Captain. We don't keep a London address here. Whoever told you this was grossly misinformed or played a joke on you. Either way, I cannot help you. Now, if you will excuse me, sir, I have other customers. Good day, sir."

Nathaniel turned around and saw a line of six people. Those closest to him did not attempt to hide their incensed feelings toward this soldier who had squandered so much of their personal time. He wondered if they had overheard the conversation. Embarrassed, he turned and walked toward the office exit. One man in line said loud enough for everyone to hear, "It's about time. You sure took long enough. Some of us have real business to tend to today." The others in line laughed at Nathaniel as he passed by. He heard a few choice remarks, too.

Disheartened, Nathaniel left the building followed by his two angry cousins. Louise was the first to register a complaint. "What was that all about? Why did you embarrass us by telling the postal worker we didn't understand the letter's destination? Why did you bring us all this way just to incur such humiliation?"

The more selfishly motivated, Margaret offered her opinion, whether or not either Nathaniel or Louise cared to hear it. "Natty, I thought you were a Christian gentleman. You treated both of us like we were little children. You forget we grew up together. What would your mother think of the way you treated us?"

Nathaniel did not respond to either set of questions. He physically heard them, but he wasn't listening. The three visitors stood near the City Hall's flagpole. Nathaniel looked up at the Stars and Bars. He felt sorry for himself. *I can't believe how they treated me in there. I'm a soldier fighting for them. What will become of us if our Southern pride keeps us from communicating with our Northern neighbors? Now, what do I do with this?* He slowly put the letter inside his shirt pocket. *Lord, how am I supposed to communicate with Eleanor Ellis?* His chest ached.

A short, round man with a dirty face, sporting a small brimmed, boulder-style hat approached the arguing threesome. He wore a dark-brown tattered suit, soiled white shirt, baggy pants held by tan suspenders, and black bow tie. As he drew near and made eye contact with Nathaniel, he spoke directly saying, "I understand you have something that you wish to send to England." His voice was rather mousy and high-pitched. His eyes were set close together and appeared small for his head. It gave him a sinister look that caused Louise to shudder, and Margaret to step back away from him in reflexive revulsion.

Nathaniel looked at this strange little man. *How did he know that I want to send something to England?* Nathaniel examined the man a little closer and decided he better answer the question, "Yes, sir. I am Captain Nathaniel Graham. I am with the 19th Tennessee Volunteers. These fine ladies are my cousins, Mrs. Louise LeConte," Nathaniel turned toward her and then to Margaret and continued, "and her sister Miss Margaret Nisbet. Who, sir, may I ask, are you?"

"Why my young Captain and to you two lovely ladies," the man bowed respectfully to both Louise and Margaret as much as his rotund shape would permit. "I am the man that you seek. I am Norman Macalister, at your service."

Nathaniel nearly jumped out of his boots with renewed excitement. Maybe it is not important how this most irritating man knew Nathaniel's need to send a letter to England. If this Norman Macalister is willing to help, even for a price, then to Nathaniel he was an angel from the Lord. Nathaniel reached for the envelope in his over-blouse inside pocket and spoke quickly, "Yes, sir. I have it right here."

Macalister stopped Nathaniel before he could present the letter, "Not here. Put it away. You want to get us arrested? If you would be so kind as to follow me to my private office, I can explain my services in detail. You will know what to expect and you can ask questions freely." He winked and smiled a broad smile exposing a missing tooth on the lower left side of his mouth. "Won't you please follow me?"

"Certainly," Nathaniel replied straightening his uniform. "Ladies, let's accompany this fine gentleman."

Louise and Margaret looked at each other and then back to Nathaniel. They both nodded agreement. Then the two men and two women walked across the dirty street, passed a gunsmith shop, headed northwest toward the livery stables and to a run-down saloon on the north end of town.

As they entered the saloon, Margaret asked, "What are we doing here?"

Macalister responded, "My office is upstairs. We can conduct business there." He turned to the bartender and declared loudly, "Hey, Charlie, what's for lunch today?"

The bartender looked up at his good friend and understood the nature of the message. Macalister had customers and he was not to be disturbed, only warned if any official interests happened to show. He responded in kind, "Not much. It's hard to get fresh anything these days. But Sally picked up a couple of chickens that we're going to fry. How does some fried chicken sound?"

"Sounds perfect." Macalister turned to his clients and asked, "Did you have any plans for lunch? You do eat lunch, don't you?"

Margaret responded for the three visitors, "Well, it is lunchtime." Margaret winked her eye at the older man. Using her fine-tuned charms she let Macalister know what she really offered, something a man like him would appreciate. Margaret was willing to give him an intimate "private" meeting, in the event the price Nathaniel had to pay to mail his letter was more than he could afford. Louise understood her sister's subtle solicitation. It completely escaped Nathaniel. Louise had another plan in mind, just in case Macalister's price rose to extortion.

Two hours later a small one-horse carriage left City Point. Nathaniel was ten gold dollars poorer. Louise was satisfied that they accomplished their goal. Margaret was thrilled that Nathaniel's letter was on its way to a girl she believed would be the future Mrs. Graham. All three were happy to ride southwest on the Petersburg–City Point Turnpike.

Chapter 12

CATHERINE'S

Rockford, Illinois, was a small midwestern town. Before the war, Rockford enjoyed several years of continuous slow yet steady economic growth. It served the many productive farms that surrounded the town. Rockford is located in north-central Illinois approximately halfway between Chicago and Dubuque, Iowa. Rockford grew on each side of the Rock River valley. The Rock River is a small tributary that flows from the northeast to the southwest into the Mississippi River near Davenport, Iowa. It is small enough that it is easy to cross and eventually bridge, yet large enough for riverboat transportation.

Rockford was more than just a stopover, or crossroads town, although it serves that purpose for both waterway and overland travelers. It had the necessary twenty-room hotel on the northwest side of the river. It was equipped with a comfortable restaurant and saloon. Another hotel was under construction on the river's southeast side. Many merchants established their businesses along Rockford's dusty streets on both sides of the river. The town's government offices, jail, post office, and newspaper are located on the northwest side of the river, and light industry was developing along the waterway's southeast side. Within easy walking distance north of the center of town, the general store and other specialty shops—such as the newly opened dress boutique—conducted daily business. However, since the Southern insurrection began hundreds of miles away, this town, like so many similar to it, had suffered the loss of many good men and community leaders.

Several townsfolk erected modest homes that expanded civilization to the Rockford landscape of rolling hills, thick woods, and spreading farms. One residential avenue called Cherry Street was cut out of this peaceful terrain about a half-mile northwest of the center of town. The home at 276 Cherry Street represented someone of better-than-average means. Resting on a small rise above the street, it was painted white, like so many in the neighborhood. From the road, a cobblestone walk led to an elegant yet welcoming front porch. It was the home of the late Lieutenant Colonel Edward Ellis and his surviving family.

The sun began to set in a mixed blue-orange, partly cloudy sky on this late May afternoon. Eleanor walked alone. Fighting back the invading grief, she turned on the cobblestone walkway that led to the front door of the quiet sanctuary she called home. She shut the front door to the pleasant world outside and surrendered to the torture that ravaged her heart and wept. *Why did you take him from us? He was a good man. He was supposed to be home with us now, not buried in the church's cemetery. It's so unfair.* Eleanor and her mother, Catherine, would place fresh flowers on Edward's grave after Sunday morning's service.

Where will I find the strength to help mother? Eleanor dropped her handbag near the front door water basin in the main floor hallway. She stopped for a second and examined herself in the wall mirror set above the water basin. She barely recognized the weepy eyes staring back at her. She removed her bonnet and hung it on one of the hooks next to the mirror. She tried to fix her hair, but gave up. She turned away from the mirror and started for the back of the house.

She passed the respectfully decorated front sitting room. *Will we have to sell our furnishings to make ends meet?* She shuffled past the staircase that led to the second and third floors, and slowly moved toward the rear of the house to the kitchen. There she would surely find her mother busily preparing their evening meal. Before she reached the kitchen entry, she sighed deeply and choked back more tears. Eleanor allowed herself one last moment to feel the never-ending sad emptiness.

Catherine Ellis heard the approaching footsteps and suspected that her daughter was home. She inquired, "Ellen, dear, I hope that's you?"

Eleanor responded, "Yes, Mother. It's me." Eleanor tried to sound happy, but her tone betrayed her. As she entered the kitchen, she forced herself to smile. She didn't want to be the center of attention, so she asked, "Did you have a nice day today?"

Pulling herself away from a large iron pot simmering on top of the wood stove, this newly widowed woman turned to her only daughter and immediately noticed her fallen countenance. Without answering Eleanor's question, and desiring not to make an issue of her daughter's appearance, Catherine asked, "What is the matter, dear? Why the long face? Did something happen at the dress shop to upset you?"

"No, Mother, I was just thinking about Father. I miss him so much. I still can't believe I'll never see him again."

"I know, dear. I miss him desperately. At night, I swear he speaks to me about marvelous things too wonderful to believe. I know it is wishful thinking. I want so much to know that he didn't suffer and that he now rests in peace."

"I try not to think about Father too much, but when I do, I wonder about many things. It really bothers me that his time of

106 · DESTINATION HOPE: SEPARATION

service was nearly over and that he could have been home with us today. It all seems like some cruel, mean prank. I wonder why God would take him from us when he was so close to coming home. I feel it's impossible for a loving, caring God to exist. If only those Rebels would see the error of their ways and stop all this foolishness. I can't bear the thought of losing Paul or John too."

"Now, dear, your father would have stayed with the army as long as the war continued. His dedication to duty is one of the honorable things I always loved about him. I know it hurts deeply, dear, and I don't pretend to understand what possible good could come from his loss, but I hope something will."

"I think I understand, Mother, and knowing how you feel about Father helps some. But I can't stop worrying about John and Paul. So much has happened since Father was killed. Our army in Virginia is so close to capturing Richmond. The war looks like it might be over soon. I want John and Paul home. I don't think I could bear another loss to our family."

"We should write the boys after dinner tonight. I worry about them, too. I think we should let them know that we are doing fine so that they don't fret over us. They have enough to think about just staying alive. We can hope that God will protect them."

"I'm glad that they haven't seen any combat yet," Eleanor added. "Remember in their last letter, how they wanted to fight? I would be very happy if they never, ever fire a shot in battle."

"What did you hear in town today? Is our army still making good progress toward Richmond?"

"Oh, Mother, yes," Eleanor's tone shifted to one of excitement. "The news is so encouraging. General McClellan has our troops positioned just a few miles from there. Several men in town think that one more strong push and he will capture the city. It seems like just days ago these same people were criticizing him for being so slow to act. Now they think the war will be over before the end of June. Many men in town want him to be our next president after he defeats the Confederates. They did talk about how a smaller Confederate army under the command of a man they're calling 'Stonewall Jackson' is winning small battles in the Shenandoah Valley. But once Richmond is captured, he will be forced to surrender, too."

"That's wonderful news, dear. Isn't it peculiar how fortunes can change almost overnight? Last month, we expected your father to return home with the war's condition so unresolved. Then, our army and navy captured New Orleans. Days ago, the news announced that our forces almost have complete control of the Mississippi River. Today we can hope that John and Paul will come home before they face the Rebels." She turned back to the stove, pulled her apron up to her face, and finished her thought. As her voice began to quiver, Catherine continued, "I only wish your father were here to see this for himself." She wept.

Eleanor knew this moment would come. It came nearly every night since they received the news that the Rebels killed her father near Pittsburg Landing, Tennessee. *How many days or weeks it will take until this pain ends?* Eleanor breathed deeply and drew from her natural gifts to help her mother through. *What if I fail her? What if I'm weak and I lash out at her when she needs my attention and company, my love and compassion? How can I keep this up day after day when I need someone to be strong for me?*

Eleanor approached her mother slowly. Eleanor was not sure if her mother needed a strong hug, a soft touch to her shoulder, a reassuring word when none seemed appropriate, or if she needed to be alone. She decided what she would have wanted. Eleanor placed her hand softly on her mother's left shoulder.

Catherine responded immediately, turned, dropped her apron, and grabbed Eleanor as if her very life depended on hanging on to her to keep her from sinking deeper into the abyss of depression swirling her downward, ever downward. Eleanor nearly stumbled, but she kept herself and her mother upright. The two women sobbed together. Eleanor knew they would be this way for a while. They probably would not eat dinner tonight.

The next morning, Eleanor woke early after another restless night's sleep. She took her time getting dressed. Business had tapered off since she and her mother opened the store. As long as she arrived before noon, that would be good enough. Besides, she could use a good breakfast. The sun began to rise and brighten her bedroom. Pondering, she brushed her hair. *What will we do if the dress shop fails? Should we sell the house? Where would we go? I suspect that our initial sales were due to the simple excitement of opening a new store. Maybe folks are showing us sympathy for Father and respect for the loss of a community leader.*

Edward Ellis had been an attorney. The young Rockford Republican Party had elected him as a delegate for their community. He was acquainted with Abraham Lincoln. During the Illinois Senate debates the fall of 1858 between Lincoln and Stephen Douglas, Ellis introduced his family to the new voice for American freedom, now the sixteenth president of a war-torn nation. Edward Ellis was extremely well thought of in his local community. Most recognized Edward Ellis as a man of solid character with a brilliant legal mind. As a lawyer, he held the reputation of a fair and aggressive trial attorney. He sustained his practice with routine actions such as preparing wills and coordinating estate settlements. He attracted clients from far beyond the Rockford area. He once collaborated with attorneys from Chicago to prepare and litigate the defense in an infamous capital murder case. Rockford would miss his levelheaded leadership on the town council.

Everything changed when Rebels in Charleston, South Carolina, fired on Fort Sumter that fateful April 12, 1861, morning. He applied for and obtained a commission from the governor to raise a regiment. To his credit, nearly every eligible man from the town and the surrounding farms enlisted to serve under his command. Weeks later, the 15th Illinois Infantry marched to join the Union troops under the command of then-Brigadier, now Major General Ulysses S. Grant. They first observed the predominant naval action and capture of Fort Henry, Tennessee, on the Tennessee River, close to the Kentucky and Tennessee border. They fought briefly at Fort Donelson, a much harder conflict on the Cumberland River, approximately twelve miles east of Fort Henry. But the regiment was decimated at the Battle of Shiloh, in the Hornet's Nest, a remote southern Tennessee forest about six miles upriver as the current flows but due southwest from the nearest town, Savannah, Tennessee. Rockford, Illinois, lost over fifty percent of its male population on April 6, 1862, and Lieutenant Colonel Edward Ellis perished with them. Eleanor grieved deeply, beyond reason, beyond consolation, the tragic loss of her father.

Eleanor and her mother decided to name the dress shop *Catherine's*. The store had been Catherine's dream since she was a young married woman, carrying her first child. Catherine would be the principal owner and seamstress. In times past Rockford ladies had come to her to make dresses for special occasions, so it seemed a natural fit for her talents. Eleanor would manage the daily operations. They opened *Catherine's* in late November 1861, just in time for Christmas. But now Eleanor found it difficult to be a businesswoman in a "man's world." She quickly learned to depend on the good will of honorable men. She understood that as a woman she had no right to vote or enter into a contract. She couldn't bring a breach of contract lawsuit if a man chose not to honor his word, her purchase orders for materials, or her schedules. She grew weary of the excuses such as, "Don't you know there's a war on?" or worse the comment, "Why don't you find a man to take care of you and quit trying to run a business?" She wanted to reply to the demeaning remarks with her own sharp retaliation, *"Don't you know there is a war on? All the good men are off fighting for the Union. Why aren't you?"* but she kept her thoughts to herself.

Fortunately, Eleanor and her mother found honorable men. For example, they leased space two streets away from Lieutenant Colonel Ellis' legal office. When time permitted, Eleanor could slip up to her father's place of business and sort through the volumes of materials left behind. She hoped to sell his collection of law books that filled one office's floor-to-ceiling bookshelves. The bound copies of cases and statutes had to be worth something, but with the war she received offers she intuitively knew were ridiculously low. She understood that a limited market existed, but she didn't want her father's life work to end up in the hands of a scavenger hunter who would not appreciate their real value. Unfortunately, time was becoming a factor. The landlord wanted to lease the space. The annual lease, although paid for in advance, would expire the end of June. He gave Catherine and Eleanor until the end of July to clear the office. After that, whatever was left he would take possession of in exchange for defraying the cost of preparing the office for a future tenant.

Eleanor reached her father's office shortly after ten o'clock. She sorted through several case files. She put them into piles for the attorneys who let her know they would accept her father's workload. Eleanor was well educated and she possessed a naturally keen mind for business. She turned cases over only to attorneys who were willing to sign an assignment agreement. Edward Ellis handled most of his civil cases on a contingency basis. Eleanor gave cases to lawyers who agreed to pay Catherine and Eleanor ten percent of the case earnings. She convincingly argued that if not for her father's successful reputation the receiving lawyer would not have the case. Also, these attorneys did not have to do anything or expend funds to obtain the case. Finally, if the clients accepted their services, then some sort of "finder's fee" would be appropriate. As she worked through the files, she came across one that caused her to pause. Her father had scribbled some interesting comments on the inside cover.

The case was titled, *"Polk vs. Waterhouse, 1860"*. It was filed as a property dispute. L. Polk, the injured party, claimed that his property must be returned based on the requirements of the Fugitive Slave Act of 1850. He further claimed that H. Waterhouse was instrumental in assisting the flight of Polk's property. Therefore, Polk was entitled to treble damages. What caught her attention was a personal note written by her father, *"How can I convince the court that the United States Supreme Court made a mistake—Dred Scott decision? How do I argue that the United States Constitution is wrong as written—protecting the institution of slavery?"* She carefully set the other files she held down onto her father's desk. Slowly she moved around to her father's office chair and sat down. The scent of her father still lingered. She breathed deeply. A memory of her father flashed through her mind. She imagined him pacing in his office and voicing some legal argument. Then she read further, *"It would take the violent removal of those slave-holding justices to change this law. This is a fight I can't win in court."* Eleanor noticed that her father dated his note to himself, April 11, 1860. *You were right, Father. It is taking a civil war to resolve this case. How could you have known that one year later war would begin over this, and two years later, you would be killed for it?*

Eleanor fought to bite back fresh tears, but her emotions broke the silence. She cried aloud, "Oh, Father, I miss you. Why?" After a few anguish-filled minutes, she calmed herself and wiped her face. She stared at the folder in her hand. She wanted to know more. She decided that she would keep this file to herself. She slipped the folder into her oversized purse, checked the time on her father's office grandfather clock, and determined that she should leave to open the dress shop for this day's business.

Eleanor managed *Catherine's*. Her mother would drop in occasionally. Catherine was scheduled later that afternoon to deliver a custom-made dress for Mrs. Prentiss, who was throwing a dinner party the following Saturday in honor of her husband's fiftieth birthday. Mrs. Prentiss would be coming into the store at 2:00 PM for her fitting appointment with Catherine. Eleanor was straightening some accessories in her back counter when the store's doorbell rang signaling the arrival of a late lunch-hour customer.

"Ellen, are you in here?" inquired Mrs. Fitzgerald, a middle-aged grandmother. "My daughter, Fanny, and I need a dress for Mrs. Prentiss' dinner party Saturday."

From her crouched position behind the sales counter, Eleanor stood up quickly and smoothed her dress. She recognized her customers immediately and responded, "Yes, Mrs. Fitzgerald, I'm here. I'm just straightening a few things. How can I help you and Fanny?"

"Can your mother make me a dress and have it ready by Saturday afternoon?"

Eleanor looked at Fanny, who simply rolled her eyes. It was clear by Mrs. Fitzgerald's statement that Fanny would need to find something to wear off one of *Catherine's* dress racks. She hoped that her mother would be forced to do the same. Eleanor replied, "I'm afraid I can't speak for mother. She has several special orders that she's filling. One dress happens to be for Mrs. Prentiss. She will be here later this afternoon for her fitting appointment. Do you think you can come back before two o'clock? My mother will be here then and you can discuss your order with her. But frankly, I don't think enough time exists for you and my mother to choose a design, purchase any needed fabric, sew the dress, and have it fitted and ready for you by Saturday's dinner. I have several attractive items here in the store that I believe Mother would still have time to alter for you if necessary."

Fanny smiled. It was the news she wanted to hear. She wanted to say something sarcastic, but instead she simply added, "Well, Mama, I'm sure we can find something that you can be proud to wear. Ellen has such lovely things. Why don't we just take our time and see what we can find?"

Mrs. Harriet Fitzgerald looked around and answered, "I suppose you're right." She sighed deeply and repeated more softly, "I suppose you're right." She turned to Eleanor and said, "Ellen, I don't want anything that's going to make me look heavier than I am. You understand, don't you, dear?"

Fanny smirked under her breath and pretended that she just sneezed. "Oh, excuse me." She cleared her throat. "Ellen, I think I would like to find something that will go with a small hoop. I'm hoping that I will be able to enjoy a dance or two during the evening. I do so love the sound of my petticoats rustling under my dress when I'm dancing."

Mrs. Fitzgerald interrupted, "I told you, dear, I don't believe Mrs. Prentiss arranged for dancing Saturday evening."

"That's not what her son told me."

Before Mrs. Fitzgerald could respond, the doorbell rang again. Everyone turned to see who came into the store. It was Mrs. Prentiss. She was more then one hour early.

Molly Prentiss announced her arrival asking, "Eleanor, is your mother in?"

"Not yet, Mrs. Prentiss. She plans to be here around one-thirty. She'll have your dress for you. Did you want to come back then? Mrs. Fitzgerald," pointing to Harriet, "wants to talk with her about a dress for your party Saturday evening."

Molly Prentiss turned to Harriet Fitzgerald and said with a condescending tone in her voice, "You don't have your dress ordered yet, Harriet?"

Harriet didn't expect this jeer, so she stumbled with her own retort, "Well, I didn't know that you would be monopolizing Catherine's time."

Eleanor recognized, *this is bad and it's only going to get worse. Why me?* "Ladies, please; we have plenty of time to make sure you both look your very best Saturday evening." Eleanor couldn't believe how petty they acted. Both women appeared primed and ready for verbal confrontation. Looking at her patrons, Eleanor realized that they had yet to suffer a loss due to the war. They couldn't recognize or appreciate the pain she carried each day. She closed her eyes and shook her head, questioning *I can't believe you are arguing over a dress.* Suffering with her broken heart, Eleanor would have to mediate this foolishness. First, she focused her attention on Mrs. Prentiss. "My mother should be here soon. She'll have your dress with her when she comes. Do you wish to stay and wait for her? May I fix you a cup of coffee or tea?

"Yes, Ellen, I think I would like a cup of tea. I feel I should stay and wait for your mother." She turned in the direction of Mrs. Fitzgerald. She continued to speak to Eleanor with a denigrating tone aimed at a woman she did not consider to be her peer, "Besides, I want to make sure that Harriet doesn't pick a dress too similar to mine."

Defensively, Mrs. Fitzgerald said to Eleanor, "Ellen, dear, Fanny and I have other errands to run. I think we'll come back later and speak with your mother then." Mrs. Fitzgerald grabbed Fanny by the arm and turned for the store's front door. The two women stormed out of the dress shop. Mrs. Fitzgerald spoke loudly as she left, "If she thinks I'll attend her husband's birthday party, she better think again."

Fanny replied, "Oh, Mother, if we don't go, I won't have a chance to dance with William."

Eleanor just shook her head. *I can't believe what I'm hearing.*

Triumphantly, Molly Prentiss declared, "Well, I for one am glad they're gone. I have no idea what came over me to invite those two busybodies in the first place. I guess I felt sorry for them. Harriet's husband is a drunk and his reputation is less than favorable in this town. If it were not for the fact that he's the only undertaker we have, no one would do business with him."

Eleanor pretended to pay attention and offered, "Yes, ma'am."

"And that daughter of hers—as I think about her now, I hope neither of them shows up Saturday night. Have you seen the way she throws herself at my William, or any boy of good reputation for that matter?"

"No, ma'am. I can't say that I have."

"Well to tell you the truth, Ellen, it wouldn't surprise me if she tried to trap a young man. You do know what I mean, don't you?"

Eleanor wished the conversation would go in another direction. She hated gossip. Something within her intuitively understood that gossip was an evil practice. However, since Mrs. Prentiss was the only other person in the store and because she was *Catherine's* most influential customer, Eleanor knew she had to humor her. Eleanor thought, *Mother, where are you?* Then, she reluctantly responded, "Yes, ma'am. I am afraid I do."

"You mark my words, Ellen, she'll be carrying some young man's child very soon, and it won't be my illegitimate grandchild, if I have anything to say about it."

Sullenly, Eleanor answered, "Yes, ma'am."

Always probing for personal information, Mrs. Prentiss asked, "What about you, Ellen? Do you have a young man in your life?"

Just then, the front doorbell rang and in walked Catherine. Quickly, Eleanor avoided Mrs. Prentiss' last question and greeted her. "Mother, I am so glad you're here. Look who's waiting to see you and to try on the gown you've prepared for her."

Catherine looked at Mrs. Prentiss and said, "Good afternoon, Molly. I have your dress right here." She proudly lifted the brown-paper-wrapped garment. "I think you will be very pleased with the fit. You will look your very best for your husband's birthday party. Do you want to try it on now?"

"Oh my, yes! I can't wait any longer. I even came in early hoping that you would too."

Catherine handed her work over to Mrs. Prentiss. She opened the package quickly, almost carelessly. Molly shook the dress so that it unfolded to its full length. She was silently awestruck by Catherine's handiwork.

In a word, the dress was stunning. Mostly, it was a creamy color. It had soft sky-blue accents streaming the full length of the dress, like ribbons of blue carnations growing out of a garden. The accents flowed along each side of the dress, starting at the shoulder and extending to the belted waistline. At the waistline, the streamers multiplied. Six equally distanced lines spread from the belt. They expanded from a quarter-inch thread to a two-inch wide ribbon at the bottom of the dress. Catherine was careful to use these lines to help make Molly appear thinner then her actual size. The design was unique compared to other popular evening-gown styles. Most dresses were layered from the floor to the waistline in repeating waterfall-type circular patterns to accentuate the hoop. Because of Catherine's approach, Molly would look sleek and elegant.

The collar lay flat and draped in a blue butterfly pattern over each shoulder, rounded across the back, and collected with a small blue ruffle in the front just below the neckline. The sleeves were puffed at the shoulder and connected to the cuffs with a sheer fabric that matched the cream color of the dress. The gloves matched the blue streamers. The belted waist pulled the dress together magnificently. The beltline was a good one-inch wide cream middle framed by quarter-inch-wide blue ribbons on the top and bottom. It all came together in the front at a two-inch-diameter cream circle surrounded by a half-inch-wide blue ribbon that matched the streamers. The full length of the dress filled a medium-size hoop and reached just above Molly's ankles perfectly. Catherine had created a beautiful work of art.

Catherine directed Mrs. Prentiss to the store's fitting room and replied, "I really do hope you like it. I added a few touches we didn't discuss as I finished the dress. I think you'll find the additions make the dress even more elegant."

Molly finally declared, "Why, Catherine, it's beautiful. You've outdone yourself. I simply love it." As they both passed Eleanor, Mrs. Prentiss continued, "Catherine, you're the best dressmaker in Rockford, Illinois."

"You mean the only dressmaker in Rockford, Illinois, don't you?"

The two women laughed as they disappeared into the fitting room. Eleanor hoped it would be a perfect fit so that she wouldn't have to see Mrs. Prentiss any time soon after today.

Suddenly, a commotion erupted in the street. Eleanor thought she heard loud voices. She looked out her front window and saw several people running toward the center of town. She pulled her apron upwards and wiped her hands as she briskly turned to the store's front door. As she opened the door, she heard a loud, young male voice crying, "Extra! Extra! Read all about it! McClellan stopped at Fair Oaks, just outside of Richmond! Rebel Command-ing General Johnson wounded in Battle! Get your newspaper. Get your paper right here!" Eleanor stepped outside and followed the growing crowd.

Chapter 13

WHAT DOES IT PROFIT?

War reached the outskirts of the Confederate capital city this rain-soaked June 1, 1862, morning. Captain Nathaniel Graham and Lieutenant Marvin Jenkins trudged through the muddy city streets as fast their tired legs and muddy boots could carry them. They walked east from the train station, passing civilians rushing west. Many noncombatant citizens moved their personal-property-laden carriages as fast as the congested traffic would allow. Others carried bundles over their shoulders and walked away from their family homes.

"What do you make of all this, Nate?" Lieutenant Jenkins asked after dodging a frightened young mother holding her baby tightly to her chest.

"I'd say our army must be in trouble. We better find our unit fast," Nathaniel replied. He prayed quietly, *"Lord Jesus, help us."* That was the best he could do. *I am scared. But I am thankful that You had Marvin wait for me in Petersburg.* Marvin told Nathaniel that Colonel Cummings had ordered him to stay. *I am glad that I'm not alone right now.* As they worked their way through the evacuating crowds, Nathanial stared at the crazed panic in the eyes of the civilians. *Are we losing the war? Will I be an outlaw for fighting for my country's political independence? Is it wrong to fight for our rights to govern ourselves?*

Nathaniel and Marvin passed the Confederacy's seat of Government. Civilians and military personnel hurried in and out of the building. Nathaniel suspected that the military members were couriers bringing status messages to the president. Then he spotted him. Nathaniel said to Marvin, "Look at the top of those stairs. It's him! It's President Davis!"

"I see him, Nate. Who's that with him?"

"I don't know. He looks old."

The aristocratic looking senior officer looked out and over the crowd of people that began to gather around the front steps of the government building. The officer held a rolled-up document in his left hand. Nathaniel assumed rightly that these were the officer's orders. President Davis said something to this officer, shook his hand, and then addressed the crowd. Nathaniel and Marvin couldn't afford to stop and listen. They couldn't hear the president's speech from that distance anyway, so they had no idea that their commander in chief announced the army's new commanding officer.

Ten minutes later, Nathaniel and Marvin reached the eastern part of the city. Several buildings showed the signs of troop occupation. Windows were broken out so sharpshooters could have a clear line-of-sight advantage. Battle trenches were dug, obstacles placed, and earthworks raised to assist the defenders slow the advancing Federal horde. Several wounded soldiers were scattered along these muddy Virginia roads. What they could see of their once-proud army did not look good. Nathaniel's faith wavered in his country's resolve to defend itself. *What happened to the fearless Confederate soldier?* Clearly, sound, uninjured men mixed among the wounded scattered on the ground. They acted like scared puppies that had just been pinned down by an aggressive dominant dog. Beaten men surrounded Nathaniel and Marvin. They would need a special leader to put the fight back into them.

Heavy Yankee cannon fire sounded just to the east. Nathaniel spoke commandingly, "If we are going to find our outfit, we'd better head that direction." *Why are our guns silent? Why don't they answer?*

Marvin responded, "I think you're right. Nate, I hope we find our boys soon. By the looks of these troops, we may be heading into our last fight."

"I hope not. We ain't been licked yet. We just put a train full of fresh troops into the field. Our boys will keep the Yankees from taking Richmond. Someone must have a plan to stop them Yankees." *I sure hope someone has a plan.*

They followed the railroad tracks that cut through the thick woods and led to the sounds of fighting. More wounded staggered toward Richmond. Nathaniel and Marvin began to stumble over the debris of battle. The evidence was scattered everywhere and led Nathaniel to believe he may have to conduct a mass funeral later this day. Suddenly a wounded, riderless horse wildly galloped out of the woods. The frightened animal ran straight for Nathaniel and Marvin. Nathaniel moved forward, threw up both arms and yelled to catch the horse's attention. "We have to stop him."

Marvin shouted, "Whoa!" He whistled as loud as his lungs would allow. The horse made a strange sound. It could have been mistaken as a woman's scream. He dropped his hindquarters, dug in his back legs, and stopped. He breathed heavily and frothed from his mouth and nostrils. With the horse halted, Nathaniel and Marvin both grabbed its bridle. Nathaniel began to inspect the animal's left side for wounds. Marvin checked its right side. It appeared to Nathaniel that shell fragments had hit the horse. The nearly crazed animal bled from several minor wounds, but none looked to be very deep.

Nathaniel stroked the animal hoping to calm it. He noticed bloody blotches spattered over the saddle and horse's hindquarter. *Where did all these bloodstains come from? The horse is more scared than injured.* Then Nathaniel saw what caused him to nearly retch. In the left stirrup, twisted and mangled, he discovered the remains of a man's riding boot, with the severed leg still inside. What remained of the lifeless limb protruded from the boot to the knee. It dangled backwards and toward the ground, completely drained. *I hope he passed quickly.*

Marvin from the other side of the horse said, "I don't think he's hurt too bad. I think he can be patched up. He should be okay."

Nathaniel replied, "I don't think his rider is. Take a look at this."

The birthday party was the main Rockford event of the weekend and seemed to be living up to its promised expectations. Mrs. Prentiss looked exquisite. Even though Molly Prentiss told everyone that this party was given in honor of her husband, it didn't take the guests long to realize that this stage was set for Molly to shine. She acted like a lady of royal birth. She reigned over all that entered her home, directing refreshments, introducing folks to one another, and attempting to make her guests feel comfortable. As she hoped, Molly's dress was the talk of the evening. Occasionally she remembered to tell her subjects that Catherine was responsible for the beautiful gown. She nearly floated on the air of self-admiration. Then, her domain crashed.

"What is she doing here?" Molly Prentiss asked her son William, who dutifully stood by her right side.

He replied, "Mother, I thought you invited Fanny and her family."

"I did, but I thought I heard that they were not going to attend. I'm not sure her mother and father are with her. Do you see either of them?"

William looked over to Fanny and smiled at her as he replied, "No, Mother, I don't see them. However, Mother, I'm glad she's here. I think I'll go welcome her to our home."

Molly Prentiss said with a firm, angry tone, "Son, please don't. She's here against my wishes. All right then, that's fine with me, but I really don't want her to feel welcome. I want her to go home. Besides, she apparently does not have an appropriate chaperon. She should go home."

"Mother, that's a terrible thing to say," William rebutted. He looked back at Fanny as she moved through the crowd greeting other revelers. He continued, "I like her, and I'm glad she's here. I'm going to say hello and offer her a cold drink. If you insist that she have an escort, I volunteer."

Molly whispered angrily, "Son, if you know what's good for you, you will stay away from that young woman. She is not to be trusted."

His mother's words blended into the background noise and were lost forever as William ignored her admonition and approached Fanny. William announced, "Who is this lovely young enchantress?"

Fanny pretended to blush at William's flattery, and then replied in kind, "Who is this handsome and chivalrous knight to come rescue this fair maid from her loneliness?"

They both laughed. William continued, "Miss Fitzgerald, I am very pleased to see you here tonight. I want to thank you for coming and for honoring my father with your charming presence." William bowed at his waist, took Fanny's right, white-gloved hand, and affectionately kissed it. He slowly turned his gaze toward his mother and smiled spitefully.

Molly turned away angrily and spoke aloud to no one in particular. "He is his father's son, after all. I'll be watching you."

Fanny responded to William, "Why thank you, kind sir, and thank your mother too, for inviting us to your father's birthday party this evening. I am very pleased to be here, too. I have so looked forward to spending this evening with you, William."

"May I offer you a glass of champagne?" William hoped he might be able to persuade her with other ideas later in the evening. Fanny didn't need his artificial help.

"Oh, yes. I would love a glass." Unlike William, Fanny's motivation was perfectly clear to her. She had an agenda of her own, and her very attractive pink dress revealed enough of her charms to help her advance it.

William bowed again, excused himself, and hurried to retrieve the refreshments.

Fanny looked around the room and noticed that there were very few young men around. The gentlemen that did attend were as old if not older then William's father, the guest of honor, William Prentiss Senior. She knew that most of the able-bodied men were away fighting the war. She had hoped that there might be a few other options to choose from, but William was attractive enough. Mostly, she was attracted to his family's wealth and name. Because of that wealth and community power, the Prentiss patriarch kept William Junior home to help run the dynasty's tool manufacturing business. This was perfectly acceptable to Fanny. As she presumed from previous encounters, William didn't have a single drop of patriotic blood flowing through his veins. He had no desire to save the Union or rush to become one of Lincoln's volunteers. He wasn't convinced that the national republic was worth the fuss. He already had plans to trade with the South should she be successful. Fanny intended to capitalize on his financial strategy.

As the younger William returned to Fanny with the requested libations, Catherine and Eleanor entered the Prentiss' front parlor.

William said quietly to Fanny, "Look who just arrived. I knew they were invited, but I am a little surprised that they would feel comfortable attending a social gathering so soon after Mr. Ellis' death."

After taking a quick sip of champagne Fanny replied, "They probably want to drum up new business. I bet they're using your father's party to advertise to these other women what they can produce. I understand Catherine made your mother's dress. It's so sad that she thinks it is a beautiful gown. I wouldn't be caught dead in a dress like that. It has such unusual lines. Although I will say, it does make your mother look younger. And just look at Eleanor. She doesn't look a bit attractive. Her dress is rather dull. I guess she's still mourning the death of her father." Fanny and William laughed.

Catherine and Eleanor mingled with several of the other women. William drank heartily and commented, "I think my mother looks very good this evening. Catherine's dress helps. But my dear Miss Fitzgerald, you are the lovely one in my eyes. It wouldn't matter what you wore. I'm sure you look beautiful even when working around your family's farm."

"Why William, that's a terrible thing to say." Fanny placed her gloved left hand just above her low-cut neckline, pretending to be embarrassed. "Are you trying to tell me that you don't like my dress? I chose it thinking of you. I so hoped you would like the way I look tonight."

"Oh, I like it very much," William smiled as he studied her from the top of her head to the bottom of her dress, pausing to watch Fanny lightly brush her left hand aside. He then continued, "Why Fanny, I believe you have a spot of champagne on your pretty pink dress."

"Where?" Fanny began to examine herself and accidentally spilled a little more of her drink on her gown. She nearly screamed.

William laughed and said, "Maybe we should find a quiet place to get you out of that dress before you ruin it altogether."

Fanny pretended to be offended. "Why Mr. Prentiss, I'm beginning to think you want to take advantage of me."

William replied, "It wouldn't be the first time now, would it?"

They laughed together. Then, William and Fanny slipped outside to enjoy the warm, late-spring evening air and each other a little more privately. Their casual disappearance was observed. Molly Prentiss would send one of her hired servants in a few minutes to find them and ask if they needed other refreshments.

Chapter 14

GENTLEMEN'S QUARTER

Catherine did discuss dresses with several women, explaining the fine points of Molly's evening gown as she mingled. She displayed her own fashion creation's special features with grace and style. Eleanor wore a rather plain looking, tan colored dress with a very small hoop. She wasn't interested in attracting attention to herself. She walked over toward William Prentiss Senior to extend her birthday wishes. Near him stood several other older gentlemen who engaged in a conversation regarding the status of the war. She heard Rockford's honorable mayor, James S. Ramsey, comment, "And what's General McClellan doing? I'll tell you what he's doing. Nothing!" He paused and noticed Eleanor approaching. He cleared his throat and prepared to address her. He stood stiffly, nearly at attention, and then bowed slightly to honor her presence. "Good evening, Eleanor. I must say you look stunning this evening."

Eleanor intuitively knew he was being kind. She also knew that she didn't dress to impress anyone this evening. She simply replied, "Why thank you, Mayor Ramsey." She addressed the evening's guest of honor, "Mr. Prentiss, I want to wish you a very happy birthday, sir." Speaking to the group she asked, "Do you gentlemen mind if I join your discussion. I am so tired of listening to what you might consider frivolous, female matters. Your opinions about the war are far more interesting."

Mayor Ramsey replied for all and said, "Eleanor, it would be our pleasure to have the honor of your company." Eleanor noticed that he didn't invite her to participate in the discussion. She simply nodded graciously.

Prentiss Senior spoke directly to Mayor Ramsey and prompted him regarding his last statement before Eleanor arrived. Opening his arms to emphasize his point, Prentiss asked, "But Jim, what do you expect General McClellan to do? He should take some time to regroup. Is anyone surprised that the Rebels would put up a stiffer fight as our troops approach Richmond? We just need to give the general a little more time. If Lincoln provided McClellan the men and supplies he needs, I'm sure he'll bring home the victory we expect. Look what he's been able to accomplish with his outnumbered force. I understand the Confederates are very confused right now. I heard Jeff Davis turned command over to old Bobby Lee. I guess Lee decided that the army was in a big mess because he's pulled his forces back to Richmond and he is taking time to reorganize. I don't think a structure change is going to make any difference. Modern warfare has passed the old man by, and he hasn't had any success as a battlefield commander."

One of Rockford's successful Swedish immigrant members, Luther Gunderson, added in his Nordic accent, "I heard recently that Jefferson Davis sent his family further south, somewhere in North Carolina. I think he already knows that the Confederacy is all but defeated."

"That's exactly my point, Mayor Ramsey declared. "McClellan should strike now while the Rebels are confused."

"McClellan is worried about the casualty count and the size of the Rebel force in front of him," Prentiss offered.

"Well, now is not the time to avoid action. Our navy has gained control of most of the Rebel coastline, our army and navy in the west have near complete control of the Mississippi River, and if McClellan will push forward, our boys will capture Richmond and this war will be over."

One of the Cherry Valley's wealthiest ranchers, Anthony Potter, affirmed, "Yes, my friends, the war will soon be over." Attempting to draw this discussion to a conclusion, he offered, "If I were a betting man, and all of you know that I am…" The men all laughed and Potter continued, "I would wager that this Rebel insurrection will be over before the end of this month."

As if on command, all the men rose their respective glasses and presented a confident, "Hear! Hear!"

Although she knew she shouldn't say a word, Eleanor couldn't resist bursting the pompous pride exuding all about her. She jumped right into the thick of this male-only conversation and interrupted, "Robert E. Lee's reputation may not be fully understood as yet, gentlemen. If you think about what he's done in his first two days of command, he's going to make McClellan's job taking Richmond harder." To Mr. Prentiss she said, "If General McClellan is worried about casualties, he's going to see them add up if he tries to storm Richmond." To the group she disputed, "If he plans a siege to starve out the soldiers and remaining population, it will take much longer than a month."

"And just how did you reach this conclusion young lady," the not-much-older, apparently wealthy and sophisticatedly attired Jason Merritt inquired. Then he turned to the other men and said, "As if she has any grasp of what she's talking about." Jason turned toward Eleanor and asked in his adopted New England accent, "Do you know anything regarding the political implications surrounding this war?"

"Well, sir, I must confess that I really haven't given it much thought," she lied. Eleanor and her father had spent many long hours discussing the gravity of what would happen should the South succeed and create a new, sovereign nation. She had developed a well-reasoned and clearly defined opinion, and she had confidence that she could withstand any intellectual challenge regarding the conflicting issues. However, she also understood her place as a woman. She knew she would have to feign naiveté to engage in this conversation.

Jason concluded that he had put this female observer in her place and turned back to the older men and attempted to prevent further interruptions by stating, "You see, gentlemen, out of her own mouth she said that she didn't give the war much thought. This war is the most important matter of our time." He chuckled and continued, "She probably thinks more about hats, dresses, and shoes, or who is going to deliver the next baby. This is exactly why women will never make informed citizens and why they should never be granted the right to vote. It must be reserved and preserved for those who can appreciate the complexity of social issues and who can render sound decisions." If these men agreed, Jason would add this position to his future political platform.

Some of the other men laughed and reinforced Jason's opinion that this was no conversation for a woman. Nevertheless, Eleanor paid no attention to their attempt to stifle her. She pressed forward with the same vigor she had watched her father display when arguing a case in court. "Well, gentlemen," Eleanor continued. Her tone was clear enough to let them know that she didn't consider their condescending attitude appropriate. "The newspaper reported that Lee strengthened the defenses surrounding Richmond. But I'm sure you already knew this." Then, she looked straight at Jason Merritt and said, "Sir, I know all of these other respected gentlemen here tonight. But frankly, who are you?"

Mayor Ramsey quickly intervened and stated, "My apology, Miss Ellis. I naturally assumed that you knew this young man. This promising future Rockford, Illinois, attorney is Jason Merritt. I'm sure you know his family."

"Of course," Eleanor did recognize him but she leaned back and pretended to get a better picture of the man. He was charming in a mysterious sort of way, and ruggedly attractive. "Yes, I believe I was told by Mrs. Fitzgerald that you would be returning to our town. You've been studying law at Dartmouth in New Hampshire, correct?"

"You are correct. I hope to begin a private practice here very soon." Self-satisfied; he took a long sip from his glass of bourbon and smugly added, "Very soon."

Mr. Prentiss interrupted this sidetracked conversation and asked, "Excuse me, Eleanor. Did you read that account about Lee in today's newspaper? I didn't see anything regarding his defensive maneuvers."

Eleanor turned her attention to Mr. Prentiss and replied, "Yes, and it included a comment by General McClellan." Eleanor gave the pretense that maybe Jason was correct in his character assassination of her and added, "I probably won't quote it correctly since I may not grasp the complexity of the matter, but the article expressed McClellan's impressions of Lee. They were not favorable, obviously, but I am always leery of someone who is so quick to render a judgment regarding another person's integrity and abilities. Wouldn't you agree, Gentlemen?"

A few of the men nodded tacit agreement, but no one was willing to agree with Eleanor. Fortunately, Mr. Gunderson broke in and asked, "What did the paper say?"

"Again, I'm not sure I am expressing the general's opinion of Lee exactly as stated in the newspaper, but he did refer to Lee as cautious and weak when he is faced with grave responsibility. I don't know how he came to that opinion. But, he also said something like he believed Lee lacked moral firmness when pressed by heavy responsibility. He also assumed that Lee would probably be timid and irresolute during the heat of battle. I suppose he knows the man better than most. They both attended West Point and served in the Mexican War, but that was a long time ago. People do change. If I remember anything about Lee from other things I've read, he has always demonstrated a consistent temperament and strong sense of duty. Surely, you remember how decisively he performed under fire during that John Brown incident at Harper's Ferry? I only hope General McClellan hasn't underestimated the man."

"Well, our little dress maker knows a little more about things then just fashion," Jason acknowledged, sounding surprised. He took a drink of his bourbon. He looked suspiciously at Eleanor wondering what sort of woman stood toe-to-toe with these recognized leaders of Rockford.

"Yes, but she's just restating what the newspaper reported, and everyone knows that they print what they want us to know," Potter interjected. "No offense, Taylor. I know you mostly reprint what you receive from the wire service."

Mr. Taylor Decker nodded that he accepted Potter's nonchalant apology. He knew better than to confront someone with the ability to buy him out and shut down the only newspaper in this young town.

Jason Merritt interrupted, "Gentlemen, maybe we should pay attention to what this patriotic woman has to say." Jason immediately recognized that he might have prejudiced himself by his earlier comments. But, he still believed his earlier statement. He would watch this woman carefully. He remembered an old saying, *Keep your friends close, and keep your enemies closer.* The next civil war might be between the sexes instead of the states.

"What do you mean?" Gunderson inquired. Then, he took a long pull on his cigar.

Jason realized that some of his captive listeners might think his withdrawal from his earlier stance a sign of weakness. Seizing the moment to practice his future political career, he decided to confuse them with a few facts mixed with reasonable speculations. He pretended to clear his throat and continued, "Well for one, she represents nearly half of our adult population. I predict that before this war is over, many women will make a substantial contribution to our successful restoration of the Union. I can think of one such woman right now. Have any of you heard of a brilliant lady who I would say could very well be viewed as an unrecognized member of Abraham Lincoln's cabinet, Miss Anna Ella Carroll?"

Eleanor answered, "Yes. She probably saved our army in the west from disaster."

Jason was very interested in what Eleanor knew for several selfish reasons, all of which he would and could easily disguise with his charm and flattery. "Miss Ellis, I am impressed with your grasp of current events. Why don't you enlighten these gentlemen and explain what you mean when you say she saved our army."

Eleanor was a little embarrassed to be the center of attention suddenly. She sincerely wished that she had stayed with her mother and talked to the other ladies about dresses, hats, and accessories, as Jason had so humiliatingly stated. She wanted to turn away and find her mother. Instead, she took a deep breath and offered her self-educated and firmly-grounded opinion. "If you please, gentlemen, as Mr. Potter already said, I do base my thoughts on what I've read in Mr. Decker's fine *Rockford Daily Chronicle*. So I suppose I am not the best source of political and military information."

Jason pressed her. He recognized that Eleanor was beginning to win the hearts, if not the minds, of these members of Rockford's privileged. "Eleanor, please don't sell yourself short. I suspect that you have something to say about Miss Carroll's contribution to our military success."

Eleanor sensed that Jason's charming encouragement was nothing more than bait to trap her. She pretended to fall for this academic temptation. All Jason's enlightened New England education didn't prepare him for her response. "Mr. Merritt, I believe

Miss Carroll's assistance preceded the *Tennessee River Plan* she submitted to President Lincoln. I understand that both Generals Halleck and Grant have publicly taken credit for this idea, which doesn't surprise me. Did any of you gentlemen ever wonder what would cause the Army of the West to suddenly drop the planned assault of the Mississippi River forts?" Eleanor's intellectual challenge surprised the men surrounding her. By changing the subject and confronting their lack of knowledge, she nearly diminished the good humor extended by her listeners.

Jason recognized the men's attitude shift. He had to intervene if he was going to glean information from the sharp mind he perceived that Eleanor possessed. Whether or not she redeemed herself in the eyes of these men mattered nothing to him. She represented a large percentage of the Northern population. He wanted to know what she thought. He fully intended to expand his budding legal practice into a political career. Eleanor could not vote, but Jason wanted to tap into her natural power of influence. He continued to sound understanding and encouraging as he prompted Eleanor further. "Miss Ellis, may I call you Eleanor?"

"Certainly," Eleanor stated, still displaying an aloof façade toward Jason. Suddenly deep inside, she felt an unfamiliar flutter. She nearly blushed. She looked down at the floor.

"Very well, Eleanor," Jason continued. "I would like to know what you've learned."

Still looking downward, she spoke softly, "You gentlemen are going to think I'm foolish."

A few chuckled, others grunted, and some just stared into the smoky air wishing that Eleanor would walk away. Still, a couple of men agreed with William Prentiss when he said that he wouldn't think her silly. Then Mayor Ramsey encouraged, "I've known you your entire life. I watched you grow up into a fine and very responsible young woman. I knew your father very well. He was my very dear friend. And the way you've taken charge of your little business, well, frankly, I don't know what your mother would do without you. Please, Eleanor, tell us what you think."

Eleanor continued to resist, "Well, I don't know." She could have excused herself and left these men but she found that she enjoyed letting them beg for her participation.

Mr. Prentiss added, "Eleanor, like Mayor Ramsey I've known you since you were a little girl. Your father was my friend, too. I think I'm speaking for all of us when I say you are very special to each of us."

Again, the men responded together affirming William's last endearing remark.

Eleanor smiled and decided to let them off easy. She relaxed her posture just a little and picked up where she'd left off, "If you will indulge me, my father first told me about Miss Anna Carroll during Lincoln's presidential campaign. He told me that she and I were alike in many ways. He said the thing he admired most about her was her sharp legal mind. She performed legal research for some pretty important attorneys, congressmen, and justices. You know, she even provided a written opinion in support of President Lincoln when he suspended the Writ of Habeas Corpus protected by the United States Constitution. My Father believed she would have made a fine lawyer. My Father believed I could, too." Sadness started to creep into her as she concluded this thought, "I guess we'll never know." She quickly got control of herself, lifted her head high and reverted to the original subject of their conversation, "If not for Anna Carroll giving Lincoln the *Tennessee River Plan*, our military leaders would have attempted to force themselves down the Mississippi River. They wanted to follow General Winnfield Scott's Anaconda Plan. More of our boys would have been lost taking the Mississippi River and its fortifications."

With a demanding tone in his voice, Potter asked, "How do you know this?"

"Simple, the Mississippi River flows from the North to the South. We need gunboats to capture the heavy defenses the Rebels built all along its banks and islands. If a gunboat is damaged, it will float further south. The enemy will capture it. We lose everything—the boat, its equipment, and, worse, our men. The advantage of using the Tennessee River, gentlemen, is"—she gave a long pause to set up her next few words—"it flows the other direction, from the South to the North."

"Surely Generals Halleck or Grant thought of this idea," Potter insisted.

"Well, if they did, my father didn't know it. In one of his letters he sent to my mother, he said that they had a sudden change in plans. Admiral Foote's gunboats were moving from the Mississippi River to Paducah at the mouth of the Tennessee River to launch an attack on Fort Henry. That was in December. Anna gave her plan to Lincoln in November. I suppose you gentlemen can draw your own conclusions."

Chapter 15

DUTIES

Captain Nathaniel Graham and Lieutenant Marvin Jenkins reached the edge of a troop encampment. They kept the horse between them; it seemed to settle the animal. The scene was a mess. The rain continued to pour, dowsing campfires. The men could neither cook nor warm themselves. Everything was rain-soaked or covered in mud. As they approached the camp, a sentry stood before them and challenged, "You boys lost your way?" The private raised his musket chest high and brandished his bayonet.

Nathaniel replied, "I am Captain Graham of the 19th Tennessee Volunteers. This is Lieutenant Jenkins. We were separated from our unit yesterday. We're trying to locate them tonight. Do you have any idea where we might find them?"

The Private shouldered his musket and saluted saying, "No one from Tennessee 'round here, sir." He proudly announced, "We're all from right here, Virginia, sir. We be part of Pickett's brigade."

Another soldier joined the guard and suggested, "Hey, Jim, why not take these officers over to our company commander? He might know something."

The private replied, "That's a good idea, Henry." He turned to Nathaniel and said, "Sir, if you don't mind following me, I'll be taking you to Captain Summers. He's my company commander. He may know where you can find your outfit."

Nathaniel thanked him and said, "Lead the way, soldier."

The young private brought his musket forward and saluted across the weapon. Nathaniel returned his salute. The private dropped his salute, performed a crude about-face in the mud, shouldered his weapon, and casually marched toward the center of the camp. Marvin said to the horse, "Let's go, boy. Maybe we can find you some fresh hay to eat." The three men and one slightly wounded horse slogged through the ankle-deep mud.

Captain Leopold Summers held open his tent flap and commanded, "Come in, gentlemen. Let's get out of this damnable rain. I think I can help you." Turning to the boy, Captain Summers said, "Thank you for caring for these officers. You may return to your post. You are dismissed, Private."

"Yes, sir," the private announced saluting.

Captain Summers returned the salute. Then he turned and followed Nathaniel and Marvin as they ducked into his tent. Once inside he stretched his aching back and said, "This rain is killing my men's morale worse than the approaching Yankees. But it is slowing down their advance. I guess we can all thank God for that. You boys came through Richmond, you say?"

Marvin answered, "Yes, sir, Captain."

"Call me Leo. We have such a mess out there, all this formality just slows us down. It's like having mud for communications. You boys missed a hell of a fight the past two days. I don't know if it was the rain or us, but the Yankees stopped their advance. What's the mood like in Richmond?"

"Not good," Nathaniel replied. "It looked to me that the citizens were evacuating. Is that how you saw it, Marvin?"

"That's exactly how I saw it. Also, we saw many of our soldiers mingling with the wounded. Looked to me like they didn't want to fight no more."

"I can't say I blame them," Summers offered. "We've been taking a beating from the Federals for weeks. The only thing we've done well is retreat. General Johnston doesn't seem to want to fight."

A memory of General Albert Sidney Johnston flashed through Nathaniel's mind. He could still see Johnston's lifeless form propped up against that large old oak tree. He wished he could remove that memory, which haunted his soul. *"Ain't it something what one bullet can do?"* Nathaniel had to shake himself to the present.

Noticing Nathaniel's glazed-over stare, Summers asked, "You OK there, Graham?"

"Oh, I ah, yes. I'm fine. I just remembered someone else I knew with the name of Johnston.

"Well, old Joe Johnston won't be ordering us to retreat anymore. He got himself wounded. The problem is, General Smith, he ain't no better. I hear he's very confused, doesn't know what to do. God knows, if we don't get a leader to command this army soon, I won't be able to keep my boys from surrendering to the Yankees just to get something to eat. I hear they have more food than they can carry." Summers paused then he continued jokingly, "Maybe that's why they move so slowly."

All three men chuckled. Nathaniel recognized that Summers was only attempting to lighten the mood. *How do I end this conversation? This man loves to talk. I need to get us back to the point.* "You say General Johnston was wounded. I hope it was nothing too serious. Anyway, if we are going to have a command change, Marvin and I best get on with finding our outfit."

"I'm sorry, Graham. I should not be going on about these things anyway. We junior officers can't do anything except obey orders, right?"

"That's why we need to get going. Do you know where we might find our boys?"

"Not exactly, but if you follow the camp and keep heading due north, you should come in contact with the new men that came in last night. I heard they fought well. They helped keep the Yankees from advancing on the main road to Richmond. I understand that Johnston was hit somewhere in that area. I heard it was bad enough to take him out of the fight, but he will be fine. You boys be careful out there, in this rain sentries can be a little trigger-happy. It was a good idea to walk your horse, too. You are less of a threat. I noticed you are not carrying a side arm, Captain Graham. Did you lose it?"

"No, Leo, I'm a chaplain."

"Oh," he paused, looked down at the moist ground inside his tent, and scratched his scruffy beard. He looked like a man deep in thought. Then he continued, "I apologize for my language, Reverend. If you think about me sometime, would you mind saying a prayer for my boys and me? We sure could use all the help we can get."

"No need to apologize. I'm sure God understands your concerns. You know, you can pray to Him for yourself. You don't need me."

"You're wrong there, Reverend. I don't even know how to pray. I wish someone would have taught me before I got myself wrapped up in this here war."

"Maybe our paths will cross again. But if you want to know how to pray, simply talk to God just like you're talking to me now."

"Maybe," he paused. He thought for a minute. Briefly, Summers considered the possibility that someone could actually talk to God. He rejected the notion and decided to send the men on their way. He continued, "You boys better get moving. It's already pretty late, and I don't think this rain is going to stop anytime soon."

Minutes later, Nathaniel, Marvin and their adopted steed trudged through the sea of tents, pouring rain, and sticky, sloppy mud.

It was a bittersweet reunion. The rain didn't stop and most of the men were trying to keep warm in their tents. Nathaniel and Marvin reported to Colonel Cummings' tent only to find that he was in an evening staff meeting. Major Patrick Duffy gave Nathaniel the strength report. Several names that Nathaniel hoped to see were missing.

"Major Duffy," Nathaniel nervously inquired. "I don't see John Countiss on this list."

"Killed in action today," Major Duffy said in a matter-of-fact tone. "You'll find his name on this list." Major Duffy handed Nathaniel another sheet of paper, the casualty list. "You better get started writing their families. They fought valiantly and died heroically for our country. You know what to say." Major Duffy looked up from the table, straight into Nathaniel's eyes, and almost in an apologetic tone continued, "Nate, I know Colonel Cummings appreciates your service."

"Have these men been buried yet?" *John was a good friend.*

"In this rain? Those that we have identified are in a barn at the edge of camp. Others are lying out in the field next to it."

"In the field? Major is that best we could do?"

Major Duffy retorted sharply, angrily. "Listen, Nate, you weren't here. We were eating Yankee shells until dark. I know this sounds bad, but we were lucky to secure as many bodies as we did. Many of our boys got left behind again. I don't know who on that list is dead, wounded, or captured. All I know is that they are not here. The only reason you're not on the list is because you had authorized leave. I suggest you do your job, Captain. And Captain, as you can see, I've assumed more regimental duties. I need more working room. You will need to find another tent."

Nathaniel was embarrassed. He just showed disrespect to his authority and friend. He swallowed hard and said, "Of course, Major. I'll take care of finishing this report. Sir, if you don't mind telling me where I can find the field hospital, I'll get right to work."

Major Duffy was satisfied with Nathaniel's response. He handed Nathaniel more pages and said, "It's good to have you back with us, Nate. I wish you had seen our boys beat back the Yankees. You would have been proud of us today." He paused, stretched, took a deep breath, and let it go slowly. Then he continued, "When you leave here, go on down to the right about a hundred paces or so. You'll pass the cook wagon and near there you should be able to see a farmhouse. That's the hospital. I'm sure the medical staff will be happy for your help."

"Thank you, sir," Nathaniel saluted smartly. He knew Major Duffy was through.

Major Duffy returned Nathaniel's salute rather casually and responded, "You are dismissed, Captain. I'll see you in the morning." He turned to his desk and picked up a piece of paper, another report.

Nathaniel stepped out of the tent and into the rain, and thought, *I missed today's action just because I believed I was supposed to mail a letter. I should have been here.* He condemned himself deeply. In a very strange way, the disappointment hurt. He walked over to the makeshift corral, unhitched his new friend and said, "Well boy, let's go see if we can find someone to help patch you up."

Marvin was about to leave when he said, "Nate, I have room in my tent. Nobody wants to share it with me."

Nathaniel humbly thanked Marvin and turned toward the direction of the field hospital. He and the horse sloshed through puddles of water mixed with mud.

Crossing the James River in a rowboat is a chore. At night it is even more difficult. Someone's life would have to be at stake to want to cross on this stormy night. Lightening flashed and thunder rolled intensely enough to make the bravest man cower at the mere thought of crossing the choppy waters. A lone man ventured forth in a small craft. On board, he carried a canvas bag. Mostly, it contained mail and a few other goods that would be of interest to a Yankee Sergeant waiting on the opposite shore.

Here the river was less than a quarter-mile wide. Thanks to Norman Macalister's business dealings, the river was free of Confederate mines and Yankee shore patrols on its north bank. Gabriel rowed with all his strength. The current pulled the little boat faster downstream then he expected. He might miss the north shore landing but he would do whatever he must to deliver his package. He cried out, "Lordy, You'z gonna hep old Gabe tonight? My Miss Mary and da boys needs me ta stay alive and do dis fer Masser 'Calister." The boat rocked violently, nearly throwing Gabriel out. One ore slipped from his left hand. He caught it before it slid away. "Whoa, that was close. You'z not hepping me much er Ya, Lordy? Got ta keep going." Gabriel pulled hard on both ores and directed the boat northward once again. His purpose was clear—deliver the mail and return with what the Sergeant would give him in exchange. He didn't care about the goods. Being Macalister's distribution man allowed him the opportunity to see his family when he would return to the south side of the river. Macalister had trade arrangements worked out in detail.

Macalister didn't care who won the war. He cared about profit and he contrived ways and means to make sure he garnered an extravagant return on his nominal investment. He spread the word through very close and trusted postal-worker friends that he could use the blockade-runners to transmit mail to loved ones who lived

144 · DESTINATION HOPE: SEPARATION

in the Northern states. He pretended that great risks existed and that many hands had to receive compensation for handling this special mail. In exchange, he charged a very large fee. His investment in this endeavor included the cost of a small rowboat, which paid for itself after the first crossing, rent of a small office above Charley's Saloon, with a little insurance money to keep Charley quiet, and a significant yet affordable fee for the Yankee sergeant. Macalister emancipated the freedman rowing for his life and put him to work as a mail sorter in the City Point Post Office, of which Macalister served as the head postmaster. Gabriel would do what Macalister asked because Macalister held the rest of this Negro postal worker's family in slavery.

Shortly after Gabriel passed the river's deeper midsection, the wind began to die and the rain turned into a gentler but steady sprinkle. It would take time before the river settled down, but for now he had two fewer elements to overcome. He remorsefully, yet thankfully, spoke to the deep-black night, "I'z sorry there, Lordy. I'z 'spect Ya'z heppin' me after all. I'z guess'n it even takes You a minute or two ta change da weatha'." He started to hum a thankful hymn, which helped settle his nerves more.

Still humming with more exuberance, he approached the north riverbank. Some twenty yards to the west up-river he heard, "Boy, you better head up this away. And quit that blasted singing."

Gabriel couldn't see anyone but he recognized the voice. He knew he should heed the Yankee sergeant's warning. They both could be shot as spies if they were caught, but Macalister assured Gabriel that the Yankee families wanted this mail and wouldn't let anything happen to their precious few modes of communication. Sergeant Norse had resolved his own set of entanglements. He found that money still worked to make folks look the other way as supplies were diverted or mailbags added to others heading north. For families separated by the war, mail was a life source, and people were willing to pay to send and receive letters from loved ones.

Macalister and Sergeant Norse had found a way to capitalize on this near-basic survival need.

A few minutes later, Gabriel reached the north riverbank, and the small rowboat eased into the soft mud. Gabriel hopped out of the bow, pulled the boat further up the shore, and tied it to a sturdy tree. He didn't realize that he was too loud for Sergeant Norse's liking. "What is the matter with you tonight?" Sergeant Norse said as he emerged from thick woods. He carried his revolver in his right hand ready to remove anyone who might object to his night work. "Why are you making so much noise, singing and dragging your boat across those rocks? Don't you know that if our pickets find us we're both dead?"

"I'z sorry, suh," Gabriel stuttered slightly. "Dis rain's got me'z worried a mite. I'z meanin' no harm."

"Well, boyo," Sergeant Norse said sternly and condescendingly in his upper-New-England accent. "You'd best be more careful if you want to see your wife and kids again." The threat was clear. Gabriel was alone in this business.

They exchanged bags quickly. Gabriel placed his new parcel in the aft of the rowboat and retrieved one more article from under the middle seat. He turned around to Sergeant Norse and said, "Masser 'Calister say dis here purse is fer you. He says to tell ya dat plenty more ta come if'n ya'z want."

Sergeant Norse replied, "You tell your boss, this war may be over soon. But so long as the army is here, I'll be here." Then he turned and disappeared into the dark woods. Gabriel untied his little rowboat, dragged it back to the riverbank, and shoved off for the south bank. The rain stopped, and Gabriel started to sing—not from fear, but from joy knowing that he would be back home with his wife and children soon.

It was another long night. Nathaniel sat and prayed with several wounded men. Some regretted that they would never be able to fight again. Several men would return to duty, given time to heal. A precious few allowed Nathaniel to escort them to the threshold of eternity. Before he left the field hospital, he gathered as much information on the men that died as he possibly could. After some much-needed rest, he would begin the lonely letter-writing task. He stepped outside and stretched. He looked up into the still dark, but now cloudless star-filled sky. *Finally, the air cleared. Maybe today will be a nice day. I have much to do.* He walked toward the tent city hoping that Marvin had taken care of getting theirs set up and that he would find it quickly. Not far away, he could hear slaves digging. He sighed deeply. *Fresh graves. I can't think about this any more. I need sleep.*

A bright, warm sunrise met the next morning. The cleansed air smelled fresh. It was a pleasure to breathe in the scent of the tall pine trees surrounding the camp. With the morning light, men began to stir. There was no rush this morning. The Yankees had pulled back. Only the most anxious expected another attack. The veterans understood this lull in the nature of fighting, and so they rested. Marvin was still green. He knew that the reason he became an officer was that he possessed a college degree. He couldn't imagine himself commanding troops in the field, shouting orders to men older than he, or imposing discipline. This morning, he simply wanted breakfast. He rolled over and noticed that Nathaniel was sound asleep. Since he had no idea when Nathaniel had slipped into his cot, he decided not to wake him. He rose quietly and slid through the tent flap. He stood upright, bent his back, and felt the bones crack as he lifted both arms and stretched. It was a beautiful, sunny day. Puddles of muddy water still pockmarked the camp, but the clear blue sky and the clean, fresh air felt very good to his filling lungs. For this brief moment, Marvin enjoyed being a soldier.

Marvin took another deep breath and smelled the air, almost like a dog trying to find his way. He caught the scent of meat cooking. His stomach rumbled and he literally followed his nose. It didn't take him long to find who was cooking. He couldn't wait to join some of the other company commanders for a hearty breakfast. He saw Lieutenant Samuel Webster from "D" Company. Webster waited in a short line. He held his tin plate ready to gather what the cooks served. Marvin approached and said, "Good morning, Sam. It sure is a fine day. Do you mind if I sit and eat breakfast with you?"

Webster replied, "Not at all, Lieutenant Jenkins. But you better get to the back of the line. If I let you in with me, we'll both end up in the field hospital, and no one comes back alive from there. These boys put up one hell of a fight yesterday and I'm sure they are very hungry."

"Don't worry. I won't get in their way. I just wanted to talk to you about yesterday."

"What do you want to know? You were there; you saw how we beat them Yankees."

Marvin was too timid to admit in front of all these men that he wasn't engaged in the action, so he responded, "Well, I just want to get your take on it, is all. Get your chow, find a place to sit, and I'll catch up to you in a few minutes after I get some food. Fair enough?"

"Sure, Jenkins, I'll see you in a few minutes. I was thinking of sitting under those shady maple trees over yonder. That okay with you?"

"Perfect. I'll be over directly." Marvin was glad to divert the conversation for now. He'd let Webster in on the details later. He really wanted to know how this fight near Fair Oaks, Virginia, went and how the men from his company performed.

Marvin walked to the back of the line of other junior officers. Most were company commanders or, like himself, a second in command. Marvin was shorter than most and he had a thin frame. His entire life he had been an easy target for anyone who wanted to bully him. He hoped the men were in a great mood. Their perceived victory seemed to be the main reason. Marvin wished he knew more so he could talk with his fellow officers, but his lack of information only increased his lack of confidence. He listened and tried to blend in with the line of men.

Captain James Nash recognized Marvin and knew that he was not engaged in yesterday's fighting. "Glad to see you could finally join us, Lieutenant Jenkins," Nash announced loud enough to make Marvin's skin crawl. Other officers turned and looked at the short, skinny, redheaded, freckle-faced, least qualified soldier in the Confederate army. "How was your little trip? Did you and your chaplain friend decide to return to the regiment now that the fighting is over?" Nash, a mean-spirited Georgian suggested, "What do you fellas think 'bout this one? He's got some nerve showing up for morning chow, don't he? Don't you boys think we should save the food for the men that did the real fighting?"

Several other officers began to laugh at Marvin. He couldn't stand the embarrassment. He felt every man's eyes under the mess tent bearing down at him, considering him a coward. He didn't know what to say in his own defense. His commanding officer had ordered him to take care of Nathaniel, but his mind went blank. He couldn't think. He just looked for a way to escape. He turned and looked at Nash fearful of what this man would say next. Marvin tried to speak but he barely squeaked out, "But I had orders."

Nash knew instantly that he had Marvin running scared. "Did you hear that? This excuse for an officer says he had orders. You bet he had orders. His own regiment commander doesn't want him any place near the fighting. He doesn't want to give the Yankees any help by having this," he paused for effect, extended his arm, pointed his left index finger at Marvin, and motioned up and down as he continued, repeating, "this officer on the field." Laughter erupted from every direction. Marvin's face turned a deeper red then the color of his hair. He mustered what little courage he had, got out of line, and walked as fast as he could away from the cause of his embarrassment. He didn't want to eat now even if he was still hungry.

Marvin quickly passed Lieutenant Webster who lounged underneath a shady maple tree. He looked up at his noticeably disturbed peer and yelled, "Hey, Marvin, where are you going in such a hurry? I thought you wanted to talk to me while we ate breakfast." Marvin pretended that he didn't here Sam. He wanted to kill Nash.

Rain fell again. By mid-afternoon, the slaves completed the trench that would serve as the final resting place for nearly one thousand Yankee troops. Nathaniel wore a handkerchief around his face to reduce the stench of decomposing flesh. He passed the rows of dead men lying on the rain-saturated muddy ground. A few Federal officers mixed with the Yankee enlisted men. Some were older, many were probably in their late twenties or early thirties, but most were young boys, no more than twenty years of age. Useful articles of clothing, especially shoes and socks, were stripped from them. Some were near naked. His duty was clear. No other Confederate soldier paid these men any respect. On the contrary, many were spat upon, bodies kicked, and valuables confiscated. Even personal items that should find their way home to grieving loved ones were taken as trophies. *Who am I to judge? I took Eleanor's letter from Colonel Ellis. The least I could have done was include it with the letter I sent to her. I wonder if she'll ever receive*

it. Will she write me and ask about her father's eternal condition? I can't think about that now. I have work to do.

The tragic reality of this great loss of life began to trouble Nathaniel's heart and mind. Nathaniel felt deeply saddened for these dead men. Nothing made sense to him. Hollow emptiness took the place of his sadness. No matter how he tried to rationalize this situation, his mind recalled the fateful words written by King Solomon of ancient Israel found in the book of Ecclesiastes, *"This sore travail hath God given to the sons of man to be exercised therewith. I have seen all the works that are done under the sun; and behold, all is vanity and vexation of spirit."* He looked up between the thick tree canopy to the concentrated cloud-covered, rainy sky above and prayed silently, *"Surely, out of this great number of men, some of them must have surrendered their lives into Your service, Father. Some of them must belong to You. Looking at these men, this is awful, horrible. Lord Jesus, there is something wrong with this war. Why are they so willing to die to keep us in their Union? How can brothers in You, Lord, kill each other so maliciously? What purpose could this fighting fulfill?*

After the slaves finished dropping body after body into the mass grave, Nathaniel positioned himself approximately in the middle of this near thirty-yard-long trench. He always felt deeply troubled by the fact that neither side had time to provide decent funerals for the nameless remains of someone's son, father, brother, uncle, nephew, or otherwise close relative. He would do his best to mark the location and the body count, but because corpses were stacked on top of each other, it was difficult to be accurate. He looked across the trench and noticed that the slaves stared back at him. They stood with their shovels ready to finish the job. They waited patiently, silently, and respectfully. Nathaniel knew that they wouldn't complain; they would stand in the rain, remove their hats when he spoke and a few would echo his final "amen" at the end of his feeble prayer. *I guess it's time to start.* He took a deep breath and began to recite the words that slowly over time were becoming meaningless to him.

"Heavenly Father, we are gathered here this day to commit the souls of these men into your eternal keeping. Father, I don't know any of them, but You do. I don't know why You took them from this life, far from their families and homes, but You do. I don't know why they fight to prevent us from governing our lives as we see fit, but You, God, judge all life and know the hearts and minds of all men. I pray, Father, that their leaders would realize the foolishness of this senseless killing, offer terms of peace, and end this invasion of our homes. I believe, Father, that You could put an end to this terrible war today, but I trust that You have a purpose for the continued loss of life. I know, Father, that You are mindful that we are but dust and that to the dust You commanded that we must return until that glorious day when You command the resurrection. As Your servant Paul once wrote, we look forward to that blessed hope, for if there is no resurrection, we are men to be most pitied. So now, dear Father, we, Your humble servants, return these bodies to the earth and pray that You, the king and judge of the living and the dead, will have mercy on their souls. In Jesus' name, the only name under heaven by which man can be saved; we commend their spirits into Your capable hands." Nathaniel paused briefly and then concluded, "Amen."

As expected, Nathaniel heard a few voices randomly repeat his concluding, "amen." Nathaniel placed his kepi cap back on his head. Across the trench, the slaves put their hats back on too. Nathaniel gave a nod to the slave directly across from him. The slave looked to his left and back to his right. Then, he began the process of covering the Yankee bodies with the muddy earth. Others quickly joined him. Nathaniel knew they would make quick work of this burial detail without further supervision. He took a step back, did a casual about-face, and began the short walk back to camp.

Chapter 16

NEW ASSIGNMENTS

The sun began to fall lower in the distant western horizon. The rain-cleansed air smelled fresh, the stench of the dead now washed away. The late afternoon grew a little cooler and more pleasant. The clearer air seemed to lift his mood. Nathaniel had received word from Major Duffy that one prisoner in particular, a Yankee chaplain, wanted to talk with someone. Major Duffy figured this assignment would be appropriate for his friend, Captain Graham. Nathaniel slowly approached the makeshift stockade. This war never seemed to exhaust itself of new experiences.

Yankee prisoners anxiously waited for the much hoped-for exchange. Mostly, the Confederate captors had treated their Federal captives fairly. They simply wanted to get back with their units. Rumors emerged that the Confederates had built prison camps in various places in the Deep South. They knew that their Federal Government constructed similar camps up North. They also knew that the practice of exchanging prisoners would soon end. Federal General McClellan hated this practice. He wanted to prevent captured Rebels from returning to the fight.

Nathaniel approached the sentry. The guard saluted and asked, "If you don't mind, Captain, what's your business with these here prisoners?"

Nathaniel returned the soldier's salute and replied, "One of the prisoners sent for me." Nathaniel unfolded the paper Major Duffy gave him just moments earlier and read the name. "He's a Yankee officer. His name is McKinley, Captain McKinley. He asked to speak with a chaplain. That's me."

"Well, I suppose I shouldn't stand between you and a man that's seeking God. Lord knows I sent a few His way the last coupla days. I wouldn't want Him telling me I prevented one of His from coming to Him. I read that part in the Bible about it would be better if I tied a stone around my neck and throw'd myself in the sea. I guess I can let you in, sir. But first, I have to check you for weapons. I don't suppose you're carrying any."

"No, son, I don't even carry a pocket knife," Nathaniel responded almost laughing,

"Then I guess you can proceed," the guard said as he shouldered his musket. "We aren't holding many prisoners here. We sent most of them fellers back toward Richmond somewhere. I don't think you'll have too much trouble finding your man."

Nathaniel stepped forward and thanked the soldier. They exchanged salutes one more time, and then Nathaniel entered the gate to the stockade. A Yankee officer approached him immediately. He looked at Nathaniel as if to size him up, or to see what sort of man dared to enter his world. He spoke loudly with a deep raspy voice worn by too many cigars over too many years. "You're kind of young to be a captain, aren't you, sonny?"

Nathaniel noticed the gold leaf on the officer's collar, came to attention, saluted and replied formally, "Major, I am Nathaniel Graham, a captain of the 19th Tennessee Volunteers. I am here to see Captain McKinley at his request. May I speak with him, sir?"

Surprised at the genuine respect, the Yankee major brought himself to attention, returned Nathaniel's salute, and replied, "Sure, Captain. I'll take you to him. He's right over here. Did Captain McKinley say what he wanted to talk to you about? I think it is a little strange that he didn't mention it to me. Certainly you can understand that I'd be curious, being the ranking officer among these men. You won't mind if I listen to your conversation, now would you?"

Nathaniel never handled rapid-fire questioning well. He always wanted to prioritize the questions and form appropriate responses so he stuttered as he attempted to reply, "No, sir, I mean yes, I mean, no, he didn't indicate what he wanted to say, and yes, I understand your concern. It is only natural. I have no objection to you being a part of the conversation. I wouldn't think that anything he would say to me would be confidential."

The major turned and pointed with his right hand toward a very old, shady cottonwood tree, and said, "Good then. We understand each other as officers. Follow me, Captain."

As they walked, the major informed Nathaniel that Captain McKinley was the regiment's chaplain and inquired about their possible prisoner-exchange status. These captured officers rested under the shade trees and as the two men came near, the major spoke commandingly, "Captain McKinley."

The captain watched the men walk in his general direction. He expected that the Rebel officer was the man he requested. He quickly held up his hand and responded, "Here, sir." Then he smartly presented a proper salute to his superior officer.

The major walked directly to McKinley, returned his salute and commanded, "Captain McKinley, I would like to speak with you for a moment."

"Of course, Major Baxter, sir," McKinley dropped his salute and began to walk toward Major Baxter and Nathaniel. Once they were all together, Major Baxter introduced the two captains to each other. They both took a second to size each other up, as if preparing for a fistfight. But in the next second, McKinley extended his right hand in greeting to Nathaniel and inquired, "I gather you received my message?"

Nathaniel shook hands with the prisoner and replied, "Yes, I did. I am curious about your request to speak with a chaplain, even more so now that Major Baxter has kindly informed me that you are a chaplain yourself."

Captain McKinley looked Nathaniel directly into his eyes and stated, "Well, Captain Graham, I suppose I should get right to the point. I was simply looking for some minister-to-minister fellowship. And frankly, I thought we could discuss viewpoints. I don't know if I will ever return home again and I'd like to have some honest conversation with a fellow believer because I am very confused about many things concerning this war."

This straight answer caught Nathaniel and Major Baxter by complete surprise. Nathaniel's mind quickly remembered the admonition General Breckinridge spoke to him in what seemed to be a lifetime ago, *"Nate, you need to really know why you are here and why we should be fighting this war if you are going to help my men."*

Major Baxter broke the silence and said, "If you boys are going to talk theology, you go right ahead without me." Captain McKinley gave his superior officer a confident affirming look and then saluted, declaring, "Sir, that is exactly my intention. It is hard for me to grasp how apparent brothers in Christ can kill each other, when there is nothing, in my humble opinion, that I can see worth fighting for. Aren't we commanded by our Savior to love each other and by doing so prove we belong to Him?"

Major Baxter returned the salute and said jovially, "This is too much for me. I'll leave you gentlemen to figure out the divine purpose of the universe."

Out of conditioned reflexive respect, Nathaniel also saluted Major Baxter. Then Nathaniel and Captain McKinley stood face-to-face. Although surrounded by curious onlookers, they stood together alone. McKinley continued, "Isn't it interesting how quickly the Holy Spirit exposes a nonbeliever's heart; they flee from any opportunity to come into His holy light." Nathaniel took note of the curious statement and reaction, but said nothing in reply.

Not far from them a large old log lay on the ground. It would make a good place to sit. Captain McKinley noticed it and suggested that they sit down. Captain McKinley was more forward in his approach to conversation. Maybe it stemmed from the fact that he had nothing to lose, now a prisoner. Or maybe he had an aggressive nature. Nathaniel couldn't quite tell, nor was he ready when Captain McKinley asked directly, "Where you from, Captain Graham?"

Nathaniel replied, "Tennessee, near the Nashville area. The town I live in is called Franklin. Before the war, I was a pastor of a small congregation. We served nearly a hundred regular members."

"One hundred?" McKinley paused for effect. "That's a large fellowship. I bet you miss your home? I sure do."

"Where are you from, Captain?" Nathaniel tried to sound interested. He suspected that McKinley wanted to discuss something other than home and family.

"I'm from Connecticut. My wife and three children live in a small town too, close to the sea. It is about a half-day's carriage ride from Hartford."

"I've never seen the sea. I was told that we are not far from the ocean in this very place. I wonder if I'll ever see it. I imagine it is spectacular."

"Yes it is. I love fishing; all the men in my family love to fish. Do you?"

"Not as much as some of my friends. We have only streams, rivers, and small lakes to choose from, but I do enjoy the peace of mind and the relaxation of being out in the country away from the demands of other people when I go fishing."

"Peace of mind, yes, that's important to me too. In many respects that's why I wanted and needed to speak with another minister."

Both men were silent and just stared at each other for an awkward moment. The real issue was about to surface. With it came an uncomfortable tension. Would they continue to unleash the anger that could not be checked by diplomatic compromise in Washington? Or would they reasonably address the volatile issues? Could two men, who by faith should be closer in their relationship than blood relatives, reach a compromise that forty years of bickering had failed to produce? Or, as Nathaniel feared deeply in his being that once again deadly pride would rule? Nathaniel swallowed hard and offered up the first verbal gesture that indicated that he was ready to engage this discussion. "Well, sir, I am here as you requested. What do we need to talk about?"

"Captain Graham," McKinley started again. "I'd like to talk with you as a brother in Christ. So before we talk about specific matters, I'd like to pray and invite Jesus to rule over our hearts and minds by His Holy Spirit as we talk. I want to pray that our fellowship will be pleasing to our Father. Also, as brothers, I'd like to drop the formality of military titles. My first name is Francis. My friends call me Frank. Is this agreeable to you? By the way, if you don't mind telling me, what is your first name?"

Nathaniel was not used to McKinley's straightforward approach. He assumed that time was a key factor driving McKinley to quick results. Nathaniel steeled himself and replied, "Everything you've suggested is fine with me, and my first name is Nathaniel. Most people call me Nate. I don't know why because I've never suggested that anyone use that name. Seems funny to me that people would just assume that it is my nickname and that I wouldn't mind or didn't care if they used it."

"Do you?"

"Do what?"

"Do you mind that people call you Nate? Does it offend you? I've met many people who don't like it when others don't refer to them by their proper name, so do you care?"

"I guess I don't. But don't you think it's interesting what folks assume?"

"Yes I do, especially about really important things. It seems people always take the easy path, even if it is wrong. It takes effort to learn the truth about a matter. I guess that's why I wanted to talk with a fellow believer in Christ. My hope is that you are a seeker of His truth."

"I believe I am."

"I hope I am, too. War has a way of distorting things. I believe I heard it said that the first casualty in any war is the truth. After this past year, I think I believe this to be so."

"I guess I haven't given it much thought."

"Well, Nathaniel, I hope you have some time available, because I've been doing a lot of thinking and I simply can't talk to just anyone about these things. I hope you won't think I'm crazy, but I can't figure out why we are fighting this war in the first place. Nothing seems to make sense. But before I bend your ear, let's take a minute and pray."

Nathaniel agreed and bowed his head. The older, gray-haired Captain McKinley took off his cap and folded it in his hands. Out of respect, Nathaniel removed his kepi too. Both sat quietly for a few seconds and then McKinley began, "Father in Heaven, Nathaniel and I stand before You in Jesus' name. We desire to receive wisdom, knowledge and understanding from You. We trust in Your word that tells us if any man lacks wisdom that we should ask for it from You and You will grant it liberally. I submit myself to Your plan and purpose for my life. I don't understand why I am in this place, but I know You do and I am thankful that You've brought Nathaniel to me so I can talk to another believer about the thoughts that trouble me deeply. I cast all my cares onto Jesus and I humble myself before You. I ask that our conversation will be pleasing in Your sight and in Your hearing, for You are the judge of the thoughts and intents of our minds and hearts. I know that You incline Your ear to listen to the prayers of Your children and I know that You will answer these petitions according to Your sovereign will. I also know that where two or more gather in Your name, Jesus, You are with us. In Your name, Lord Jesus, we commit these things into Your capable hands." McKinley paused, took a deep breath. Relieved, he ended his prayer sighing, "Amen!"

Nathaniel was a bit confused by the content of this prayer. He never heard anyone pray with such depth of spirit before. Since he didn't hear anything that was objectionable, he pensively said in agreement, "Amen."

A hawk flew overhead and screeched as if it agreed with both men. McKinley looked up toward the sky. He knew that what he was about to say would be awkward for someone who hadn't taken time to meditate over these issues. But he desperately needed to deliver his soul. He longed for truth to set him free. He wasn't looking to Nathaniel for answers; he looked to his Redeemer. But he understood that God uses others to sharpen his understanding regarding many issues. He only hoped that God would answer his prayer and use Nathaniel as the Holy Spirit directed. He stood, stretched, folded his hands behind his back, and began to pace. Nathaniel watched McKinley collect himself and, after a few silent seconds passed, McKinley stopped, lowered his head, sighed deeply, looked directly into Nathaniel's eyes and said, "I know God intended for me to be captured. Even I understand that these men will need a shepherd to tend to their yet unrealized spiritual needs. I do submit to His will. I suppose I now have something in common with His early disciples."

Nathaniel looked at McKinley and asked, "What's that, Frank?"

He chuckled and said, "Well, Nate, they kept winding up in prison."

They both laughed and Nathaniel said, "You and your men might be exchanged."

McKinley pursed his lips thoughtfully, gazed back up at the sky, shook his head negatively and said, "I really don't think that is God's plan. General McClellan ordered that all prisoner exchanges be stopped because he was tired of letting your boys go only to have to fight them again, and yet again. No, Nate, I'm afraid the fighting is over for these men and me. I have but one personal hope and that is, I want to survive to see my home and family again. But if that is not His plan, then so be it."

"Well, Frank, the way this war is going, I don't think you'll have to wait too much longer. It seems to me that you Yankees are winning every fight. Richmond is just a few miles from here. The way I see it, one real strong push and your boys could take the city. Then I'll need you to come visit me in a Federal prison."

McKinley shook his head again and said, "I don't think so. Last night I had a dream. I won't bore you with the details, but I believe it was from the Lord. From this dream, I concluded that this war is going to go on for a long time. I believe it will be years before we see the end, and unspeakable multitudes will die because of it. Our young nation is being baptized in blood."

The truth of this last statement penetrated Nathaniel's heart. Deep inside, he suspected this very same thing. Out of curiosity he asked, "Did God show you who wins?"

McKinley smirked and replied, "I only wish He had. No, He has His own purposes for this war. That is another reason why I need to talk with you."

Nathaniel leaned back slightly, defensively, and replied, "Frank, if you think I know the outcome of this fight, you've got another

NEW ASSIGNMENTS · 161

think coming to you. I sure don't have any idea how this whole mess is ever going to be settled, unless you boys go home and leave us alone to live our lives as we see fit."

Nathaniel stepped into the heart of the matter. It was deep and it smelled bad. It struck a foul discord in Frank and he turned to look Nathaniel directly in the eye as a parent scolding his child. He stroked his beard and let his anger subside. Penitently he responded, "That's the problem, isn't it? We won't simply go away. Why do you think that is, Nate?"

"I believe you Yankees want to conquer our lands. Many of our people believe that your leaders of commerce want to control our agricultural production and that all this rhetoric about preserving the Union is just a cover-up for colonial conquest."

McKinley held his tongue for a second, then responded calmly, "Nathaniel, I assure you that this is not the case. Preserving the Union is the one and only driving force behind our cause. I am very close to those who make political decisions in my town. They are men of honor, character, and trust. We want to see our country restored, not divided."

Defensively, Nathaniel summarized, "You're telling me that the only reason you are here is to make our country rejoin yours? I find that very hard to believe. It doesn't make any sense that you Yankees would go to such extremes just to keep us part of your government. There must be another motive, something very deep and sinister that you are just not aware of yet. I'm sure your bankers and business leaders want to control our lives so that they can make more profits. I don't believe that they care about the rights of the people and their respective states. We must be free to choose for ourselves, be responsible to ourselves, and to govern ourselves."

"I can see that you've given this some thought, Nate. However, your conclusion is wrong. Keeping America one nation is my reason for being here. I believe God created our country and our constitutional form of government to be a light of liberty to the world—" McKinley paused because he wanted his next point to be clear. He took a breath and continued his comparison, "—just as the gospel is the light of salvation to a lost soul. I know many might disagree with this opinion, but I believe God created our nation, a free people, to be His tool to spread His gospel."

Nathaniel really wasn't listening. He continued to defend the proud Southern position, "That's why we created our own Constitution. We know which way is best to conduct our lives. So why can't you accept that, stop this foolishness, and go home? I'm sure in time we'll all learn to get along as two separate nations."

McKinley realized that he was not getting through so he decided to take a different approach. He tried another analogy, "I don't think so, because we are one nation, one people. Have you ever been to Europe?"

Nathaniel shook his head, "No, I haven't. Before the war, I never left Tennessee."

"Well, Nate, some of the nations in Europe are smaller than many of our states, and they border one another. Those people don't get along, haven't gotten along, and may never get along. Every time they have a disagreement, they split up and create a new nation. They establish new boundaries and become further isolated from one another. They never force themselves to resolve their differences."

Nathaniel could not see anything wrong with people separating for their own reasons, so he questioned, "Why should or would they want to do that?"

McKinley was prepared with his answer, "Because each time they subdivide, they weaken themselves. And if you keep demanding an independent Virginia or Tennessee, it won't be long before your Confederacy will divide itself further. We are a strong nation united and we should do everything possible to stay that way."

Nathaniel challenged, "Including invading our homes?"

Captain McKinley countered, "The way I see it, you're more concerned with blaming us for prosecuting this war then you are in identifying the problem and fixing it so that we can stop fighting it."

Nathaniel's irritation with this discussion grew. He could not control the anger that sprung from deep in his gut, so he retaliated, "The problem is that you won't leave us alone."

Captain McKinley recognized Nathaniel's agitation and chose a third direction. "That's not the real issue. Are we or are we not going to be one nation? That's the issue, Nate; the Union is like a big family, a unique marriage relationship. Are you married?"

Nathaniel seemed to calm slightly as he answered, "No. I hope that God will bring a woman into my life someday, but now doesn't seem like the right time."

Captain McKinley became hopeful and continued his new thought, "Well, as a young pastor, I'm sure that you understand that you don't break up a marriage just because of disagreements. Divorce may be a convenient solution but it certainly can't be the right one. Would you agree?"

Finally, Nathaniel relaxed his defensive posture and replied, "Yes, I do. I have preached Christ's teaching on marriage several times."

Confident that he was on the right path, McKinley pressed his point. "Then you know that a husband and wife must choose to work together and press through the disagreement until they find a compromise and a place of peace. In like manner, if we break up into sovereign states, then how are we different from Europe? Then what would America stand for? Nothing. As I said before, throughout their history, disagreements resulted in the separation of people groups. They became bitter toward one another and war erupted. They separated and became weaker. Nate, can you realize that we are stronger as a union and weaker divided. Didn't Jesus say, 'Every kingdom divided against itself is brought to desolation; and *every city or house divided against itself shall not stand?'* President Lincoln understands this truth and that it applies to an individual, a marriage, and even a nation. Doesn't the scripture teach that God blesses those brethren who dwell in unity? It is bad enough that families are split over this war and family members are actually fighting against each other because of the disagreement. But here we are, both of us professing to belong to God's family, and you wear the uniform of the South and I the North. Don't you think something is terribly wrong with fellow believers in Christ killing each other over non-eternal issues? The politics of this life are temporal, they are not eternal."

Trapped in the Southern mindset, Nathaniel responded, "But we don't want you Yankees telling us what to do and how to live our lives. You invade our land and demand that we submit and subject ourselves to an authority that is not justly in power and that does not have the consent of the people."

Captain McKinley slipped and countered, "We didn't fire on Fort Sumter."

Nathaniel shot back, "Lincoln provoked it with his inauguration speech."

Captain McKinley argued indisputable facts, "But many states seceded after the election results were known. He didn't say anything right away. South Carolina never gave him a chance."

"Lincoln only had forty-seven percent of the popular vote," Nathaniel countered with an equally valid fact.

"He had the electoral votes."

"The election was all wrong to have three Democrats and one other. The people didn't have fair choices. The Black Republicans won unfairly."

Captain McKinley stopped himself. He realized that the conversation had deteriorated into the typical circular arguments of the past decades, but he couldn't stop as he continued, "How do you know that God didn't appoint Lincoln? How do you justify your actions against Romans 13 and Galatians 5?"

"We are a free people and we have the right to defend ourselves against tyranny, aggression, and invasion. You people in the North really started this mess."

"There, you have proven my point. You want to blame someone and break the Union rather than fix the problem."

"What is the problem?"

"Are we different people groups or are we all Americans? If we are all Americans, why are we killing each other?"

Both men stopped talking as if this last statement found its mark in both their hearts. After a long moment of silence, McKinley continued, "Nathaniel, please pray and think about what we've talked about today."

Still defensive, Nathaniel answered sharply, "I will. Is there anything else that you want?"

"Yes, as a matter of fact there is. As I said, I believe God showed me that this is going to be a very long war. In the fighting the other day, I lost one of my most important possessions. If you please, Nate, could you do me one favor and find me a Bible? I still have some money. I'll gladly give you all I have so that I can have His Word with me on this next appointed journey."

Somehow, Nathaniel seemed to understand that this ended their discussion. In a brotherly response and without hesitation he stated, "Here, Frank, take mine."

Captain McKinley received Nathaniel's Bible graciously. Then, he extended his right hand in thanks. Nathaniel took it and shook the man's hand respectfully. There was no anger toward him even though he still disagreed deeply. They parted. Nathaniel turned and walked toward the gate. He was touched by the fact that this man could resign himself to the will of God so easily.

Nathaniel padded his tired bent-over body back to Major Duffy's tent. He tried to clear his troubled mind. The conversation with Captain Francis McKinley turned over and over again in his thoughts. He couldn't avoid the reality that he couldn't justify the war on eternal, heavenly, or biblical authority, only natural, earthly, temporal and political. He recognized that Scripture declared clearly that the kingdoms of this world are not now but someday will become subordinate to Christ. Obviously, no one earthly government is superior to another in comparison to the Kingdom of God. He wanted to stop thinking altogether as he reached Major Duffy's tent. He pulled back the flap opening and leaned in to see Major Duffy still working.

"Major Duffy," Nathaniel announced his return. "I've finished speaking with the Yankee chaplain. I spoke with a few of our men, too. Do you mind if I return to my tent and get some rest?"

"Nate! Am I glad to see you! We don't have time to rest. Our new senior commander reorganized the entire army. He's calling us the Army of Northern Virginia. We must break camp here and move to a location north and east of here." With excitement in his voice, Major Duffy announced, "We've been assigned to General D. H. Hill's Division."

Chapter 17

SHIFTING TIDES

The sun broke through early morning clouds after a night filled with pouring rain, violent thunder, and flashes of bright lightning. The air smelled sweet, fresh, and clean. Eleanor threw open her bedroom windows and greeted this Thursday, the 26th day of June, with renewed vigor and a sense of expectation she hadn't felt since that terrible day when she'd learned of her father's death at Shiloh. What was this feeling? Could it be joy? Why is today so different, why now?

Eleanor turned her thoughts to her brothers, Paul and John. As she looked up at the near-cloudless beautiful deep-blue sky, she wondered what they were doing this bright morning and if the sun shone on them too. Mostly, she hoped they were both safe. Then she thought briefly about what she should do about her father's office. Time was running out. However, she dismissed this problem as she turned her attention to the dress shop's inventory. In a strange way, she actually looked forward to going to work this delightful early summer day.

She continued to gaze out her bedroom window and drank in the morning splendor. It seemed to spring hope in her soul.

The birds seemed to sing louder. The flowers in the fields seemed more colorful, and the trees seemed to dance in the breeze as it blew through their branches and broad green leaves. Eleanor felt happy and she didn't care why. She heard noises coming from the main floor below; her mother was preparing breakfast. She quickly pulled her robe over her shoulders, gathered the sash about her waist, tied it snug, and bounded down the staircase to wish her mother a wonderful good morning.

Partway down the stairs, the image of Jason Merritt flashed through her mind. She tried to ignore it. She even slowed her pace to help her divert her internal energy to her brain to help her remove the picture of his charming, smiling face. However, the thought took control of her thinking. She felt differently, too—in a word, silly.

Excitedly, Eleanor nearly shouted, "Good morning, Mother," as she entered the kitchen. She took a deep breath through her nose and as she exhaled she declared, "Smells delicious." Then she asked, "What are you cooking for breakfast this beautiful morning?"

Catherine turned from the corner woodstove and said, "Good morning, dear. Did you sleep well? You look—," Catherine paused and looked deeply into Eleanor's eyes, as if she saw something she'd never seen before. After a long, almost awkward second, Catherine tried to continue, "You look—," she paused again.

This prompted Eleanor to ask, "What, Mother, what do I look like? Do I have something on my face?" Eleanor turned to run to the parlor and look in a mirror. But before she could leave the kitchen, Catherine stopped her.

"No, dear, there is nothing wrong with your face. You just look happy. I can see it in your eyes."

Eleanor quipped, "I do?" She smiled a broad smile, chuckled a little almost under her breath, and agreed, "I suppose I am. It's a beautiful morning. The sun is shining brightly, the air smells sweet and clean, and the field is filled with corn stalks and wild flowers. It's nice to see."

Catherine continued to examine her daughter and said, "No, it's something more than all that. No, it is something else."

Eleanor tried to direct the conversation onto another path. "Well," she started deliberately. "The war is going well and it looks as though it will be over very soon. Then Paul and John will come home, and at least we'll all be together again."

Catherine thought about Eleanor's reply for a moment and said, "No, that's not it either. I can't explain it, but you seem to have a sparkle in your eye."

Eleanor nearly blushed at this news. What did her mother see? She tried to dismiss the remark and said, "Oh, Mother, please! If anything, I'm just happy. For a change, I'm looking forward to going to work, not feeling sad, and thinking about and missing Father. Is it so wrong to feel happiness, to see a new day, and to have hope for that day? It has been nearly three months since he died. I'm not saying that I've forgotten about him, he just wasn't preoccupying my thoughts this morning."

Catherine turned back to her cooking and sighed, "I suppose you're right. Maybe a day will come when I too will greet a new day like today with hope for the future." She breathed deeply and began to sob.

Eleanor hurried to Catherine's side. She gave her mother a warm, comforting embrace and they wept together. Eleanor's new day of hope turned to mourning once again.

After a few minutes, the two women wiped their tears, blew their noses, and returned to their respective tasks of getting ready for the day. They chatted casually as they ate the small feast Catherine prepared for breakfast and enjoyed fresh, hot coffee. But Catherine couldn't leave the subject alone. At one point during their light conversation their eyes met and Catherine announced, "There it is again."

Somewhat dumbfounded and caught off guard, Eleanor replied, "Where? What's it again?"

Catherine winked at her daughter and said, "That sparkle in your eyes."

Both women laughed aloud for a brief moment. Once they composed themselves, they sat quietly, sipping what was left of their coffee. Each in her own way wondered what Catherine saw and what it could possibly mean.

It was a few minutes after the noon hour. The sun seemed to be directly over Rockford, Illinois. Hot, humid air fell heavily upon the town. A single horse-drawn carriage rolled by Catherine's Boutique. Dust rose a few inches from the street, then fell quickly back to earth after the buggy passed. Heavy boot steps could be heard clomping along the boardwalk in front of the dress shop. A young gentleman approached the store's front door and opened it. The bell above the door rang announcing the entrance of a potential patron. Jason Merritt closed the door behind him and called, "Eleanor, are you here?"

Eleanor was in the store's back storage area. She heard the doorbell ring and instinctively dropped sorting through newly arrived dress accessories and turned for the store's front. But as soon as she heard an unfamiliar male voice call her name, she stopped in her tracks. She wondered. An expectancy rose in her, another feeling foreign to her for the past several months. *Who could this man be?* She smoothed her dress, checked her hair in the mirror near the doorway that separated the front from the back of the store, and called out, "I'll be with you in just one moment. Feel free to look around." She really wished that she had installed the small window between the rooms so she could sneak a peek before venturing out of the protection and isolation of the store's backroom. She took a deep breath and, with anxious anticipation, she stepped forward to greet her visitor.

Jason stood straight, arching his back, which increased the appearance of his slightly higher than six-foot stature. He looked directly at the doorway from where Eleanor's voice came. He anticipated this opportunity to join a social call with a business proposition. He believed that Catherine and Eleanor could benefit from his intended offer; however, he more greatly appreciated the benefit it would bring to his plans. If by chance he could spend some personal time with Eleanor, even better. From the party, he formed an impression that she could be pleasant, possibly even inspiring company.

As Eleanor appeared and walked through the doorway, Jason's eyes lit up. She looked stunning, very different from the other evening. As their eyes met, Eleanor stopped and both stood silently for an awkward second. Jason wanted to speak, but his words stuck in his throat. Clumsily, he removed his gray, medium-length top hat.

Eleanor calmly broke the stillness, "Why Mr. Merritt, how nice of you to drop in. Is there something I can help you find? Are you shopping for a dress for someone, perhaps your mother?"

Jason caught himself staring at the young woman who stood across the vast sea of dresses, hats, and other items whose description or purpose he couldn't explain. He had to shake himself back to the present and explain his reason for seeing her. Somehow, he didn't expect her to have this impact on him. After all, she is just a woman.

Eleanor continued, "Are you all right, Mr. Merritt? I never expected you to be one lost for words, sir." She snickered slightly under her breath and looked down at the floor to break the eye contact and, hopefully, ease the tension.

Jason composed himself, cleared his throat, and broke through his nervousness by stating, "Miss Ellis, good day to you."

"Good day to you, sir," Eleanor replied quickly. Then she repeated, "Now, is there something I can help you find, Mr. Merritt?"

Jason responded, "No, Miss Ellis. I am not here to shop for articles of clothing, for my mother or for anyone else, for that matter. I happened to be in the area and when I saw your store, I started thinking about the other evening. You sure made fools of several pillars of our fair community."

"Now, sir," Eleanor began with a sharper tone. "That matter is not worthy of further discussion. I should think one would not wish to waste one's time on such trifles. If that is the subject matter you wish to discuss with me, then I suggest, sir that this is neither the time nor the place."

Clearly, this was not going well and Jason needed to change the subject from small talk to the real purpose of his visit. He responded in as dignified a manner as he could under the circumstances, "Yes, Miss Ellis, of course. Certainly, I do have a matter of greater importance I wish to discuss with you. If you don't mind, I'll get directly to the point?"

"No, sir, I don't mind at all," Eleanor nearly interrupted. "In fact, I am now quite curious as to what brings you into my shop today. So, sir, please do go on."

Jason realized that he might not be able to control the conversation as he had done with so many people, especially women, in the past. He furrowed his brow reflectively for a second, then he continued, "Yes, Miss Ellis, I will state my purpose. I have a business proposition for you and your mother to consider. I believe it will help both our respective interests. Are you interested in what I have to say?"

Eleanor gazed at Jason for minute, searched his eyes for any hint of insincerity, leaned back just a bit, and thoughtfully replied, "Yes, sir, I do believe I wish to hear more about this, 'business proposition,' as you call it. Since you say it could help both my mother and I, maybe we should include her in this discussion. She will be here shortly. But maybe we should set an appointment so that we could spend more time to—" Eleanor stopped in mid sentence. She nearly blushed because she couldn't believe what she almost said. Then she quickly clarified, "I mean so we could have plenty of time to discuss the matter with my mother."

Jason felt confident that Eleanor took his bait. Now he needed to set the hook. He encouraged, "That is a perfect idea. I wish I had thought of it myself." He pretended to pause in thought, but so far things were working out better then he planned. He pressed on with his ruse, "Yes, Eleanor, that is a wonderful idea indeed. Maybe we could meet one morning for an hour or so before you normally open the store. How does that sound?"

Eleanor thoughtfully replied, "Let's see, I guess that would be around nine o'clock in the morning. Is that what you had in mind, sir?"

Jason smiled as he answered, "Yes, I think that would be a very good time for me."

Eleanor saw the smiling face she pictured in her mind that morning. She stumbled over her own words as she asked, "Do you have a place in mind?" Eleanor paused herself and then teasingly, almost flirting, she clarified, "I mean, for this 'business' meeting?" Eleanor looked away quickly. *Where is this coy behavior coming from?*

Jason acted as if this thought suddenly came to him, "I have an idea. We could meet at your father's office. As I understand, it is close to your store here, is that correct?"

"Yes. It is just down the street, closer to the center of town."

"Very well then, we have a time and a place. All we need to do is set the day. Can you think of a day, say early next week that would work best for you and your mother?"

Eleanor didn't want to sound too eager so she offered, "Of course, Mr. Merritt, you must realize that I have to speak with my mother first; however, next Tuesday, the first of July, seems as though it could work out well for both of us."

"Certainly, Miss Ellis, I do understand. Then I will wait to hear from you to confirm our meeting plans?"

"Yes, sir, Mr. Merritt. I will send you word in a day or two."

"Then, I will beg your leave to go for now." Jason bowed slightly at his waist, and lowered his head. As he straightened himself, he put on his gray top hat and tapped it into place on his head and said, "Good day to you, Miss Ellis."

"Good day to you, Mr. Merritt. But before you leave, would you be so kind as to provide me with a few more details regarding our meeting? Surely you understand that my mother will ask me questions. If we need to prepare, having more information about the issue would be helpful."

Jason knew he could dismiss himself. He turned to leave, reached for the store's front door, opened it, stepped into the threshold, turned and looked at Eleanor and answered, "Why Miss Ellis, I am interested in taking over your father's legal practice and the lease of his office. We can discuss the details next Tuesday morning. Unless I hear otherwise, I will see you and your dear mother then. Until then, Miss Ellis," Jason nodded, "Good day." He quickly stepped outside and pulled the door closed. He smiled at Eleanor through the door's glass window, turned toward the center of town, and walked quickly away before Eleanor had a chance to react.

Eleanor stood motionless just inside her store. Her mouth dropped open, but she was speechless. What just happened? Why was she suddenly both curious about and angry with this man? *He wants father's practice and office. How could he presume to be so bold?*

While Eleanor stood gazing out the window, looking in the general direction into which Jason had disappeared, the store's door opened and the doorbell rang loudly again, right above Eleanor's head. Catherine's entrance startled Eleanor, and shook her from her thoughts.

"How are you, Eleanor dear," Catherine asked, noticing her daughter's shaken countenance.

"Oh, Mother," Eleanor quickly responded. "You gave me such a fright; nearly scared me to death, coming in so quickly. I was looking out the window but I didn't see you coming."

"I should say so; you look as if you'd seen a ghost or something. What has you so upset, dear? Didn't I just see that nice young man—" Catherine paused and looked down at the store's floor as she shook her head as if to waken some past memory. "What's his name?"

"Jason Merritt," Eleanor answered.

"Yes, that's it, Jason. Did he just leave our store?"

"Yes, Mother, he did," Eleanor replied sharply. She strongly suspected what came next and became exasperated with her mother.

"Oh, isn't that nice? Did he come to visit you, dear?" Catherine knew her daughter very well so she pretended that she really didn't care what Eleanor's answer would be to her purposely-probing question. Catherine casually strolled to the store's rear counter. She carried an armful of new fabrics for yet another stunning garment masterpiece. She muttered under her breath, "Thank God so many women are enslaved to fashion."

Eleanor retorted forcefully, "No, Mother, he didn't come to visit just me. He wants to discuss something with the both of us. He called it a 'business proposition' and it concerns the lease of father's law office."

"Oh, that's too bad, dear," Catherine wanted to plant a few suggestive seeds into Eleanor's mind. She knew well enough that if she could cultivate the thought, it could take root and Eleanor's general attitude for this man might change.

Eleanor's temper flared, "Too bad! What do you mean, too bad?"

"Well, I just thought it would be nice if he had stopped to simply see you and the two of you had a few minutes to talk about anything other than work. He seems like a nice young man who also appears to have a real bright, successful future in front of him."

Eleanor caught her mother's not-so-subtle hint. She placed both hands on her hips, nearly snorted from an internal emotional burst of anger, and started to march directly for Catherine and a face-to-face confrontation. "Now Mother, you stop this matchmaking idea right this instant. I don't want you dreaming up some romantic notions for my future. I don't need a husband. I'm quiet content with my life just as it is."

"I wasn't thinking anything of the sort," Catherine replied defensively. "I was just thinking out loud. How could you think that I would plan such a thing? I just said I think that he's a nice young man. He's obviously interested in you."

"Mother, you can't mean that, you don't know that," Eleanor responded sharply.

"Elli dear, you said yourself that he wanted to speak with both of us. He certainly could have come a few minutes later to catch you and me in the store together if he really wanted to speak with me too. He's been around town long enough to know folks' routines. Besides, a mother knows a few things more about life then her daughter, no matter how smart or self-educated you might be.

Eleanor could tell that this conversation was going to get nasty. She wanted to restrain herself. She didn't want to upset her mother, but out it came, "I wish you'd mind your own business and stay out of mine."

"Why Eleanor," Catherine declared, "I've never heard you talk to me this way." Wounded, Catherine looked down at the floor and continued wagging her head. "If that's the way you really feel, maybe I should just go home." She turned toward the rear of the store, walked quickly through the passageway, and headed for the rear door.

Eleanor's entire being instantly filled with deep anguish and guilt. The shame drove her to yell to Catherine, "Mother, please don't do this." Eleanor heard her mother's footsteps grow distant. "Mother, please wait." Then, Eleanor heard the locking bar on the rear door lift. "Stop!" she cried. Eleanor strode toward the rear of the store and shouted, "Let's talk—" The slamming of the door stopped her cold and her voice simply faded away with, "—about this." Once again, she stood silently with her mouth wide open. *What did I do? Why did I upset her? I know better. Should I chase after her? What more could go wrong this day?* Eleanor glanced at the calendar that hung on the store wall behind the counter.

Chapter 18

CHICKAHOMINY BLUES

Finally the rain stopped and the sun broke through the still-gray midday sky. Both the Beaver Dam Creek and the Chickahominy River were at or near flood stage. Some of the low-lying temporary log roads built by the Federal Infantry were actually underwater. The Yankee supply wagons were bogged down. The higher ground near Mechanicsville offered little relief from the swampy surroundings. Here sat the Union Army's Fifth Corps, waiting, always waiting to hear some news. Maybe they would receive orders to advance in some new direction. Their mission was to anchor the extreme right flank of McClellan's army and to protect the rear supply line from the occasional Rebel raiding party. But mostly, every day was met with new degrees of boredom. The only action these soldiers saw was the long march from Hampton Roads near the Southern point of the Chesapeake Bay through the swampy woods on both sides of the muddy Chickahominy River. Another wagon was nearly ready to carry supplies to the main body a few miles south of the river. John and Paul Ellis returned to their routine of loading and unloading wagons with the necessities of army life on this grimy Virginia peninsula.

"These cartridge boxes seem to get heavier each day," Private John Ellis complained as he lifted an ammunition case from the stockpile.

"Your whining won't do no good," John's older brother Paul replied. He took a drink from his canteen.

The sun began to beat down hard on John's back and sweat dripped from his forehead. He arched his back and turned toward Paul who leaned against the side of a covered wagon. "Paul, I hate this here army. I want to go home. I want to see Mamma and Elli. All we do all day long is move supplies from one pile to another or one wagon to a stack or another wagon. When we aren't doing that, we're marching through this God-forsaken swamp. When we stop, we set up camp. We get up, tear down the camp, march some more, set up another camp, and move supplies. I wonder if anyone really knows where we are. Most of the army is on the other side of that smelly, muddy river. We're stuck over here far away from everyone and everything. Hell, our boys could have captured Richmond by now and we'd never hear anything about it."

"Well, little brother," Paul replied condescendingly. "It's probably best that you aren't anywhere near the fighting. You're such a dang fool you'd go and get yourself killed before the first minute of fighting passed."

Both boys laughed. John quickly defended, "You may be right, but I'd go down knowing I bravely faced the enemy. You'd turn tail and run for your life."

Paul thought *we talked about this very thing before*. Then he replied, "You know as well as I, we don't know what we'd do. We've never been close to any action. Guarding these supply lines against the wild animals looking for food has been our biggest fight. But you know that it is important that we keep our supply line flowing," Paul admonished. "When Little Mac begins the real seize of Richmond, we'll see plenty of action."

John asked, "Do you think the Rebs will come out from behind their trenches and fight again?"

"I doubt it," Paul stated strongly. "The rumor I hear is that the Rebels new commander, old Bobby Lee, is called the 'King of Spades' by his own men. I heard that Lee seems content to build up Richmond's defenses. He won't come out and fight us. He'll sit behind his mud fortress and wait for us to come root them varmints out of their rat holes."

John shouldered another cartridge box and carried it toward the wagon as he said, "Well, I'm real tired of this whole mess. I still want to go home."

Paul added, "I think this war will be over soon. Then we can go home and tell everyone in Rockford how well we marched, how we learned to sleep on the ground, how we forced ourselves to eat lousy food, how we learned to dig sinks and live in the rain, wind and mud. My God, you couldn't ask for a more exciting life than the army life. If the Rebels don't kill us first, surely the boredom will."

"I know what you mean, Paul. I really do." John took off his kepi, wiped the sweat from his forehead and looked southward deep into the encampment. Rows of tents scattered the higher ground around Mechanicsville. Many idle soldiers lingered in front of or near their tents cooking a meal, playing cards, or just lying under a shady tree. Some sat on the wet ground; others found a wooden box to use as a chair. Several puffed steadily on a pipe filled with old, stale tobacco. Another day in camp with nothing to do except watch the day pass.

Suddenly, a flock of birds took flight just about twenty-five yards to the north of Paul' and John's location near the supply wagons. John said, "I wonder what spooked them birds. I bet a panther is roaming those woods. Or maybe, it's a small bear!"

Paul decided to make himself comfortable and sat on the ground. He leaned up against the wagon's rear right wheel and folded his arms to take a nap. He pulled his kepi down low to shield his eyes from the sun. From under his cap he replied drowsily, "Yeah, maybe. He won't come for the wagons in the middle of the day. I'm going to take a little rest. You OK to stand guard by yourself?"

Before John could answer, a sound bellowed forth like that of a banshee released from a thousand years of captivity in hell. For months the frustrated Confederate troops had retreated and fought vain rear action defensive maneuvers. They backed themselves into Richmond. Their new leader knew they were like a serpent that coiled into a fierce striking force ready to unleash its pent-up strength. Transformed into a cornered, wounded, and desperate animal with nothing left to lose, the Rebel army struck vengefully with all its remaining strength.

The terrifying sound caused Paul to jump to his feet. Both John and Paul stood and looked in the general direction from where this strange noise came, but it filled the air. It was very hard to discern from where this frightening, blood-curdling scream sprang. Paul remembered several Yankees trying to describe the sound of the Rebel yell. They swore they'd never forget the fear it drove into their hearts. Some said it was an odd blend of screams, yelps, barking yaps, squealing pigs, Indian whoops, and excited hollers. It could be heard for miles and it meant only one thing, Confederate soldiers were attacking in great force. Paul wondered as he spoke to John, "Do you think that's the Rebel yell? Do you think the Johnnies are coming this way?

Out of the trees they came, rank upon rank, thousands as far as Paul or John could see. This was no raiding party of General J.E.B. Stuart's Cavalry. This looked like the entire Confederate army heading straight for their supply station.

Bugles sounded, orders shouted, and young, frightened drummer boys beat out the assembly command. John and Paul nearly banged into each other before they collected themselves and ran to retrieve their muskets and cartridge belts. They were seeing the elephant for the first time and from John's point of view, it sure looked like June 26, 1862, was going to be his last day on Earth.

"Paul," John shouted, "We should pull back across the creek and up that hill where more of our regiment is posted."

Paul was tamping tight a miniball into his musket, preparing to fight right where he stood. He looked at his younger brother and yelled loudly above the gathering storm, "You might be right, little brother. Appears if we stay here, we're sure to be killed. No officers are around to tell us what to do. Let's get!"

Both boys grabbed what they could and ran as fast as their legs would carry them. They crossed Beaver Dam Creek and, hopefully to safety.

The Southern troops charged into combat screaming out the now infamous Rebel yell. They willed themselves forward into the face of intense Yankee fire. The first Federal defensive line poured out a sheet of lead resistance. The Johnnies faltered and fell back. The Confederate officers gained control of their men. They rallied and charged again. They crossed the creek toward Yankee guns unlimbered, loaded, and ready to fire on the oncoming surge of butternut and gray.

The Confederate soldiers continued to yell, willing their attacking ranks up the hillside. Shot and shell rained down upon them from the Yankees dug into a strong defensive position on the rise above Ellerson's Mill. But these soldiers of General A. P. Hill's Division were not to be denied. These troops were ready for this fight and they were glad to be on the offensive for a change.

Confederate General Robert E. Lee ordered the attack on Major General Fitz-John Porter's Fifth Corps, which was vulnerable and exposed, alone on the Federal right flank, north of the Chickahominy River. Before taking command, General Lee was responsible for supplying the Confederate army. He knew that the Yankee supply line was its life source. He intended to cut that life source. Lee's men were ready to throw the Yankee invaders out of Virginia. They would pay any price, kill or be killed.

The Rebels rolled up the hillside like a tidal wave. Massed together, their officers shouted encouragement, "Keep up your pace, lads!" "Forward, men! Keep pushing forward!" "Let's go, boys!"

Shells exploded in the ranks and opened huge holes in the lines of troops. Some men simply disappeared, as a great flame extinguished by a greater wind. Others fell to the ground, some missing limbs, others ripped apart at their centers. A few were thrown down unhurt by the concussion alone. Once they recovered, they stood to their feet as best they could and then forced themselves to rejoin their comrades and press up the hill in the face of murderous Yankee cannon and musket fire.

Nearly a full regiment of one thousand Rebels reached the Beaver Dam Creek. The trees surrounding the area slowed their progress, but once they reached the creek, they ran across as fast as they could. Several went down in the muddy water. Blood began to run with the creek toward the Chickahominy River. A color bearer went down in the bloodstained slime. A musket dropped by his dying body and a young soldier stripped the battle flag from his hands. The dying man lifted his head for a brief second to see the face of the boy that took his honor forward. He didn't know him. Life passed from this torn and broken tent.

Another regiment crossed with much less resistance. The one that preceded them took a vicious pounding. The wounded and scared moved down the hill toward the creek and away from the Yankee line of fire. Officers yelled at the obviously unhurt and commanded them to fall in with their own companies. A young private, scared beyond reason, kept running. A lieutenant yelled, "Fall in, private or I'll shoot you!" The private kept running. The lieutenant fired one shot in the air and shouted, "Boy, the next one will be in your back if you don't stop now!" The private reached the creek and began to cross. The lieutenant lowered his pistol, took aim, and fired. A shell burst in the tree next to the lieutenant sending shell fragments all around. The explosion killed him instantly. The private fell dead, next to the slain color-bearer face down in the bloody, muddy, creek water.

The Rebels came with the strength of a full division, approximately five thousand men. They attacked with incredible zeal, but their losses were staggering. General Porter's Fifth Corps may have been vulnerable, but it was prepared. The Union troops cut down trees and made protective rifle pits. They held a good defensive position. They were ready should a flank attack come, and it came. Because of their readiness, they suffered fewer than four hundred casualties—killed, wounded, and missing—during a full afternoon and evening of fighting.

General Lee's army suffered nearly one thousand, five hundred casualties. Confederate bodies covered the southeast bank of the Beaver Dam Creek. Mathematically, Lee should have considered this a terrible defeat. Other men would have withdrawn, thinking his enemy too strong to remove. Maybe it was his strong faith in God, or maybe he was simply denying the facts, but Lee thought differently.

The Federal line above Beaver Dam Creek held. Porter's men fought effectively. The men realized that they had beaten back the enemy. They could see the bodies of the fallen in the dimming twilight. They watched the Rebels withdraw back to Mechanicsville. They believed that they had won a tremendous victory. But they didn't know the real character of their commander, Major General George B. McClellan. This man was easily intimidated. He was a very effective organizer, a good talker, but not a man of conviction and action. Consequently, Lee achieved his desired result.

McClellan believed that Lee outnumbered the massive one-hundred-thousand-man Federal army, two-to-one. Otherwise, Lee would not commit forces to an attack. Timidly, he ordered Porter's Fifth Corps to withdraw to a stronger defensive position near a farmland area called Gaines' Mill. A high, broad hill overlooked all approaches from which Lee's perceived huge army might attack. It also protected the bridges across the Chickahominy River. Under the cover of night, Porter reluctantly surrendered the field his men fought so well to hold. The once jubilant Yankees marched away in the dark. With each step, their resolve fell. Lee would resume his relentless attack at his first opportunity the next day.

Chapter 19

BREAK THROUGH

June 27, 1862

Dearest Louise,

We had some success yesterday. I don't have time to write any details because we are expected to march within the hour. Give my love to Margaret, your dear mother, and your father. Marvin wanted me to tell you that he's doing well and hopes that you would let Margaret know this for him. He said he'd send her a letter too. I'll write again as soon as time permits.

With loving affection,
Nathaniel

General Daniel H. Hill's Division left Mechanicsville, Virginia, around midmorning. The nearly five thousand soldiers marched for about three hours without stopping, even for water, this hot summer day. Company commanders would send runners to fill canteens as they crossed creeks and streams, but they kept marching as the day grew hotter and the air thicker.

They passed Gaines' Mill and turned east toward Old Cold Harbor. The sounds of intense fighting could be heard to their right and to the south. Every man in line knew that he'd be in the thick of battle too, and very soon. The Yankees were dug in and determined to repeat their tough stand of the previous day. General Robert E. Lee was even more determined to dislodge the Federal force and drive it further away from Richmond. Contrary to his Union counterpart, Lee would make any sacrifice to meet his objective.

Nathaniel marched with his company. *Lord, I am scared. I feel like I might upchuck. I hope I'm ready.* He looked at his men. *I am grateful for these men. I can see their resolve etched on their faces. They're ready. They'll do their duty. They'll drive the invader out of their homeland.*

Company "H" passed an abandoned two-story home. It may have been a very nice, even charming dwelling prior to the Yankee occupation. Nathaniel said to his first sergeant, "Look at what those Blue-Bellied ruffians did to this property."

Sergeant Perry replied, "Looks to me that nearly every window is broken out. The front door is smashed and splintered."

"They must have used some of the picket fence for firewood. Do you see that ash heap?"

"You see that, sir?"

Another casualty of war fell on the front lawn. Obviously, the family dog had tried to defend the home from the armed strangers. The poor loyal defender of his master's home was shot through so many times his remains were barely intact. Maggots made quick work of the carcass.

Nathaniel gazed at this four-legged fallen hero. *What unchained cruelty crushed this poor animal? What monsters could do this awful thing to a defenseless dog? We have to drive these godless sinners from our beautiful southern land.*

Orders came to form into a line of battle. Lieutenant Marvin Jenkins drew his sword and pulled his revolver. As he moved into a command position, he passed Nathaniel doing some of the same preparation maneuvers and said, "I sure hope I don't let the boys down, Nate. Please pray for me that I stay strong for them. You know what they say about me in the camp and all."

Surprised by this, Nathaniel had to think quickly of a reply while he dealt with his own sense of inadequacy. "You'll do just fine, Marvin." Nathaniel hoped that his words of encouragement for Marvin would help himself. "I'll pray for you. You know I will. Please pray for me, too. If we just keep heading through those woods and up that hill, we'll surprise them good. Once the Yankees see us coming, they'll run away for sure. They always do when we catch them unaware. I'll see you at the top of the hill, Marvin." Nathaniel extended his hand and they shook hands earnestly.

"I'll see you at the top," Marvin repeated, releasing his clasp.

The order to move forward came at approximately three-thirty in the afternoon. Quietly, at first, the battle line moved forward into the woods. After they advanced several minutes in the thick woods, Nathaniel's company began to ascend the hill. Just yards ahead, they could see the enemy's handiwork. They cut down trees to form a clear kill zone. Near the crest, those trees were gathered together to form a strong defensive breastwork. *I think the surprise flanking maneuver worked,* Nathaniel observed. *The Yankees don't seem to know we're coming right for them.*

Nathaniel's assumption was very wrong. He heard the first Yankee solid shot bark from behind the breastworks. They knew the rebels were coming, and they were ready too.

Suddenly, a volley of musket fire fell upon the Confederate ranks. Cannon shot split trees and opened great holes in the battle-line formation. It was nearly impossible to keep the ranks in order. The thick woods and steep grade of the hill were entanglements and obstacles enough; but coupled with the rain of lead falling hard all around, it was all Nathaniel could do to encourage his men to remain steady.

Then it happened. That banshee yell started to Nathaniel's right and, like a powerful tidal wave, it moved through his men and out to the companies to their left. It seemed to energize the men, and as they yelled, they began almost automatically to run up the hill.

The Yankee fire began to take its toll. Men fell all around Nathaniel. He remembered a few verses from the 91st Psalm, *"Thou shalt not be afraid for the terror by night; nor for the arrow that flieth by day; nor for the pestilence that walketh in darkness; nor for the destruction that wasteth at noonday. A thousand shall fall at thy side, and ten thousand at thy right hand; but it shall not come nigh thee."* Nathaniel stiffened himself and yelled, "Keep going, boys! Keep going!"

Several men from Nathaniel's company sought protective cover behind some of the larger trees. Nathaniel let them squeeze off a round, and then he approached one large young man as he began to reload his musket. "Mark," Nathaniel interrupted. "We must keep pushing forward, up the hill. The Yankee sharpshooters will surely pick you off if you remain here." Nathaniel looked Mark in the eye and declared respectfully, "You're a good man, Mark. I know I can trust you."

"Thank you, sir," the young private saluted. "I'm ready, sir."

Nathaniel smiled at him and said, "Okay, then, if you're ready, let's go!" With that, they rushed toward the Yankee stronghold together.

Mark ran right in front of Nathaniel. As he crossed, Mark was hit directly in the chest. The impact of the .57 caliber miniball exploded his sternum and threw him back on top of Nathaniel knocking them both to the ground. It took a few seconds for Nathaniel to pull himself together. He pushed the young man off his chest, rolling him down the hill a foot or two. He checked the boy's condition. He was gone. If Mark had not been directly in front of Nathaniel, their positions would be reversed. This reality sunk deep into Nathaniel's heart. Nathaniel swallowed hard and then spoke softly, respectfully, "Thanks, Mark. You gave your life for your friend. I trust you're saying hello to Jesus right now. I might see you both real soon." Nathaniel was still a little shook. He needed to take stock of the immediate situation. From this perilous position he could see that the hill got steeper and the Yankee fire hotter.

My boys are stopping. I have to move them forward. No one's running, but we can't stay here. The men of Company "H" sought cover behind trees, rocks, or the bodies of fallen friends. They returned the Yankee fire as best they could. Nathaniel didn't need to shout encouragement or orders to keep firing. The men fought heroically.

"We're too far from the Yankee line to be effective," Nathaniel yelled to Sergeant Perry.

Perry agreed, "Sir, we need cannon support to drive the Yankees away from their breastworks."

"If we don't, our fight ends here." Nathaniel looked to his left. The rest of the regiment continued to advance up the hill. He saw Marvin wave his sword in a circular motion above his head. "Lieutenant Jenkins is pushing his company forward." *Marvin's doing just fine.*

"Ewell's Division is putting up a severe fight on our right, sir. They're about to reach the clearing. Sir, if we don't move forward, we'll be cut down."

"Or put our advancing flanks in jeopardy. Sergeant Perry, let's push our boys forward."

Sergeant Perry looked around quickly and replied, "We sure ain't doing much good here. We might as well push on and see how many Yankees are really up there. It'd be a dang shame to be held back by just a small company of Blue Bellies."

Nathaniel smiled and said, "I agree. Major Duffy should be just over to our left a little bit, just beyond Lieutenant Jenkins' troops. Sergeant, find Major Duffy and suggest to him, with my compliments that the charge be reordered. We must rally now. Do you understand?"

"Yes, Captain."

"Now, Sergeant, please keep your head down. I need you alive to deliver this message. I know I can depend on you. Also, tell Major Duffy that I will wait for a bugle command. Is this clear, Sergeant?"

"Yessir, Captain."

Nathaniel quickly looked past his sergeant in the direction he was sending the man. It would be dangerous. Marvin's company had also stopped, and now "G" Company took a severe pounding too. Then Nathaniel looked squarely into his sergeant's eyes and commanded, "Move!"

Sergeant Perry rolled over onto his stomach and looked up the hill at the Yankee position as if he were looking for a break in a summer Virginia torrential downpour. Then he looked to his left, pushed himself up, and in a crouched posture ran in the commanded direction. He hoped that he would find Major Duffy alive so he could deliver his burden. Strangely, and much to his and Nathaniel's surprise, his movement did not attract the anticipated Yankee fire. Within a couple of minutes he located Major Duffy, who had reached the same conclusion and decision.

"You tell Captain Graham to get his men ready. I'm giving the same orders to all my company commanders. Tell him that I'll sound the advance in five minutes from right now." They checked their timepieces.

"Five minutes," Sergeant Perry acknowledged. "Yes, sir!"

"Go!"

"Yes, sir, Major Duffy, sir," Sergeant Perry saluted, nearly knocking his kepi from his head. He turned and ran as fast as his legs would carry him back to his captain to deliver the orders.

Major Duffy turned to his first sergeant, Carter, and inquired, "You heard my instructions?"

"Yes, Major."

"Pass the word to my other officers. We will push off again in force in a few minutes on my command."

Sergeant Carter was off. Lead filled the air. Major Duffy watched another tree shatter from a shot of Yankee artillery. They had found the range. It wouldn't be long before they would be hit with the full force of their massed field batteries. More shells fell, pounding the hillside. His regiment was taking a terrible beating. However, the extreme left was free from this cannonade. Where was General Jackson's division? They were supposed to be there. He grabbed the shoulder of another young soldier who had just fired and was beginning to reload his musket. "Son," Major Duffy shouted above the fierce noise. Major Duffy made direct eye contact with the private. He waited a second for the startled, dazed glare to pass. "I need you take this order to Captain Graham on our right, just over there. Do you see that large boulder jutting out of the ground?"

The private looked, saw the big rock, and replied, "Yes, sir. I see it."

"Good. Now, son, what's your name?

Private Beecher, sir, Sam Beecher."

Major Duffy wanted to know this young man's name before he sent him deeper into harm's way. He wanted to extend greater respect to this soldier, knowing that right now he needed nothing more. Major Duffy continued, "Sam, somewhere over there you will find Captain Graham. Tell him you have new orders from me. Tell him, when he hears me sound the advance, he is to order his men this direction and close ranks with us. Tell him to move his company to his left and to follow us. Do you understand my orders, son?"

"Yes, sir. Captain Graham is to move his men this way."

"Good, son. Get going as fast as you can." Major Duffy looked Private Beecher directly into his wide eyes and finished, "Sam, we don't have a moment to lose."

The private forgot to salute. He turned and ran. Before Major Duffy could react, the boy was gone. Then another shot exploded just to his right, splitting trees and sending shrapnel in all directions. He couldn't see through the smoke if his runner survived the blast.

"...Jesus wants to reunite you with your father, and the Lord will not let me rest until I tell you. I humbly request your permission to write to you and your mother further. I would be happy to discuss any questions you may have regarding your father or about any matters I raised by this letter.

Very truly yours,
Nathaniel Thomas Graham, Captain
Chaplain, 19th Tennessee Volunteer Infantry
Army of the Mississippi
Confederate States of America"

Through swelling tears Eleanor looked up from the letter at her mother. Eleanor was silenced by its words. *What could this possibly mean?* Tears streamed from Catherine's eyes. *I fear this letter must be reopening scarred-over pain-filled, devastating wounds, buried deep in Mother's heart.* Eleanor suspected that Catherine's pain was just as real as the fact that her husband's remains rested in the church cemetery.

Choking back her own emotions, Eleanor said, "Mother, I'm so sorry. Maybe I shouldn't have read this to you."

"No, dear, it is wonderful to hear this news," Catherine replied through sniffles and sobs. She took a second to blow her nose and wipe her eyes. Then she continued, "It is an answer to my prayer. We must write this chaplain and inquire further, and we must thank him for what he's done for us."

Eleanor was stunned. For a second she looked at Catherine with her mouth wide open. Then Eleanor rebuked, "Mother, you can't be serious? Didn't you hear me say that he's a Rebel?"

Calmly, Catherine replied, "Yes dear, I heard you. It doesn't matter to me who he is. He knows things about your father that no one else could possibly know. I have a million questions, and this man may have a few answers. We must sit down and write him tonight, immediately after supper."

Eleanor still couldn't believe her mother's insistence. She looked at the envelope and offered another excuse, "Mother, look at the postmark date. This letter was mailed over a month ago. With all the fighting that's taken place around Richmond, it may be impossible to get a letter returned to him, if he's alive."

"I understand, dear," Catherine responded softly. "But he went to so much trouble to write to you—to us. What could be the harm in sending him a thoughtful reply and thank him for his kindness to us."

"Kindness?" Eleanor nearly lashed out at her mother. "Those Rebels killed my father. Have you forgotten that fact, Mother?"

"No, dear, I haven't forgotten. My heart breaks every day when the thought invades my peace. I wonder how many more hearts will break before this meaningless war is over. When it does end, we will have to learn to live together again as one nation. Much will have to be forgiven."

"Forgiven?" Eleanor fumed. "You must be out of your mind with grief. I will never forgive any of them. If you want to write this devil, go right ahead, but don't ask me to help you." Eleanor threw the letter onto the parlor floor, turned, and stormed out of the room. Catherine walked over to the letter, picked it up, looked at it briefly, and then clutched it to her heart. This was an answer to her prayer, and she would write a reply that evening.

Five minutes seemed like hours as shot and shell continued to fall upon his men. He ordered the wounded courier, Private Beecher, to the rear. The boy wanted to stay and fight, but his left arm was badly damaged. Nathaniel concluded that he would lose it if he survived the hospital. Then he heard the sound he waited impatiently for as it pierced the roaring confusion. The bugle orders were a welcome sound. To his left, he could make out the sound of Marvin's somewhat higher-pitched voice shouting, "Let's go boys. Charge!"

Nathaniel yelled, "Oblique left! Forward!" What remained of Company "H" rose up as one and shouted the now famous Rebel yell. They moved just as Nathaniel ordered, exactly as they'd practiced in drill those endless months in training camp. Nathaniel couldn't help but feel a strong respect-filled, deep sense of pride well up within his chest as his men responded flawlessly.

The sudden regrouping maneuver seemed to stun and confuse the Yankee fire for a minute. Quickly, the Confederates were clear of the artillery pounding. It would take the Yankees several minutes to redirect their gunfire. The Yankee infantry rifle fire even slowed for an instant. Although Major Duffy had only been in a few engagements, he understood that it was common for men to simply watch what their enemy did and attempt to figure out what would come next. The brief respite ended with a renewed flurry as musket rounds filled the air, slapping the trees, penetrating the ground, ricocheting off rocks, and hitting his men.

Closing ranks strengthened the attack. As Colonel Cumming's regiment pushed forward, they continued to move to their left. Soon they would reach the extreme right flank of the Yankee line. They pushed themselves hard, firing as they advanced. They no longer sought shelter from the rocks and trees. They moved faster than the Yankee artillery could adjust their fire. They could clearly see the top of the hill and the thin Yankee line. They could break through the breastworks and the clearing beyond and get behind the Yankee defenses.

Several hundred Confederates poured over the Yankee rifle pit. Those Bluecoats that remained were either killed, captured, or ran. A dozen Yankees formed a single firing line in the clearing above and prepared to face the Rebels. Colonel Cummings ordered the formation of his own firing line, nearly one hundred muskets. The small band of Federal troops fired while the Rebels prepared. A few men were hit. One was killed instantly. But mostly the frightened Yankees missed their intended targets. The Confederates returned one volley. Most of those boys in blue fell to the ground. The two that remained standing turned and ran for safety. The Rebels began to cheer. They had broken through, but at an extreme price.

Colonel Cummings ordered Major Duffy to direct the regiment to commence firing on the Yankee line facing Ewell's division. As Colonel Cummings surveyed the situation through his field glasses, he saw Yankee reserves approaching quickly in his direction. They came in great strength. Cannon were turned and preparing to fire on his position. Clearly, his men were outnumbered three-to-one, and without artillery support he knew that his men could not hold this spot for very long. "What could have happened to General Jackson and his division? They should be coming up the hill behind us now. We could sweep these Yankees from this entire hill. Where is Jackson?"

"Colonel, we've damaged the enemy."

"Yes, Major. They're diverting resources this way. We don't have to win the battle for the army. I think we've done all we can."

Major Duffy offered his assessment, "Sir, it doesn't look too good for us here. Colonel, I don't see any reserves from General Jackson's division coming this way."

"I know, Major. I don't think we can hold this position long without support. General Jackson's division should have been here by now." Colonel Cummings stared at the approaching threat through his glasses and yelled, "Orders!"

A sergeant stepped forward and said, "Yes, sir!"

Colonel Cummings wrote a quick note and gave it to the sergeant, commanding, "Take this to General Hill as fast as you can! Move out, Sergeant!"

His sergeant saluted, which Colonel Cummings returned sloppily. The sergeant handed his musket to another soldier and ran back down the hill his fellows fought so hard to ascend.

Colonel Cummings turned to Major Duffy and ordered, "Have the entire regiment form a tight firing line behind these breastworks here. Wait for the Yankees to come closer, another fifty yards. Order the men to fire at will."

The regiment formed quickly. The approaching Yankees formed their own line of fire. The next few minutes would be close and deadly. Muskets were leveled and aimed. Both lines fired at the same instant. Through the gun smoke, Colonel Cummings heard the sound of lead slapping the breastworks and the flesh and bone of his men. Some screamed out in pain, others fell dead where they once crouched or stood. He heard his officers shouting commands up and down the line, "Reload!" "Fire at will!" The scene repeated itself again and again.

Then, he heard that awful distant barking sound of cannon fire. Several shells hit the breastworks, exploding and tearing men apart. If they stayed much longer, what remained of his regiment would be destroyed. The Yankee gunners were very good. He couldn't wait any longer for orders from his general, or for the missing support he was promised. General Jackson failed to arrive with his division. Someone would hear about this later. For now, Colonel Cummings must decide. "Bugler," Colonel Cummings shouted. His bugler approached and saluted. Solemnly but firmly, Colonel Cummings ordered, "Sound the withdrawal!"

Chapter 20

NEW RECRUITS

The Confederate army under General Lee's command claimed a genuine victory after the battle around Gaines' Mill that long five-hour Friday afternoon of June 27, 1862. Shortly after General D. H. Hill's and General Richard Ewell's divisions withdrew, Lee ordered General John Bell Hood and his division of Texans forward into the Federal center. The Texans broke through the weakened Union defenses, captured several Yankee batteries, and took many prisoners. The Federal Army's Fifth Corps, commanded by Major General Fitz-John Porter, fought well and repulsed four separate assaults before the Texans breached the Yankee defenses. Pushed back and beaten, the Union troops retreated during the cover of night again. It was an awful, terrible, demoralizing forced march. Because they had to cross the Chickahominy River to reach safety, the troops could only move a few hundred feet and then wait for wagon traffic to clear the few available bridges. Their withdrawal took all night, while General Lee's men rested.

News of this second defeat reached the War Department in Washington, D.C. Before long, it would reach all the main northern newspapers. Lee would not let his men rest for long, nor would he offer the Yankees peace. Lee pushed his force southward in a great chase of McClellan's grand army. On Saturday, June 28, Lee hit the Federal troops at Savage Station, about five miles south of Gaines' Mill. The Union forces retreated so quickly that they left their supply depot, field hospital, and thousands of wounded troops in the hands of the advancing Rebels. The Yankees stopped long enough to destroy ammunition before moving further south toward the James River and an escape to safety.

Lee attacked again on Sunday, June 29, at White Oak Swamp, approximately six miles south of Savage Station. Lee could not force the fleeing McClellan into a full engagement. The Federal commander would only commit his Fifth Corps to provide rear guard cover. McClellan kept pushing his army southward to the James River. Porter's men fought well and repulsed the Confederates repeatedly. The Yankee infantry could not understand why they retreated after each fight. These boys in blue believed they had won repeated victories.

Another three miles closer to McClellan's chosen place of escape, Harrison's Landing on the James River, the Federal Army's battered Fifth Corps, prepared a defensive position around a place called Frayser's Farm, near Glendale, Virginia. Relentlessly, Lee hurled two divisions at Porter's defenses in an attempt to cut them off from McClellan's main body. Lee hoped to destroy McClellan's Fifth Corps and force him to turn and face Lee's Army. Again, Porter's troops fought valiantly and repulsed the Confederate advances. Saved by his now-seasoned Fifth Corps, McClellan ordered Porter to retreat under the cover of darkness to a stronger defensive position on top of a large rise called Malvern Hill.

Stars filled the sky. Most of the Confederate troops rested. Several men were too restless to sleep, even though they had fought the Yankees for nearly six days without rest. They were ready to finish the work and push the Federals out of Virginia.

Marvin found his friend Nathaniel and asked him to take a walk. He needed to talk.

"Nate, thanks for seeing me for a few minutes," Marvin started as they shuffled behind their encampment and headed toward an old farmhouse. "I know how busy you are taking care of the casualty details and all."

"What's on your mind, Marvin?" *I wonder what's bothering him. At night, we often talk freely about many things. We've talked just about everything since our college days back in Tennessee. But this is something different, distant, and dark. Marvin's been cold and formal lately. Why is he so aloof? What happened to our friendship?*

Marvin started, "You know Captain Nash, don't you?"

"Yeah, I sure do. He's not my favorite member of this regiment. So what's he got to do with anything?"

Marvin scratched his neck behind his left ear and continued, "Well, he doesn't think much of me as a man, let alone an officer in this here army."

"I am surprised that you're worried about him," Nathaniel had heard a few rumors around camp. "I wouldn't think too much on what he says or does. He is more mouth than man. He seems to be angry at everyone for all the wrong reasons. He's said a few things about me, too."

Marvin stopped and turned to Nathaniel and continued, "Nate, I really don't care for the man myself. It's a shame that he's still alive. I don't think he'd be much of a loss if he took a bullet through his black heart. But I just want to know your honest opinion about me. I respect you and I expect you to tell me the truth. These last few days have been more than any of us could have expected. We've been fighting every day for the last six days, and it doesn't seem that we've seen the end of this yet. You've seen me with my company. How am I doing, really?"

God spoke to Nathaniel's spirit and made it clear that Nathaniel held Marvin's manhood in his hands. He had to be honest. The truth would set Marvin free. Nathaniel took a deep breath and exhaled loudly as he spoke, "Marvin, you sure didn't beat about the bush. You went straight to your point. I suppose that's one thing I can say that proves you've done well."

"How so?" Marvin's hopes were stirred.

"Marvin, I've known you longer than anyone in our regiment. I've seen you at your worst. I remember when you couldn't even speak for yourself back in college. These past few days have been hard on us all. But I watched you lead your company up the hill at Gaines' Mill, I saw you shoot and kill two Yankees at Savage Station. You pushed your boys through the mud at White Oak Swamp, and now we rest on ground held by our enemy just hours ago. None of these things make you any better of a man. What proves to me that you're a real officer is the fact that you are still here and you've been faithful to our cause of freedom. It doesn't matter what anyone else says about you, and it doesn't matter what you think of yourself. You're still here. You fought alongside the men you lead. No one can ask any more of you. You are doing your job, and if you weren't doing it well, they wouldn't follow you."

Marvin was quiet. He seemed to be taking every word deep into his soul. Then he replied, "Nathaniel, thanks, I trust you. I trust your judgment." He paused and turned to look Nathaniel in the eye and said solemnly, "If I die in this war, if I fall tomorrow, could you say those words at my funeral, those that you just said, so others will know that I'm not a coward? You know me. You understand that I am afraid, but I am and I have always been faithful. I want others to know that about me."

Nathaniel looked at his long-time friend and simply replied, "Yes. I will."

Both men turned back toward their encampment. They walked slowly, lost in their own thoughts about this conversation as they listened to the night symphony of crickets, frogs, and owls. Suddenly they heard funny noises coming from a nearby barn.

Nathaniel looked at Marvin and asked, "What do you think that is?"

"Sounds like some kind of animal, maybe a dog, inside that barn. I wonder what's got it so upset."

"Let's go see what's making such a fuss."

Marvin pulled his revolver. The barn was badly damaged from that day's fighting. They walked slowly, cautiously, to the south-facing wall and large entry doors. Nathaniel pulled the board that locked the doors. Marvin covered their approach with his gun. Nathaniel pushed the right-side barn door open. A terrible odor filled the air. It was black inside. They could hear the whimpering sounds better now. Clearly, more than one animal was in distress. They sounded like puppies. Nathaniel found an oil lantern hanging on the inside wall by the door. He asked, "Marvin, do you have a match?"

Marvin responded quickly, "Yeah, here, let me have the lamp." Marvin holstered his revolver, and in a few seconds he had the lamp lit and the light trimmed. Once their eyes adjusted to the light, they both wished they never entered. The Yankees had used this barn as a field hospital. They didn't have time to dispose of the hundreds of limbs that littered the bloodstained floor. Straw absorbed most of the blood. The barn smelled of decay. Nathaniel looked at Marvin. "If I fall in battle, I hope I die. I'd hate to be subjected to this barbaric medical treatment."

"I know what you mean." Marvin just stared at the carnage.

The puppy cries pierced their ears. They looked in the direction from where the sound came and stepped carefully over the remains beneath them.

Marvin pushed a large bale of hay away from the front stall. It must have been left there to keep the puppies from roaming freely. Once again, the cruelty of this terrible war appeared before them. Two puppies were obviously dead. Three were trying to nurse from their mother. She was wounded, badly. She'd taken a bullet into her chest near her left shoulder. She panted heavily as she gave what life she had left to her young. Nathaniel responded automatically.

"Marvin, try and pull those pups away from their mother. She needs our help. Be careful, she may fight us, but I don't think she has the strength to last too much longer."

"What do you have in mind?"

"I'm going to try and carry her out of here. Doc Jones patched up our horse, Max. Maybe he can save this poor girl."

"I don't know. She doesn't look too good to me. Maybe we should put her out of her misery."

"I'll let Doc make that call."

Both men approached the animals as quietly and gently as possible. Nathaniel tried to speak soothingly to the injured mother, "Easy, girl. We're not going to hurt you. Just take it nice and easy," Nathaniel spoke to Marvin but in the same tone so as not to arouse her. It didn't work.

The Black Labrador looked up at Nathaniel and started to growl. She lifted her head and snarled, showing her teeth. She was going to fight. She probably knew instinctively this would hasten her own death. She was determined to protect her puppies. She struggled to get to her feet, causing the chest wound to gush. Her legs just shook. She couldn't even carry her own weight.

The pool collected in the straw. "She's lost too much blood. She'll be dead soon. Okay, I need to think what to do. Marvin, we're not going to try and remove her or her puppies."

"I thought you said you wanted to take her to Doc Jones," Marvin protested.

"I changed my mind," Nathaniel replied. His heart broke for the animal that had only minutes left. "We're going to let her go peacefully. I'm going to try and get her to lie back down."

All Marvin could add was, "Be careful. She still has teeth."

Nathaniel sat on the ground a few feet away from the dog. This seemed to calm her, or she simply lost her strength. Still breathing heavily, she looked at her small brood, and then with a sad appeal in her eye she looked directly at Nathaniel. They both knew this was her end. With an extremely heavy sigh, she nearly fell as she laid herself back down on the barn floor. Nathaniel inched closer to her. She gave no resistance, only whimpered in pain. Nathaniel scooted next to her head and began to pet the poor animal. She accepted his touch. She needed his touch. The puppies bounced all around her, yapping at her as if demanding her to get up and play. The one brown-colored puppy pulled on her tail, growling ferociously, trying to get his mother to move. She couldn't. The two black puppies gave up and started to wrestle with each other. Then the moment arrived when life passes, the way of all flesh. With one last long exhale, she slipped away. Nathaniel continued to stroke her head and neck. A tear fell from his eye. The little brown puppy stumbled over to his mother's face and sniffed her carefully. Marvin surveyed the entire scene and asked, "Now what do we do?"

The newspaper boys ran out of the *Rockford Daily Chronicle* like a buffalo stampede. They knew that they would sell a lot of papers this day. The shouting began immediately.

A boy quickly reached one street corner and yelled, "Extra! Extra! McClellan pushed back on the Virginia Peninsula!"

Another shouted from the opposite corner, "The Union army is in full retreat! Read all about it!"

"Lee defeats McClellan at Gaines' Mill!" cried a third. "McClellan blames Lincoln! Get your paper here!"

In seconds, men and women surrounded these and other newspaper boys. Rockford citizens hungered for the latest information about the war. Newspapers were unfolded and the printed words digested as quickly as the populace could consume them. Soon horrified gasps, or phrases like, "Oh my Lord!" and, "No, this can't be!" filled the air. The news shocked and stunned a people who had made plans for the victory that seemed to be just days away. Eleanor and Catherine joined the untold millions of Northern inhabitants that now wondered what this turn of events could mean.

"My God, Mother, it says here that the Union Army's Fifth Corps took a heavy beating from the attacking Confederates," Eleanor read aloud to Catherine. She continued, "The losses were heavy on both sides," she lowered her paper. "Mother, Paul and John are assigned to the Fifth Corps," she nearly gasped.

Catherine remained unusually calm for this news. Her sons were clearly in harm's way, possibly both casualties. She looked at her daughter and demanded, "What else does the newspaper report? Please do go on, dear."

Eleanor searched for where she'd left off and tried to see if there were any names of the fallen before she read further. She didn't see any names other than those of the respective commanding generals. Finding her place, she continued, "Okay, Mother, here the paper states that Lee's Rebels attacked on June 26th and he continued to press his advance against our boys for the past four days without stop. He keeps attacking the same Fifth Corps under the command of Major General Fitz-John Porter. After each attack, Porter retreats. His Corps is protecting McClellan's main force from the greater danger of Lee's superior numbers. McClellan's army is in full retreat to the James River and, hopefully, safety." Eleanor paused. "Mother, how are you taking this news?" *Where are the names?* She asked, "Do you want me to continue, Mother?"

Catherine shared her daughter's concern and replied, "No dear, I think I understand what is being reported. Do you mind looking for a list of casualties, dear? I'm sure both Paul and John are fine; otherwise, a uniformed service man would have already found us and let us know if something had happened to either of them. You remember how we found out about your father. We knew before the newspapers reported the information. I am concerned about some of our neighbors. I haven't seen Harriet Fitzgerald for a day or two. I usually see her in town. Or, she stops in here at our dress shop. Sometimes, I see her working in her garden on my way home. The weather has been too nice for her to stay stranded in her house unless she's sick, or worse. I haven't seen Fanny lately either, come to think of it."

Eleanor, still stunned by this recent news, briefly forgot that other families had sent their sons, brothers, husbands, and fathers to fight to preserve the Union. This day could be a very dark one for Rockford, Illinois. She continued to scan the newspaper for more information. While she looked, Eleanor offered, "With this news, should we call off our meeting with Mr. Merritt tomorrow?" *I hope you say yes. I can't think of a good reason to meet with him.*

But Catherine failed to comply. "Why no, dear," Catherine sounded insistent. "There is absolutely no reason why we should delay this meeting another second longer. I think it is important that we keep our appointment tomorrow morning."

This news further surprised Eleanor. *Where does she get her strength, and clarity of thought in the midst of all this new confusion?* Eleanor simply continued, "Well, OK Mother, if you think you are up to the meeting then we should go."

"Yes, dear, I see no cause to disappoint Mr. Merritt. Now please, dear, keep looking for a list of casualties."

Eleanor replied, "I think I just found it."

Chapter 21

ONE SUMMER EVENING

Nathaniel, Marvin, and Major Duffy thoroughly enjoyed playing with the three puppies. The three men decided that each one would take and care for a pup. Marvin chose the black male. Major Duffy wanted the black female. That left Nathaniel with the one brown male that had seemed so attached to his mother. He had tried so hard to stop Nathaniel and Marvin from burying her with his dead siblings in a shallow grave just outside the barn. Nathaniel seemed to sense that this one was special and that he would need a little more attention.

Marvin scrounged a few scraps of food from the regiment's cook, and with the introduction of a little hardtack, the puppies seemed to be okay with the absence of their mother. The two black puppies loved to wrestle with each other. They would be hard to keep apart. The brown puppy simply rested in Nathaniel's arms. *I fear we are in for a long night.*

Shortly thereafter, a young private looked into the tent and asked permission to speak with the company chaplain. He looked at the scene in Nathaniel's tent and excused himself, "Sirs, I don't mean to interrupt, but I was wondering if'n you know where I might find the company chaplain?"

Marvin pointed at Nathaniel and stated proudly, "You found him, soldier. That's Captain Graham. He's our chaplain."

Major Duffy commanded, "Lieutenant Jenkins, let's take these new recruits outside and see if we can get them properly outfitted to serve in this here army."

Marvin nearly laughed aloud but replied, "Yessir, Major, sir. That sounds like a perfect thing to do. We should put them through some close-order drill."

Major Duffy picked up his puppy and said, "I agree Lieutenant. Let's go."

Marvin picked up his. Then he turned to Nathaniel and asked, "Do you mind if we take yours along with us?"

Nathaniel responded favorably, "Lieutenant Jenkins, that is a splendid idea. Please do." And with that, Nathaniel helped Marvin gather the little brown puppy into his other arm. The two puppies stared at each other with a look on both their faces that seemed to wonder what would happen next. In the next second, Nathaniel and the young private were alone.

"What's on your mind, soldier?" Nathaniel asked in a rather matter-of-fact tone that subtly indicated that he really didn't want to be disturbed at this moment, but he would tolerate the meeting.

The private had removed his kepi and was twisting it between his hands. He was nervous or maybe even scared about something. He looked down at the ground and shook his head from side to side as if fighting some internal battle that raged within. "I'm terribly sorry, sir," he started. "Maybe I shouldn't have come. I'll just leave, sir. I'm terribly sorry to have bothered you." The private turned around to leave.

Nathaniel suddenly felt terrible. He recognized the conviction of the Holy Spirit. The feeling wasn't condemnation, which would make him feel less of a man, but it was conviction, which let him know that he simply needed to change his mind about the current situation. Nathaniel quickly responded, "No, son, please stay. Besides, I haven't dismissed you, now have I? Sit down here." Nathaniel offered his field-desk chair, a flimsy fold up canvas stool.

The confused young man nearly forgot all the military protocol drilled into his brain. He then realized that he was speaking with an officer and decorum returned. "Sir, forgive me, sir. Thank-you, sir, may I speak freely, sir?"

Nathaniel took a good look at him in the lantern light and acknowledged, "Yes, Private. As Lieutenant Jenkins said, I am the chaplain for the 19th Tennessee Volunteers and anything you say will remain just between God Almighty and us. Do you mind if we pray together first? I think it will help both of us be in the right frame of mind."

The private stated clearly, "I would like that very much, sir."

Nathaniel tilted his head and thoughtfully asked, "What's your name, Private?"

"Jennison, sir, Private Edwin Jennison," the private announced, somewhat muffled. "I'm with an outfit from Georgia. Captain Nash is my company commander. I believe you know him, sir."

"Edwin, may I call you Ed?" Nathaniel posed.

"That's fine, sir."

"Good, and Ed, yes I do know Captain Nash." *He's a mean one, but I better not think about him.* "Now, Ed, let's pray together." Both men bowed their heads in humble submission to God. Nathaniel recited a brief prayer that got directly to the point of their meeting. After they both said their respective, "Amens," Nathaniel continued, "Okay, son, what's on your mind? What do you want to talk about?"

Still twisting his kepi, Private Jennison choked out, "I just feel so uncertain about this whole thing."

"I'm sorry, Ed. I'm not sure I follow you."

"Well, sir."

"Call me Nate." *Everyone else does.*

"I'm sorry sir, I'm sorry, Nate. Well uh, I'm really not sure that we're doing the right thing. I mean I know we are supposed to be fighting for our independence, like our founding fathers did in the great war for independence against England. But I think the situation is different and I'm not sure God is on our side this time."

"What makes you think that, Ed?" Nathaniel listened as Private Jennison talked. He was just a boy. He didn't even need to shave yet. Nathaniel noticed Private Jennison's thick dark-brown, almost black hair. Jennison's thick, bushy eyebrows shadowed his dark-brown eyes. His eyes had a sunken sadness about them, as if he intuitively knew that something frightful and terrible would soon befall him. God had given him a small nose, very thin lips, and a slight cleft in his chin. Nathaniel recognized something nearly sinister in his expression, as if he represented a generation that would be lost for eternity, a hopelessness that could never be erased. As he spoke, he handed Nathaniel a photograph that he had had taken in Richmond just a few weeks before.

With the picture exchanged, Edwin finally got to the matter on his heart and mind and asked, "Sir, could you help me write a letter to my mother? I can't make the letters and words very good. I ain't had much schoolin'. We didn't have no time for that sort of thing back in Georgia."

"I understand, son. We all have to do the best we can with what God gives us." *That was shallow. I wished I'd just kept my mouth shut.*

Private Jennison continued, "I'd like to send that picture to her, too."

He has that same haunted sadness in this photograph. Nathaniel nearly choked. *How can I send this portrait to her? What if he falls in battle? This picture would probably increase her overwhelming sorrow. Maybe it might just help.*

"Okay, I'll help your write the letter, but, Ed, I want to ask you a question about yourself before we write to your mother. Is that okay?"

"Yes, sir, go right ahead."

"I'd like to know if you know Jesus as your personal Lord and Savior."

"Oh yes, Captain. I know that my Redeemer, Jesus Christ, lives."

For the first time, Nathaniel saw light and life in this young man's eyes. This change in countenance confirmed to Nathaniel what he needed to know. He continued, "That's wonderful, son. I'm glad to hear and see this for myself. When we write to your mother, it will be wise to make sure that we add this information somewhere in the letter to remind her to whom you really belong, and I know that it will be a comfort to her if this war should continue much longer."

"Thank you, sir, I think that's a good idea." Private Jennison paused and then asked, "Could we get started, sir? It's getting late."

"I agree, son. If you don't mind, I'll need my chair."

Private Jennison stood quickly and said, "Thank you, sir. Here's your chair."

For the next hour, Private Jennison talked and Nathaniel wrote. Nathaniel made suggestions once in awhile to help a sentence make better sense. But for the most part, every word poured forth from deep within Private Edwin Jennison's heart.

June 30, 1862

Dear Mother,

As you may have already heard, we have been fighting hard for the past several days. I do believe that we shall continue this for a few more—perhaps starting again tomorrow. Thus far, I have endured this fiery trial without mishap. My spirit is strong within me, and it quickens my step as we continue to march into the face of our enemy. By God's everlasting grace I have not fallen ill to the "soldier's disease" that seems to plague so many just before we engage in battle. But it is not my place to judge; just know that I am well. Lest I shall not be able to write you again, I feel compelled to send you the photograph I had taken and to write a few lines that may fall under your eye, should I be no more.

These passing days have been met with reported success, and many of my fellows are filled with cheerful glee at our apparent victories. It is as if they have not seen for themselves the severe conflict and death, which may soon befall even me. As our Lord said in the garden, "Nevertheless, not as I will, but as Thou wilt." If it is necessary that I should fall on the battlefield for my country, I am ready. But I do have some misgivings about and a recent lack of confidence in, the cause in which I am engaged. Do not worry; my courage does not halt or falter and I will do my duty. I will make you most proud.

I know how strongly our way of life now leans upon the triumph of the Confederacy. I am very much aware of how great a debt we owe to those who went before us through the blood and suffering of the Revolution. I am willing—perfectly willing—to lay down all my joys in this life to help maintain this Confederacy and to pay that debt. But, mother, I fear that my love for our new country may be misguided.

I cannot describe to you my feelings on this calm summer night. Nearly two thousand men are sleeping around me, many of them enjoying the last, perhaps, before that of death. I am suspicious that death is creeping behind me with his fatal dart while I am communing with God, and you. I know that He has called me to this place and I have obeyed. My desire to honor Him is stronger than my fear of death. I do want you to understand what I believe He's shown me.

When I left our home to join the army, I did so with much ambition. Like so many with me, I thought as the Holy Scripture teaches that, "If God be for us, who can be against us?" I want to live and die by this truth, but my eyes see something very different.

Mother, I've seen with my own eyes how well the Yankee soldiers fight for a cause I do not understand. I am convinced that no one could fight as well as they do unless God were with them. Clearly, God cannot be for both sides of this war. I do not understand why they continue to retreat. I fear that our army and our country is being drawn into a great trap of divine judgment, like God did to many of the heathen nations of Old Testament days. I must say that if the Yankees win this war, I know it is God's will.

Please forgive my many faults, and the many pains I have caused you. How thoughtless, how foolish, I have oftentimes been. How gladly would I wash out with my tears every little spot upon your happiness, and struggle with all the misfortune of this world, to shield you and my dear little brother and sister from harm, but I cannot. Should I fall, I must watch you from the spirit land and hover near you while you buffet the storms with your precious little freight and wait with sad patience till we meet to part no more. Mother, please do not mourn me dead. I may be gone from your sight but know that I will wait for you, for we shall meet again.

> *Your loving son,*
> *Edwin*

"What do you think, Pastor?"

"I think it's a fine letter. I know it will be a comfort to your mother, if—you know—if you do fall. But can I ask you a question?"

"Yes, Captain."

"Do you really believe that our fight for independence is wrong?"

"Yes, sir, I do. I know that many of those men we been killing belong to Jesus, just as we do. I don't think He's happy about that."

Nathaniel finished preparing the letter for mailing, sealed the envelope, handed it to Private Jennison, and said, "No, Edwin, I don't suppose He is."

Nathaniel and Private Jennison said good night. Both men stepped outside of Nathaniel's tent. As Private Jennison walked away into the night, Nathaniel looked up into the star-filled sky and suddenly felt haunted by several memories. The image of dead Lieutenant General Albert Sidney Johnston flashed through his mind. He heard, *"Ain't it something what one bullet can do?"* Then, he heard the voice of Brigadier General John C. Breckinridge echo, *"Nate, if you're not sure, how do you expect to help any of us? You of all people should know why you are wearing the uniform of the Confederacy."* Finally, he recalled the potentially prophetic words from that Yankee prisoner, Chaplain Captain McKinley. *"I believe it will be years before we see the end, and unspeakable multitudes will die because of it. Our young nation is being baptized in blood."*

Chapter 22

TRANSACTION

It was another muggy morning. Marvin had been up since long before sunrise; the puppies kept him up most of the night. He decided to have breakfast as early as possible, then try to secure a few extra scraps for their new tent mates. Nathaniel got a few hours' sleep. He forced himself to write those awful letters for Colonel Cummings to sign, if time permitted.

"Are you going to be okay, keeping a watch over these two?" Marvin asked. The puppies were already playing with each other.

"Sure, Marvin," Nathaniel confirmed. "How much trouble can they get into, anyway?" Nathaniel almost bit his tongue. *I can't believe I just asked such a stupid question.*

Marvin laughed and replied, "Oh, I'm sure that they'll think of something. You better watch your boots. I think your boy has his eye on them."

Nathaniel dropped his quill, picked his shoes off the ground, and put them on his bunk. Triumphantly he said, "There, that should keep him out of trouble." He looked at Marvin, smiled, and asked, "Can you bring me a plate when you come back from the mess tent?"

Marvin proudly stated, "I already decided to take care of that little detail. I was going to bring breakfast for all of us."

"Thanks, Marvin, I'm sure we'll be right here."

Marvin slipped out of the tent and headed for the chow line. He felt pretty good this morning. He had performed well the past few days. Nate was right; Marvin's company had shown him genuine respect. He began to respect himself. He didn't have to walk far to the mess tent. The cooks were up before dawn, too, preparing captured Yankee food supplies for the men. There was plenty to eat for everyone.

Marvin walked quickly back to his tent carrying two plates stacked with cooked meat, scrambled eggs, fried potatoes, and piping-hot flapjacks. Captain James Nash and two of his friends happened to be on their way to the mess tent. Nash started his ridicule campaign even before they passed each other. "If it isn't the worst officer in the Confederate army," Nash announced loudly. "And look at him gentlemen; he's carrying two plates of food when he doesn't deserve even one." The two officers with Nash laughed and gave Marvin a condemning look.

Marvin chose to defend himself and stated, "If you please, Captain Nash, this other plate is for Captain Graham. He's busy with an important detail and I promised to fetch him some grub this morning."

Nash puffed up his chest and said, "Well, now. Our little Lieutenant has finally learned some proper protocol. Oh, by the way Jenkins, I heard that you and your holy friend found some puppy dogs last night. That pile of food meant for fighting men wouldn't be going to feed your brood of mongrels now, would it?"

"Captain Nash," Marvin started. "As I just said, sir, this plate is for Captain Graham. Now as for my breakfast, if I choose to let the puppies have a little, don't I have that right? Aren't we fighting for the right to do with our own what we think is best?"

Nash narrowed his eyes and said, "I suppose you do." Then Nash continued with a hostile tone, "But that don't make it right, taking food meant for us and giving it to some mutts. And I'm telling you, boy," Nash stuck his finger a few inches in front of Marvin's nose, shook it, and continued, "You better hope I don't catch them damned dogs running around loose and stealing food from my boys. If I do, I'll shoot them on the spot."

Marvin was shocked by Nash's last statement. He knew he'd better leave before he started a fight he couldn't win. Nash might be an evil man, but he outranked Marvin. Pretending to respect Nash, Marvin swallowed hard and said, "I understand, Captain. May I have your permission to leave, sir?"

Nash replied, "Yes, Lieutenant, you may go about your business. Just keep them mutts out of my sight."

Marvin attempted a salute as best he could while holding both plates of food. Quickly he turned and walked back to his tent. He decided right then that if they were close in the next battle, if the confusion was anything like he'd seen these passed few days, he'd put a bullet into Nash. "Maybe two or three," he muttered.

It was another beautiful summer midmorning in Rockford, Illinois. The sun drove away the morning mist, and by ten o'clock, most of the local citizens were busy with their day's activities. The townspeople prepared for that Friday's Independence Day celebrations. Red, white, and blue banners and buntings decorated the buildings. The busy folks did their very best to keep the streets as clear of litter as possible. Even with the news of the military setback in Virginia, the good citizens of Rockford believed that McClellan would turn things around. Somehow he would find a way to defeat the Rebels. Besides, the news from the Western campaigns remained positive. Everyone anticipated news of total

Union victory on, or before, Friday. In one two-story office building near the Rockford town square, three people concluded a fruitful business meeting.

Jason Merritt stated, "Ladies, I am so glad that we discussed this matter today. I will draw up some papers that represent our discussions and agreement for your review. If these meet with your satisfaction, we can meet again and sign the contract. I'm sure that the revenue stream this arrangement creates will provide generous financial security for many years to come, if not for the rest of your lives."

Eleanor countered, "Yes, and clearly you benefit by assuming my father's cases, his library assets, and his reputation that goes along with this office."

Jason pulled back saying, "And that is why I consider your sacrifice in this endeavor a true business investment, for which you shall be compensated."

Catherine interrupted, "Children, please. I am satisfied that what we've accomplished this morning is truly wonderful for us all." Catherine stood from her chair and smoothed her dress. Then she continued, "I'm sure, Mr. Merritt, that everything will be in proper order when you present the final agreement. I have confidence in you, sir. Now I'd like to present another small matter for the two of you to discuss."

This caught both Eleanor and Jason by surprise. Catherine turned to leave and as she made her way to exit the office, she announced, "Eleanor, dear, please show Mr. Merritt the letter you received. I would like his opinion on whether or not a response is in order."

Jason quickly replied, "I'll be happy to take a look at it for you, Mrs. Ellis, and I will give you my professional opinion."

Eleanor was stunned. She stood rigidly and simply did nothing.

As Catherine departed through the door's threshold, she commanded, "Now, dear, don't just stand there; show him the letter. I know you have it with you."

Catherine pulled the office entrance door closed behind her. Her steps echoed on the hardwood hallway, but the clopping sounds quickly faded as she disappeared down the stairs to Rockford's main street below.

Inside her father's—soon to be Jason's—office, Eleanor fumed. *Will mother never stop her meddling? Do I have to leave my home, my town, this place I love, to live and enjoy life?*

Jason Merritt examined the obviously furious woman that stood only a few feet away from him. Looking at Eleanor, he decided quickly that he should keep quiet. She began to mumble angrily so he concluded that it would be in his personal best interest to speak only if asked a direct question. Slowly he turned his gaze toward the dark walnut wood-paneled office that would soon be his home away from home. He absorbed various unnoticed details offered in this large law office. The pride that filled his heart began to permeate his entire being. He pivoted away from Eleanor and walked over to the large wooden desk that would serve his future legal practice and hoped-for political career. He knew he could bring his Democratic Party back to its proper place of rule over the masses and iron-will control over their meaningless lives. He considered the transaction negotiated this day a small victory for his chosen political affiliation. After all, he now assumed the legal practice from a true leader of the valueless, upstart, and destructive Black-Republican Party. He grasped the back of the wooden chair lined with thick dark-brown leather and stroked the chair as if it were a precious sculpture or a favorite pet. He surveyed the room further and smiled.

The décor expressed a man's world. Clearly, the former Mr. Ellis, Esquire, kept the local taxidermist busy. Hunted animal trophies consisting of a few deer, an antelope, a fox, and even a black bear surrounded him. In time, he could take full credit for bagging these beauties. A large portrait of Mr. Ellis filled the wall opposite the large paneled windows covered with thick dark-blue curtains. The portrait would have to go.

Suddenly he heard, "Have you heard a word I've said?"

Eleanor looked at him with her head cocked to one side slightly, her hands placed on both hips, and she projected the most condemning expression he'd ever seen etched on a human face. Jason didn't know what to say. How did he fail to listen to his new business partner? He tried a feeble response. With false dignity he replied, "Yes, Eleanor." He choked and tried to clear his throat, "I understand that you would rather not discuss the letter in question at this time."

Eleanor adjusted her stance. She slightly extended her hip to her left. Her mouth dropped open and her expression changed from contempt to disbelief. She turned away from Jason's face, threw her arms into the air, and barked, "I can't believe this!"

"What?" Jason asked the fatal word.

"You have no idea what I just said to you!"

"Why Eleanor, what ever gives you that impression?" Jason dug himself unwittingly deeper into a pit of lies.

Eleanor turned back to Jason and gave him a deep piercing stare before she protested, "Well, I guess you got what you wanted. I see no useful purpose to continue our discussion any further. Draw up your agreement. I'm certain my mother will sign it. It doesn't matter what I think about all this," waiving her arms as if to emphasize the grandness of her father's former place of business. As she grabbed her personal things from one of the large guest chairs, she concluded furiously, "Good-day to you, sir!"

Eleanor quickly turned and stormed out of the office, slamming the entrance door behind her. Jason stood behind the desk, mouth opened wide, wondering what had just happened.

Eleanor had nearly reached Mulberry Street. *Darn it, I really wanted Jason's opinion about that letter.* She slowed her descent and stopped just a few steps before the staircase reached the main floor below. *What should I do? I can't go back now.* Her head tilted as if to hear a soft distant voice. She even spoke as if answering someone's question, "Well, I didn't expect mother to bring up the matter. And the manner in which she introduced the subject caught me completely by surprise. No, I really didn't mean to be so short with him. But, he was so rude. He didn't listen to me. It's not my fault. He needed to be corrected for his selfish behavior."

I need to go to work. She took a few more steps. "Though, he did offer to help. Maybe he simply misunderstood me. After all, he hardly knows me." She stopped, turned and looked up the stairs. Jason was not there, as she hoped. Then she jumped to a conclusion saying, "But he should know how I feel, and he should understand me. He would have if he had listened to me." The suppressed anger returned full force. *Forget him.* Without hesitation, she started toward the street.

"Eleanor," she heard Jason's voice behind her. "Wait," he pleaded. "Please, let me read the letter. It will only take a few minutes. Then you can be on your way. I'm sorry, Eleanor, I mean Miss Ellis. I meant no disrespect." Jason knew he couldn't afford to offend this woman, a perceived key to his future success. He could fake sincerity better than anyone and he was certain no one could appear more honest.

Eleanor smiled. *Well now, I think I just leashed this reckless beast. It feels good. Careful now, keep your distance. Don't let a girlish crush take over.* She slowed her steps, stopped, and gradually turned around to see the face she now desired to see again.

Eleanor kept her eyes on the stairs directly in front of her and slowly let her gaze rise with each step until the man was in view and their eyes locked for a moment's stare, each looking for something more.

Jason started down the hallway staircase saying, "Miss Ellis, please won't you return to the office?"

Eleanor said nothing. She watched Jason approach and waited. He would have to do one thing more before she would consent.

Unknowingly, Jason extended his hand in an expression of gracious surrender. *Good. You finally did the right thing.*

"Please, Miss Ellis," Jason implored.

Eleanor responded with a minor protest, "I can depend on you to give me your full attention, Mr. Merritt?"

Jason smiled warmly and replied, "My undivided attention, Miss Ellis. You have my word as a gentleman."

Eleanor took his hand formally allowing just her fingers to touch his palms lightly. The instant touch thrilled her inside, only she never let even an extra breath escape as her heart began to race. Quickly she lowered her head as if to check the difficulty of the staircase ascent and replied beneath her bonnet, "Very well, sir."

Jason knew he had this woman. He would not let go of her hand. He knew that with a little patience he would lead her to his bed, but that would have to wait for now. He must conclude the office transaction and let some time pass first. Thinking ahead, he looked forward to the day when he would take her for his own pleasures.

"Fire!" Major Alexander yelled as loud as he could so that the commanders of the twelve batteries of four cannon each could hear his command. In rapid succession each Napoleon brass cannon belched forth its fiery death to rain down hot sixteen-pound cast-iron explosive shells on a twenty-thousand man one hundred-gun enemy that sat ready to defend a high mile-wide hill.

Paul's and John's regiment was posted in the center. The first volley sailed well over their heads. Explosive shells blew earth in all directions. Most fell doing little damage other than opening huge holes in the ground. For now, the Federal force was intact. John observed the cannonade overshot and said to his older brother, "They sure wasted those rounds."

Paul quickly pulled him down and corrected, "You better keep your head down, little brother. The next round will likely take it off. They won't miss us for long." More cannon pops could be heard from nearly a mile away. Paul continued, "Stay close to the bottom of this trench, John. I think they've got the range on our position this time."

Sure enough, Paul was deadly correct. Just six days before he was a green recruit. Now he was a seasoned veteran. Alternately, shells crashed into the trees and ground near them. Some fell into the log breastworks that protected their rifle pits. The killing began. Other shells fell deeper to the rear than the first volley. Some hit near Union artillery batteries, loaded and ready. The Yankee gunners stood and waited for orders to return the Rebel fire. With this close blast, the orders came.

A few yards to the right of the brothers, a shell detonated, blowing a hole in the breastworks. The explosion threw logs, debris, and bodies of men in all directions. John, forever driven by his curiosity, looked up and then over toward the wreckage as dirt fell around him and said, "Poor souls."

Paul added a simple, "Yeah." The shelling continued with deadlier accuracy. Paul continued, "It looks like many will pass over this day."

John replied, "I pray for Ellie's and Mother's sake that neither of us join that harvest."

"Amen, little brother, amen," Paul replied soberly. He reached over to John, grabbed his brother's hand, and grasped it tightly for just a quick but meaningful moment. Each army shelled the other for more than an hour.

Chapter 23

SCHEME

Jason finished reading the letter. He placed it gently on the desk in front of him and slid it a few inches toward Eleanor as if to say, you can take it now if you want. Eleanor left it alone. She hadn't quite finished studying Jason's facial expressions that accompanied his silent reading of the strange correspondence. Jason looked up, their eyes met again, Eleanor's emotions ignited, and Jason simply, calmly said, "Well, that's very interesting. I'm not sure what to make of it exactly."

Eleanor remained composed outwardly and said, "What do you think about all the things he said about my father and God and praying with him? And why didn't he write to my mother? Why did he write to me?"

Jason hadn't thought about that. This bit of information helped him form an opinion based on his own ways and means. He replied, "Eleanor, I can't speak to his assertions and speculative conclusions about your father and eternity. I suggest you speak with your family minister, Reverend Kelley, I believe. Isn't his son a junior officer in your father's unit?"

"Yes, you are correct," Eleanor assured.

SCHEME · 225

Jason nodded his head in acknowledgement and continued, "OK." Then, Jason stood up and began to pace in front of the office window. "However," he spoke slowly and paused to allow time to prepare his line of reasoning. He looked at the street below as if he searched for an answer and then continued, "As far as I can tell, he may want to communicate with you for his own personal gain."

Eleanor's curiosity sparked. Without thinking she replied, "What do you mean?"

Jason smiled and stared at the street. "As I see it—," Jason paused again for effect. He was now comfortable with the story he concocted. He could and he would project his own cunning plans upon this Rebel. Thus he might divert any potential mistrust away from him and all further attention on to this intruder. Jason turned away from the window and looked directly at Eleanor and continued, "He wants something in return. You'll have to trust me, Eleanor. I know men because I am one. I know how we think. I've been trained in the legal profession to know that all men are potentially bad and the really bad ones love to disguise themselves as being very good."

This line of thinking was foreign to Eleanor. Confused, she asked, "What are you trying to say?" She believed Jason meant something more. If she only knew what he was postulating. But her emotions controlled her now. She could never believe that the man who stood before her would lie to her.

Jason closed the trap door and let her get used to her new surroundings. He enjoyed bathing in her gaze. He could almost see the feelings of admiration that filled her eyes and emanated from her voice. Jason continued keeping his eyes on Eleanor as he paced and used animated motions to emphasize his points. He sowed his seeds of rational lies saying, "It's really quite simple Eleanor. This Rebel knew that your father was a ranking officer in the Union army."

"So?" Eleanor quizzed.

"First," Jason answered. "Your father's military rank indicates that he most probably received it based on economic status, a political connection, or both. I understand that the process for appointing military officers is the same in both the North and the South. To receive a commission as high as the one your father held, a man must be well-connected politically and securely established financially."

"I don't understand," Eleanor confessed.

"Well, your father's position in the army is something we know he knew. But Eleanor, we know nothing about this man. We don't even know if he is who he claims to be, do we?"

Eleanor lowered her head and answered, "No, I guess we don't. But—," Eleanor hesitated. She raised her head and again looked into Jason's eyes and asked, "Why would he send this letter? He seems so sincere."

Jason quickly tilted his head to his left, raised his eyebrows in the same movement, and declared, "Frankly, Eleanor, that's the part that concerns me and convinces me that this man wants something more than he lets on here."

Captivated, Eleanor inquired, "How so?"

Jason continued to spin his web of intrigue, "Just suppose with me for a minute."

"Go on," Eleanor encouraged.

"Let us assume that this man is a scoundrel, a practiced thief. After the fighting at Shiloh, he rummages through the pockets of dead soldiers looking for anything of value."

Eleanor protested, "I can't believe that there are men like that."

"Believe me, Eleanor," Jason insisted. "They are more numerous than we know. History has recorded repeatedly that rogues canvassed battlefields after combatants left. They robbed anything and everything they could find. I studied a case in law school where this mortician absconded with private property he discovered on

SCHEME · 227

the person of the remains. This was a man in business to protect the interests of the bereaved. A suffering widow remembered her passed husband had an expensive gold watch in his pocket after the mortician took him away for burial preparation. She prosecuted him. If she hadn't, the grave robber would have become unjustly enriched with a gold watch above his normal fee." Jason paused. Then, he continued jokingly, "Maybe that's how they garnered the name 'Undertaker' in the first place."

Eleanor giggled at this thought and almost cooed, "You're a ghoul." She smiled, thrilled at the mystery he portrayed as he unfolded its details.

"I'm just telling you the truth about a well-documented case. I'm sure I can find it in this beautiful and bountiful law library surrounding us."

Eleanor assured, "There's no need. Please do continue, sir."

Jason picked up the letter and continued, "Well, getting back to our Rebel outlaw here, let's say he searched your father's pockets and found something that tells him that the dead officer has a family."

"I wrote my father a letter. He was supposed to come home soon. I never expected him to come home the way he did." Eleanor felt that old pain of loss, but she continued to show interest in Jason's story telling.

"Exactly!" Jason snapped his right finger. He continued, "This thief, this evil robber of the dead, finds your tender letter written to your dear father. I can see him reading it. As he does, he examines your father and learns as much about him as he can and devises a plan to take advantage of the man's family."

A little skeptical now, Eleanor asks, "How can you think that from this letter, and how can you be so sure?"

"Eleanor, honestly, I'm not sure," Jason realized that these were the first words of truth to come out of his mouth since he started his host of lies. He knew he must mix truth into his story to render a ruse of credibility. Satisfied with his progress he continued, "But I want you to notice two things." Jason picked up the letter and gave it to Eleanor.

Taking the paper and keeping her eyes fixed on Jason, she responded, "OK."

Jason enjoyed this opportunity to practice his immature courtroom presentation skills. He now addressed Eleanor as if she were on a witness stand as he probed for facts. He nodded to her and with his eyes directed her to look at the letter. Then he began, "First, what's the date of the letter?"

Eleanor didn't need to look at the paper. She knew it and quickly relied, "May 25, 1862."

Jason encouraged, "Very good. Now, when did the battle of Shiloh happen?"

Eleanor recalled everything she'd learned and summarized, "It took several days before both sides finally stopped to regroup, but the fighting began on April sixth and for the most part it was over on April seventh."

Jason was trilled with how quickly she grasped information and interpreted the facts. His respect for her intelligence continued to grow as he stated, "That's precisely how I understand the course of the events myself. Now, do you see the gap in time?"

What, does he think that I can't see the obvious here? I guess I'll play along. "Yes I do, and I've thought about this issue myself. My mother and I talked about it and we decided that anyone would be uncomfortable writing a letter like this and that it would naturally take some time to compose."

Jason could see this point of view, but he challenged her thinking saying, "Although I greatly appreciate your willingness to give this criminal the benefit of the doubt, I'd like to suggest another point of view for your consideration. Let us suppose that if the date is accurate—I have my own personal doubts about that—but let's assume for argument's sake that it is accurate. The date alone

SCHEME · 229

suggests plenty of time to create a believable story. I know I would have had the time to research enough information about how a man died in battle and discuss with a clergyman how to disclose this matter with a family member."

"I'm not sure I believe you yet," Eleanor stated. But it was too late for skepticism to protect her vulnerable mind. *I feel I can trust him. It is exciting to think he's uncovered something very dark and sinister.*

Jason continued his line of reasoning saying, "Well, my second point might help persuade you. Notice how he brings the letter to a close— '*I humbly request your permission to write to you and your mother further. I would be happy to discuss any questions you may have regarding your father or about any matters I raised by this letter.*' Notice that he implies that he has more information about your father and that he'll only disclose it if he's allowed to continue to correspond with you and your mother."

Eleanor challenged, "Isn't he just being polite? After all, he did ask permission to communicate further."

Jason gazed up toward one of the hunting trophies. He looked at the fox and continued, "Maybe, but I think he's trying to set up a future exchange of some kind."

Eleanor picked up Jason's point and asked, "You mean extortion, don't you."

Jason smiled. He recognized that she was both sharp and naive. He would flatter her brilliance and manipulate her inexperience as he continued, "He wouldn't be the first evil man to take advantage of a widow and her children. Fortunately, for you and your mother, you had the good sense to ask my assistance. Because you acted responsibly, his plan, if it is his plan, will not succeed."

"But why would he write to me and not directly to my mother?"

Jason wanted to be careful not to demean her now. He softly replied, "It's simple, really. Your name is on your letter to your father. You became his open door of opportunity." Jason completed his thought, *as you are mine now.*

Eleanor mused and said, "Well, Mr. Merritt, that is a pretty incredible story." Eleanor folded the letter and started to put it away into her handbag. As she did, she continued, "I'm still not sure that I believe this tall tale of yours. It's a very interesting speculation, but don't you think it is a bit too much?"

Jason was prepared for this question before he started his staged production. He offered his counter, suggesting, "Well, there is one sure way to find out if I'm right or if I've misjudged this man."

"And how is that, sir?"

"Write him back," Jason closed the cage on his prey. "Let him know that you want to know more. Compare it to what you know from other information you've received about what happened to your father and to what we've just discussed. It won't take too long to expose this beast for what he really is."

Eleanor took it all in. She was securely hooked, and Jason would let her swim freely for a while until he decided the time was right to reel her into his boat. But for now, the answer was simple, just as Jason suggested. *I could write this Nathaniel, or whoever he is. I can find out if he really is a chaplain.* She closed her purse. *Jason's probably right. He's a common thief.* Eleanor stood from the guest chair, walked over to Jason, and shook his hand in gratitude. She turned and walked gracefully away from him. She exited the office entrance door she violently slammed earlier, turned, smiled ever so sweetly at Jason and said, "We must speak further about all of this. Thank you," she paused briefly, then she spoke clearly, "Jason."

The door closed gently behind her. Once again he heard her steps on the wooden floor fade from his hearing. This time her steps were much softer. When he could no longer hear them, he smiled broadly, looked back at the fox, and said, "I got her."

SCHEME · 231

Wednesday morning, July 2, 1862, began quiet, soft, peaceful. This muggy summer morning was so still only a few sounds of nature broke the silence. The dead lay all about this swampy, thickly-wooded wilderness. Some had smiles on their faces as if to accept their final moment on Earth knowing they departed to a much better place. Other faces were horribly contorted as if the death agony had been cut deeply into their final understanding of eternal life as natural existence escaped from their damaged bodies.

Nathaniel helped his slightly wounded friend to the regiment's field hospital. As they hobbled and stumbled across the sea of dead, they came upon one Confederate soldier that had his back against a tree with his arms folded calmly across his chest. If not for his swollen appearance, they could have easily thought him to be asleep. He had placed his musket next to him, propped up against the tree. It seems that he simply sat down, resigned himself to his end, and died.

Marvin spoke up, "I'm sure glad you found me, Nate. I don't remember much from yesterday. How did we do?"

Nathaniel knew there would be time later to answer his friend's questions. However, Nathaniel did reply, "Let's get your arm looked at, then we'll talk."

Marvin was too week to argue. He'd sustained a small shrapnel wound in his right forearm. A piece of jagged Yankee grapeshot found the fleshy muscle part beneath the bone. It hurt worse than it actually looked, but Marvin had lost a lot of blood. Jokingly, Marvin said that he now had a true battle honor. However, both men refused to voice the main worry, that Marvin might lose his arm.

Behind them about one-half mile, an open field was covered in an unusually thick summer morning fog. It was as if God did not want anyone to see what He saw. But a good father knows a time comes when he must teach his son certain cruel lessons of life so that the boy can fully develop into a man. The foggy shroud slowly lifted on a truly horrible, ghostly scene.

Nathaniel's regiment was part of Brigadier General Daniel Harvey Hill's division. Lee ordered Hill to lead a full frontal assault up the long open approach, a killing field that led to the top of a fortified Yankee defensive center on a natural plateau called Malvern Hill. Hill's division was shattered. The entire unit was nearly destroyed under the deadly-accurate Yankee artillery fire. Over five thousand, five hundred Confederate dead and wounded covered the ground. The wounded slowly crawled toward the woods that protected their comrades in the hope that they would find safety and help. Many didn't make it. Marvin was fortunate that Nathaniel found him in this sea of dead and dying.

Every now and then, the quiet would be interrupted by a single Yankee musket shot, ending a Rebel's struggle for survival. Yankee sharpshooters showed these men no mercy. If they spied movement, they'd use the slowerman for long-range target practice. Hill, an aristocratic nobleman of strong moral character observed this nightmare through his field glasses and commented to one of his staff officers, "This is not war, this is murder." And so it was.

Of the seven days, this last fight saw the most severe combat. Clearly, the Rebels were soundly beaten. But once again, Major General George B. McClellan snatched defeat from the jaws of victory. His army was victorious, but he was defeated. He was a man that could organize a strong fighting force, but he didn't know how to use it. If anything, he needed someone to lead him, or point him in a direction. Lincoln tried, but McClellan's pride and his gross disdain for Lincoln would not permit him to listen to his commander in chief. His scorn for the man overcame his respect for the office.

SCHEME · 233

As he withdrew his Grand Army of the Potomac, he flooded the ever-present news reporters with false information that the enemies that controlled the White House lost his campaign. Like all unrepentant men, he refused to recognize that he might be responsible for the bitter failure, or blame himself. As such, Lincoln moved to replace McClellan. He needed to find a man who could and would fight.

Confederate General Robert E. Lee chose to re-fit his torn-apart army. He had lost one third of his total strength in the past seven days of fighting. Nearly twenty thousand soldiers under his command were declared dead, wounded, captured, missing, or otherwise unable to return to service. But he had succeeded in the minds of the Confederate people, too proud to look at the facts.

McClellan's huge force lost approximately one-tenth of its strength. A strong fighting force remained more than double the Confederate strength. It didn't matter. As Nathaniel learned these facts, he wondered if God had spared his country.

Southern pride poured out into the streets of every city, town, hamlet, and village as news of Lee's crushing victory spread. They were convinced that God had performed a miracle likened unto David defeating Goliath.

That night during a few quiet moments, Nathaniel read Revelation, chapter 16, verses eight and nine. He set his Bible aside and wondered what God spoke to him this night. *"And the fourth angel poured out his vial upon the sun; and power was given unto him to scorch men with fire. And men were scorched with great heat; and blasphemed the name of God, which hath power over these plagues: and they repented not to give him glory."* Nathaniel decided to return to the duty at hand.

The casualty list began to grow. Some names were moved from missing to dead or wounded. Some wounded moved to dead, but the number of men no longer available for service was dramatically larger than the aftermath of Shiloh. Major Duffy had to take care of higher-level staff details. Colonel Cummings had been wounded severely. He was not expected to live, let alone return to duty. Nathaniel assumed some of Major Duffy's regimental duties, which were dispersed among the other surviving junior officers. But no one else would write the letters. That fell upon Nathaniel's shoulders. Unfortunately, there was one he couldn't bring himself to write, not this night anyway. It may be many nights before he could write to the mother of Private Edwin Jennison.

Chapter 24

THE VIEW FROM CITY POINT

Seagulls filled the rain-soaked sky while formations of pelicans skimmed the surface as they patrolled the Chesapeake Bay shoreline. The scavenging fowl followed the wake of a long line of steaming transport vessels, hoping to snag the latest piece of stale bread thrown into the sea. The ships towed barge after barge upstream away from Rebel guns and to safety carrying thousands of soldiers, horses, equipment, and supplies. The defeated, not-so-grand, Army of the Potomac limped back to Washington.

The forlorn military armada inched along this inter-coastal waterway for several days and finally the nation's capital city appeared in the distant horizon. Before long these sea-weary soldiers would be able to walk on dry ground again. The battered Fifth Corps, which protected the army's withdrawal and kept it from complete destruction, now had the honor of being the first to reach Washington, D.C., and to be humiliated by a disapproving public. For most, their complete loss of military pride didn't matter anymore. Some of the men were sick of the war, many troops no longer believed in the cause to save the Union, and nearly all of them just simply wanted to go home. They witnessed firsthand the foolishness of trying to save something that was hell-bent committed to not only reject and prevent its salvation, but also willingly chose to destroy it.

Two such men hung their heads low over the starboard gunwale of their barge. One just threw up his breakfast, his wounded and aching right arm protected in a sling. The older spoke quietly to the younger, "Are you all right, little brother? How's your shoulder holding together?"

Spitting, John replied, "Oh, I reckon I'll be fine once I can get off this here scow. When I get home to Rockford, I'm going to stay on firm, dry ground. I hope I never see the ocean again. If I never step foot on another boat for the rest of my born days, that will be just fine with me."

Paul still wanted to know more, so he repeated, "And how's the arm?"

John looked at his right side, shrugged his left shoulder and said, "I guess it'll be okay too. I won't be loading supplies or digging any sinks for a while. That's good. I suppose Ma was right about one thing."

"What's that?" Paul asked.

John coughed a little and then answered, "I was real upset after we buried Pa. I remember Ma saying to me that the family would be fine. We needed to carry on in his honor. She said, 'You can always find some good in every bad thing.' I guess getting out of some of the work is a good thing."

Paul tried to encourage his brother and said, "Well, I think you're gonna get one of your wishes granted here very soon."

John spit some more matter from his mouth and tried to clear his throat as he asked, "What do you mean?"

"I can see the unfinished dome of the Capital building way over there," Paul pointed.

John just turned his head a little to his left and said, "Oh, now, isn't that just wonderful." John spit again. "Yep, I can see it for myself, the great seat of our stupid government." John spit once more into the boat-disturbed waters and said disgustingly, "Cowards all, especially Lincoln."

Paul quickly replied, keeping his voice low, "I agree with you. I heard they cut off our supplies and reinforcements to protect themselves back here in Washington."

John asked, "Where did you hear that?"

Paul turned to look around to see if anyone appeared to be listening to their conversation. He didn't need to worry. No one cared. Satisfied they were speaking privately, he answered softly, "While you were lounging at the field hospital, I spoke with a sergeant from 'A' Company. He said he'd talked to a newspaper reporter who heard this from his newspaper office back in Philadelphia."

John said quietly, "I wish we could get out of this army. I want to go home. We should leave the Johnnies to themselves. I'm beginning to think they're right about our government being tyrannical. They sent us down there to fight and then they cut off our support. Maybe we should march on Washington and throw the bastards out. You remember what Eleanor said after Pa's funeral—at least with two separate countries, we'd have peace."

Paul summed up their conversation and tried to calm his brother saying, "I'm beginning to wonder just whose side our Government is on in this here war. If they're not on ours, and they say they ain't on the Johnnies', then they must be concerned only about their own doings."

Both men leaned quietly against the barge's railing and watched the bay waters pass below them. John threw up again.

"Oh Mother, would you please stop making such a fuss," Eleanor demanded.

"Now, dear, I just want you to look your best tonight. It's important for a young lady to look and feel beautiful," Catherine encouraged.

"Mother, I don't intend to make myself into something I'm not. Besides, he just asked me to join him for dinner."

"That's exactly my point, dear," Catherine continued. "You are going to be seen with a gentleman of good reputation in a very public place. You must be properly dressed for this occasion."

"It's not an occasion, Mother," Eleanor protested. "It's just dinner."

"Trust me, dear, it's never 'just dinner,' as you insist," Catherine instructed. "Further, you have a reputation as a lady to uphold and it won't hurt our little dress shop's business if your evening gown becomes the talk of Rockford, now will it?"

"I see, then, I am your advertisement this evening," Eleanor interpreted, somewhat hurt at the thought that her own mother would exploit her this way.

"No, dear, not at all. Eleanor, I just feel you should look out for your future. He's a good man and he will be a good provider. He seems very interested in you. If you look as beautiful as I know you are, his interest may grow into something more…" she paused for effect, "…lasting."

"You make it sound as if I look attractive enough he might ask me to marry him. Is that it?" Eleanor's anger lashed out as she continued, "I'm sorry, Mother, but if I were interested in this man, or any man for that matter, I'd want him to want me for who I am as a person, not a beautiful ornament. This just seems like manipulation to me."

Catherine cocked her head to her left as she continued to fashion the dress to enhance Eleanor's charms, then she responded, "One never really knows about these things. But it won't hurt him if your beauty causes him to desire you for his future too. And if you'll excuse me for saying so, dear, I can tell that you're interested in him, even if you won't admit to it."

Eleanor almost pulled herself out of the dress with that last comment from her mother. She shouted furiously at Catherine saying, "You are impossible!" She stepped back from her mother's reach. Exasperated, she floundered as she spoke, chopping her sentences, "What? What makes you think? He's just a man. I never declared any affection. Why, I have a notion to send word to him and call this whole evening off."

Catherine realized that she struck a sensitive nerve. Desiring to reconcile, she apologized saying, "I'm very sorry, dear." She looked into her daughter's sad and angry eyes and said, "I didn't mean to upset you. I just want you to be happy again. And I've seen how happy you become when you spend a little time with him. I just want this evening to be a pleasant one for the both of you."

Eleanor could see the love and sincerity flowing from her mother's gaze. Compassion for her mother filled her heart and she reached for her to embrace. The two women gave each other a warm hug and Eleanor quietly said, "It is a beautiful dress, Mother. I will wear it proudly for you tonight. If Jason likes it, I will consider that an added bonus."

With that, they both laughed for a brief moment. Then, they returned to the task at hand. Catherine worked to straighten the hem on Eleanor's left side. Eleanor smoothed the dress with her hands and looked at herself in the full-length mirror. *Mother has done it again. It is a beautiful dress. I suppose it makes me look my best. I wonder how this evening will go.* She smiled.

General Robert E. Lee had a significant problem that he had to address if the army under his command would truly be as successful as the Southern city newspapers publicized. What the enraptured reporters failed to say was that the Confederate Army performed poorly as a unit. They could only see the fact that the Yankees had fled back to Washington, D.C. They really didn't know that a duped Federal military commander ordered the retreat because he really didn't have the stomach to fight. Lee knew the truth. He saw the true metal of those people in blue uniforms. If properly directed, they could and would fight. He also recognized that his little army must be better prepared and organized to have a chance in the next soon-coming battle.

The first, and easiest, problem he addressed was his own general staff. Captain Walter H. Taylor was intelligent and energetic. Taylor's desire to please his commander flowed from his God-fearing desire to serve his general as if he were the Lord, and this manifested in the conduct of his daily duties. Unfortunately, to be received by the aristocratic division leaders he needed to carry the grade of a field officer to represent the voice of General Lee. Lee prepared the justification and the promotion to the rank of Major. Lee's recommendation was approved and Taylor was commissioned instantly.

The bigger problem manifested during the touted success of the now-known "Seven-Days Battle." The organization of the army, if it could be called that, consisted of individual divisions led by equally individualistic and even eccentric division commanders. Lee found himself directing the greatest number of high-strung troop-commanding West Point-graduate general officers per square yard of any army ever assembled. Each man believed he could do a better job of leading the whole army than his "respected" peers or aged commander. Lee had to bridle their egos without damaging any. God gave Lee the capacity to mold the army and its leaders into a lethally efficient fighting unit.

Lee gave each general a fair evaluation. Daniel H. —his friends called him, "Harvey" —Hill, "Stonewall" Jackson's brother-in-law, was one of many devoted Christian men who used his acid tongue too often. A forty-year-old North Carolinian, he was a caustic hater of all things Northern. He criticized anyone or anything that caused him displeasure. Hill suffered from a spinal ailment, which gave him an unmilitary bearing whether mounted or afoot. A hungry-looking man with haunted eyes and a close-cropped, scraggly beard, he took a fierce delight in combat—especially when it was hand-to-hand. He proved impatient and frequently took battlefield matters into his own hands.

James Longstreet proved to be the most reliable and balanced field officer of the lot. He lost most of his family, wife included, to illness, yet he pressed through his ponderous moods and struck a fine balance between aggressive and reserved fighting tactics. Lee began to refer to General Longstreet as his "war horse."

Ambrose Powell Hill was an aggressive fighter. However, he tended to allow his hot temper to get out of control. J. E. B. (Jeb) Stuart was flamboyant. He never seemed to grow out of his boyhood enthusiasm for adventure. He was perfectly suited as the commander of the Confederate cavalry. Richard Ewell was too reserved. He failed to garner the respect of his peers or subordinates. They called him "Old Bald Head." His lack of hair gave him a "bird-like" appearance and, all too often, he reported sick for duty, which did not sit well with his subordinates, peers, or commanding general.

Thomas "Stonewall" Jackson was the last and probably the strangest of them all, a man of fire and brimstone straight out of the Old Testament. He often called his division the "Army of the Lord." Compared to D. H. Hill, he proved himself capable of operating independently within the boundaries of issued orders.

These were the men the Confederacy gave Lee to lead the Army of Northern Virginia. The sheer size of the army required a change in its organizational structure. Further, the Southern population perceived the Seven-Days Battle as a great victory. As a result, Southern pride and the ranks began to swell again. New volunteers and draftees entered the service, and others returned who had previously lost heart and simply went home. Before long, Lee looked at an army nearly ninety thousand strong.

For Lee, the Seven-Days Battle convinced him that he must improve command communication for better fighting coordination between units. He understood that his smaller force needed this change. He hoped that better and faster direct orders would help his men strike severe blows against their enormous enemy. He decided to divide the army into two distinct corps. Promoting Longstreet was the easy decision. Lee offered him command of the larger First Corps. After several sleepless nights of self-deliberation, Lee decided that Jackson would receive command of the Second Corps. Jackson could be counted on if independent action were required. However, he performed poorly during the Seven-Days Battle. Generals D. H. Hill and A. P. Hill argued that they performed better, which was true. But fortunately for Jackson, he and Lee shared a similar attitude in faith. Jackson openly demonstrated his deep desire to serve God, as did Lee. Further, Lee understood that Jackson longed to be a man of honor above all others, one to bring glory to his Lord and Savior. This may have been the deciding factor. Lee prepared the promotion requests to President Davis, who in turn submitted them to the Confederate Congress for approval. Both Longstreet and Jackson received the rank of lieutenant general. The First Corps would comprise three divisions, and the Second, two. With that, Lee accomplished his reorganization objective.

"Dat be da last of dem, Masser 'Calister, suh," Gabriel said as the two men watched the last Union troop transport, escorted by a Federal gunboat, steam down the James River to the Chesapeake Bay.

"In a way, I'm sorry to see them go," Macalister said as he patted his pants pocket full of Yankee gold coins.

Gabriel noticed Macalister's motion, protecting a small portion of his recently and illegally obtained wealth at the expense of Gabriel's life. Satisfied that he had served this evil man as best he could, and unfortunately assuming that his job was done, Gabriel asked, "What's ya gonna do now, Masser 'Calister, now dat da Yankee man gone away?"

The smallish, rotund, balding man rocked up on his toes and back again just to stretch and see downstream a bit farther. Then he replied, "Oh, this." He paused. "This is just a minor set-back, Gabriel, a small bump in the road to prosperity, if you can understand my meaning. A good business man always prepares for contingencies."

Gabriel didn't understand this man and his use of fancy words, so he simply asked, "What's dis con-tin-gen-seas?"

Macalister smiled a perfectly sinister grin and instructed, "Other plans just in case the first idea fails or doesn't work out quite as well as originally expected." Proudly he continued, "I know exactly what we're going to do next."

Surprised, Gabriel stumbled over his own words as he replied, "Next? We? I tawt we'z dun wit da Yankee man!"

Macalister's smile broadened, as he answered, "Not at all my friend, not at all. They have mail to send and receive just as much as our fine, upstanding Southern citizens, and we're going to make sure that they get it. Only it's going to cost both sides more now that our handy channel has been, shall I say, moved to a less convenient, and higher risk location?"

Both curious and anxious, Gabriel asked, "Jus' what yew'z got in mind, Masser 'Calister, and how duz I fit in?"

Macalister looked off into the distance and slowly replied, "Well, boy, I'm not going to tell you everything just yet, but trust me, there will be plenty of money for you to earn. I know how badly you want to buy your family's freedom."

Gabriel removed his hat and scratched his head as he answered, "Yassuh, Masser 'Calister, I duz. But what?" Gabriel paused.

"But what?" Macalister echoed. "Speak up boy! What's on your mind?"

Gabriel hesitated. He thought long and hard how to ask his question. "Well, suh, what 'bout dat Yankee sir-gent you need? Ain't he gone 'way, too?"

Once more, Macalister smiled and continued, "As I said, boy, a good business man prepares for contingencies. Don't you worry about our sergeant friend. Money can work wonders, even in the Yankee army. Our man will be in the right place when the time comes for us to deliver the mail again."

Gabriel turned to look down the river and wondered just what new risk Macalister planned for him. Silently he prayed, *Lordy, please protect my wife and chill'n, and me too. Sometimes, I think this man wouldn't care a snip if'n I got kilt doing his evil work.*

Camp life settled into the routine of close order drill, inspection, drill, fix equipment, drill, clean and repair uniforms, drill, eat, drill, sleep, drill, cut hair, drill, write reports, drill, write letters and drill some more. The perceived Seven-Days Battle victories brought some slack to heavy discipline, but for the most part, time passed with mindless activities and abundant boredom. Nathaniel's newfound friend, Buster, the chocolate Labrador puppy, took what little free time Nathaniel could find for himself. Buster had grown quite a bit in the last few weeks since that fateful day when Nathaniel rescued the little fella. His chocolate-colored smooth coat glistened in the afternoon August sunshine as they played a happy game of tug-of-war.

Nathaniel discovered three things about this ball of four-legged energy. One, Buster loved to retrieve anything. If Nathaniel threw it, Buster would go after it, find it, and bring it back. Nathaniel didn't think this too unusual. *After all, he is a retriever.* But, Buster didn't always bring the retrieved item right back. Sometimes the cry of a bird or a strange noise from camp would distract him. Sometimes Buster would bring it close to Nathaniel and hold it. He wouldn't let go of the stick, or pinecone, or whatever Nathaniel pitched. Nathaniel took it all in stride and figured Buster would learn.

The second thing Nathaniel realized was that Buster could continue this activity endlessly. If Nathaniel tried to stop and perform his assigned duties, Buster would start barking at him in his high-pitched puppy voice until Nathaniel either put Buster in his pen or resumed the game of fetch. Nathaniel was sorry he had praised Buster that very first time he tested Buster's inbred talents. Even now, Buster was Nathaniel's largest distraction, keeping him from completing his responsibilities—writing letters home about lost sons, brothers, fathers or husbands.

It was another hot, dry, dusty, August afternoon. "Stonewall" Jackson kept his Second Corps boys very busy. Rumors ran through the camp like wildfire. Most of the men believed that they would launch another forced march to somewhere north of Richmond. These ideas had to be rumors because Jackson rarely told anyone, even his closest staff members, what might be his next move. Nathaniel wanted to finish writing a letter to his two cousins, Louise and Margaret, before supper. But Buster would have none of that. He crouched with his tail wagging high above his arched upward hindquarters. His front legs were lowered so that he could spring into action the instant it was required. He barked and growled and made other sounds that made Nathaniel and others who heard Buster swear that the puppy was trying to speak English. Nathaniel was tired. His right arm and shoulder ached from throwing the hide-covered pinecone under Buster's left paw.

This peculiar habit Buster displayed was the thing that fascinated Nathaniel most. Often Buster would bring the retrieved article and drop it right at Nathaniel's feet. Nathaniel praised Buster, and if he happened to have a little extra hardtack he'd give him a small reward. But when Nathaniel would reach down to pick up the prize, Buster would quickly step on it with his front left paw and hold it down tight. He'd keep his eye fixed on his captured property, wagging his tail happily, waiting for Nathaniel's next move. Nathaniel tried all kinds of distractions, but nothing would work to cause Buster to give up his catch. Finally, Nathaniel tried standing erect with his hands placed on his hips showing Buster that he would not move. Once convinced that the game would not continue until he released the toy, he'd remove his paw, step back, let Nathaniel to reach down, pick it up, and toss it again.

"What am I going to do with you, Buster?" Nathaniel asked the little chocolate Labrador.

Buster cocked his head to one side and pulled his ears back as if to say, "I don't know." But then he responded with a series of barks and yelps that almost expressed those very words, except he seemed to add, "Just pick it up and throw it."

Nathaniel put his hands on his hips and questioned further, "How am I supposed to throw it if you insist on standing on it?"

Finally, Buster got the message and released his grip on the leather-covered pinecone that Nathaniel had stitched together for his little friend. "It stinks," Nathaniel exclaimed. It was moist from Buster chewing it, but the puppy loved it. Whenever Nathaniel was near, Buster could be seen holding it in his mouth waiting for his master to throw the funny looking little ball so he could go chase it with all his might.

Nathaniel picked up the slightly soggy orb and tossed it as far as he could into the thick woods on the edge of their camp. Buster tore off as fast as he could run and dove headlong into the underbrush. Nathaniel just smiled as the chocolate tail disappeared from his sight. This war was terrible, but Buster gave Nathaniel some daily joy in the upside-down world in which he found himself.

Chapter 25

AUGUST 1862

August 1862 brought a shift in the weather. The hot, steamy air of July, fueled by near-daily rain, turned even hotter, still filled with life-draining humidity. But for now, the rain stopped. Within a few days, the roads dried and the heavy air soon became heavier, filled with dust from the new replacements that marched and drilled everyday. The veterans attended to the routine necessities of camp life. They patched uniforms, read and wrote letters from and to loved ones. Many tried to find shade from the brutal heat and penetrating sunshine that sapped all energy from both man and beast.

Rumors filled the camp, energized from newspaper reports that praised the exploits of the Southern war-fighters. The daily reports ridiculed the ineptness of the Northern military leadership, or condemned the less-than-human qualities of the mercenaries in blue uniforms. Most Southerners believed that the war would be over shortly, no later than the approaching harvest season. Some understood that this was wishful thinking. A few realized that it would not be over until one side completely conquered the other.

The President of the United States of America, Abraham Lincoln, demanded results. More importantly, he demanded victories. The President of the Confederate States of America, Jefferson Davis, felt relieved that his capital city had been spared. Union General George B. McClellan withdrew to the safety of the defenses surrounding Washington, D.C. Southern General Robert E. Lee prepared for another Yankee assault and speculated from where it would come.

Lincoln had to do something to achieve the Federal Government's objectives. General McClellan seemed content to keep the "Grand Army of the Potomac" as concentrated and intact as possible to avoid any further damage. Lincoln needed a leader who would use the resources at his disposal. He wanted to find a man who would not complain and constantly demand more men, supplies, and equipment. The commander in chief and his appointed field marshal were diametrically opposed to each other in opinion regarding how the war should be prosecuted. Something must change if the Union were to be preserved. Lincoln believed that it would take an aggressive use of force, not merely a demonstration of rarely used superior capabilities and resources.

Lincoln made up his mind. McClellan had to go. Once the Army of the Potomac was reasonably safe and bivouacked around the Federal Capital, orders were written and dispatched transferring nearly all of McClellan's fighting force to Major General John Pope. General Pope gained Lincoln's respect because he had conducted a successful campaign and capture of Island No. 10, a highly fortified defense of the Confederacy's main supply artery, the Mississippi River. Furthermore, the Union Army's General-In-Chief, Major General Henry Halleck, recommended Pope as the man who would get the job done. Established with the reputation of an aggressive fighter, General Pope was given the new assignment to crush Lee's Rebel Army of Northern Virginia. General Pope commanded a sizable and formidable force of his own. He and his army were stationed northwest of Manassas, Virginia, the same location of the war's first major battle of consequence.

Davis, on the other hand, was inspired by the deemed divine intervention and turn-about in the fortunes of war. The Confederate government never ceased its call for support from its citizens from across all of the Southern States. No matter how small the event, the newspapers filled the Southern population with flattering reports of each Confederate victory or exploit. As a result, the people responded with new regiments that the government could not house, clothe, or equip. Men flocked to service fearing the war would be over before they got a chance to fight. The expectations that filled the military camps and Southern towns ranged from the unlikely future Federal assault to the hoped-for Federal appeal for peace and recognition of the new independent southern nation. Davis hoped that victory was at hand. His commander of the Army of Northern Virginia did not share his optimism. He prepared for another massive Yankee attack and he guessed correctly that it would come from Pope quartered near Manassas. He called on his generals and laid out his plans.

I think it's hotter and more humid today than any other this summer. The sun has only been up a few hours and it's already sticky this morning. The heat is making me bone weary. Now I have these strange orders. No one else received orders like these. What could they mean? Had someone brought charges against me? What transgression did I commit? Maybe, I'm being transferred to another outfit. Did something terrible happen to Mother? Stop it! Get hold of yourself. For all you know, this could be a pleasant surprise, like a promotion. What you do know is that you don't know anything so stop this foolishness.

"Good morning, Max. Looks like you and me have some work to do this morning." Nathaniel mounted his horse and settled into the saddle. "You're doing really well, big fella. Maybe I'll get used to putting my foot into this left stirrup," Nathaniel shuddered.

"Let's go, Max. We have to go to a place I've never been before. I hope this map is accurate."

Max just breathed heavily as if he paid attention.

"Looks like we are headed for a spot a mile or so due north. It's supposed to be some clearing. I just hope it's not in the middle of some mosquito-infested swamp." Horse and rider entered the thick woods. "So far so good, this looks like the right path. This old winding, rolling one-lane road is supposed to connect Ellerson and Mechanicsville. It sure is well worn on both sides of the middle rise. I imagine it saw heavy traffic during the Yankees' push to Richmond." *Was that just a month ago?* He pressed forward, consumed with the many memories of the recent heavy fighting and the loss of so many friends.

The steady rhythmic clopping of Max's hooves along the dusty way, coupled with the banging of Nathaniel's canteen against his saddle, made for an amusing percussion. Added to this from overhead, Nathaniel heard the rapid clamoring against a tall pine tree of a determined woodpecker. Nathaniel took a deep breath and absorbed the piney aroma that filled the air. Suddenly, a large grasshopper jumped and fluttered a good ten feet in front of Max. It repeated this futile attempt to escape demise several times until unexpectedly a strong breeze gusting from west to east drove the creature into the safety of the woods. Nathaniel said to Max, "I guess Jesus had to help that little one get out of our way." Max just took a deep breath and snorted loudly as he exhaled. The wind continued to blow stronger and Nathaniel listened as it sounded like a rushing river through the treetops. He looked up and watched the tall pines sway as if dancing to some sweet music only they could hear. *I wonder if it will rain again soon.*

Nathaniel and Max came to a low-lying point where the trail crossed the narrow, swift-running Beaver Dam Creek. So many streams and tributaries ran faster and higher than normal from all the rain over the previous weeks. Many had crested, but by this time this creek just ran fast within its overgrown banks. As he eased Max forward toward the water, Nathaniel caught a glimpse of a doe in the woods licking its very young fawn. Nathaniel quietly halted Max. "Max, do you see that?" Nathaniel whispered. "That little one can't be more than a few days old." Nathaniel smiled. "I hope none of our boys spot them. Fresh roasted venison would taste good, but not at the expense of killing this mother and her young."

Max fidgeted. He breathed heavily and lowered his head to grab a quick grassy snack. The doe turned her ears toward the potential threat. Her ears moved back and forth alternatively, trying to locate the new noise. Nathaniel praised his creator whispering, "Thank You, Lord Jesus, for letting me see these magnificent animals." Then the doe spotted Nathaniel. She took a few guarded steps in his direction. She got a better look. Nathaniel returned her stare. *I mean you no harm, dear lady of the woods. Take your baby where you will.*

Just then Max's impatience got the best of him and he breathed heavily again, snorting and vibrating his mouth with a loud bellowing. The fawn bolted. The doe stood statuesquely still for another instant and then turned and bounded up the hill after her fawn. In another second, both disappeared into the thick, dark woods. Nathaniel patted Max's neck and said, "Well, you sure scared them away. Let's go boy." Nathaniel gave the reins a shake and lightly kicked Max's sides. They crossed the creek and pressed on to the clearing.

Nathaniel passed under a low-hanging tree branch, which caused him to duck and lean awkwardly off to his left side. He held tight to the saddle horn. "That one almost knocked me down. Whoa, Max. Hold up. What's that just off the trail? Looks like battle debris. Let's have a look see." Nathaniel stood in his stirrups and tried to get a better view. "I can make out a broken wagon wheel partly buried in the hardening dirt." He reined Max to the right and walked him into the woods. He could see more debris scattered about. "There must have been some hard fighting here, Max old boy." He didn't stop to get down, and he was just about to return to the trail when he saw a ragged blue uniform that looked like it was propped up against a large oak tree. "I better take a closer look at this one." Nathaniel and Max rounded the oak tree. "This is no surprise. We've seen similar things before, haven't we, Max?" Below him rested the skeletal remains of a Yankee, probably wounded in battle and left to his fate. "Sir, I don't have time to care for you today, but I'll do what I can later." He wheeled Max about and headed for the trail.

Nathaniel reached the clearing several minutes before the appointed time. Other officers were already there. They all milled about. Some had struck conversations with others, and some stood or sat alone. More arrived until the clearing held more than fifty officers of various ranks. *That's odd. 'Most everyone wears a chaplain's insignia. What could this possibly be about?*

Nathaniel dismounted and tied Max to a low-hanging branch on a sturdy maple tree. He walked slowly toward two other chaplains who were standing and talking to each other. Both men had their arms folded across their chests. Nathaniel recognized one man. He was the chaplain for another regiment in Nathaniel's division. As Nathaniel approached, the chaplain recognized Nathaniel too and called to him in his deep western-Tennessee tone, "Hey, Graham, what do you make of this? Have you ever seen so many preachers in one place before?" The two men laughed. Obviously, they understood this as some inside joke to which Nathaniel was not privy.

Nathaniel replied, "Maybe the army doesn't need our services anymore, Captain Wynette?"

"Yes, Graham, we've considered that possibility. It does seem that the Lord has shown everyone, even President Lincoln, whose side He favors. It would be redundant for us to try and speak better of it than the Almighty has already done on the field of battle. Wouldn't you agree, Josh?" The other man nodded affirmatively. "Oh, Graham, I'd like you to meet a friend of mine and member of our convention from the great state of North Carolina, Major Joshua Adams. He is the pastor of a rather large congregation in the mountain town of Asheville. That's probably why he outranks us!" Everyone chuckled at that last comment. Major Adams and Nathaniel shook hands, each sensing the other man's grip. Nathaniel looked deeply into Major Adams' eyes. He saw that genuine "light" that Nathaniel had learned to look for in any man who claimed to know and represent Jesus. Within a quick moment, Nathaniel had received that inner witness, that intuitive knowledge, that this man too loved the Lord and would willingly give his life in service to his creator and redeemer.

With the greetings exchanged, Nathaniel briefly looked at each man and attempted to answer Captain Wynette's last question. He stated with no degree of certainty, and without a hint of humor, "If you want my opinion, I think this army will be on the move again real soon. I guess our generals must be expecting a high number of casualties." Both Major Adams and Captain Wynette caught the spirit of Nathaniel's comment and quickly sobered up their respective attitudes as they absorbed the truth of Nathaniel's words.

Pesky insects swarmed all around the men as they talked. Captain Wynette swatted a mosquito as it bit the back of his neck. He pulled his slightly bloodstained hand down in front of him and said, "This one has had its last meal." Suddenly they heard the sound of horses and riders. They approached the clearing from the dusty road that led northward into the thick, dark woods. All the officers turned to face the sound and possible threat. Those who talked stopped. Those who sat stood. Many carried side arms and pulled them from their holsters. They readied themselves just in case their worst unvoiced fear came true. Could a deep probing Yankee cavalry patrol ambush them in this remote spot far from their main encampment?

Their anxiety intensified as the next moment passed. Then the lead horse and rider appeared. A small column followed. They were shielded from sight from the dust being kicked up by the lead horse. The shade was so thick it was impossible for Nathaniel to make out the colors. Eventually, those closest to the riders began to relax their defensive posture. Then the lead horse and rider broke into the clearing and the sun shone down upon the man. Those that followed fanned out into a "V" formation behind him and they walked their respective steeds to a slow, relaxed halt.

The officers standing in the clearing were both speechless and motionless. A few gazed upon the lead general officer, awestruck by his presence. Then one officer on the ground came to his senses and yelled out, "Gentlemen, ten-hut!" In an instant, their military training overcame their temporary mental paralysis and, within a second, every officer on the ground snapped to attention and offered the commanding figure the requisite military courtesy.

The mounted general leaned forward in his saddle as if to get a better look at the men in front of him. Then, as if satisfied with what he saw, he brought himself up into a seated position of attention and returned their salute. In a flourish, the standing officers dropped their arms, remained in the position of attention and waited the next command.

The general officer could easily have been mistaken for a Yankee. He wore his mud-stained dark-blue Virginia Military Institute kepi with an equally stained VMI dark-blue blazer and trousers. Fortunately, even the men who stood before him and who had never met or seen the man personally, knew him by his legendary description. The man did have soul-piercing steel-blue eyes.

This man won the hearts of every Southerner. Lieutenant General Thomas Jackson, now known affectionately by all as "Stonewall" Jackson, sat atop his red quarter horse, Little Sorrel. He let a slight smile appear behind his heavy dark-brown, gray-speckled beard. "At ease, gentlemen," Jackson spoke commandingly. "I want to speak with you about a matter that General Robert E. Lee and I consider to be of extreme and grave military importance. We must act immediately."

"Do you recognize this place?" Macalister asked, hoping he would not need to waste time explaining this detail to Gabriel. Unfortunately, as Macalister looked into the face of his obliging servant, he could see the glazed-over expression that let him know that the map on the table meant nothing to Gabriel. Macalister restarted his instructions with his typical demeaning attitude toward the man who was helping him become wealthier than he ever could have hoped. "I see you don't really know how to read a map," Macalister continued. "I guess I'll have to explain each step to you. I can't afford your getting lost tonight. It would cost me too much money to train a new man. And think of your poor wife and children, Gabriel. They need you to know where you're going so you can come home and eventually buy their freedom." Macalister controlled Gabriel with a different kind of slavery. He had the man's attention. Macalister took his finger and pointed to the spot on the map that showed City Point and stated, "We are here. This is our town, City Point."

Gabriel followed with his eyes and then bent over real close to see the small writing on the map. Once he figured out what the words said he stood upright and proudly exclaimed, "I see it now, suh! What's this other stuff?"

Macalister swept his hand along the drawn snake-like figure and said, "This wide curving line is the James River. It says so right here." Macalister pointed directly to the place on the map where the river's name was printed. Gabriel bent over again so that he could better read the legend. He grunted an affirmation and then straightened back up to look at his boss. Macalister became curious about this repeated behavior. He let his eyes squint, furrowed his brow, brought his right hand up to his chin and decided to ask, "Are you having trouble seeing the words? Do you have to get that close to the map to read it?"

"Yassuh, Masser 'Calister, suh, I'z must get real clos't ta da letters ta make out what dey sez," Gabriel humbly admitted.

Macalister immediately recognized that his impairment could lead to a disaster if Gabriel didn't see well enough to keep himself from getting lost. How had this man survived all his years? He asked, "How were you able to get across the river if you couldn't see where you were headed?"

"Masser 'Calister, suh," Gabriel started. "My eyes haven't always bin dis bad. I grew up in these here parts. I'z know'd boat sides of da James, around deez City Point area. I'z doesn't need ta see'z dat good to find my way."

Macalister felt a bit better, but he still had doubts. He pressed for more information. "Do you know this area as well, down river here," pointing with his finger, "where it ends?"

Gabriel leaned down to see where Macalister held his finger, compared it with the City Point depiction, scratched his head, and pulled himself upright to respond, "I'z never bin down to any place called Fort Monroe, suh."

Macalister's anxiety began to reach its peak. He nearly shook inside. Suddenly, he feared that his fortune would cease to grow. To make this work, he would have to become more involved. He'd have to invest more of his personal time and physical presence. He didn't want to do this because he knew it increased his personal risk. He could take Gabriel to get spectacles made so he could see well again. That would be easy to justify if he could find a doctor willing to help his Negro employee. He made a decision, but he needed more details. "Tell me, how long does it take you to cross the river from our spot near City Point?"

Gabriel was almost proud of his ability to navigate the river. He replied, "Well, suh, it 'pends on da weather. Dat one night, back a few weeks, took longer den most. But, if'n the weather is clear and the river running in its reg'lar way, I can make it cross in less den one hour."

Macalister looked at the much wider gap in the James River between the Confederates' side of the river across from Fort Monroe. Judging by the comparative distance, he guessed it would take Gabriel much more than two hours to cross by rowboat. Somehow he would have to get by the Yankee boats that patrolled the river. Macalister didn't know the nature of the waterway there. He'd have to learn if it was rough or steady. Plus, if Gabriel didn't know the area, he could easily get lost. If that happened, Macalister's enterprise would be lost with him.

He dismounted. He held onto the saddle's horn for a second and bowed his head as if in prayer. He was. Then he let go of his horse's saddle, turned, and began to pace as if inspecting the troops before him, which still stood at attention. With his old VMI dark-blue kepi pulled tight just above his eyes, he spoke to these men of God commandingly, "Gentlemen, be at ease!"

As if it were difficult to do so in the presence of this legendary figure, the men reluctantly released their tense, fixed posture and a few even began to relax. The celebrated General Jackson stood before them. His dark-blue wool over-blouse was noticeably dirty and stained. His riding boots appeared to be well worn. When they looked into his eyes, they could see the passion that burned deep within him. Unquestionably, a real leader stood before them.

To help those that were still obviously anxious, Jackson relaxed his own posture. He removed his riding gloves, which revealed the wound he had received on his left hand. It happened at the Battle of Manassas on his wife Anna's birthday, July 21, 1861, the day he earned the nickname "Stonewall." He tucked his gloves into his belt and folded them neatly. He looked up at the surrounding trees and blue cloudless sky, took a deep breath and began to speak from his heart. "It is a beautiful morning today, isn't it, gentlemen?" He didn't wait for a reply, but some of the men affirmed his statement. After a short pause, he drove straight into his message. "Gentlemen, you hold the keys to our success in this conflict for our nation's survival against the Yankee invaders of our blessed land. These cowards who claim to be our brothers have come down here and greatly disturbed our peace-loving, God-fearing people."

This firm introduction took most of them by surprise. Several men began to look at each other with bewilderment etched upon their faces. Jackson continued, "I am quite certain that all of you are familiar with the passage from God's Holy Scriptures where our Lord instructed the chief apostle, Peter, in the use of the keys to the kingdom of heaven found in Matthew's gospel account, chapter 16, verse 19?" Jackson stopped for a moment to let them remember. Then, he pressed forward to make his point, "Gentlemen, I wish you to consider this verse in the context of this war. Our enemy has great resources. We must prevent their use against us. Our men must be set free, if you don't mind my paraphrase, to act boldly in battle. You hold the keys to inspire bravery. Our men must carry the fight to the enemy and destroy their will to fight. If we are successful on the battlefield, the Northern people will weaken and stop this tyrannical and illegal war of aggression. I believe that the Bible shows us example after example of how God Almighty uses small bands of faith-filled men who are willing to fight bravely. He calls them to face their enemies of greater numbers. He fought for them each time they obeyed His command. You, gentlemen, can instill in our men the spiritual courage to accomplish this mission. By His mighty hand, we will prevail."

Jackson took a deep breath. He spoke with increased passion as he continued to pace. He acted like a caged animal that looked to be set free. He scanned the eyes of each man with his own piercing gaze as he drove home his message. "I ask you men to aggressively invite our troops to attend worship services. I expect you to preach the gospel. I want you to help our men come to know our Lord and Savior, Jesus Christ, in a personal way. I believe that once a man knows Jesus personally, that man is truly alive. I hope they learn to love Him more than life itself, more than wanting to live life for themselves. In this, they will become willing, living sacrifices for Him. This will give them the courage to fight for Him and each other."

Stonewall came to the difficult part of his speech. He knew he must be very clear. "I know that you men come from different backgrounds and denominations. I understand that you emphasize different things in your respective interpretations concerning doctrine. I myself have very strong opinions, but we must put these differences aside. We must be in complete unity about one thing." Jackson hesitated for just a second and then nearly shouted with great exuberance, "Jesus is Lord!"

A few words of agreement like, "Amen," or "Yes, sir," could be heard. Some echoed Jackson's zeal; while other words were muttered throughout the small crowd.

Jackson clasped his hands behind his back and continued to pace as he spoke, but just a step slower now. "I will announce that you have my full support. I want a revival to spread like a wildfire throughout this army. General Lee shares this desire. He and I have spoken at length about this and we believe, regardless of your particular persuasion, our men need to know that they are eternally secure before they face the enemy. Is this point clear, gentlemen?"

It was crystal-clear and all the men answered excitedly in near unison, "Yes, sir, General sir!"

Jackson continued, "I want souls saved for our Lord. I want His kingdom advanced more so then I want our army to advance on our enemy. You have been called by the Lord to preach His Word. I expect you to do it with vigor." Jackson stopped and faced the men who had gathered in a slight arch around him. He continued, "I am aware that our Lord said that His kingdom is not of this world. If it were, His servants would fight. I know that many of you believe strongly that you should not take up arms yourself." Jackson's eyes met Nathaniel's. Jackson's eyes penetrated Nathaniel's spirit as if Jackson could see right into Nathaniel's soul. The stare lasted less than a second, but it felt like minutes to Nathaniel, as if General Jackson had singled him out. Of course, Jackson did not intend to address anyone individually. Consciously, Nathaniel did feel a pang of guilt as Jackson continued to encourage these men of God. "I want you to understand that I respect your views and I will not impose my own on you. However, I want those of you who hold to this position to consider meeting with me privately so that we can discuss this further."

Jackson turned and looked toward his staff. He held up his right arm and pointed as he spoke, "Gentlemen, please see my adjutant, Captain Pendleton. Hold up your hand, Captain, so these men can recognize you."

Captain Sandy Pendleton obeyed instantly and raised his right hand and held it high for a long minute even as Jackson turned back to face the group of Second Corps chaplains. "You can make an appointment to meet with me through Captain Pendleton. I expect to hear from you within the next three days."

Jackson placed his hands behind his back again, took a deep breath, raised up slightly on his toes, and then settled back squarely on his feet and concluded, "Gentlemen, I expect each of you to have an inspiring sermon prepared for Sunday's service. I will visit each of your services as the weeks pass. I expect nothing less of you than what the Lord would. Preach His Word so that the men come to know and love Him. Do you have any questions?"

The voices that responded stated that they understood their leader perfectly. With that, Jackson brought himself to attention. His men reciprocated immediately. Jackson scanned them one last time and then finished, "Gentlemen." He paused, took one more deep breath then said, "You are dismissed."

Salutes snapped to his honor. Jackson returned to his horse and mounted the animal. Stiffly, he sat at attention and returned their salute. The meeting was over. Jackson wheeled Little Sorrel to his left. His staff followed, and in less than a minute they all disappeared into the thick woods. The men stood there motionless. They gazed at the spot in the woods where Jackson and his staff had entered the woods. Each man pondered the words he'd just heard.

Chapter 26

UNCERTAINTY

The Rockford Hotel's Garden Room was the finest restaurant in town. The locals claimed that it offered the best food and the best service. The garden atmosphere furnished a most romantic flair. One wing of this elegant dining room spread over a thirty- by twenty-foot rectangle and the second wing covered a twenty- by twenty-foot square. Together, they formed an "L" shape. The kitchen was located at the inside junction of the "L" to better serve both wings. Each had a modest and tasteful candle-lit teardrop-shaped crystal chandelier. The ornate crown molding revealed hand-carved artistry, a variety of flowering plants. The dining area was further accented with an assortment of live plants and fresh-cut flowers in a variety of eye-pleasing arrangements. The aroma from several potted gardenia shrubs and small rose bushes filled the air.

Approximately every four feet along the walls stood walnut facings about twelve inches wide that extended from the base of the crown molding to the broad baseboards at the floor. Four feet from the floor, light-colored panels displayed the characteristic beautiful grain of solid oak between the walnut planks. Above the oak panels rested decorative mirrors, smoked with a floral design that filled the rest of the wall space. On each walnut plank, set at eye level between the tables, oil lamps burned softly, providing just enough light for the respective dinner patrons to have a relaxed environment in which to enjoy their evening meal as well as each other's company.

By design, Jason Merritt wanted to impress his dinner guest. He hoped to raise her expectations for a secure future. More importantly, he intended to keep her for himself. He prided himself for being a man who got what he wanted, and as a young man, he set his goal to become a prominent political leader. He knew that to secure his position of power, he needed a strong, spirited woman committed to stand beside him, even if it were only for appearance's sake. He knew nothing of God's eternal purpose for joining a man and woman together as husband and wife, nor did he care to learn, because for him God was an old-fashioned notion only for the ignorant. Jason Merritt was now the product of a new age of enlightenment—a man of reason, educated with the most modern understanding of science and economics from one of the nation's finest and most progressive New England universities.

However, he recognized the many personal benefits marriage could bring. He believed that perception of truth was more important than integrity. If people perceived that he maintained a stable family life, then they might believe that the future Congressman or Senator Merritt could be trusted with representing their political and economic interests. To him, obtaining and retaining power was all that mattered, and he would say anything, promise everything, knowing he did not have to deliver on anything, just to convince people he cared about them. In this way he would steal their right to vote by his crafty speech and oozing charisma. But for this night, he simply hoped to steal one heart. He wanted Eleanor to be treated like and feel like a queen—and maybe, someday, a First Lady.

The woman who sat across the table from Jason impressed him. He barely noticed the beautifully decorated dinner table with its crystal centerpiece that contained the dozen long-stemmed red roses he ordered. Jason Merritt also failed to observe the accented floral tablecloth with an array of colors that adorned it and somewhat matched the carved pattern in the crown molding above him. Eleanor brought these things to his attention. All he could see was a lovely creature who shared a delicious dinner with him. This night her beauty nearly took his breath away. For the first time since he met Eleanor, he saw a radiant woman. He let himself stare into her light-brown eyes and found an enjoyment being lost in her returned gaze. He felt almost silly inside. He began to let himself drift with the emotion of the moment. Then, as if a voice spoke to him to wake up, he acknowledged this fault and forced himself to snap out of the trance. Love is for the weak-minded; power is for the strong. Even the strong needed the support of a strong image, and he would have that image securely established as quickly as possible. He was prepared to advance his position this very night.

The dinner went smoothly. Although a dozen other tables enjoyed similar dining pleasures, the prearranged extra incentive offered to the headwaiter the day before now paid off handsomely. It was as if the two of them had the entire place all to themselves. The roasted duck was delicious. As they sipped several glasses of wine, they shared a good hour's worth of small talk and laughed over old family stories. And the crazy First Lady, Mary Todd Lincoln, provided numerous funny tales. They spoke seriously about the immediate need to end the war quickly so that Eleanor's brothers could come home.

Jason had just agreed with Eleanor saying, "We simply should let the Confederates have their own country," when dessert was served. Placed before both of them was a thick three-layered piece of rich, chocolate cake.

This looks tasty. I think I will enjoy this immensely. Before Eleanor took her first bite, she changed the subject, "You'd be very proud of me, Mr. Merritt!"

Jason, somewhat surprised, asked, "And just how is that, my dear Eleanor?"

"Well, I did it, just as you suggested. I wrote that Confederate fellow a reply today. I dropped it in the post office on my way home from the dress shop this afternoon." Eleanor took her first bite and hummed with delight.

"You don't say?" Jason didn't really expect her to do this. He didn't like the idea of her engaging in any form of communication with any other man, especially one who might be a threat more than just a physical enemy. He hid his displeasure well.

Eleanor failed to detect any change in his manner. She used her fork to cut another small sliver of cake from her slice. Before she placed the delicate morsel into her mouth, she said proudly, "Yes I did, and I'm very glad that I did. If the man is a cad, as you predict, it won't be long before we find out the truth." She placed the second piece of cake into her mouth, smiled, and opened her eyes wide, raising her eyebrows to emphasize the sweet taste she enjoyed. Then she closed her eyes to savor the moment and said, "This is so good! You really should try it." Then she returned to her main point, "However, the postmaster charged me extra for sending a letter South and also told me that there was no guarantee that it would ever reach the addressee. I don't care. I'm just glad I had the courage to send it." Eleanor quickly took another bite.

Jason was disappointed because he considered the strong possibility that the man was an honest Southern gentleman. To protect his interests he knew he had to change the subject, and quickly. He simply affirmed, "Well that's very brave of you, Eleanor. I hope we do find out the truth soon. Yes, I am proud of you. That's one of the many things that I've come to admire about you. And because I've grown so fond of you, I have a very important question to ask you." Jason reached his right hand across the table and grasped Eleanor's left hand. At the same time, he reached his left hand into his jacket's pocket.

"Where did you find him?" asked Colonel Blair, commanding officer of the Fort Monroe garrison.

"He was wandering around in the woods just northwest of here," a young lieutenant replied. "One of our pickets found him. He was carrying this big bag with him."

"I gather you're pushing me for that promotion again. What's in the bag?" Colonel Blair directed with his head toward the large burlap sack that lay on the wooden floor of the colonel's office next to the lieutenant's left foot.

"Mail, sir, all from Rebels addressed to folks in the north."

"You don't say?" Colonel Blair's curiosity piqued immediately. An idea began to take form.

"Yes, sir. Seems to me we caught ourselves a smuggler, the best kind of contraband. Do you want to set the slave free, Colonel?"

Colonel Blair turned and stared out of his office window that overlooked the waterway where the Chesapeake Bay and James River met, and continued, "I might. Have you looked at any of the mail in that bag?"

"No, sir. I assumed it was against the law," the lieutenant defended his lack of initiative. "I just looked at the mailing and return addresses on the envelopes."

"I'm surprised you restrained yourself. Well technically, Lieutenant, you are correct," Colonel Blair assured. Then, he stroked his clean-shaven chin and continued, "Yes, you did the right thing. But it is Rebel mail and I'm not sure that our rules protecting the mail from tampering apply."

His colonel's last comment confused the lieutenant so he asked, "What do you mean, sir?"

The idea matured in Colonel Blair's mind as he proclaimed, "I'll tell you what I mean. Lieutenant, I want you to look through this bag and let me know if you find any mail with return addresses from leaders in either the Rebel government or military officers. Don't rule out family members. Wives and children or other relatives might have some information that could be useful, too."

The lieutenant finally caught the colonel's intention. They held an opportunity to gain some valuable intelligence about what the Confederates were thinking. He would be happy to help discover their next move. Given the large casualties already suffered in what appeared to be a lost cause to everyone who wore blue, these Federal officers must exploit every advantage. However, he still needed direction regarding the Negro. He wasn't a prisoner, he wasn't a runaway, he wasn't quite sure what he was or what they should do with him. Clearly, they just couldn't let him go, so he asked, "What should I do about that slave out in the waiting area, sir?"

Colonel Blair's idea morphed into a plan of action so he commanded, "Bring him in, I'd like to ask him a few questions."

"Yessir, Colonel, sir!" The young, overly enthusiastic red-haired, freckled-face lieutenant saluted smartly, performed a flawless about-face, took a few steps, opened the office door, and commandingly ordered, "Sergeant, bring the man into the colonel's office."

A few seconds later, a large, muscular older sergeant entered Colonel Blair's office followed by a musket-armed private who looked about eighteen years of age. A hand-tied Negro followed the boyish private. A very dirty armed private pushed the prisoner through the doorway. Colonel Blair concluded this soldier probably captured the detainee during the night. Once inside, the two privates stood close beside the tall, bone-thin Negro that kept his head down and eyes fixed on the wood-plank floor in front of him.

He was noticeably scared. Colonel Blair correctly assumed that this Negro probably thought that he had seen his last day on Earth.

Colonel Blair was an honest and genuinely kind man at heart. He felt real compassion for the poor soul that stood shaking before him. Colonel Blair rose from his desk chair and proceeded to walk around his desk to get a better view of the frightened man. As soon as he recognized the ropes tied around the man's wrists, he ordered, "Sergeant, remove the bonds from this man. We have no need of them here."

The young Lieutenant protested slightly stating, "Sir, we didn't want him to escape. We thought this might help us keep hold of him."

Colonel Blair reacted firmly, "Would you treat him like a dog on a leash? And where do you think he's going to go? The man is scared to death. He's probably been mistreated his entire life. It's time someone showed him a little kindness. Now remove those ropes, or do I have to do it myself?"

None hesitated. The younger officer gave his sergeant a look of scared urgency. In turn, the brawny sergeant pulled his knife from his leg strap and quickly cut through the ropes with a few hard and fast slicing motions. Gabriel breathed deeply, greatly relieved, and rubbed his sore, slightly rope-burned wrists. Colonel Blair hoped that this frightened man believed that just maybe he would see the next day's sunrise.

The Yankees had stockpiled equipment, supplies, and food all around the Manassas Junction train station. More war materials remained inside boxcars in the rail yard. It was too much to believe. The fast marches and countermarches executed by Jackson's "Foot Cavalry," the Second Corps of the Army of Northern Virginia, through the rolling hills and valleys east of the Shenandoah mountain range resulted in what could be considered a miracle. The Confederates captured Major General Pope's logistics stores with practically no Yankee resistance. The food alone could feed them and General Longstreet's larger First Corps for the rest of the year. This would ease the burden on the battle-pockmarked Virginia farmland already stripped by both foraging forces. But General Jackson had other plans.

Jackson understood that his corps' survival depended upon speed. Lee's strategy broke from all traditional military training and logic. He split his outnumbered forces and sent Jackson's twenty-five thousand ahead of the rest of the army to perform this harassment while the rest of Lee's force moved west around the Shenandoah mountains and would converge from the west through Thoroughfare Gap.

As tempting as this great prize might be, Jackson's men needed to remain light for their mission to have its tactical effect. Unfortunately, Jackson failed to communicate the breadth of his rationale even to his closest staff members. Thus, the troops could not understand his apparently unreasonable command. They simply couldn't believe that these "spoils-of-war" couldn't be moved back toward Richmond or to the starving towns just south of their present location. Consequently, the orders to destroy the supplies were not received with warm affection. If they only knew the strength of the Federal army marching in hot pursuit to destroy them, they'd finish this job quickly.

The fierce independent spirit that motivated these men to fight this rebellion frequently manifested itself, even against the officers that led them. So the men first gorged themselves on pork, beef, and amazingly, New England lobster tail. They stuffed their packs and wagons with as much as they could carry. Then they brought in the torches.

"Sure is a pity to send all of this fine food up in smoke," Marvin sighed, but still very grateful to have enjoyed a filling meal for the first time in many weeks.

"I guess General Jackson doesn't want the Yankees to have their supplies," Nathaniel tried to defend his commanding general. However, he did wonder aloud, "If we can't take these materials and provisions back to Richmond, —" Nathaniel stopped his thought and never finished his sentence. *I'd better watch what I say. I'll have a bigger problem addressing this to the troops in my next sermon. I can't let disloyalty take control of my thinking. Sunday will be a test of my resolve. How am I to motivate the men if I'm struggling with this decision? I need a Scripture to steady my mind.* Nathaniel recalled the passage from Second Corinthians, chapter 10, verse 5, *"Casting down imaginations, and every high thing that exalted itself against the knowledge of God, and bringing into captivity every thought to the obedience of Christ."*

Nathaniel's train of thought was broken as Marvin coughed, "We've got to move away from this smoke." The wind blew directly toward them. "Seems," Marvin nearly choked, "the wind's," Marvin covered his face with his handkerchief and muffled, "shifted."

Nathaniel was having great difficulty breathing, too, but managed to shout, "Let's go!"

The two company commanders turned away from the raging inferno and thickening black smoke coming from the burning railroad cars. The consuming flames seemed to swallow them whole. Nathaniel and Marvin waved to their troops to move away from the area. Suddenly one of the railcars exploded with such force it sent debris thirty feet into the air and in all directions. The men were thrown to the ground by the sheer concussion.

Marvin shook himself back to his senses. He called to Nathaniel and yelled, "Seems like your big friend up in the sky got us out of harm's way just in the nick of time."

Nathaniel was dazed. He just looked at Marvin, not really comprehending what he said. He slowly looked around. Some of his men were beginning to pull themselves together. He barely heard a few choice expressions about the foolish Yankees mixing munitions with food or other supplies. *I can't hear anything but loud ringing. My head, oh God, it hurts.* Nathaniel felt for a wound. He gazed at the destruction. *If we hadn't moved when we did, we'd all have been killed accidentally, needlessly.* Nathaniel reached up to a soldier who tried to pull Nathaniel to his feet. Another train car exploded. Then, everything went black.

Chapter 27

CHASED

The dusty roads had turned into a muddy quagmire as a torrential rain poured relentlessly down upon the driven march-weary Federal troops. Murmuring filled the ranks. They marched without stopping except for regulation-required breaks. Soldiers, soaked and sullen, reached Manassas Junction to find their supplies and equipment destroyed. Railroad cars burned completely. Only the iron trucks remained, distorted by the hellish heat that once engulfed the metal wheels. If not for the rain, it was possible that some of the remains would still be smoldering.

Disheartened, the overburdened Yankee infantry received orders to march on to destroy the cowardly small band of Rebels that had once been so near. Again, Union officers proudly concluded that they could smash Jackson's detached force if they moved swiftly. Unfortunately, the scent of victory that attracted them to move quickly north from Manassas Junction to Suddley Springs was the bait for a trap that a very wily, old gray fox, General Robert E. Lee, intended to snap closed around them.

"We've been marching for three whole days, and now we're moving out again," John complained. "First we head west, then we go south. Then we turn around and march north. I am so sick of this army. No one knows where the enemy can be found, so we walk in circles because our stupid officers don't know which way to go. Our president fires the only general who knew what to do. That idiot stays in the protection of Washington, D.C. He knows nothing of military matters. Worse yet, he gives the army into the hands of an egomaniac. Pope will get us all killed."

Paul's usually stable mood was downtrodden too, dampened even more by the pouring rain, sloppy mud, loss of provisions, and his own growing disgust. He only grunted an agreement and then followed with his usual question to his younger brother, "How's the arm?"

"Oh, it's okay," John assured. "My feet hurt so bad I don't even think about my arm at all anymore. I wish we'd take a long break, but then I'd rather keep walking then rest in the mud."

"I sure hope the rain stops," Paul added. "I think a big fight is brewing just ahead. I'd hate to fight in the rain."

"I think you're right about the coming battle." Bitterly, John continued his grumbling, "We've sure got ourselves into one big mess. I hate this business."

John's anger started to get the best of him. Paul recognized that he'd better quiet his younger, impetuous brother, "Me, too, but it's best not to talk about it. Just march! We'll have to stop for the night if we don't find the Rebels somewhere up this road."

"I guess you're right about that too," John finished. He always had to have the last word, even if it was a meaningless one. For the rest of the day the rain fell as thousands of Yankee soldiers marched over the now-hallowed ground where the first major battle of this sixteen-month-old war had been fought just a little over one year earlier. Many of their ranks had already forded that infamous creek called "Bull Run."

"Son, that's a very interesting testimony. I don't question your views whatsoever. I hope you know that. However, I do disagree. I respect you and I won't ask you to violate your personal convictions. But I do expect you to obey and give orders on the field. If we march into battle, I expect you to march with your company."

"General Jackson, sir, I already do just that. I've never shirked from my duties."

"I know. Reports from your fellow officers attest to your bravery in the face of the enemy. I respect your choice not to fire a pistol or strike with a sword. I believe that matter is between you and our Lord. I also believe you can lead with honor even if you refuse to take the life of our enemy. I expect you to make sure your men are placed in the best possible positions to inflict the most damage on our foe. That is your duty as a commanding officer. Do I make myself clear?"

"Yes, sir, General Jackson, sir," he replied, grateful that he would be allowed the privilege of continued service.

"Then, Captain, I expect you to do your duty. You're dismissed."

Salutes were exchanged and he left the house's bedroom that had been quickly converted into an office for the Second Corps commander. He exited the house and noticed that a very thick fog had settled over the open field spread out before him. He walked into the cloud and discovered the acrid smell of gun power and the odor of burning wood. It wasn't fog but smoke that surrounded him. To his far right, he heard thunder.

The booming noise called to him like a siren calling to a lost sailor searching for a safe port. Drawn deeper into the smoke, he eventually came across a group of slaves preparing a mass grave for fallen Yankee soldiers. One slave said, "Dee'z men be a fight'n to keep da states together. It don't make no sense."

Another gravedigger responded, "Yassuh, and Southern boys fight to protect they'z land." He paused for a second and then continued, "And to keep us on it. Dat don't make no sense neither. I can't understand how any man who calls he'z self a Christian can hold another brother in Christ in bondage. I'z can't read dat good, but I'z hear'd it say'z in da Bible that it t'was for freedom's sake that Jesus died to set us free."

"Amen!" the first slave agreed. "And, how can a man dat calls he'z self a Christian keep another man a slave who Jesus has set free? Dat don't make no sense, neither." Then he asked a chilling question that went directly to the heart of the matter. "How can they'z kill each other, you know, fellow Christians, with such rabid-dog hate? Don't Jesus say Christians supposed to love each other? I don't understand this mean hate. This here war makes no sense at all."

Not one slave noticed the man that stood by them and listened to their conversation. More booming sounds from the distance called him to move on in that uncertain direction. He walked on into the thickening smoke.

Suddenly the smoke cleared. He saw a tent. It looked strangely familiar, so he pulled back the entrance flap and leaned forward to have a look inside. The smoke was now inside the tent. As he tried to look around, he heard a familiar voice say, "Come in, come in. I'm very glad to see you again. Take a seat." It was General John Breckinridge. The man was puzzled by his presence. What was General Breckinridge doing in Virginia? Wasn't he somewhere in western Tennessee? But he couldn't bring himself to ask these questions aloud. He just adjusted the chair across from the general's table and sat down. He tried to make himself comfortable. General Breckinridge took a drink of coffee from his tin cup. Then he asked, "Have you figured out why we are fighting this war yet? Do you remember what I told you? I believe this war is about power and who is going to control it. Whoever controls the power, the

Yankee Republicans or us righteous Southern Democrats, gets to create the reality for our nation. What do you believe?"

He sighed heavily and replied, "No, sir, I just don't know. I'm not real sure what I believe anymore. I can't make any sense of it all. This war seems like a big mystery, one for the ages. I know the Lord knows and I've been praying that He'd grant me understanding. But so far He's been very quiet."

General Breckinridge looked him squarely in the eyes and commanded, "Then, son, you'd better get back out there and find out, and real soon. Go on now!"

Despairingly, he shrugged and made his way out of the tent. The booming continued and the smoke returned, enveloping him thicker than before. This time it burned his lungs as he breathed. He coughed violently. His head hurt badly and he began sweating heavily. He rubbed his burning eyes. He couldn't see but he could hear the crunch of footsteps coming toward him. He tried to focus on the tall and very thin figure of a man that approached and finally came into recognizable view. He couldn't believe what he saw. The boy's ashen face revealed a countenance that was even more sunken and haunted-looking then the night they first met. The boy's eyes held a doomed, distant stare that sent a chill up his spine and caused him to want to turn away from the boy. But no matter how hard he tried to run away, he was fixed in this place, face-to-face. Then the boy spoke in a distant echo and raspy voice, "Sir, thanks for helping me write that letter to my mother. I'm sure it was a big help to her. I didn't get a chance to properly thank you before, sir." Then, the boy passed him by and disappeared into the heavy smoke.

He stood motionless, speechless. It was Edwin Jennison, the young private from Georgia, killed in action at Malvern Hill. Seeing and hearing this apparition could mean only one thing, he must be dead too. But he felt alive. The great pain he felt in both his head and chest must mean that he's still alive. The booming continued. He walked on deeper into the smoke to a destination unknown.

He looked, and just ahead of him, prancing with his head up and tail wagging, Buster appeared. He seemed to be in a hurry to go somewhere. As he followed his nearly full-grown pup, the smoke cleared again. Another small farmhouse sat before him. Buster bounded up the steps, then curled up on the front porch. He walked up the stairs. The front door opened. He felt invited so he stepped inside. He walked past the front parlor on the right and a dining room on the left. He reached the kitchen at the rear of the house and saw a small table set with a hot meal for two. It looked like roasted chicken with mashed potatoes. The aroma caused him to feel very hungry and for a second he forgot about the pain in his head and chest.

"Sit down," a quiet deep-baritone yet soft and friendly voice commanded. He naturally hesitated but then grabbed the back of the chair, pulled it away from the table, and quickly sat. He was nervous because he could see the other side of the table, but not beyond. It appeared to him that he was alone, except for that voice. He looked at the bountiful food before him and picked up the knife and fork and started to attack the chicken. Then he paused, put the utensils down, and quickly uttered a prayer of thanksgiving for this wonderful meal.

"You're welcome," the voice declared.

He stopped himself from placing a piece of chicken in his mouth and said, "I'm sorry. I do appreciate the meal. I haven't been offered a supper this good in months. I guess I forgot my manners. Thanks again."

"You already thanked me when you prayed."

This statement stunned him. To whom was he talking? He looked quickly around the room. He saw no one. He put the fork back down on the plate and started to push himself away from the table, scared.

"Where are you going?" the voice inquired. "I know you are hungry and you said yourself you haven't had this fine of a meal in some time."

"I should be getting back to my unit."

"I agree. But I think you should eat something first. You need food for strength. After all, I prepared this meal just for you, Nathaniel."

"Who are you? Where are you?"

"I am right here. My sheep know my voice."

"You say you've been carrying mail back and forth between our lines and the Rebels for several months?" Colonel Blair couldn't believe what he was hearing.

"Yassuh, I has," Gabriel replied, still scared and uncertain what would become of him.

"And you give the mail to one of our men, he pays you, and you give the money to your boss? Don't you mean your master?"

"I'm not a slave!" Gabriel defended almost angrily. "Masser 'Calister set me free long ago. I still work for him at the post office cuz he still owns my wife and chill'n. But he promises to let me buy they'z freedom if I duz dis extra work for him. I'z earnt extra money and soon I'z might has 'nuff."

Colonel Blair's plan took further shape. "I see," he said. "Tell me, do you know the name of the man you exchange the mail with?" he asked, getting right to the point of his larger concern.

"No, suh, I don't ask cuz Masser 'Calister saz I don't need to know."

Disappointed, Colonel Blair chose another path of questioning, "Can you describe him to me?"

"Well, suh, he'z a real angry man. He always looks mad and he'z always yellin' at me. He'z a real big man, bigger than me, and his uniform has stripes on he'z sleeves."

"That could be twenty percent of the men under my command," Colonel Blair spoke aloud, but he was really talking to himself.

"Scuzz me, suh? I don't understand," Gabriel tried to cooperate. He hoped that by doing so he might just live to see his family again.

"Never mind what I just said," Colonel Blair was a little angry with himself for voicing his frustration. He needed to put a stop to whoever was profiteering by this scheme. However, if he didn't get this situation under his control, he might not be able to bring his military strategy to fruition. Regardless of his perceived problem, he still needed more information. He decided to continue the questioning, "Go on Gabriel, please. Tell me what else you know about this soldier."

"I'm sorry, suh, I don't have much else to tell," Gabriel declared, disappointed he didn't pay better attention. He hoped that he didn't ruin his improved standing with the colonel. "You see, suh, we always met at night. It was hard to see what he looked like."

"Very well," Colonel Blair walked back to his desk and sat down. He offered Gabriel a drink of water, which Gabriel took and drank quickly. As Colonel Blair watched Gabriel down the cool water, he decided to disclose his idea. "Gabriel, I have a proposition for you, one that I think you will accept because I think I have a way to free your family faster than under your current arrangement. Are you interested in what I have to say?"

Gabriel nearly dropped the cup of water. His eyes lit up as he responded enthusiastically, "Yassuh!"

Chapter 28

SHAMEFUL BEHAVIOR

The air smelled fresh from a recent rainfall. The cloudy night's sea breeze cooled his sweating forehead. He perspired more from anxiety than from the hot, humid August blackness that surrounded him. Many things could go wrong and he might be killed. He sat as quietly as possible; however, the sounds of night echoed from every direction. Crickets chirped, mosquitoes and other insects buzzed, the wind blew through the treetops, plus an occasional hoot from a distant owl rang out a chorus that caused him to quake with tormenting terror. Fear always got the best of him. The only way he knew how to combat it was to hum a spiritual hymn. He chose "Rock of Ages" to help calm his shattering nerves.

"Stop that fool singing," Sergeant Norse whispered as forcefully as he dared without shouting. He pushed his way through the thick peninsula foliage trying hard not to make too much noise as he approached the small clearing near the riverbank. "How many times do I have to tell you that you can't be making no noise, you have to be quiet? No one's supposed to be out here that ain't looking for trouble." Suddenly he broke through the last few branches and slowly approached Gabriel, cursing under his breath as he crossed the rocky shore.

When Sergeant Norse saw the extra mailbags piled in the small boat, he smiled. Quickly, he assessed his earnings and changed his tune. "Since I heard the signal from your boss the other night, I expected to see you soon. I thought you'd of been here last night. If you could tell time and get that fool singing under control, you'd make a first-rate soldier."

Pretending to be glad to see the Yankee warrior, Gabriel responded, "I'd much like that, suh. Do you think I could be a soldier?" he asked, knowing the probable answer.

"There ain't no way you, or any darkie for that matter, would ever be a soldier in my army," Sergeant Norse confirmed Gabriel's expectation. "Besides," Sergeant Norse continued cynically, "Who's going to carry the mail and make me a rich man if you were allowed to join? You want to see your wife and kids free don't you, boyo?"

"Yassuh, I'z duz," Gabriel responded humbly. Then he perked up announcing, "Suh, I'z got da mail and a pouch from Masser 'Calister in da boat over yonder. Duz you have any ting for me to take to him?"

"Yep, two full bags. I think the word is spreading that mail can be moved quickly between the two countries. And we are ready, willing and able to help folks do just that, right boyo?" Sergeant Norse looked around thinking he heard something back in the thick trees and underbrush, behind and to his left. He started to pull his revolver when suddenly a wild boar popped out of the wilderness undergrowth and headed for the river and a drink of water. Troubled by this brief disturbance, Sergeant Norse remembered the great risk he took. He looked back at Gabriel and ordered, "Well, boyo, you'd best be fetching that mail for me."

Frightened, Gabriel replied, "Yassuh. I'll go ta git dem, right 'way, suh." Gabriel moved toward the spot directed by Sergeant Norse.

Norse held his revolver at the ready. Something made him feel uneasy, as though he was being watched. He looked all around, but in the darkness he couldn't see much at all. He'd felt vulnerable before, but this was stronger. He couldn't shake his deep gut sense of imminent danger.

All was still. He could hear the sound of the water lapping against the shore. The boar had disappeared back into the woods. He heard it grunting and crunching through the underbrush. Gabriel walked back from his boat carrying the first bag of goods. He made his own assorted unpleasant noises that surely would attract unwanted attention. But something was wrong. He could feel it.

"Bring that bag and follow me," Sergeant Norse ordered.

Gabriel protested as Norse moved back toward the woods away from the little rowboat, "But, suh, I'z need to git back to da udder side wit da mail before da sun come up. It take long time to cross from here. And Masser 'Calister, well suh, he'd be real mad if'n the Rebel soldiers captured me. They'z maybe send me'z back to slavery."

"This won't take long. I need your help over there." A second later they both disappeared into the thick woods.

"What do mean you told him that you'd think about it," Catherine exploded. "What is the matter with you? What is wrong with you? Are you insane?" Catherine threw her dishtowel down to the kitchen floor and stepped aggressively toward her daughter.

Eleanor started to back away but stumbled into one of the kitchen table chairs defending herself, "But, but Mother, I—"

"Don't you 'but Mother' me," Catherine interrupted angrily, wondering if her plans for her daughter had just been ruined. Attempting to repair the breach, she asked, "Do you have any idea how he might feel right now?"

"Him?" You're not serious." *You asked for it, Mother. If a fight is what you want, I'm ready.* "What about my feelings? I'm not sure how I feel about Jason, and I'm definitely not going to marry a man just because he is available, is considered a 'good catch' in your mind, and offers me a beautiful ring to adorn my hand so that I can become his ornament."

"It's called a marriage proposal, dear," Catherine said in a condescending tone.

"I know that, Mother. I'm not stupid as you obviously must think!"

"Don't take that tone with me, young lady. I can see by your face you're angry. How dare you presume to know what I think," Catherine responded with corresponding anger in her eyes. She continued, "Don't put words in my mouth!"

The argument grew with increasing hostility. Both women's faces turned fiery red. Eleanor countered shaking her finger into her mother's face, "You haven't answered my question. Why do you care more about his feelings? Did you and Jason plan this whole thing? It wouldn't surprise me. You still want to control my life. This is so manipulative. Did you promise him that I would say yes? What did you think? If I saw the ring I'd immediately melt and accept his proposal? Do you really believe that I am desperate to get married?" Eleanor turned away from her mother and choked back tears that began to flow. With her back turned she fired her last shot before her emotional dam broke, "Or are you desperate to get me married? That's it isn't it, Mother? You want me to be cared for so that you'll no longer have to worry about me, especially if I'm married to a wealthy man. I guess it wouldn't hurt your future either!"

Eleanor was done. Catherine started her defense. She wanted to say that she loved her daughter and that she only wanted what was best for her, but Eleanor anticipated her mother's next move and held up her right hand behind her toward the sound of her mother and commanded, "Don't say a word, Mother. Right now, all I feel is hatred for both of you!" Her emotions overcame her. Feeling betrayed, Eleanor walked quickly toward the kitchen door and covered her face with her hands. Sobs began intensely. Once she reached the stairs that would take her up to her bedroom, the flood of emotions poured free. She climbed the stairs as fast as her feet could carry her.

Catherine stood alone in her kitchen, completely misunderstood, shocked, and sinking deeply into an uncharted heartache.

August 28, 1862

Dear Mother,

I know it has been many days since I last wrote to you. John and I have been marching with our unit every waking minute since we left Washington over a week ago. This is the first time I've had an opportunity to write. I hope this letter finds you and Eleanor well. Please don't worry about us. We will do our duty and we will keep our promise to honor our country and the blessed memory of our father.

I must confess that I've become weary of this war and I want it to end. I am willing to let the Rebels have their own country. The loss of life that we continue to suffer doesn't seem worth saving the Union.

I do have some good news to report this evening. Today we ended our march with a stroke of providential good fortune. This turn of events gives me renewed hope that we might gain an advantage and maybe even victory. We believe we trapped the famous General "Stonewall" Jackson and his detached army. We've nearly got his men surrounded. I believe that in the morning we will crush his small force with our overwhelming numbers. Hopefully, if we are successful, we will crush the enemy's will to continue this foolishness.

John's arm is healing well. He hopes to be fit for real action again very soon. He still complains about everything. He really dislikes army life. I don't think he will ever change.

Please continue to pray for our safety, that we will come home very soon.

Your loving son,
Paul

Dawn broke and a heavy fog hovered above the ground making it just as difficult to see in the morning as it had been during the night. Coupled with the thick forest and dew-drenched underbrush that surrounded them in the swamp, they could barely see a few yards beyond the culvert they nestled in throughout the long dark hours. The increasing daylight did little to heighten their spirits or to ease the tension of the situation. Morning birds welcomed the new day with song. Their sweet melodies replaced the frightening noises of night.

Neither man slept. Sergeant Norse restrained himself from killing Gabriel who constantly complained throughout the fitful night as they protected themselves from an unseen danger. The small dip in the ground provided a hiding place that could be easily defended, if necessary. Finally satisfied that all was well, Sergeant Norse holstered his revolver.

Gabriel broke the silence once again, instantly annoying Sergeant Norse as he protested, "Now I'z really in trouble. Masser

'Calister going to beat me good and probably my family too, for being so late."

"Shut up you fool. You've got nothing to worry about so long as I'm able to make excuses for you."

"How'z yuz gonna' do dat? 'Sides, I cain't cross da river in the daytime. I'd be caught fo' sure. And what 'bout my boat?"

"You tied it up good and tight didn't you?"

"Yassuh, I'z did, but we'z 'long way from it and I'z not sure, which way'z ta go."

Sergeant Norse pointed, "Just head that way. You'll reach the river soon enough. Once you're there, you should be able to find your boat. And while you're waiting for nightfall, you can rest."

"But what 'bout Masser 'Calister? He'z still gonna be real mad at me!"

"You leave him to me," Sergeant Norse stated proudly. "You've got no cause to worry. I'll give you a note that you can take to him, and I'll write it so that he'll know that it came from me. I'll explain everything to him and how we had to take extra precautions to avoid capture. You'll be fine. Besides, this is our first exchange in a long time and at a new spot on this river. He's got to expect delays once in awhile. He wants to keep this business going. He won't hurt you; you're the one that makes the crossings."

"I'z s'pose you're right."

"Of course I am. Yes, your boss must expect the unexpected."

"I'z tink he'z calls dem con-tin-gent-seas."

"What did you say, contingencies?"

"Yassuh. He'z sez day are udder plans when tings go wrong."

Sergeant Norse mused, "I guess you could say that's what we have here, one big contingency." He sat down on a stump and chuckled, "Contingencies." He pulled out a note pad and a small pencil from his vest pocket and scratched out a quick note to his business partner. He folded it and gave it to Gabriel. Once satisfied that it was time to go, he ordered Gabriel to head for the river.

Gabriel climbed out of the natural depression and walked south hoping that he'd find his boat but more worried that this Yankee might get away. He'd fully expected to be captured during the night, but the soldier had found a safe hiding place. Well, he'd done what he'd promised to do. It was up to that colonel to keep his word.

Gabriel walked a few yards away from the gully, and he was about to disappear into the thick woods when he heard a strange, gruff voice behind him say, "Where do you think you're going?" Gabriel thought the question was spoken to him so he turned around. He saw several armed Federal soldiers pointing their muskets directly at Sergeant Norse.

"What's you got in all them bags, Sergeant?" another soldier asked.

"It's none of your business, sonny," Sergeant Norse countered. Then he dropped the large mailbag he just shouldered and challenged all of them, "You boys on patrol or are you deserting?"

Another voice came from the woods, "They're on patrol under my command, Sergeant. We've been looking for you." A young, redheaded, freckle-faced lieutenant stepped out from his observation point, moved around his big sergeant and smiled as he approached Sergeant Norse. "It looks to me that you've got some real explaining to do. I'm sure Colonel Blair will be very interested in what you have to tell him."

Other soldiers arrived and escorted Gabriel to the point of capture. The young lieutenant said, "Thanks for your cooperation. Men, make sure to give him something to eat and see to it that he gets safely back across the river with the mail."

Sergeant Norse instantly realized what was happening and quickly pulled his revolver and yelled, "Why you double crossing—"

It happened so fast. The shot rang out but it was not carefully aimed. The private standing just to Gabriel's left had moved a step closer toward Sergeant Norse and partially shielded Gabriel. It was just enough. The bullet slammed into the boy's chest knocking him back into Gabriel and both men fell to the muddy ground.

Another soldier behind Sergeant Norse reacted quickly and clubbed the traitor in the back of his head with the butt of his musket. Sergeant Norse fell to the ground too, but he would recover in time.

The incident was over. Birds flew quickly away from the loud noise, many chirping their protest at the disturbance. The fog began to lift and the sunshine broke through the dense forest while another young life slipped into eternity.

"Here they come boys," Marvin yelled as he walked the line behind his men entrenched along an unfinished railroad embankment. This was a strong natural defensive position. The thick woods just to their rear hid the Confederate reserves massed together and waiting to engage the approaching enemy as soon as the Blue Bellies fully committed themselves to fight what appeared to be a small force. The Confederate artillery opened fire and began to punch deadly holes in the massed wave of blue that rolled toward them across an open, unprotected field.

The thunder of hooves could be heard to Marvin's left. He looked and saw General Jackson and his staff approaching. Jackson was in the process of checking the readiness of his nearly two-mile-long defensive position. As he approached near the center of his battle line, he came to a halt right in front of Marvin's men who were busy loading their weapons and preparing to meet the Yankee advance. Jackson took his field glasses from their case and peered intently toward the approaching horde. Yankee cannon fire exploded near, but their artillery officers still had not calibrated the range accurately. A few more rounds would correct that defect.

"By God Almighty, do you see that Mr. Smith?" Marvin could hear General Jackson speak excitedly to one of his aides.

"Yes, sir, I do, sir," Captain Smith replied.

Jackson pulled his glasses away from his face. Little Sorrel wanted to move, but Jackson held him with a firm word, "Whoa." Then, he turned to Captain Smith and commanded, "Mr. Smith, give these orders directly to Colonel Pendleton. Tell him to direct his fire on those massed troops moving there to our left. I want him to drive them toward our center. Do you see them, son?"

Captain Smith replied, "Yes, sir, I do. That large square, sir."

"Yes, Captain, that is correct." Jackson paused and then continued, "The idiot is using one of Napoleon's outdated infantry maneuvers. He's probably jammed an entire division together. They can't move quickly, turn efficiently, or fight effectively from that position. Yes, Mr. Smith, make certain that Colonel Pendleton fires at that group and tell him to fire at will. Don't spare a round of solid percussion shot. We'll break them apart and smash them badly, bunched that tight together. Make sure to check for damage before you report back to me. You'll find me near our right flank. Do you understand my orders, Captain?"

Captain Smith saluted crisply and answered emphatically, "Yes, sir!"

"Then, get going!" General Jackson commanded, returning his aide's salute.

"Yes, sir!" Purposefully, Captain Smith wheeled his mount and disappeared into the woods behind Marvin's company.

Jackson lifted up his face toward heaven and prayed loudly, "Thank you, my Father for showing me that a well-trained and highly-maneuverable small force can beat a larger and slower one any day." Then General "Stonewall" Jackson turned toward Company "G" of the Nineteenth Tennessee Volunteer Regiment and asked, "You men of the great state of Tennessee ready to fight this beautiful day that the Lord has made?"

Marvin proudly replied for his company, "We're ready to send them back to Washington today, sir!"

Jackson shouted, "Send them to their maker, and may God have mercy on them, for we shall have none!"

A loud, enthusiastic cheer went up for their commander. Jackson turned to his remaining staff, held up his right hand and commanded, "Let's go, gentlemen. We have work to do this very fine day." A minute later, they were gone from sight heading toward the right flank near Grovetown. The Yankee bombardment continued and grew more intense with each passing minute.

Marvin heard the reassuring commands of fellow officers of brother units to his left and right. Marvin echoed the same. "Steady, men! Hold your fire! Let them come in a little closer!" Marvin pulled his revolver from its holster and held it just above his head. Yankee artillery projectiles began to rain down just in front of their position. It was hard to see through the smoke and debris. Still, orders to fire had not yet come. Marvin commanded again, "Steady, boys!"

Then it began to Marvin's left. A volley of musket fire released at the blue mass, maybe five thousand fighting men moving directly toward him. "Now!" Marvin yelled as loud as his lungs and vocal chords could stand. "Open fire, boys! Let them have it!" An explosion erupted and a hail of bullets ripped into the concentrated blue troops. Many fell, but the mass kept moving. Grapeshot exploded in the Federal ranks tearing men to shreds. The concussions forced them to shift more toward Marvin's position. "Reload!" Marvin ordered calmly. He was a seasoned veteran now. The fighting still scared him, but he'd learned to control the paralyzing nature of this demon. However, he knew in the deepest part of his gut he wasn't prepared to die. He hoped this would not be his day.

Chapter 29

REBELS EVERYWHERE

The musket fire was hot and furious. Shells exploded all around him, sending men and horses in all directions. As quickly as they could recover, the ranks closed on the holes made by the enemy fire. The Yankees were close to the Confederate entrenchment when suddenly that hellish-banshee scream, the now infamous "Rebel yell," blew out of the woods just in front of the deep-blue line. With them came an equally demonic volley of lead, ripping into flesh and bone and sending many to the ground forever.

"My God! Where did they come from," Paul cried aloud. He didn't want to speak; it just came out. He was sure other men in his closed ranks thought the same thing. Paul's good friend, Sam caught a round in his left shoulder, nearly separating his arm from his body. Instinctively, he dropped his musket and grabbed his shoulder. The bayonet just missed Paul's right foot.

With this new thrust and threat of Rebel relief, the Yankee advance faltered. Quickly, the officers responded to this stall and rallied their men. After a struggling moment, the blue mass pushed forward again. Paul was scared. This was the tightest grip of fear he'd ever felt. Wide-eyed, he thought of his little brother, John, held in reserve with the other recovering wounded, safe. For that he was grateful. At least both of them wouldn't be killed today. Death surrounded him, just as real as the constant popping musket fire deafened him. The burning gun-smoke stung his eyes. The exploding shells of percussion and grapeshot shook the earth beneath his stumbling feet. A bullet zipped by his right ear. He felt its heat.

Fear grabbed Paul's heart in a painful vise and he dove to the ground. A private right behind him was hit in the head. Paul recognized the thud and crack and somehow he knew that round was meant for him. The private grabbed his head and dropped his musket, which landed on Paul. Next, the now lifeless young man fell on top of Paul. The boy's blood poured out onto Paul's back and then spilled to the ground pooling on both sides of him. Fortunately, the boy's body shielded Paul from the next cannonball that fell just a few yards to his right side. It sent more Yankees to their respective ends and Paul felt shrapnel hit the covering corpse as earth and rock rained down on top of Paul and his protector. Paul began to condemn himself for his cowardice, but he couldn't bring himself to his feet. He shook with fear and cried as he watched his fellows enter the fiery mouth of hell just a stone's throw from his spot on this Virginia field.

"Fire at will, boys," Marvin yelled. He squeezed off a round from his revolver, hitting a Blue Belly, dropping him in his stride. Marvin felt a bullet whiz by his left ear. Reflexes caused him to duck low. Once he recovered, he stood, walked to his right, and yelled, "Keep up your fire, boys. Pour it into them. Send them to hell!" Marvin pointed toward a hole in his line created by a shell blast vaporizing the men who were there a second before and yelled, "Reserve squad, fill that hole." Instantly, six men quickly moved into position and began shooting. The Yankees kept coming, closer, ever closer—too close. What should he do? Marvin looked to his left and right. As far as he could tell, the line held. He was determined to hold too. "Let 'em have it, boys!" Marvin fired another round stopping a Federal less than ten yards from his company's position.

Paul watched his regiment get close to the Rebel line. The fighting was intense and disorganized. Men used muskets as clubs. They fought hand-to-hand. Shells rained down, killing friend and foe alike. It was mayhem. Men dropped like harvested corn stalks. The scene seemed to play out for hours, but only minutes passed before men in blue started to turn and run. A Yankee officer yelled to rally his men, but it was to no avail. They sensed that they were beaten and backed away from their enemy without orders. Then they broke and ran. Another officer on horseback rallied a group close to Paul's right. The officer was able to turn them back into the fight. He had them form a crouched firing line. They reloaded their muskets and returned the Rebel fire. Their volley got the attention of the Confederate defenders who replied in kind. Another wounded Yankee fell near Paul. Paul crawled over to the man. As soon as their eyes met, they instantly recognized one another. The injured man cried, "Paul, thank God. Help me, please!"

Paul acted. He grabbed his friend and suddenly he had renewed strength. He had purpose. He would save his friend. He yelled, "I'll get you out of here, Henry!" Paul struggled but was able to hoist Henry onto his back. He moved quickly toward their Federal lines. He could see another division moving toward him and thought *they are too late. They can't help. They'll be massacred, just like my friends.* Paul said nothing. He stumbled toward the field hospital jostling Henry on his back.

Cheers went up all along the line. The Rebels had beaten back the first wave. They thought that they had won the day. But this day had just begun and another Yankee division advanced toward them. Marvin quickly assessed his company's strength. They'd taken a considerable beating but they held. He counted his losses—six dead, seventeen wounded. All of his men held their positions in line, even the wounded. He was very proud of their work.

Orders came for them to check their ammunition. A few minutes later, it was clear. They would need more and very soon if they were to beat back the approaching Federal assault. Marvin reacted quickly and commanded, "Take cartridges from the dead and pass them around." He looked at the wounded. They were being treated but as soon as Marvin had their attention he asked, "You wounded men, can you load rifles for the others?" All responded affirmatively. Even bandaged and bleeding they wanted to stay and fight.

Marvin knew he had to get help. He moved toward his left along the forest side of the railroad cut and sought out Major Duffy. He feared that the other companies suffered similar casualties. As soon as he found him, Marvin asked respectfully, "Major, sir, we're going to need more ammunition, sir! Can you send some our way, sir?"

"I am well aware of the situation, Lieutenant," Major Duffy replied. "I've sent for provisions. Ammunition cases should be here very soon. Get back to your post, Lieutenant. I'll make sure you and your men get what you need."

Marvin saluted smartly and responded, "Sir, yes, sir! But, sir, we're going to need reinforcements, too."

"I know Jenkins. Get back to your men."

Marvin hurried back to his company. The shelling continued and seemed to be growing in intensity again. The next Yankee division reached Rebel musket range. The firing began heavily once again. Marvin hoped that the ammunition would come soon, now would be better.

Marvin pondered the situation. He watched the next massive blue wave approach steadily. He realized that if the Yankees had coordinated their attacks better and sent this next division into action sooner, his men would have been overwhelmed. He wondered if reserves were available.

Once again, Marvin heard the distant thunder of Yankee cannon. They unleashed a mass barrage. The scream of the incoming projectiles signaled that these would be close if not right on target. Knowing that the Federal gunners were very good, Marvin commanded, "Take cover, boys! Get down!"

Most of the men barely had a second to react. The shells slammed into their line, throwing shattered bodies and debris in every direction. The explosions punched jagged holes in the Confederate makeshift breastworks.

Another round hit with similar deadly effect, then a third. The few minutes of this killing cannonade seemed to last for an hour. Painful screams of the wounded and dying softened even the hardened veterans. The officers did their best to encourage hearts that began to faint. Marvin ordered, "Steady, men! Get ready, boys, and take careful aim. Hold your fire. Make every shot count!"

Marvin heard another thundering sound; this time it came from behind him. It wasn't Confederate cannon, but horses. He looked and saw Jackson and his staff approach. This time they didn't stop. Jackson had a determined look on his face as he passed. His eyes seemed to be blazing with extreme intensity. Marvin had heard that Jackson's blue eyes got bluer in battle, but this time he saw it for himself. The man seemed possessed with a passion for fighting. It was inspiring, and Marvin felt a renewed strength.

Marvin turned to the business at hand. He assumed that the left flank needed Jackson's attention. He hoped that the Yankee's would head that direction. But if they hit his line again in the center, he was ready. He didn't want to think of the possibility that they might break through. He steeled himself and encouraged his men as he watched the second blue mass move right for his position.

A few more minutes passed. Again Confederate batteries answered and more lives disappeared. The smoke became so thick it was hard to see. Marvin couldn't tell where the Yankees headed, but it didn't matter. The intent of the massed formation was to act like a hurricane and cut a wide swath through the Rebel defenses. It was clear that Marvin's men would be in the thick of this storm again. The haze lifted confirming Marvin's prediction.

"Get ready, men!" Marvin yelled. He heard similar commands to both sides of his company's position. "Aim!" Confederate artillery fired at will, blasting as fast as the gun crews dared. They poured water on the barrels to prevent overheating. Marvin waited for the shelling impact. The blue horde was less than one hundred yards away, well within effective range. At the second of detonation, Marvin shouted, "Fire! Let 'em have it, men!" The Rebels were settled from the earlier action. This time, their first volley was more deadly. Yankees dropped and several regimental colors fell too. "Second rank, fire!" Another musket blast erupted and more Federal troops fell, but those that survived kept moving forward, unwavering.

"Reload! Fire when ready!" Marvin commanded. Random musket popping now took the place of the massed blasting, but it seemed to have little impact. The blue mass continued to roll toward the Confederate center. Their intent was clear. The Yankee objective was to break the center and split the line in two. It was a good plan, but it required rapid reinforcement. Marvin could see beyond the huge square and again the field was open. A trailing support division would be sufficient, but none appeared. Marvin wasn't sure if this was lucky for his comrades or stupidity on the part of the Union generals. It didn't matter because the fight was in front of him. He had to hold, but his line was thinning fast. He needed ammunition and reinforcements—now!

Marvin grabbed Private Clarke on the shoulder just after the man squeezed off a round knocking down a Blue Belly. Marvin pulled him out of the firing line. "I need you to take a message for me. Find Major Duffy. He's over there," Marvin pointed with his sword to the left of their line. "Request from the Major, with my compliments, for more ammunition. Also, request that more reserves be brought to our position immediately. Do you understand my orders, Private?"

"Yes, sir!"

"Go!"

Private Clarke saluted across his musket and turned to run. Marvin watched to make sure he ran in the right direction. He moved quickly for more than ten yards and then a Yankee cannonball exploded right on top of him, splitting him into tiny fragments. Instantly horrified, Marvin's spirit sank. He'd just killed that boy. But worse, precious seconds had just been wasted. For the first time in his life, Marvin prayed, "Oh God, forgive me! We need Your help. We need Your help now!"

Another shell exploded nearby, knocking Marvin to the ground, but it shook him back to the urgency of the moment. His men fired wildly, furiously, and deadly—those that remained anyway. He got up to a crouched posture and moved back to his men. He approached another private. He hesitated. Could he send another? He must. Then, he heard horses approach from the woods behind him. It was Jackson and his staff again. He couldn't hear over the deafening roar of battle but he could see Jackson waving commands emphatically. Suddenly Marvin felt an intuitive sense that his prayer had been answered. He furrowed his brow and briefly considered this possibility, but dismissed it and immediately returned to the business of killing.

Jackson shifted his force to meet the threat. A full regiment of fresh Confederates moved quickly out of the woods and crowded into the firing line. They began blasting at the Yankees who were less than twenty yards from the railroad cut.

The concentrated fire felled dozens. This time the impact caused them to slow their advance for a moment. Federal officers quickly ordered their men into a firing line formation. Even with men dropping all around, they organized, took aim, and fired a return volley that caused equal devastation in the Rebel ranks. Men all around Marvin were hit, some killed instantly. Marvin heard bullets zip past, slamming into the trees behind him with random thwacks that sounded something like a bad drum roll. Other thuds he recognized, mini-balls crashing into flesh and muscle. Others sounded like the cracking of a tree branch, bone being shattered as lead hit and struck deep into human limbs. Still the Yankees pressed forward, stepping over their fallen fellows left from the first assault. This small patch of Virginia soil would cost extravagantly. The day had just begun.

"We're almost there, Henry," Paul yelled to the man he carried. Henry groaned. Paul wasn't sure if Henry acknowledged him or if the moan was pain. Paul's back ached, his legs hurt, and his strength was nearly gone. "We're going to make it. Stay with me Henry."

The field hospital was swamped with wounded already. It would be impossible for Paul to get Henry looked at any time soon. Men were scattered all over the ground. Painful groans echoed all around. The smell of death hung in the air, choking Paul's natural instinct to breathe. The man on Paul's back seemed heavier. Paul needed a place to put Henry down.

Paul found an orderly and asked, "Where can I put my friend?"

The orderly stood, looked around and answered, "What's the matter with you? Are you blind? Can't you see what's going on around here? Just find a bare patch of ground and lay him down. I'll get to him as soon as I can." But the orderly didn't care to look at Paul's burden.

Paul was confused and ashamed by his cowardice. He needed to find redemption. He desperately sought relief from the plaguing guilt more than he searched for a spare patch of grass. No matter how hard he tried, Paul couldn't shake the haunting guilt. It hurt more than the growing ache in his chest. It was heavier than the man on his back. It demanded that he do something, and fast.

Paul looked around the shack that served as the army's hospital. Beyond the bombed-out shelter, Paul spotted a grassy area not yet populated with wounded men. Paul moved that direction and said, "I'm going to put you down over there, Henry." Paul reached the spot and carefully let himself down onto one knee. He gently slid Henry off his back and eased him down to the grass. As he did, he said, "I'll try and get someone to come over and care for you right away."

Paul's kepi sat over his eyes. He lifted his hat and looked at Henry for the first time since hoisting him onto his back. Henry's face told Paul that the whole effort had been a waste. His eyes stared blankly into the sky. His mouth was open and the color of his face had already changed to an ashen orange. Henry had passed several minutes earlier. Paul covered his face with his hands and began to weep bitterly, not for the dead soldier at his knees, but for his shame.

"President Lincoln must be removed!" Clement L. Vallandigham bellowed during his prepared speech before a large Chicago audience of Democratic Party faithful members. Vallandigham was the self-appointed leader of the radical, antiwar wing of the party, *"The Sons of Liberty."* As if directed, the crowd cheered with wild enthusiasm. "How many more of our sons, brothers, fathers, neighbors, and friends must be crippled, captured, or killed needlessly?" Vallandigham yelled rhetorically. "We just lost nearly fifteen thousand good men at another disaster in Virginia at the same battlefield where we suffered our first major humiliation. The overall casualty count is now close to seventy thousand with no end in sight. We all know that Mr. Lincoln provoked our Southern friends and neighbors to fire on Fort Sumter." More cheers erupted. As soon as the crowd quieted he continued, "He didn't need to start this war. Lincoln failed to use diplomatic pressure from England and France to negotiate a compromise to the slavery question and the preservation of the Union. No! He rushed us into this war. We were ill prepared to fight; we were untrained to prosecute a war of conquest. Virginia could have been our strong ally and voice of reason to the other Southern States. North Carolina was willing to speak calm to the other cotton-producing states. Lincoln has left them no choice. They were forced to fight against us because we invaded their lands." He paused to give the people a chance to soak in his message and then he instructed more passively, "I've corresponded with many friends and past colleagues that reside in Virginia, North Carolina, Tennessee, and Georgia. Their expressed sentiment is crystal clear. They want to negotiate for peace, a just and lasting peace." Then he shouted again, "Isn't that what we all want?"

The crowd responded, yelling various affirmations.

One voice declared, "We should impeach the fool!"

Another bellowed, "He's using this war for his own benefit!"

A deep-baritone angry voice cried, "He's destroyed our Constitution and our country!"

A woman shouted, "He's killing thousands of our young men, with no end in sight!"

Vallandigham took control again, waving his hands just in front of him to signal that they needed to quiet themselves. Then he continued in a calmer voice, "My friends, we have a plan. Several governors and congressmen know we can cripple this president if we succeed in gaining several congressional seats this November. I am seeking your help to become the next governor of Ohio. Can I count on your support?"

A voice planted in the audience yelled, "You can count on me, Clement!" As obedient sheep following a shepherd, other voices parroted similar declarations.

Vallandigham smiled his approval and finished, "Together, we can force President Lincoln to bring this war to a quick and peaceful end!" With that, he stepped away from the lectern and down from the gazebo's platform. He began shaking the hands of visitors and admiring fans. One in particular moved in close to the guest speaker and quickly introduced himself saying, "Sir, I'd like to support your campaign. How can I help you?"

The question was music to the politician's ears, more pleasant then the marching band that began to play a lively rendition of the "Battle Cry of Freedom." A lovely young lady sang its inspiring words and many in the crowd joined in enthusiastically. Vallandigham looked at the young man. His first impression was favorable. The young man was obviously well educated and finely polished. Vallandigham could read the unabashed political ambition glowing from his eyes and said, "Follow me, son. We'll talk some more after this show is over."

Chapter 30

REGROUP

S o what do you want?" The kind, deep voice probed.

"I'm not really sure," Nathaniel replied sheepishly. *Who are you and what do you want with me? Why do you care about what I want? What business is it of yours anyway? You have control over me now, why don't you tell me what I want.*

"I know you know, and I also know that you are sure. You just need to be honest with yourself and me. Now would be a good time to start."

"But it all seems so selfish."

"Maybe, but if you don't speak the truth, you won't be able to live the truth. So, what is your deepest desire? What do you think will really make your life whole?"

"Well," he paused. "I guess I want," he hesitated longer.

"Go on."

"I just want to live a normal life."

"Okay, that is a good start. What does it mean? What does a normal life look like to you?"

"I'd like to get married, have a family, and maybe own a small farm."

"Is there anything wrong with these desires? What's keeping you from them?"

"Well for one, I'm trapped here and I don't know how I got here. I don't know where here is, how to get out of this place, or even if I can."

"Do you want to get out? I mean do you really want to go back to the life you were living and start living your dream from that point forward?"

"Maybe not the exact life I was living. If I could, I would change some things about myself. I don't like the way I behave sometimes. Everything in life is so confusing, hard, painful."

"So maybe you don't want to go back. You feel safe here, don't you?"

"Yes, but as I said, I'm not sure where 'here' is? It doesn't seem to be anywhere. I'm not sure if I can trust this safe feeling. If I could leave, I still don't know how."

"You don't know or you don't want to?"

"What? Why do you keep asking me the same question?"

"Anger, good, now we are getting somewhere. You are starting to be honest."

"What do you mean? You see, this is exactly what I meant. Life is too confusing, who can understand it? If you want honesty, you're going to get it."

"What do you want?"

"I want to understand why must there be so much suffering. I want life to mean something." Nathaniel yelled, "I want to live."

"Okay."

Oh, God, my head hurts. I've never felt pain like this before. Where did that white-shadowy figure with no face go? Oh, God, no, I can't see. What is that warm wet thing on my face? I think I hear voices.

That thumping, I think it's my heart. I'm alive? I'm breathing, but that hurts too. I can't move my arms or legs. How can I stop that wet thing from hitting me? What is happening to me? Oh, God, everything hurts. Jesus, don't let me go to—.

Nathaniel opened his eyes.

"Well, look who just woke up? "We were sure worried about you. I began to lose hope that I'd ever see you awake again. Buster, give him some breathing room. Stop licking him. You're about to drown the poor man. This fool dog won't leave your side, no sir. Buster's been here, next to you day and night since he found you. He won't leave you, not even to eat. I've never seen such loyalty in a puppy before. Nate, you with me?"

Buster, oh, your breath is—. *Stop licking me.* "Marvin, is that you? I can't see very good."

"Yeah, it's me. You've been out for some time, several days. You missed the big fight. You'd a been real proud of your boys. We beat the Yankees so badly, I'm sure they're gonna call it quits. I wish you could've been there, seen your boys in action. It was a real hullabaloo." Marvin noticed Nathaniel wince and asked, "You OK? You look like you're in a lot of pain. After I came to, it took me a while to find you. When I did, I thought you were dead."

"My head hurts real bad," Nathaniel replied softly. Buster yelped, sending a piercing, painfully-high pitch knifing into Nathaniel's eardrums. "What happened to me?"

"I don't rightly know," Marvin replied.

I heard this before. Nathaniel found strength in his right arm. He picked it up from the cot, reached and felt the thick bandage wrapped around his head.

Marvin continued, "Like I said, when I woke up, you weren't anywhere near me. If not for Buster boy here, I'm not sure we'd ever have found you, least ways not nearly as fast. You were buried alive under a pile of broken stuff, mostly Yankee equipment. The worst was a large wagon wheel that fell right on top of you. But this dog of yours, he just dug and dug through the entire mess. Then he began to bark. He kept it up until Bailey joined him. The both of them dug and barked. I started yelling at them to stop their foolishness, but then I caught on to what they were trying to say. When I got to them, they had uncovered one of your legs. Buster had grabbed on to your pants and was trying to pull you out. I yelled for help and we got you free. I know this may not be what you want to hear right now, but you are lucky to be alive."

I don't feel lucky. Nathaniel reached and hugged the puppy's head against his pain-filled chest and grunted to let Marvin know that he was listening.

"The back of your head had a pretty deep gash."

Nathaniel imagined the damage and tried to pay attention.

"Some of the wood that fell on top of you was still smoldering. You have some bad burns on the back of both your legs. Doc said that if you ever regained consciousness, you'd be in pain for a long, long time, maybe months. I guess this here war is over for you."

Nathaniel closed his eyes. The pain was beginning to be more than he could bear. *I don't want to go home.* He groaned a response as if to say, "Go on."

Marvin didn't want to tell his best friend anymore, but he knew Nathaniel would want the truth. Marvin believed Nathaniel would take the real bad news best if it came from him. Marvin's face turned sober, sullen, withdrawn. Then he continued, "Doc says you may never walk again. He just doesn't know how badly the wagon-wheel hub hit you in the back. He says there's no way to tell if you're back is broken.

The pain, shock, and heavy sorrow took its toll. Nathaniel drew one gasping, pain-filled breath and lost consciousness again.

Marvin yelled, "Doc!"

The late summer evening was cool and clear. It was a good time of year to be in Chicago. It wasn't too hot, and not too humid. Some thought that it was the perfect time to be busy planning the future.

The rally ended early enough for the main party faithful to adjourn to the hotel's restaurant for a late meal. Jason Merritt had accepted Clement L. Vallandigham's invitation and thoroughly enjoyed the steak dinner and several glasses of imported burgundy. After dinner, the planners of the nation's future took to Vallandigham's spacious suite. It included two adjoining rooms. The hotel converted one into a temporary office and the other into a comfortable conference room. Some conferees sat around the large cherry-wood table. Others found places to relax in comfortable chairs or sofas. They sipped whiskey and smoked cigars as they plotted their next move. Jason was thrilled to be included and only briefly wondered why.

Jason watched Vallandigham address his visitors. He was a striking man, distinguished in every manner. He kept his dark-brown hair cut neatly, a medium length that covered half of his ears, and he wore it parted high on his right side combed to the left. He had a pleasant egg-shaped face, but his light blue eyes were tired. He showed signs of a man willing to make any self-sacrifice necessary to achieve his goals. Jason decided that Vallandigham was the man he would emulate.

Jason noticed an odd, nearly ironic feature. Vallandigham wore his beard in the exact same style as the man he wanted removed from the White House's Oval Office. Like Lincoln, Vallandigham had a mole on his right cheek. Jason shrugged and simply decided that this was one of life's strange little coincidences.

The fiery, yet stately Vallandigham set the overall meeting objective, "Gentleman, we must win as many seats as we possibly can in both houses this November. We must regain control of our nation. The Black Republicans are ruining our country, killing our people, and destroying our tenuous relationships abroad."

Several voices in the smoke-filled room echoed his sentiment. "We need to take back Illinois for the Democratic Party and never let it go again. If we do that, we'll send a message to that devil Lincoln that he can't even deliver his home state," James Dailey a rather rotund and sweaty, short, balding man cried out.

"If we win seats in Ohio, Massachusetts, and New York, we'll crush those stupid Republicans," Donald Hastings added. "Lincoln will have no power. Then we can bring this foolish war to a just and peaceful end."

An angry voice yelled from a dark corner of the room, "Why wait until November? I say we kill congressmen from states that have Democratic governors. They will appoint our own people to fill the vacancies."

No one objected to what Jason considered a shocking statement. Maybe they were drunk and didn't care about possible assassination conspiracy consequences. Possibly a more intoxicating spirit—the overwhelming passion for power—held them captive. Jason absorbed the moment, embraced the possibilities, and smiled.

Coldly, another voice stated, "Why stop at a few senators and congressmen? We should kill Lincoln. He's the cause of this war."

Several men grunted their agreement. A small man sulked in a smoky, shadowy corner and took the last statement to heart. An act like that would surely guarantee him fame. He would go down in history, a man no one would ever forget.

Vallandigham brought the men back to the main theme and declared, "Gentlemen, those are all fine ideas. I appreciate your passion to do what is best for our nation and its future. Let's put this energy to work. We need to expend ourselves from now until the November elections. So long as the Federal Army shows itself incapable of stopping 'Bobby Lee,' we will win back our seats in

Congress." He paused for a moment and then added enthusiastically, "Agree?"

All of the men agreed loudly. Some mimicked Vallandigham's enthusiasm; others mumbled or grunted their assent. But all of them felt very proud of themselves and their plans. They believed that the war would be over by Christmas, even if it meant that the Southern Confederacy would be a separate nation. Peace at any price was more important than unity.

Late summer heat collided with early cooler fall air. During the night, rain fell for the first time in two weeks. It brought a chill as it subsided. A thick fog replaced the morning rain and hid the sunrise from this mid-September morning.

Marvin crutched his way from his tent through the heavy mist to the field hospital where he spent most of his day talking with his friend who started to show signs that he might make a full recovery.

Bailey bounced along his side. The black Labrador puppy ran back and forth through the camp making friends with soldiers along the way. It was easy for Bailey to keep up with his master who couldn't move very fast, walking with the funny sticks. Along the way, Marvin and Bailey came face-to-face with Captain Nash.

"Where are you and that mangy mutt going today?" Captain Nash challenged, as if Marvin needed to report to this man.

Respectfully and with correct military bearing Marvin replied, "Sir, I'm going to the hospital to have my wound redressed. It's still oozing some, and my bandage needs to be replaced."

Nash furrowed his brow and gave Marvin an angry stare as he looked down at Marvin's leg. He grunted disapprovingly as he continued his inquisition. "I guess I can let you go. It's too bad that the bullet didn't hit you in the head. This army would be better off without you and that dog around. How many times do I have to tell you to keep that damned dog away from me? He's nothing but trouble. Didn't I tell you that I'd shoot him if he got in my way?"

Marvin defended his four-legged friend, "He ain't bothering nobody else in my outfit and besides, the boys really like having him around."

Bailey sat next to Marvin and looked up at both men talking. He panted freely and his big pink tongue hung out one side of his mouth. He sensed the loud man's anger. Instinct told him to stay away from the mean one.

"I guess I'll let it go, again! If you weren't starting to show some worth to this army, I'd shoot you both right now and be done with you. At least you stopped a Yankee bullet from hitting one of our real fighting men." Captain Nash looked suspiciously at Marvin and breathed heavily as he finished granting Marvin permission, "Go on about your business, and keep that damned dog away from me!"

Marvin clutched his crutch tightly and rendered a sloppy salute, holding his right hand loosely against the brim of his kepi. Captain Nash seemed to recognize the feigned respect. He didn't return Marvin's salute and grumbled as he passed Marvin, "What an idiot. We'd all been better off if you'd been killed."

Marvin replied, "Thank you, sir." He dropped his salute, spat on the ground, repositioned his crutches, and hobbled toward the camp hospital. Bailey followed, wagging his long, black tail.

Several paces later, Marvin said to Bailey, "Don't you worry none, boy. If that bad man ever tries to hurt you, I will kill him." It was more than an idle threat in Marvin's heart and mind.

Nathaniel woke up. He stared at the mud-stained canvas roof above his head. *I feel better today. I'm glad it's cooler.* He looked around the open-sided shelter that served as the Second Corps field hospital. *I don't think I'll ever get used to that smell. I wonder who died in the night.*

The numbers in the hospital decreased daily. Some men were finally well enough to travel and returned home. Many died of their wounds or secondary infections caused by their weakened conditions, a few like Nathaniel recovered slowly, and still others were strong enough to return to duty. Each day, the overall scene improved.

I do believe Doc will release me to return to duty soon. Nathaniel came from a long, near-death sleep to an alert, ready-to-act man who had no idea how sick he had been. *My head still aches, but I want to get up and walk some around some more today. I want to get out of here. I hate this place. I can't believe how much I feared it.*

Nathaniel pulled himself up onto one elbow. His motion woke Buster. Instantly the puppy was on his feet and looking into the eyes of his best friend. Nathaniel reached with his right hand and patted the chocolate Labrador on his squared head. Buster lifted both front paws onto the cot's edge. "Easy, boy, stay down," Nathaniel said anticipating Buster's move. He held the puppy down and smiled at the young dog. Buster licked his master's left hand. Nathaniel watched two orderlies remove a dead man's body. *Another loss, too bad. I suppose I should be grateful to be alive, but why did I get a second chance? I guess I shouldn't think too much on it.*

Look who's coming. Nathaniel looked into Buster's big, brown, happy eyes and said, "I see your brother coming to visit us again."

Buster closed his panting mouth and cocked his head to one side. He raised his ears trying hard to understand the sounds that came from this creature he attached himself to affectionately. Nathaniel sat upright. He reached behind Buster's floppy ears and scratched, much to the puppy's delight. Buster tried to mouth Nathaniel's left hand to show his appreciation, but suddenly his master stopped the wonderful touching and made another loud noise.

"Morning, Marvin," Nathaniel waved. Buster turned to look.

"We'll be moving out soon, I can feel it!" Marvin said mystically, as he sat down on the tree stump that served as a chair near the foot of Nathaniel's cot.

Nathaniel challenged, "That don't seem right." "Didn't you tell me that General Lee was wounded in the last fight? We shouldn't move out until he's well."

"Oh, he's well enough," Marvin quickly countered. "He rides around camp in an ambulance making sure everyone sees him. He's proving to all of us that he's one tough 'Old Granny.' He's got that wagon set up like a rolling staff office. You should see him try to read reports with those two thick bandages on his hands."

An orderly came to redress Marvin's leg. Nathaniel interrupted the procedure and asked him, "Do you know the extent of General Lee's injuries?"

The orderly stopped what he was doing and answered, "He's got one broken wrist and the other one is badly sprained. He'll be fine in a few weeks."

Nathaniel asked skeptically, "Are you sure?" *Why are you being hard on this man? He's just doing his job. Ever since that haunting dream, I question everything.* With a mean expression on his face, Nathaniel inquired, "How did it happen? Do you know?"

Marvin just shrugged his shoulders and looked foolishly uninformed. The orderly didn't have much to add but sheepishly, simply offered, "Sir, I'm not sure if what I heard is accurate. But I was told that one of our own men caused the accident."

Nathaniel shot back, "That's a lie!"

Nathaniel's accusation stunned Marvin, but he defended the soldier and interrupted, saying, "Let the man tell it, Nathaniel. My word, what's gotten into you? You know as well as I that anything is possible in war. You, more than anyone, should know that by now." Marvin turned to the orderly and said, "Please forgive my friend. He ain't been himself lately. Go on now, tell us what you know."

The orderly swallowed hard and looked fearfully at the angry man in front of him. Then he turned to Marvin and said, "There's not much to tell. As I said, I don't know how true this is but after the fight was over and the Yankees skedaddled back to Washington-town, General Lee was standing by his horse. I think it was the next day. Anyway, some of our boys thought that General Lee and his staff were Yankees and fired at them. Lee's horse jumped and bolted. General Lee's hands were wrapped in the reigns and the horse dragged him for a ways. That's how I heard it happened. He's lucky he wasn't hurt worse."

Nathaniel shook his head and thought, *he's lucky?*

"I'm not interested, Mother," Eleanor replied firmly as she straightened garments on a rack of clothing near the dress shop's front entrance.

"But you must go, dear," Catherine insisted. "Your father was a strong supporter of the Republican Party in this state. Many very important people got behind your father's promotion of President Lincoln when he was just a political nobody."

"Important to you, maybe," Eleanor challenged. "I don't see what any of it has to do with me."

"Not a thing," Catherine assured. "It's just that Mayor Ramsey asked us if we'd make a showing at the fund-raiser benefit dance. Many folks consider your father a hero. It would look favorable for the party if his widow and daughter appeared in honor of his memory. God knows, the party can use all the help it can get right now, the way the war is going so badly."

"So now you want to use me to raise money?" Eleanor snapped. "Is there no end to your manipulations? First you try to arrange a marriage between Jason and me, and now you want to parade me around to raise money for the political party that is destroying our country and losing the war! At least that is one thing on which Jason and I agree. Mother—" Eleanor straightened her back and placed her hands on her hips, "—if I go to this fund-raiser, will you promise to stay out of my life?"

Catherine was stunned again. She couldn't believe the changes in her daughter and that her child would talk to her in this disrespectful manner. Didn't Eleanor realize that she wanted a good life for her daughter? She hung her head down and consented, "Yes, dear, I promise." No sooner did those words leave her mouth, she perked up again with a fresh thought, "But I just know you will have a wonderful time!"

Eleanor returned to sorting through the clothes as she answered, "We'll see, Mother." Eleanor rolled her eyes and sighed deeply as she finished, "Now, Mother, can we finish getting this store ready so we can open for business?"

"Yes, dear," Catherine breathed easier and walked back to the counter to make sure the cash drawer was in proper order. She smiled, knowing that she had won a small victory. *Jason will be pleased.*

The nation's capital city was coming apart at its seams. Washington, D.C., was flooded with tens of thousands of disheartened troops from the retreating Army of the Potomac. Furthermore, newspaper reporters from across the country, as far away as San Francisco, and some from Europe swamped the halls of government. All these mixed with angry citizens who attempted to receive an audience with any public official who would rise to the surface long enough to cross the streets swollen with idle people.

Through this sea of madness rode the president on a black horse that was too small for his extraordinary long legs. He needed a man who could restore order to his beaten and battered army and who might return some hope to Washington, D.C., and the rest of the country. He humbly sought the service and support of the man he'd removed from command just weeks ago. Lincoln reined the small black horse to a stop in front of the residence of Mary Ellen and Major General George B. McClellan.

Chapter 31

PARTY POLITICS

The sound of an army of seasoned warriors on the move broke the peace of the Shenandoah Valley. Through this breadbasket of Virginia snaked a long, winding gray and butternut line. It marched methodically through the rolling hills, lush valleys, thick forests, and clear, fresh streams of this northwestern portion of the most prominent Confederate State. The people who resided in this territory were loyal to the cause of saving the Union and bitterly divided among themselves whether or not to secede. But after President Lincoln provoked the good citizens of South Carolina to fire their guns at Fort Sumter, and the North cried out for revenge, fate was sealed for these Virginians. Eventually, proud patriotic voices cried aloud for liberty and that it would be better to die fighting for one's freedom then to submit to tyranny.

Now they, with many others from sister Confederate States, moved in an orderly manner, but their steps were far from precision drill. Occasionally an officer or a hardened noncommissioned veteran would use his power of persuasion to encourage some who showed signs of weariness. They carried all that they possessed either on their person or on the noisy, clanging wagons that followed close behind each regiment. The early September sun burned hot upon the men, horses, and mules that labored northward. It was near midday. A rest would be needed if they were to continue another mile. Most of the thousands had no idea where they were headed, nor did they care.

General Robert E. Lee submitted this idea to advance north to President Davis, who approved the plan after questioning it in detail. Lee hoped that his army in the east, combined with a similar move by General Braxton Bragg in the west, would encourage England and France to recognize the Confederate States of America officially as an independent sovereign nation-state. Lee convinced Davis that English and French officials would see that the Confederacy acted like a nation. It not only had the will to defend itself but the strength to take its fight to the enemy on their soil. If accomplished, Abraham Lincoln would be forced to negotiate a quick end to the war.

Finally, the orders came down the line. The march halted and the men scattered off the dusty road to find a shady tree to rest beneath, maybe even grab some much needed sleep. Nathaniel dismounted Max and walked him into the woods that bordered each side of the Valley Turnpike. He tied the horse up to a tree surrounded by grassy undergrowth. Before Nathaniel secured the animal, Max began to gorge himself on the sweet greenery. Nathaniel let the large steed graze freely. Nathaniel's legs were still stiff from his injuries and lack of use. He was grateful that he didn't have to walk, but riding hurt his back and tortured his burned legs. He limped toward the regiment wagons and eventually he found the old buckboard that carried his faithful friend Buster. Nathaniel was hot, tired, thirsty, hungry, and in pain. He knew that the pups would be hungry and thirsty, too. He would share what little fresh water he had in his canteen with the dogs. As he approached the wagon he called, "Buster, Bailey! You boys awake?"

As if on command, two Labrador puppy heads popped up over the side of the buckboard. Both dogs panted heavily, responding to the hot, humid, heavy, dusty air. They fixed their gaze on the approaching man and their tails began to wag rapidly.

Nathaniel reached the wagon and quickly patted both dogs on their respective heads. As Buster tried to mouth Nathaniel's right hand, Nathaniel asked, "You boys want some water to help you cool off?"

Bailey cocked his head trying to understand the words. Buster was so happy to see his master he jumped out of the wagon. Nathaniel caught him in mid flight, which caused a stabbing pain in his lower back. He just grunted and quickly put Buster back in the wagon saying, "Easy, Buster, easy now, boy! You'll get your chance to play."

"Okay, Buster, just settle down. Where's that little wooden bowl we use to feed you boys." Nathaniel reached into the wagon and found their dish. "Looks like these flies are finishing off your leftovers." Nathaniel shook it and scattered the pests. He pulled the stopper off of his canteen, and poured some warm water into the basin. Both dogs tried to lap up the water as it fell into the basin, splashing some of the life-sustaining liquid. Nathaniel chided angrily, "Boys, you're spilling the water. Stop it!" That dark venom spewed out again. *Where is that coming from?*

"Easy, Nate," Marvin called. "They're just puppies. They don't know no better."

Nathaniel turned to greet his friend, but the friendliness he once knew was no longer evident in him. He just hung his head, silently ashamed at his own behavior.

"Nate, what's gotten into you lately?" Marvin asked sincerely, knowing that his friend had changed dramatically since that terrible day a little over one week ago. "You ain't yourself. You've been so mean; I think you should stop being the regiment's chaplain."

"Maybe I should."

That response surprised even Nathaniel, but Marvin quickly challenged, "What? You can't be serious. I was just funning with you to try and get you to snap out of your doldrums. I didn't really mean anything by it."

"But maybe I should, Marv. I don't think it's fair to the men when I have so many doubts myself."

"Nate, you're talking crazy. Why, I don't know another man in this here army, or anywhere else for that matter, who knows the Bible as good as you. You'd be wrong to quit preaching. It's what you love to do. It's what you were made for, and you know it."

"Not any more." Nathaniel stopped scratching Buster's right ear, turned around, and walked away. *I can't shake that dream. It felt more real than just a dream. I nearly died. Most men soften, but what's happening to me?*

Marvin stood with the puppies, staring at his friend as he gingerly left. Marvin was stunned and speechless. Buster jumped out of the wagon and happily hurried after his forlorn friend who ignored him altogether.

Once again, the Rockford Hotel's main ballroom served the local community's Republican Party's campaign fund-raising dinner extremely well. Small by a larger city's standard for an event forum—like nearby Chicago—the elegant room comfortably served the one hundred or so contributing guests.

The wait staff stretched themselves more than usual. Each server handled three to four round tables of eight diners. By design, the center of the room provided a nice focal point for folks to mingle. A large, twelve-foot-by-twelve-foot beige polished-marble square covered the middle of the hall. Directly above, an elaborate oil-lit crystal chandelier hung majestically and ruled the banquet lounge with its light.

Opposite the French-style entry doors, a small stage consumed most of the far wall. A lectern stood in the center of the stage, used by the evening's guest speaker who frequently gestured to the portrait of Abraham Lincoln hanging on the wall directly behind and above him. A large stone fireplace commanded the left exterior wall. This warm September evening the fireplace remained cool. Two large picture windows framed it. Thick cranberry-red draperies drawn ceiling-to-floor covered the windows. Unfortunately, the expensive window dressings clashed badly with the red, white and blue bunting that hung, just above door height, all around the room.

In the far left corner, a curved, dark-walnut railing separated the room and stage. A string quartet occupied this somewhat isolated spot. They continuously played softly so as not to overwhelm the deals being worked on the floor.

Cigar smoke filled the room as waiters scurried about providing adequate liquid refreshments to the donors and other honored guests. Through the haze and commotion, he spotted her, standing to the right of the stage near one of the kitchen access doors. She cheerfully spoke with the evening's host and master of ceremonies. He approached cautiously. The last time they spoke, the conversation had failed to go as well as he planned. Fortunately, the local leader of the Rockford Republican Party, Mayor Ramsey, had finished extending his personal gratitude for Eleanor's gracious appearance and left her for another conversation. Now he moved quickly to close the gap. Confidently walking up to her, their eyes met and he declared, "Good evening, Miss Ellis. I am very pleased to see you here tonight."

"Why I can't believe my own eyes. Mr. Merritt, it is good to see you, too. But, I must say, I thought you were a die-hard Democrat and that you hated all Republicans. I can't understand why you spend your busy time with me because if I could vote, I'd vote Republican. What on earth are you doing here?" Eleanor asked the man who had made his intentions known to more than Eleanor and her mother in recent weeks. This further embarrassed and infuriated her as bits of gossip grew like an aggressive cancer and eventually reached her ears.

Jason smiled, waved at another influential member of Rockford's financial community, and answered, "You are correct, my dear lady. I have come to learn what my political enemies plan so that I can help my party counter their moves. They are such trusting fools. They think that just because I'm here, I am one of them. It will be easy for me to gain the information I need."

"You, sir, are a cad," Eleanor rebuked teasingly letting him know that in a way she really didn't disapprove and that she too still had interests in him. "Just what do you hope to learn?"

"Well, first I want to find out who they intend to promote for both houses of Congress," Jason stated under his breath and craning his neck to get a better look at another man.

"Then, I suppose, you will uncover as much dirt as you can on these men?" Eleanor probed.

Jason smiled and added, "And if we can't find any real facts of indiscretion, we'll make up plausible stories to call their credibility into question. They will have to spend their precious limited resources defending our false accusations."

That's an odd thing to say. No, it's terrible. Who is this man? Maybe Republicans act the same way. I guess it's not that important. After all, he's just a man.

Catherine nearly floated up to the engaging couple. Smiling, she spoke to them happily. "Now isn't this a wonderful sight, you two together in a lovely setting like this." Catherine waved her shawl-covered right arm as if to put the elegant grand ballroom on display for first-time visitors. She turned back to the pair and then looked directly at Jason and asked, "Did you enjoy your dinner, Mr. Merritt?"

"Yes, ma'am, I most certainly did. The roast beef was done to perfection. And I couldn't agree with you more that the present company makes the evening even more perfect. Oh, and please Mrs. Ellis, call me Jason. I think we are close enough friends, nearly family, if you will do me the honor," Jason paused to make it clear to whom he directed his last few words. Smoothly he continued, "I think it's fair to dispense with all formalities."

"You're so sweet, Mr. Merritt," Catherine chuckled and acted embarrassed. "I mean, Jason. Isn't he sweet, Eleanor?"

I know what you're doing, Mother. But for father's sake, I will play along. I don't want to start an argument. Cheerfully, Eleanor replied, "Yes, Mother, Jason is a kind and considerate man. We have been enjoying a pleasant conversation about the political campaign."

Assuming that she understood what the conversation was about, Catherine added, "Oh, my, wasn't the speech by his Honorable Thaddeus Stevens inspiring? I do believe he is a wonderful congressman. I think your father would approve of his nomination to return to Washington on behalf of Pennsylvania. If he were alive, I'm sure he'd promote Mr. Stevens' candidacy."

Jason questioned, "You really think he's the best man for the job? Don't you think his views are a bit radical? Really, do you think the way to end the war and restore the Union of the United States is to conquer and punish the South? And his idea about putting Negroes in the army to fight for their freedom and equality, it's nonsense. That craziness will surely infuriate even the moderate Southern slaveholders. With that kind of talk, how can we ever hope for a fair, negotiated peace?"

After being bombarded by so many questions, Catherine retracted her own thoughts and sheepishly replied, "Well, what do I know?" Then she defended herself, saying, "I'm just a woman and not very well-versed in these matters as you men seem to be. I'm not really interested in such things," Catherine confessed.

A little surprised at her mother's submissiveness, Eleanor asked, "Mother, then why do you think Father would have supported Mr. Stevens?"

Catherine gathered her thoughts together quickly and replied only to her daughter, "Well, dear, he seems to say the things your father used to say. I remember him quoting President Lincoln when he ran for Congress before the war, '*A house divided against itself cannot stand.*' Mr. Stevens seems to support the conviction that we must be one nation, no matter what the cost."

Jason couldn't help himself and interrupted, "Even at the cost of your own sons?"

Both women were stunned by the abrupt, rude question. Catherine breathed heavily and brought one gloved hand to her mouth to cover the fact that her lower jaw had just dropped with a gasp. In disbelief, Eleanor took a step back away from this man who spoke so presumptuously, so arrogantly. Suddenly, she felt strongly that this dinner party should be over for her and her mother. There was something that troubled her deep in her soul and she desperately felt a need to speak to her father. She wanted to run, but instead she spewed a strong rebuke, "How dare you talk to my mother like that. If I were a man, I'd demand satisfaction for the dishonor you just displayed."

Jason was taken by surprise by Eleanor's response. He didn't think he'd done or said anything wrong or that wasn't true. In fact, he believed that Eleanor agreed with him and that he was helping Catherine clarify her thinking on the cost of the war. He knew it should stop immediately, if not sooner. Without acknowledging that he possibly did anything wrong or was willing to take responsibility for any harm committed, he defended himself saying, "I'm sorry if I offended you in any way. I was just—"

"Just what?" Eleanor stopped him cold and wouldn't let him finish. "What business is it of yours to tell my mother, or I, what sacrifices we're willing to make. My mother lost her husband, I lost my father, and you've lost nothing or anyone. It's my guess," her voice became louder, "you've profited by the war and will most likely continue to do so. This terrible war may take my brothers, too. Cost what it may, if slavery stands between preserving our nation and your Rebel, slaver friends, then I say, let this hateful and peculiar Southern institution, the source of all our trouble, be destroyed."

"But surely you can't mean—"

"I'm not exactly sure you really belong here, Mr. Merritt," stating his name formally, knowing others watched and listened. *I hope you are embarrassed. But, I suspect it is impossible to shame the shameless.* She finished sharply, "I think you should take your leave of this place, sir!"

Jason stared at Eleanor with a puzzled expression on his face. Then he looked at Catherine. She was biting back tears. She buried her face into her handkerchief. He turned back to Eleanor. He was dumbfounded. He felt rejected again. It stirred anger deep within. He was just trying to help, but obviously these simple-minded people just didn't understand his goodness. He decided to withdraw and said, "I see that you don't have it within your heart to forgive me, so I will bid you ladies good evening." He bowed slightly at the waist to feign respect, turned and walked away. He wanted this woman who spoke her mind. He wondered how he could win her heart.

As she watched Jason slink away, Eleanor said to her mother, "Do you believe the nerve of that man?"

Catherine choked back her tears and quivered, "Please, dear, take me home."

Eleanor looked at her mother who was flushed with emotional pain. God only knew the pang in her widow's heart for the memory of her beloved husband. It stabbed deeper for her two sons who marched into harm's way again. Eleanor took her mother's arm, breathed deeply, and sighed. Intuitively, she knew the war was far from over. Eleanor wished she could do something to bring it to an end. If only Paul and John could come home, they could relieve her mother's pain.

As the two women left the hotel, Eleanor wished she could talk to her father.

Chapter 32

INVASION

W hat did you find?" Paul asked, skeptical but excited at the same time.

Corporal Bart Mitchell of the Twenty-seventh Indiana Regiment repeated his claim confidently to the small group of infantry soldiers gathering around to hear the strange news. "I'm telling you, fellas, we found operation orders signed by old Bobby Lee himself. I read a little of the writing. It said on the top of the page, *"Headquarters, Army of Northern Virginia, Special Orders, No. 191.* I was with Sergeant John Bloss at the time. If you don't believe me, you can ask him yourselves. He'll vouch for me."

Private Scott Adams asked, "Where did you find them?"

A new recruit, Private Tommy Wiles, impetuously replied for Corporal Mitchell, "You had to have found them somewhere along the Frederick Road. After we broke camp near Clarksburg, Maryland, this morning, we marched northwest on the Frederick Road, which connects Clarksburg and Frederick. My guess is that we were somewhere near Urbana."

"Let Mitchell finish," Staff Sergeant Tim McCoy came to Mitchell's aid. "Boy, you need to learn to speak only when spoken to, understand?" McCoy tolerated the kid, but he needed the information Corporal Mitchell had to report. McCoy was a very large man, one of the tallest in the entire army. Many teased him that he was a natural target for the Rebels, but he was a seasoned veteran who had fought in the Mexican war and he knew how to keep his head down in a fight. He gave Mitchell a reassuring gaze to continue.

Mitchell recognized McCoy's nonverbal command and continued, "We just came over that high ridge yonder."

Private Wiles broke in again, "That's Parr's Ridge."

Sergeant McCoy turned to the private and with his deep, gruff command voice nearly shouted, "Who cares, Private know-it-all? I need Mitchell's information about those papers. I'm ordering you to keep your mouth shut."

Mitchell continued to disclose the details, "When we broke ranks to eat and rest, we went foraging for food in those wide-open meadows." Mitchell pointed to the ridge as he continued. "Just beyond one of the cornfields, we saw an apple orchard and beyond that we could make out a small farmhouse and barn. Sergeant Bloss hoped we might find some chickens. He wanted some fresh eggs."

Private Wiles could not control himself and interrupted again, "Problem is, most folks 'round these parts took much of their livestock as they hightailed further north. They feared the Rebels were coming to take their livestock and anything else they could steal."

Sergeant McCoy's tolerance ended. He yelled, "Will you shut up and let Mitchell talk?" It seemed that the extremely hot afternoon weather made everyone short-tempered.

Corporal Mitchell spoke freely, "We passed through a wheat field that was partly harvested. It looked like the folks just up and left in the middle of bringing in their crop. I guess our replacement is right about the locals. Anyway, a large maple tree stood near the

328 · DESTINATION HOPE: SEPARATION

barn and we spotted a Confederate officer's jacket hanging on one of the lower branches."

Paul chose to show an example of proper military behavior for the aggravating Wiles. He asked respectfully, "Is that where you found the orders, Corporal Mitchell?"

"Yes, they were rolled up around some cigars in an inside pocket of that Reb officer's jacket. Either our approach startled 'em to run away from that farm or the dumb secessionist officer forgot his clothes. Any old way, he left a complete set of operational orders addressed to General Daniel Harvey Hill. The orders included troop movements and schedules for the likes of Longstreet, Jackson, and Stuart."

John asked, "Do you really think they are real?" Before he let the corporal answer he added, "You know, they could have been planted there expecting to be found to cause us to make a bad decision."

"I don't know about that." Corporal Mitchell scratched his head, then he defended himself again, "All I know is that when we showed them to Captain Barton, he decided on the spot to forward them up the chain of command. I bet they are being reviewed by old Mac and his staff right now."

The small group of men seemed to grunt or nod their respective approval of the situation. Paul added, "If that's so, and those orders are genuine, old Mac will know what to do with them. I heard that he was at the 'Point' the same time that old gray fox was there. Maybe he'd be able to authenticate the writing."

Sergeant McCoy jumped in, "Boys, I'm glad that long-legged fool, Lincoln, had enough sense to put McClellan back in charge. With him in command, we have a real chance to beat them Rebs once and for all."

Not everyone shared Staff Sergeant Tim McCoy's enthusiasm. However, they all pretended to agree, and all of them hoped that they could end this terrible war with a decisive victory over the

South and her best commander. Maybe they could all go home before Christmas.

The road wound down through the thick forest toward the river that separated the North from the South. During the night, General D. H. Hill's division reached the other side. Their orders were to cross the Potomac River near Leesburg, Virginia, at Ball's Bluff, the site of an early Yankee blunder. No bridge spanned this point in the river to help speed the army northward. However, it was shallow enough to ford and it had a landmass near the middle of the river to help conceal the army's movement. It would take longer and extra effort would be needed to help the heavy supply wagons, but stealth was more important than speed on this clear September night. Many men stripped to their undergarments and carried their shoes, trousers, packs, and muskets over their heads and waded into the cold water. The remaining force of General Robert E. Lee's Army of Northern Virginia invaded the border state of Maryland.

Nathaniel rode Max stoically, silently, a stern look etched on his face. Rarely did he challenge the strategy and leadership of this army, but his mind began to wander as he struggled to stay awake. He needed sleep. He looked at the building clouds that gathered to block the moon. *It might rain today; that would help hide us.* His company reached the Potomac River's bank. Small waves beat along the rocky, muddy shoreline. He gave Max a sound encouraging kick and whistled to move him forward into the water. After the horse took a few steps into the river, Nathaniel felt the cool water cover his feet, then his legs that still burned. *This feels very good on my legs.* Then, another thought hit him as if it came from a divine messenger, *This is wrong!*

Soldiers can and will endure most anything and everything as long as letters from loved-ones arrive regularly. This September afternoon was no different. Marvin stood anxiously with other men from his regiment. He hoped to receive a letter from his mother. She always wrote encouraging words that strengthened him, but he desired a note from his father, one that would say, *"I'm proud of you, son."* Bailey sat by his side, panting and wagging his long black tail in the dust. The puppy had grown quickly and would soon reach his full height and length. Because food was scarce, he was too thin for his age, but otherwise he seemed healthy and happily received the small provisions from his master's hand. Bailey waited for food.

As men heard their names called, they shouted back to the mail officer. Quickly, he would hand the correspondence to one of his three aids who, in turn, would make sure the parcel reached its proper recipient. While Marvin listened for his name, he heard, "Graham, Captain Nathaniel Graham."

Marvin hesitated. "Bailey, what do you think? Ol' Nate's asleep in our tent. I guess I better fetch it for him." Marvin threw up his hand and called out, "Here, sir!" To this, Bailey added his own barking, which gave the surrounding soldiers a good reason to laugh.

Marvin and Bailey pushed through the small crowd of men to take the single envelope from the private standing at the rear of the mail wagon. The private briefly examined the letter's return address and said, "I don't know if I should give this to you, Lieutenant."

"Why not," Marvin challenged.

"Well, first of all, sir, you ain't Captain Nathaniel Graham, now are you, Lieutenant Jenkins?"

"He's my friend and tent-mate, Private," Marvin responded indignantly. "I think you know that too."

"I do know that, sir," Private Sutter defended smugly. "But there is something here that bothers me, and I want to hold this letter and let the captain decide if it should be released into your hands. I can't believe it made it all the way here without being challenged or stopped altogether."

"You can't stop a man from receiving his mail!" Marvin insisted. "You have no right or authority!"

"Maybe so," Private Sutter stated, confident that he held an exception in his hand.

A few minutes later, the mail officer, Captain Boyd, yelled out, "That's all for today fellers. Tomorrow is another day." He commanded, "Dismissed!"

The men grumbled their respective disappointments and dispersed to return to their duties. Captain Boyd turned to the growing scrap at the rear of his wagon. "What's the matter here, Private? Why aren't you letting your superior officer have his letter?"

Private Sutter immediately assumed correct military posture, turned and looked up at his commander, and replied, "Captain Boyd, sir, I was about to explain that to Lieutenant Jenkins."

"Go on," Captain Boyd encouraged as he climbed down from the wagon. "I'd really like to hear this myself."

Private Sutter swallowed hard, uncertain if he was in trouble. He considered the possibility that he was about to receive a commendation for his keen eye, tenacity and perseverance. He wasn't quite as confident as a few minutes before when he'd stood up to Marvin. He waited for Captain Boyd to straighten himself after his quick descent and then he spoke up clearly, "Well, sir, first I explained that the letter is addressed to Captain Graham, not Lieutenant Jenkins here, sir."

"Private Sutter, you've been doing this duty for a long time now, son, and you know full well that we let friends and relatives pick up mail for each other. What else is the matter?"

"Sir, it's the return mailing address."

"What about it?"

"Yeah," Marvin interjected. "Who's the letter from and what's the big hullabaloo all about?"

"Lieutenant Jenkins, I'll handle this," Captain Boyd spoke firmly but respectfully to Marvin to let him and the private know clearly who was in charge of this discussion. He turned to his man and commanded, "Now, Private Sutter, do finish your explanation for us."

Private Sutter held the letter up to his commander and pointed at the return address saying, "See for yourself, sir, the letter comes from Illinois. It's a Yankee letter!"

Later that evening, Nathaniel explained his side of the story to Captain Boyd and General Jackson's adjutant, Captain Sandy Pendleton. The oil lamps inside Captain Pendleton's tent burned evenly, with minimal flicker, casting clear silhouette movements for anyone who might observe from outside. Nathaniel stood quietly as Captain Boyd presented his facts regarding the potentially dangerous letter. Captain Pendleton listened carefully and then asked Nathaniel to speak freely.

"Honestly, Sandy, I really didn't expect a response when I wrote to her," Nathaniel defended.

Captain Sandy Pendleton proved to be a very capable young officer. He won the confidence of his commanding general; not many men did. As Jackson's aid, Pendleton was well versed in military protocol. This situation presented something new. He called upon his whole experience to render a sound decision. Based on Boyd's statement, Pendleton didn't think the matter required anything more than this evening's informal investigation. He sat behind his field desk and decided to re-create the timeline, hoping it would shed some more light on the subject. "When did you write this girl, Nate?"

"I decided to write to her shortly after the battle of Shiloh. I finally got around to it and finished it on the train from Corinth, Mississippi, to Chattanooga this past May."

"I am curious; how did you manage to mail it?" Sandy probed, keeping his eyes fixed on Nathaniel's.

"I gave it to the Postmaster at City Point, Virginia. A post office worker at the Chattanooga, train depot gave me his name and said he'd be my best bet for sending my letter up north."

"No doubt," Captain Pendleton stated. He decided to send this information forward and have this character investigated further. Now he needed to pry a bit deeper. "And what is the name of this postmaster in City Point?"

"Macalister, sir, Norman Macalister," Nathaniel answered quickly. "He charged me ten gold dollars to mail it. I think it is extortion." Nathaniel could tell that Captain Pendleton was considering some action so he added, "If you need more information about him, I'm sure I can write my cousin who lives in that area and ask for her help."

"I don't think that will be necessary," Captain Pendleton responded. He wrote a quick note in his logbook, contemplated how he might proceed, and then returned to the business at hand. "Do you mind telling me why you wrote this girl? It seems rather odd to me that you would write someone you don't know personally, especially a Northern girl you've never met."

I've been asking myself the same question. I don't know what motivated me to write to her. I wish I had a good answer. "Sandy, I thought my intentions were honorable and I believed that I was obeying what God wanted me to do."

"Fraternizing with the enemy," Captain Boyd accused. "You mean to tell me that God wanted you to befriend some Yankee girl! That don't make no sense! For all we know, she's Lincoln's kin."

"Take it easy Captain Boyd," Sandy tried to calm the situation. It was tense enough without railing accusations. "Go ahead, Nate, what drove you to write her?"

You're not going to believe this. I'm not sure I do. Nathaniel took a deep breath and started, "You see, Sandy, I was with her father when he died. He was a Yankee colonel. Ellis was his name. He showed me a letter from his daughter, Eleanor. In fact, I still have it if you want to see it."

Sandy shook his head and said, "No need. So, what happened?"

"Well, I made a promise to this man just before he passed on."

"Good riddance, I say," Captain Boyd interrupted.

Captain Pendleton furrowed his brow and spoke sternly, "I've had about all I'm going to take from you, Captain Boyd. I suggest that you remain quiet." Captain Boyd was shocked at Captain Pendleton's remark. He quietly decided to obey. Then Captain Pendleton turned again to Nathaniel and encouraged, "And what was that promise, Nate?"

"Sandy, I—" *I think I'm about to disclose a sacred trust.* "I promised him that if I survived this war I would find Eleanor and explain to her how he came to salvation in the Lord Jesus. I said it just as he died. I don't even know if he heard me, but I know God did."

"Oh brother! Do you believe this dribble?" Captain Boyd mocked. "I would have put a bullet right between his eyes and sent him on his way."

Nathaniel turned to him and defended earnestly, "I know it sounds funny to you. I can see how it might. But at the time it seemed like an honorable thing to do." He turned to Captain Pendleton and said, "It may have been a mistake in judgment on my part to write to the girl. I take full responsibility for any crime I may have committed."

"I'm not sure you committed a crime, nor do I question your judgment. God only knows what I would have said or done if I'd found myself in a similar situation," Captain Pendleton stated, surprising Nathaniel and Captain Boyd even more.

"What do you mean, Sandy?" Captain Boyd challenged aggressively. "He has committed an act of treason, consorting with the enemy. Providing them aid and comfort, you know. He should be brought up on charges, tried, convicted, court-martialed, and hanged!"

Captain Pendleton looked sternly at Nathaniel's accuser and commandingly stated, "I've had all I'm going to take from you, Captain Boyd. Do you understand me?"

Defensively, Captain Boyd responded, "But Sandy, you can't mean that it's all right to correspond with the Yankees?"

"I didn't say that, Captain. What I mean is that there are thousands of people on both sides who have family members, friends and all types of acquaintances that have been torn apart by this war. I'm confident that they all feel a need to hear from them. One day this war will end, and maybe, God willing, very soon. When that day comes, we will need men like Nate here who know how to bring reconciliation."

Captain Boyd's mouth was stopped. He couldn't believe what he'd just heard, nor did he have any comprehension why reconciliation with Yankees might be important.

Nathaniel breathed a sigh of relief. *If only he knew how confused I've been lately. I don't think I understand reconciliation anymore.* "Sandy, I appreciate your confidence, but lately, I've seriously considered giving up the ministry. I don't know if it's the war, or what, but I seem to have lost my faith. Don't get me wrong; I still believe in God, but something is missing. I don't know what it is. I don't know where to look for it, and I'm not sure how to pray. None of the things I relied on in the past help."

Captain Sandy Pendleton heard Nathaniel's plea and made his decision. He picked up the unopened envelope from his desk, stood up, and approached Nathaniel to speak to him man-to-man, face-to-face. He said, "Nate, I can't help you in your search for answers to your questions. In my humble opinion, those things are between you and the Almighty. What I do know is that war accelerates everything, makes exceptions for many things, and exchanges rules and regulations for what is expedient. In this case, I'm sure you acted out of a trusting heart toward God with care for this girl," he tapped the letter in his left hand, then held it up to make his final point. "It's probably no coincidence that this arrived for you at this time. Maybe an answer is in here." Sandy grabbed Nathaniel's right arm and put the letter in Nathaniel's right hand. "Go about your business, Captain." Sandy took a step back and snapped a proper salute.

Stunned, Nathaniel responded appropriately in kind. *What just happened? I can't believe I'm holding this letter. I thought for sure I'd be clapped in irons. Jesus, thank you. I received your mercy through Sandy. You've set me free. I suppose if I write Eleanor again no one will mind, not officially anyway.*

Later that night, Captain Boyd expounded his version of the day's events to his friend, Captain James Nash, who soaked up the information. Nash concluded that Marvin, Nathaniel, and their damned dogs, all had to go.

At the same time, in another tent not far away, Nathaniel pored over Eleanor's letter. He read it and re-read it.

August 1, 1862

Captain Graham,

I must admit, your letter was a complete surprise to my mother and I. We are grateful that you took the time to express

*what you believe about my father. However, sir, you are our
enemy and I do not have any reason to believe a single word
of your—I must say—fantastic story.*

*We all would like to believe that one day we will once again
see our departed loved ones. But I am a realist, and I think any
hope for an afterlife is simple deluded wishful thinking.*

*I am willing to give you the benefit of the doubt. I am also
willing to let you write to me again. I am curious about this
salvation idea you seem so sure of for my father, a man who
was dying and probably needed hope to let himself pass. I want
to remind you that I find your credibility to be lacking. For all
I know, you are a charlatan playing on the emotions of women
who have suffered loss. But if you can present a logical argument that would prove or at least persuade me to understand
how a person like my father could know that "salvation" is
real, I will consider your points for myself.*

*Respectfully,
Eleanor J. Ellis*

*She will accept letters from me. I don't care what she thinks of me;
my reputation doesn't matter.* Nathaniel picked up the letter and held
it to the lamp light. *She doesn't believe that God provided salvation
for us, yet she wants to learn about eternal things. This is exciting.* For
the first time since he regained consciousness, Nathaniel smiled.

The next day, the Second Corps was on the move again. General
Jackson split his divisions and positioned them along the hills
surrounding Harpers Ferry, Virginia. This was one of the quickest
battles of the war. The town surrendered with very little resistance

and the military stores fell into Jackson's hands. Upon receipt of General Lee's latest orders, Jackson left General A. P. Hill's division behind and moved the rest of the Second Corps, with all possible speed, to Sharpsburg, Maryland.

Chapter 33

NEWS

O h my God, Mother, listen to this!" Eleanor shouted as she burst through Catherine's Dress Shop's entrance. Eleanor didn't wait for a response from her mother. She kept shouting, "The Rebels invaded Maryland and Kentucky!"

Catherine quickly walked from the back of the store bewildered by her daughter's wild announcement. "What, dear, what did you say?"

Eleanor held up the newspaper bundled in her left hand and continued to speak excitedly, "Mother, the newspaper says right here—," she reached with her right hand and opened it. Quickly she stepped toward the service counter and placed the paper down so they could read it together. The headline was clear, "Rebel Invasion!" Outside their shop, newsboys yelled the same information.

Catherine stared at the words on the page as Eleanor read them aloud. "Confederate General Robert E. Lee advanced his Army of Northern Virginia into Maryland. Elements of his cavalry are reported to be roaming freely throughout southern Pennsylvania.

General Braxton Bragg marched the Army of Tennessee into Kentucky."

Catherine gasped, "Kentucky! Oh no! What if they cross the river into Illinois?" The bell over the entrance door rang announcing a visitor, but neither woman noticed. Catherine continued as she looked around the store and fear gripped her heart in a merciless vice. "What will we do? Where will we go? The boys are far away. The army won't let them come home to help us."

"I'll take care of you two ladies," a familiar male voice announced confidently. Both women turned about and saw him walking toward them, smiling. "Don't you worry one bit," Jason said. "Our boys will stop them before they reach the Ohio River, and even if they manage to get a raiding party across it, I will take you out of harm's way."

Catherine breathed a sigh of relief and nearly ran to greet Jason. "Oh, Jason, thank you so very much for thinking about us."

Jason seized this opportunity to win their forgiveness. He played upon their deep need for security and attempted to be reassuring. "Mrs. Ellis, Miss Ellis." Jason looked directly into Eleanor's eyes. "I do hope that by now you'd know that I would never let anything bad happen to either of you."

Catherine graciously thanked Jason again. Eleanor acknowledged his declaration with her eyes and then quickly turned back to the counter and the newspaper. She found where she'd left off and read an eyewitness description of the Rebels as they marched through Maryland, *"They were the dirtiest men I ever saw, a most ragged lean and hungry set of wolves. Yet there was a dash about them that the Northern men lacked."* Eleanor's thoughts drifted away as the continuing conversation between Jason and her mother faded from her hearing. *I wonder if he's with them.*

Most of Lee's available force, approximately thirty-two thousand actives, held positions in and around Sharpsburg, Maryland, a very small town located along one of the many bends in the Potomac River. A large creek, called "Antietam" by its Indian name, wound through the farmland outside of the town and emptied into the Potomac River south and east of the town. The 1860 census numbered the male population at approximately six hundred and fifty. Most founding community members came to this quiet location to take advantage of the natural hot spring. The local legend claimed that the spring water held healing properties. The military hordes that now surrounded this quite, peaceful farm community came for other reasons.

General Lee decided to stand and fight here. Federal Major General George McClellan approached slowly with a force that neither leader knew exceeded twice the size of Lee's men. General Lee assumed that the ease with which General Jackson took Harper's Ferry meant that the Yankee army's will to fight had been damaged, maybe beyond repair. He further concluded that success on Northern soil would force the end of this terrible war. General Lee calculated what he might gain by what he might lose and decided that the potential results were worth the risk. He erred on all counts. The Federal army and the people of the North were ready and determined to fight and to win.

Eleanor continued, "This report says that Confederate officers are purchasing supplies with worthless Rebel currency."

"That's stealing, no matter what they think," Jason asserted.

"What does the paper say they are taking, dear?"

"It says that they are buying shoes, clothing, food, and livestock from the surrounding Maryland and southern Pennsylvania farms and towns."

"Those villains can't expect to get away with this. Once our fighting men hear about this, they will destroy the Rebels for sure."

"I do hope God will keep Paul and John safe from harm."

Eleanor gasped.

"What is it, dear?"

"I can't believe this."

"What, Eleanor? Let me see it," Jason grabbed the newspaper and began to read.

Eleanor looked at her mother and said, "If there is a God, they deserve His wrath. Mother, what they've done is unimaginable. They don't deserve to govern themselves."

"What, dear, what did they do that's upset you so?"

"I don't believe it either," Jason found the report. "They've rounded up every Negro man, woman, and child they found, many of them born 'Freedmen,' and herded them like cattle back to Virginia and into slavery. Even worse, these barbarians summarily executed those too old or sick to be of any use."

Catherine nearly fainted. "I need to sit down. Eleanor, please, dear, get me some water."

Eleanor rushed to bring her mother a cup of cool water.

Jason continued to expound on the article, "The Rebels continue to pillage our towns even as our troops mass along the rolling hills east of a little town called Sharpsburg. Our leaders are calling for the destruction of slavery and demanding that Lincoln declare it the sole purpose for prosecuting the war."

Neither Catherine nor Eleanor listened.

A very strange column of captive Negroes walked reluctantly toward General A.P. Hill's encampment near Harper's Ferry. The ruthless afternoon sun beat down upon these dispossessed men, women, and children. They carried little more than the clothes they wore. Some women carried their infants who wailed their discomfort. These poor souls looked terrified.

The Rebel soldiers failed to show mercy. They had refused to provide food, water, or rest since dawn when they began the desperate forced march southward. The new masters herded their captives toward the slaughterhouse of slavery.

Nathaniel and Marvin watched the approaching masses. There had to be a thousand or more. Nathaniel echoed the words that penetrated his thinking when this invasion of Maryland began. "This isn't right," he muttered.

"What, what did you say?" Marvin asked. Bailey began to bark at the intruding long line of strangers. Buster just looked around with a wondering look on his face.

Nathaniel swallowed hard. *Why did I say that?* Defensively he replied, "Nothing."

Marvin challenged his friend inquiring, "I thought I heard you say, 'This isn't right.' I'm sure that's what I heard. So tell me, what's not right?"

Marvin had heard him correctly. *Why am I so impulsive? Why can't I keep my thoughts to myself? It's because I know this thought wasn't mine. But how am I going to convince Marvin?* "I guess I don't know why we need to take any Negroes."

Marvin had already assumed Nathaniel's response and he was ready for the justification. "They take ours from us, don't they," Marvin posed. "It's only fair that we take back what rightly belongs to us. Chances are, most of them are runaways, and even if they ain't, I seem to recollect that you once preached that God destined the Negro for slavery!"

Nathaniel swallowed even harder now. *My own preaching condemns me. We no longer share the same conviction. I can't voice why I think taking these Negroes is wrong. Maybe someday it will be clear to me. I'm just not so certain anymore.* "I understand what you are saying, Marvin, but deep inside I think we as a nation should conform to a higher standard if we are to secure the Lord's blessings in this business."

Being concerned about God's opinion was a foreign concept to Marvin. He dismissed his friend's comment as that from a crazed man and assumed Nathaniel had not recovered from his head injury. He simply stated, "Nate, this is war. We have to do what we have to do to survive. It changes all of us. You've changed, I've changed, the nation has changed. If we don't preserve our way of life, we'll lose everything. I believe you were right about the fate of darkies. We're just doing God's will here."

The column moved closer and began to pass them. Nathaniel quickly remembered his early days of ministry training. Yes, he'd taught the very principal parroted by his friend. Yes, he'd changed. But something else pulled at his heart and mind. He just didn't know what to do with these new thoughts that attacked his traditionally held views. Reluctantly he acquiesced, "I suppose you're right. We've got other things to worry about this day."

As Nathaniel concluded their short debate, a Confederate sergeant broke off from the column and approached a soldier near the edge of camp carrying a box of cartridges to distribute to his company. The two men exchanged words. Then the man burdened with the wooden crate pointed with his left elbow in Nathaniel and Marvin's general direction. The sergeant indicated an apparent grateful comment and then he began walking directly toward the young officers.

Marvin noted, "Looks like that sergeant is coming this way."

"Appears so," Nathaniel replied. "I wonder what he wants."

Confederate soldiers under the command of Major General Daniel Harvey Hill fought a delaying action on and near South

Mountain against overwhelming odds. Wave upon wave of Federal advances were repulsed for nearly an entire day, buying General Robert E. Lee's widely divided army time to consolidate near Sharpsburg, Maryland. The fighting lasted until dusk. Lee's gamble worked. Hill's division kept the Yankees bottled up on the main road and caused their ever-cautious leader to slow his advance. General Hill retreated under the cover of darkness to protect what remained of his division. In their haste to withdraw, Hill's men did not have time to properly care for their dead and severely wounded.

On both sides of the pass, freed Negroes, dubbed contraband by the Federal army, dragged dead Rebels toward a burial trench. The faces of these bodies became blackened and bloated as they began to decay in the hot sun. These departed sons of the South looked almost like Negroes themselves. Several had arms and hands lifted and fixed toward heaven as if pleading to live. The boys in blue were happy that their enemy paid a dear price defending this mountain road. Irreverently, the Yankees passed the dead soldiers.

"We've got the Rebs on the run," John declared among the many cheers of his fellow soldiers. The Fifth Corps just passed through Turner's Gap and viewed the destruction of the recent action.

Paul presented a voice of reason and responded, "I wouldn't be too sure, little brother. I think old Bobby Lee has a big surprise planned for us just up this road a short ways. Do you think they'll just run back to old Virginia?"

"I sure do. I bet old Mac is driving them right into the river." John panted as they quickened their uphill march. They didn't want to miss any of the approaching fight. "It don't seem right," John added. "Why should we be stuck at the end of the line?"

"I'm sure we'll be fighting them Gray Backs soon enough," a young Kelly Hess interrupted. He was a brand new recruit, a boy fresh off a farm near Rockford, barely eighteen years old. In his zeal he foolishly added, "I can't wait!"

"Don't be in such a fool hurry," Sergeant Richard Holmes replied. "You boys keep it quiet."

"I've had it with those two and their stupid dogs," Captain James Nash declared. "Did you see them walking around the camp? We work while they take their dogs for a stroll." The seed of jealous hatred that Nash absorbed on the train to Richmond sprouted and developed into a strong root of bitterness. It blossomed and spawned evil.

"But what can you do?" Captain Boyd inquired. "They seem to have the favor of General Jackson, some of his staff members, and Major Duffy. Doesn't the 'Duffer' have one of the pups from the same litter?"

"I don't care," Nash snapped. "Graham's the only one who seems to have that old Tom fool's eye. The other one, Jenkins, he's just no good. If it weren't for Graham, I'd have put the idiot out of his misery long ago. Now some of our boys think he's some kind of hero because he held his line after his company ran out of ammunition at Second Manassas. He ordered his troops to throw rocks and use their muskets like clubs to fight off the Yankees. In the fight, he got a small wound in his leg. Everyone thinks he did some great thing. As far as I'm concerned, he just followed orders. In my mind, he's still worthless. I should shoot him the next chance I get."

"Why waste a good bullet on him?" Boyd laughed.

"I thought the very same thing," Nash sat back on his bunk and took a long draw on his cigar. He followed the sweet-smelling smoke trail as it drifted toward the tent-pole opening at the tent's peak. Then he continued his thought, "You know, Jenkin's life is no more significant than this smoky vapor," he waved the cigar to disturb the smoke's natural assent. "He'd be lucky if he survived this next fight that's brewing, don't you think?" He paused for a moment, then concluded, "If he happens to be in a thick firefight, who is to say that a bullet in the back of his head wasn't from a Yankee."

"I'd like to do the same thing to Graham," Boyd added, influenced by his friend and still angry that Pendleton let Graham go.

"You'll have to hope that the Yankees kill him," Nash shook his head hoping to convey to Boyd his idea wouldn't work for Graham. Then he explained, "Jackson keeps his blue lights fixed on that boy. He'd know if something happened to him. Jackson don't seem to pay it no mind that the preacher boy doesn't carry a gun." Nash watched his cigar smoke trail rise again as if he gained clairvoyance from the haze. "You know, Boyd, there is something wrong with old Blue Light. I know most of the South loves him and thinks he's the best warrior general in the entire Confederate army. But if you think about it, he's just a fortunate fool. I heard that he was the worst professor at the Virginia Military Institute. They let him teach because he was a war hero during the fight with Mexico. The only real reason he's gotten to be the commander of our corps is because old Granny Lee likes him."

Nash took another long pull on his cigar, savored the taste and aroma, and then his eyes lit up with a completely new thought. He stared into the thick smoke as he exhaled. Boyd recognized that his friend's mind was working and asked, "What are you thinking, Jim?"

"It's like they have this exclusive club. They watch out for one another, they promote each other, and we do all the dirty work so they don't have to. I've never seen either of them use a weapon, have you?"

"Can't say that I've ever noticed one way or the other," Boyd scratched the thinning hair on his balding head. "But what difference does that make? It's not like I run in their circles. And besides, generals are not supposed to be in the middle of a fight anyway."

Mean-spirited, Nash shot back, "Graham ain't no general, but somehow he's one of them. Something ain't right about this and I aim to get to the bottom of it. What did Pendleton say about war exchanging 'rules and regulations for what is expedient?' I have an idea. You can look at their mail."

"I can't do that. I can't tamper with the mail. I think you'll just be wasting your time. Just shoot them and be done with it." Boyd paused, "Wait a minute, you might have something here. I would love to trap Graham. I bet he'll tell his Yankee girlfriend something that could get him hung."

"If you find something on Jenkins, let me know. Jenkins, Graham, and their stupid, chow-stealing dogs need to go. We'd all be better off if they were gone."

Boyd nodded his head in agreement and asked, "So what are we going to do?"

Nash stroked his beard as he answered, "You can start tracking Graham's mail. This coming fight should provide me many good opportunities to remove Jenkins. But if not, maybe a letter might give me something to get him court-martialed. Nash grinned as a sinister picture took shape in his mind. He smiled and took a long satisfying draw on his cigar.

Chapter 34

BATTLE PLANS: TUESDAY, SEPTEMBER 16, 1862

eneral Jackson's Second Corps arrived in Sharpsburg by midday. Except for General A. P. Hill's division, the Second Corps neared one hundred percent strength, approximately seventeen thousand men. These veterans understood the severe penalty for straggling. Before dusk, tents dotted the Potomac River side of the town. Jackson's Second Corps occupied the north, or left flank of General Lee's small but quickly consolidating thirty-two thousand man Confederate Army of Northern Virginia. Tension filled the air. A fight brewed and everyone could sense it. Most of the men busied themselves with routine activities. Not a single unit drilled to prepare for the fight. They all knew what to do, what was expected of them, and what the cost of failure would yield. Each man embraced his fate and prepared to face it.

Approximately two and one-half miles northeast of Sharpsburg, forward elements of General George B. McClellan's massive United States Army of the Potomac, over eighty-seven thousand strong, began to take up positions along the large hills that overlooked the town and their namesake river just beyond. McClellan and his staff occupied a modestly-furnished farmhouse. From this rear position, they prepared expansive battle plans. Scouts bore various reports regarding Rebel troop strength, positions, and movements throughout the day. As conflicting and confirming bits of information filtered into the planning meetings, McClellan adjusted his deployments. The captured orders were extremely helpful; however, McClellan did not know that Lee learned of his lost orders and moved quickly to strengthen his positions. McClellan recognized General Lee's vulnerability, but with each new report he over-inflated Lee's strength. McClellan, deliberative as always, recalculated, re-planned, and repositioned his troops, established a massive reserve, and stalled making command decisions. When he finally issued written orders to his corps commanders, they were vague and confusing regarding the placement of his forces, timing of troop movements, and coordination between respective corps. His men were ready to fight, but once again McClellan hesitated.

General Robert E. Lee moved decisively. His orders were clear and simple. He placed most of Jackson's men on his left flank. In the center, Lee merged one of Jackson's divisions with elements from Longstreet's First Corps. The rest of Longstreet's men protected the right flank. Lee made it clear that he intended to fight. The Army of Northern Virginia would not retreat across the river to relative safety.

Lee recognized that he had a weakness in his center. Major General D. H. Hill's Division, what remained of it, occupied a section of that center along a deeply worn wagon trail. His men fought a costly delaying action at Turner's Gap on South Mountain. They were tired from their deadly work two days earlier, purchasing for General Lee precious time to prepare for this battle. Placed in the center, Lee hoped that Hill's Division would participate little if any in the coming fight. If necessary, Lee could pull troops from his flanks to reinforce this natural defensive position.

General Lee, with Longstreet by his side, rode to meet with General Hill face-to-face. Lee knew the man needed personal encouragement. He decided to provide Hill motivating respect and approbation. He believed he owed it to Hill, specifically this day. Lee found Hill, sitting on his horse, giving orders to his brigade commanders.

"Gentlemen, this road should give you excellent cover should the Yankees come this way," General Hill instructed. He turned in his saddle and looked directly at Brigadier General Rodes and stated, "Robert, I've placed you and your men in the center of our line. I expect you to hold it at all possible hazards."

General Rodes, a man of few words, simply nodded acceptance of the assignment. Then he verbally responded, "You can count on my men, sir."

Hill continued, "I don't need to remind any of you how important it is to hold this road. We have few reinforcements behind us to stop the Yankees from splitting our army in two, if they break through here. Does everyone understand?"

All of the brigade leaders acknowledged affirmatively. General Hill took another moment to look each man in the eye and reaffirmed everyone with his confident contact. Then Hill concluded, "Very well, then, my compliments to each and every one of you. Make sure that your men get plenty of rest and food. Give your pickets clear orders to stay alert. We need an early warning of any Yankee movements this way. We don't want those Blue Bellies catching us by surprise."

"No, sir," Colonel John B. Gordon shouted. Confidently, he stated, "Don't worry, sir; we will hold this road all day! Besides, them damned Yankees are too proud and foolish to sneak up on us, sir. They always announce their coming with drums and bugle calls, sir. If we don't see them, we'll surely hear them, sir!"

The other commanders chuckled their agreement, but not too loudly, just in case Gordon's rash boldness was received poorly. Hill put his commanders at ease when he joined the laughter. Then Brigadier General George B. Anderson reasoned, "Maybe so, gentlemen, but even a dog can learn to approach danger differently after he's received a few regular beatings."

Gordon countered, "Yankees ain't as smart as most dogs, General."

General Ripley agreed, "You are right about that, Gordon."

Everyone present except for Generals Lee and Longstreet laughed in response. With that final moment of levity, General Hill finished his exhortation and asked, "Gentlemen, may we take a moment to pray?"

Each man removed his hat and bowed his head reverently. Hill proceeded, "Gracious Heavenly Father, we believe You brought us to this place far from our homes to take the fight to our enemy. We beseech Your mercy and ask that You would look favorably upon Your servants. We entrust ourselves into Your keeping. Should You call us to our eternal home, we ask that You would comfort our loved ones. We ask only that Your sovereign will be done and we believe that it is to set our country free from the tyranny of the despotic northern aggressors. In that mighty name of Jesus, we petition Your throne. Amen!"

All the men repeated in agreement, some more enthusiastically, "Amen!"

The officers returned their caps to their sun-beaten crowns, and then Hill commanded, "Gentlemen, take your positions." They exchanged salutes and the men, now dismissed, moved to their respective posts. General Hill wheeled his horse around and formally greeted his commander. "General Lee, good day to you, sir, and to you too, General Longstreet."

General Lee replied for both men, "Good day to you, General. That was a very fine speech and prayer you gave your men, sir."

"Thank you very kindly, General Lee. I do appreciate your approval. It means a great deal to me coming from you, sir."

General Lee nodded, shifted in his saddle as his horse, Traveler, kicked at the ground, while Lee continued, "I and this army are greatly indebted to you, sir. Generals Longstreet and Jackson have reported to me the fine work you and your men did at South Mountain and specifically at Turner's Gap. Without your help, this army might have been destroyed and with it our hope for the independence of our nation. I do want to thank you for your services."

Hill straightened himself in his saddle and said with all the sincerity he could muster, "Thank you, General Lee." Hill paused. Then he quickly made eye contact with General Longstreet and repeated, "And thank you, General Longstreet."

General James Longstreet, Pete to his close friends, simply nodded and chewed on his cigar. General Lee took command of the conversation and casually stated, "General Hill, if those people," pointing toward the Yankees on the hills to their east, "come this way en masse, you be quick to send word to me. I want to provide you with as much support as you may need. I don't expect you to hold this place all alone."

With renewed confidence, General Hill replied, "General Lee, we will hold this road to the last, sir!"

"Very well," General Lee responded. He determined that his visit was successful and that his purpose satisfied. "I know that I and this army can depend on you and your men, General Hill."

"Yes you can, sir!" Hill declared.

"Then, if you need help, I can expect to hear from you?" Lee asked just to make sure his meaning was clear.

"Yes, sir," Hill acknowledged. Then he added, "As Colonel Gordon said, we won't let the Yankees get past this road, General Lee. To make sure, I will have couriers at my side ready to dispatch directly to you if trouble comes my way."

"Very well then," General Lee replied. "Good day and Godspeed to you, sir!"

"And Godspeed to both of you!" Hill replied, and saluted.

Salutes were exchanged and Generals Lee and Longstreet turned their respective mounts to the right and rode back to town. With some distance between them and General Hill's battered division, Longstreet inquired, "I was just wondering from where do you intend to draw reinforcements?"

General Lee also recognized his vulnerable condition. He took a deep breath before replying, "Only God Almighty knows the answer to that question, Pete." They rode on silently, both contemplating what the next day would bring.

"Our orders are to set up camp here," Captain Adams barked. "The rest of the army is pushing forward up this road. We've been ordered to hold back, to be a reserve unit. Spread out, but set up your tents in company formation. You never know when we will be ordered to move out. Be ready to move fast. Dismissed!"

John and Paul's company shuffled off the road in an orderly fashion and began the routine of setting up their tents. John asked, "How long do you think we'll hold up here?"

"It might be a night," Paul suggested. "I hope it won't be more than that. No way to tell for sure."

"It's pretty clear, Captain Adams doesn't know anything."

"This looks like a dry, flat spot," Paul noted.

"Pastureland, I'm glad they didn't stick us over in one of those corn fields."

Minutes passed, arms were stacked, and temporary quarters rose in the quiet field. It would be suppertime soon and, shortly thereafter, nightfall. Thick clouds filled the sky, cooling the air, filling it with a growing aroma of rain nearby. The men scrambled to raise their tents. No one liked sleeping in the mud.

John pulled a tent stake tight, and as he hammered it into the ground, he voiced his opinion, "I think we're going to see one hell of a fight real soon."

Paul just shook his head in disbelief because John always seemed to come out with wild notions. He didn't really want to ask, but he did. "OK, John, just what makes you so sure?"

"I don't know how to explain it," John conceded. "What I know is that I can sense it deep inside my gut."

"That does not make any sense to me at all," Paul challenged. "You can see that the army is bedding down for the night; you can hear that it's quiet just over that hill, too. You clearly can't taste that a fight is coming; you can't touch it or smell it either. So what gives you any idea other than that crazy head of yours that a big fight is coming? Isn't it possible that the Rebs will just run back to Virginia?"

John was convinced that he had to try to help his older brother understand. "The best way I can explain it is like this—you know how you can smell the rain in the air, right? And because we live outside so much, we know it is going to rain soon, right?"

Chapter 35

A HOPE FOR FREEDOM

The sergeant approached Marvin and Nathaniel. Clearly, he intended to speak with them. The two officers watched him with growing curiosity. He reached easy conversational distance and came to a halt. He drew himself up into attention, saluted across his musket, and reported his intentions, "Sergeant Jones, sirs, beg to report!"

Both officers returned the sergeant's salute and Marvin replied, "Go on, Sergeant." Marvin crossed his arms and leaned back a bit to look important in the eyes of the noncommissioned officer.

Nathaniel noticed Marvin's posture change. *Yes, I guess all of us have changed.* He remembered how scared of everything and everyone Marvin had been. *He was just a boy then. He is a seasoned, battle-tested veteran now.*

The sergeant continued, "Well, Lieutenant, sir," speaking directly to Marvin in a distinct deep Louisiana Cajun drawl. Marvin and Nathaniel recognized that they must listen carefully to understand the mixed English-French dialect. "We've captured a bunch of runaways."

"I can see that, Sergeant," Marvin looked over at the mass moving into the town. Then Marvin asked, "What's that got to do with us?"

"Sir, may I speak freely?"

Marvin uncrossed his arms and realized that Sergeant Jones still stood rigidly at attention. He decided to put him at ease. "Yes you may, and please stand at ease."

"Thank you, sir," the sergeant acknowledged as he relaxed and rested his musket by his right foot. "You see, Lieutenant, one of them darkies keeps complaining that we've kidnapped him and many others that he claims were freedmen. He says that they have rights as citizens of Pennsylvania, and a whole bunch of other foolishness. He keeps demanding to talk with an officer. He wants to speak directly to General Lee hisself. Would one of you be so kind and help me with this real uppity one? I'm afraid he might stir up the rest of them. We ain't got time for no riot."

Neither Marvin nor Nathaniel knew what to make of this strange request. Marvin turned to Nathaniel and feigned proper military protocol, "What do you think, Captain?"

Keeping in step with Marvin, Nathaniel responded, "I'm not real sure, Lieutenant." Nathaniel turned his attention to the soldier, "Sergeant," he began.

"Yes, sir," Sergeant Jones quickly replied.

Nathaniel looked at him inquisitively and asked, "What did you say your name was, son?"

"Sergeant Jones, Leroy Jones, sir. I'm with the 6th Louisiana Infantry, Hay's Brigade commanded by Colonel Strong."

"Very well," Nathaniel replied. *What am I going to do with this Negro? I guess I can listen to his complaint.* "Thank you, Sergeant. I am Captain Graham. This is Lieutenant Jenkins." Sergeant Jones acknowledged by nodding his head. Nathaniel continued, "Now, who is this Negro that claims to be a Pennsylvanian?"

"I don't know his name, sir," Sergeant Jones admitted. "Frankly, sir, I can't understand much of what he says. He speaks like most Blue Bellies I've captured, maybe better. He's one uppity darkie. He keeps using words I don't understand. Ain't sure they'z English. He keeps saying he's entitled to a 'hay-be-us-carp-us,' or something like that. Since when is a slave entitled to anything? That's what I think. But I'm just a soldier and I want to shut him up, deliver these slaves to someone who'll ferry them back where they belong, and get back to the rest of my unit. I think a big fight is brewing back up that road and I don't want to miss it."

Nathaniel looked down the hill at the massed Negroes filing into the town and asked, "Can you bring him to me?"

"Yes, sir, thank you, sir. I'll fetch him right away, sir."

Nathaniel mused, then chuckled as he commanded, "Tell him you've found an officer who is willing to talk with him. I may not be General Lee—"

Marvin laughed, causing Nathaniel to pause.

Nathaniel smiled as he finished, "But I am willing to listen to his grievances."

Sergeant Jones brought himself back to attention, saluted across his musket, waited for Nathaniel to return his salute, took a full step backwards, performed an about-face, and hurried down the hill toward the herd of Negroes that were being corralled into Harper's Ferry. Nathaniel and Marvin watched as Sergeant Jones disappeared into the crowd. Marvin questioned, "What are you going to say to the darkie?"

"Don't know," Nathaniel shrugged his shoulders. "I suppose I'll just listen to him."

"What if he demands to speak with a higher-ranking officer?"

"I'll see what he has to say first. I am concerned that he might know a thing or two about the law. Not too many folks know what a writ of habeas corpus is."

"You're right about that," Marvin affirmed. Then he confessed, "I don't know what it is."

"It's a Latin term that basically means to produce the body. It's used as a legal term to give an arrested man a chance to have his case quickly heard in a court of law. If the judge determines that he's been wrongfully held, the man can be set free from jail."

"Where did you learn that stuff? You ain't no lawyer."

"I thought I wanted to be," Nathaniel stared up into the sky. "Do you remember when Lincoln had all the Maryland legislators arrested right after the war started?"

Marvin removed his kepi and scratched his head. "Yep, I seem to remember that the dictator did that."

"And he banned the use of habeas corpus to keep them held in Federal prison. Lincoln acted like a despot, not a president. He must be stopped. That's one of the reasons I felt compelled to join the army."

"Maybe you should have become a lawyer."

Sergeant Jones appeared again with a tall, thin Negro in tow. They both marched quickly up the hill, and Nathaniel finished his thought, "I guess God had other plans for me."

Marvin nodded, affirming Nathaniel's comment. He observed the pair approach and said, "When they get here, I'm going to head back to my company and get my men ready to move out. Do you want me to take Buster with me?"

Nathaniel handed Marvin Buster's lead. Then he thanked Marvin and asked, "Will you get my boys ready too?"

"You can count on me. I think that sergeant is right. We're going to be in the thick of it real soon. We better be ready to march. You may need to learn how to use that piece I got out of one of them Yankee warehouses."

"Marv, thanks for your help. I won't be long."

The two officers made a show of military protocol for the approaching pair and exchanged salutes. Marvin turned and walked toward the encampment being happily pulled by Bailey and Buster.

Nathaniel turned his attention to the sergeant and Negro. *He is well dressed. That's a fine black suit. He doesn't carry himself like a slave. He walks like one who knows who he is, where he is from, and where he is going. He displays an air of confidence. What sort of character is he? What does he really want?*

Sergeant Jones came to a halt, saluted across his musket, and declared officially, "Captain Graham, this slave is Jonah Benjamin. He wishes to speak with an officer. May he speak with you, sir?"

Nathaniel hesitated. He examined the captive. Nathaniel took a deep breath and answered, "Yes, Sergeant, I will speak with him. You are dismissed. I'll see to it that he is returned to the group in town."

The Sergeant breathed a small sigh of relief. He was finally relieved of this nagging burden. He saluted smartly again and said, "Thank you, Captain." Quickly, Sergeant Jones departed from their presence.

Nathaniel returned his gaze toward this tall one, looked into his dark eyes, and asked, "Jonah Benjamin, did I hear that correctly? Is that your name?"

"Yes, Captain. That is my given Christian name." Jonah Benjamin spoke with the clearest English Nathaniel had ever heard from a Negro. He had a deep, smooth, inviting voice that further exuded the confident character that Nathaniel already detected.

"The sergeant told me that you wanted to speak with an officer."

"Yes, sir, and if at all possible, I would like to speak with your Army's Judge Advocate General."

This statement caught Nathaniel completely by surprise. The Negro who stood before him was no ordinary darkie. *I don't think he's a runaway. By the looks of him, he never picked cotton. How would he know to ask for legal counsel?* "I'm not sure that your request can be granted. You may not realize it, but the Judge Advocate is concerned only with matters of military discipline. You are just a runaway slave being returned to your rightful owner."

Calmly, Jonah Benjamin declared, "I have never been a slave, sir. I was born to free parents in Lancaster, Pennsylvania."

He's never been a slave. Why is he here? I best listen to this Negro's story. What if we've made a terrible mistake? Nathaniel took a deep breath and continued attempting to belittle, "That's a very good story, boy. Why should I believe you?"

Jonah maintained his composure and respectfully replied, "I suggest that you ask any of my people, those whom your soldiers kidnapped. They will confirm what I am saying to you, sir!"

"It would be easy for you to cook up a story with your friends," Nathaniel continued his smug tone. "And just what do you mean, 'my people'?" Nathaniel challenged.

"I am the pastor of a small congregation in Chambersburg, Pennsylvania. We were taken prisoner during our Sunday morning church service. I freely admit that some members of my little flock are runaway slaves; but most of us were born and raised freedmen. Because we refused to identify them for your soldiers, they took us all captive."

Nathaniel was shocked at this last claim. *This can't be. No, I don't believe it. But why would he tell such a grand lie?* Nathaniel removed his kepi and wiped his sweating brow. The heat from the late afternoon sun bore down on him making him feel even more uncomfortable. Jonah didn't seem to mind it at all. Nathaniel looked at a nearby cluster of trees and commanded, "Let's go over to those shady trees."

They did not speak while they walked. Once under the trees, Nathaniel found a stump to sit on, and he motioned to a nearby log for Jonah, but he remained standing. He simply stated, "I prefer to stand, sir, if you don't mind." Nathaniel reluctantly concluded that this was no ordinary slave. It also appeared to Nathaniel that this one told the truth.

Nathaniel decided to change the direction of his inquisition. "You say you are a pastor," Nathaniel restated. "How did you receive an ordination?"

Calmly, Jonah returned to his story, "As I said, I was born in Lancaster, Pennsylvania. My parents were William and Mara Benjamin. They were both freedmen and upstanding, hardworking members of the Lancaster community. Both have passed over, but while they were alive, my father worked for an undertaker and my mother worked for the town's best hotel."

Nathaniel stroked his no-longer clean-shaven chin. He was still not sure what to make of Jonah. He simply said, "Go on."

Jonah continued to look straight into Nathaniel's eyes as he continued, "As a boy, I went to school and earned top marks. When I became a young man, I continued with school and I worked at the livery stable. I worked very hard and earned enough money to help my family get along. I was the only boy of five children. When I finished school, several folks from Lancaster helped by speaking well of me. Eventually, Gettysburg Lutheran Seminary offered me a scholarship. They wanted to provide higher education opportunities for Negroes. I accepted the challenge. University studies were difficult, but I applied myself and graduated with honors. After I graduated, I was offered the associate pastorate position at the Lutheran Church in Chambersburg, Pennsylvania. I have been serving the Lord there for over five years. A little more than a year ago, our senior pastor died. Many didn't want me to become the senior pastor, but the congregation decided to let me assume the position. Is there anything else you need to know?"

Nathaniel stared at this well-spoken creature. He was satisfied, but uncertain what to do. He stated, "I'm not sure I can do much for you or your congregation, Jonah. I must confess I find your story amazing. But I do believe that there may be a reason why you and I are speaking with each other." Nathaniel assumed he had the answer and continued, "You see, I am a pastor, too. My small Baptist church is near Nashville, Tennessee."

"Nashville. I know where it is. It is the capital city of the state of Tennessee, is it not?"

"Yes it is, and it is a beautiful city, settled along the banks of the Cumberland River."

Sensitive and soft spoken, Jonah thought it best to return to the main subject. He stated, "I do apologize, sir. I believe I interrupted your thought."

"No need. As I was saying, I served there before the war started and now I am a chaplain in the army. It is altogether possible that the Almighty arranged this meeting."

Jonah's eyes lit up for a second as the hope of freedom sprang forth. Nathaniel caught his changed expression and quickly countered, "Jonah, there is nothing I can do for you or your people. Our law is clear. If we find runaways, we must return them to their owners if possible. If not, they are sold at auction. Since you provided them safe haven, you're guilty of aiding their escape, punishable by death. If you were a white man, we'd summarily execute you. Because you're not, we can let you live as a slave. You should be thankful."

Jonah could hold his tongue and temper no longer. The arrogance in Nathaniel's tone had to be challenged. "Captain Graham, why should I be thankful? You can't believe that I, or any man, would want to trade freedom for a life in bondage! Death would be welcome over slavery!"

"Now you better watch what you say, boy," Nathaniel became defensive and resorted to deeper arrogance. "I could have you shot, or I could shoot you myself right here. No one would care one twit!"

Jonah was fearless and pressed the matter further. He approached Nathaniel saying, "I said it and I meant it. Death would be better than bondage. I think you're correct believing that God ordained our meeting. But I think it is for different reasons than you assume. You claim to be a chaplain. I suspect that you should be familiar with the apostle Paul's letter to the Galatians?"

Nathaniel tried to calm his boiling anger as he replied, "I am."

Jonah peered deeply into Nathaniel's eyes. "Captain, I am a Christian, saved by God's grace and the finished work Jesus performed on the cross. He was brutally tortured and died for my sins."

Nathaniel acknowledged, "He did that for me too."

"Then sir, I ask you," Jonah was not about to let up now. "Did Jesus die for all mankind?"

Nathaniel answered mechanically, without hesitation or thinking, "Of course."

"As a man, I recognize that it was my sin that nailed Jesus to that cross. I repented of my sin and I received His free gift of salvation. His work transforms a mere man who is dead in his sins to become alive to God. Do you agree?"

Nathaniel had to agree with this line of reasoning, but so far, he could only nod. Jonah continued, emboldened by the truth, "So only men and women can receive salvation, not animals, correct?"

Again, Nathaniel nodded. Something made him feel uncertain deep inside his chest. He was dealing with a thinking being.

Jonah quoted, "Stand fast therefore in the liberty wherewith Christ hath made us free."

Nathaniel finally spoke, "Galatians chapter five, verse one. I know it well."

"Then I ask you, Captain, how is it that one brother in Christ can with biblical authority hold another brother in Christ in bondage when Jesus died to set all captives free? We are all men, not animals, captured by sin. Jesus purchased my freedom and yours with His blood. It is His truth, this truth that makes us and keeps us free. What gives you or any other Christian the right to treat me like a dumb animal of instinct and keep me, a fellow believer, in slavery? I think Fredrick Douglas said it well when he stated that any Christian who holds another in captivity, that man's Christianity is false!"

Quiet!" Nathaniel yelled. "I'll hear no more of this!" Nathaniel pulled Marvin's recent gift from its holster, and pointed it at Jonah's face. "I should shoot you right here, right now. You're nothing worth saving." *Is he a man? No, it's not possible. He's one smart Negro.* "Move!" Nathaniel commanded heatedly.

Nathaniel marched Jonah down the hill back to the main part of town. Jonah walked with the same confidence he displayed earlier. Nathaniel kept his Colt pointed at Jonah's back. *Why isn't he afraid?*

As they walked, Jonah said, "You may place me in bondage Captain, but God Almighty will set me free at His appointed time."

"Quiet I said," Nathaniel fumed.

"Go ahead, shoot me if you must," Jonah said calmly. "You will have to answer before the Judge of all mankind for how you treated His lowly ones. I've heard you Southerners say that you are fighting for your rights. Like it or not, because the Confederate army kidnapped us and is enslaving us, you solders just made this war all about slavery. God will rescue His people from bondage and He will choose the way He will deliver us from the sin of slavery. He will choose the man through whom He will work His sovereign will. Just remember what He did to the Egyptians, Captain Graham."

Nathaniel said nothing. They reached the area where the Rebels held the other Negroes. Nathaniel turned Jonah over to the soldier in charge. Jonah began to mix with the others who had found places to rest before they moved deeper into Virginia with the wagon trains full of supplies from the arsenal at Harper's Ferry. As Nathaniel left, he commanded, "Keep a close eye on that one. He's a troublemaker. Feel free to shoot him if he causes a problem."

Nathaniel walked quickly back up the hill toward the camp. He observed dark storm clouds gathering. *The prophet Jonah brought a clear warning to the people of Nineveh. Lord, did you send this Jonah to me?*

"General Lee, we were fortunate that General McClellan didn't attack us today," Major Taylor observed as he straightened maps and reports in his commander's headquarters.

"Yes, Major, he probably took the entire day to prepare his battle plans with his staff. God has spared us, granting us precious time to position our troops."

"We are ready whenever the Yankees attack."

"We must learn from his mistake. He failed to act swiftly. Had he attacked us today, he could have taken our entire army piecemeal."

"Well, sir, most of Jackson's Second Corps anchors our left flank near the Dunker Church along the Hagerstown Pike, and General Longstreet's First Corps holds strong natural defensive positions in our center and right flank."

Lee paced; he folded his hands behind his back. "With the Potomac River at our back, I've left this army no avenue of escape. Major, we will have to fight to survive."

"Yes, sir. We're ready. If the Yankees attack in the morning, our boys will give them what for, sir.

General Lee wished he shared his adjutant's enthusiasm.

Darkness fell on this quiet small farm community. The campfires of the contesting armies dotted the surrounding countryside and looked like a ground-based constellation. An early autumn rain began to fall, distorting the flaming images.

Major Duffy sat at his field desk in his regimental headquarters' tent near Harper's Ferry. He stroked Maggie's back and scratched her ears while he reviewed his regiment's troop-strength reports. The regiment needed to be ready if called upon in the morning. Maggie settled down and curled at his feet, took a deep breath, exhaled loudly, and let herself fall asleep.

Of the more than one thousand men that had left Mississippi a mere four months before, Major Duffy's outfit had less than eight hundred active for fighting. He greatly missed his mentor, Colonel Cummings. He hoped that he would never forget the things Colonel Cummings taught him about command. Of the twenty-plus sick and wounded that could travel with the army, two company commanders, Nathaniel and Marvin, were still unfit for duty. Major Duffy would command his friends to stay with the ill and injured in the rear and simply be available to help care for the men that would soon fall.

A band of rain beat heavily upon a tent pitched several miles east of Antietam Creek. John kept talking to his older, sleepy brother. John could feel the tension building as rain pounded their little shelter. Paul felt lost and alone, still haunted by his own cowardice. He demanded with a false bravado, "John, please go to sleep. I'm tired. I don't care what tomorrow brings. If we fight, we fight. If we die, we die."

John wouldn't, couldn't let it go. He didn't understand his older brother's lack of concern for what their end might do to their mother and sister. John acquiesced, "I just can't stop worrying about Ma and Ellie, but you're right, we need to get some sleep.

If we march into action tomorrow, we need to be rested, ready. Good-night, Paul."

Paul rolled over on his cot and responded in kind, "Good-night, John. We'll speak more of this in the morning."

Paul pretended to drift off to sleep, but fear took control. John stared at the canvas sheet inches above him that prevented the rain from hitting him in the face. Sleep eluded both men.

Sometime after midnight, Major Taylor left Lieutenant General Robert E. Lee alone in his tent. An oil lamp hung from the tent's center cross-pole and burned steadily, softly illuminating his field headquarters. He had distributed battle orders earlier. He knew his men would follow them without question. Lee made a few final entries into his logbook and closed it for the night. He took his chair and set it near the middle of his tent. Then he opened one tent flap and let the cool, moist air fill his lungs. The rain slowed to a misty drizzle. He turned and paced back and forth inside his tent for a few minutes. He stopped, looked up toward Heaven, closed his eyes and sat down into his chair. He bowed his head and prayed. Settled that God held the future in His capable hands and that He would accomplish His purposes, Lee breathed deeply, satisfied that the Almighty heard his prayer. With his eyes still closed, he finally sat upright, crossed his legs, relaxed, and looked outside of his tent toward a bright light in the east. Somewhere beyond the blaze the Federal army encamped just over the far ridge.

Confederate Brigadier General Roswell S. Ripley ordered his men to ransack a lush family farm and meticulously kept farmhouse. Second-generation immigrants, the Mumma family, owned the property. They were pillars in this very religious community of Dunker's, pacifists who simply wanted to live their lives separated from the rest of the self-consuming world. They wanted nothing to do with this terrible war. General Ripley's men stripped the Mumma farm of all valuables, livestock, and harvested food. As if this were not enough, General Ripley decided that the Mumma barn and farmhouse posed a strategic threat. He concluded that these buildings would provide a perfect shelter for Yankee snipers. He ordered his men to set fire to these structures in the early, pre-dawn morning of Wednesday, September 17, 1862.

Many Federal troops and Northern newspaper reporters observed this horrible atrocity. Shortly thereafter, telegraph wires carried the story. Within hours, a cry for retribution reached Abraham Lincoln who pressed General McClellan for action. This news filled the Federal military with rage and purpose, more so than ever before. Prior to this morning, they marched to save the Union. Now they wanted to destroy the enemy and everything the South represented.

Major General George B. McClellan signed the order, folded it, and stuffed it into the envelope addressed to Major General Joseph Hooker. He called for a courier and commanded him to deliver the dispatch directly to General Hooker as fast as possible. Moments later, General "Fighting Joe" Hooker moved his First Corp, approximately eight thousand, five hundred men, into attack position along both east and west sides of the Hagerstown Pike, just north of David Miller's farm and cornfield outside of Sharpsburg, Maryland.

Many miles away, Eleanor slept soundly, peacefully, in her bed. She dreamed, and in her dream she is confused. It is a future time. She searches through a town she does not recognize, for what she can't determine. She has a strange encounter with a man she's never met. "Yes, I can help." She falls deeper into a restful sleep.

Marvin breathed deeply and began to snore to the rhythm of the heavy raindrops tapping gently on the tent canopy. His back turned away from the dim oil lamp that sat on Nathaniel's small writing table.

> …*It is a few minutes past three in the morning. I know I should be sleeping. A horrible fight is coming. Everyone can feel it. Some other terrible sense of foreboding grips my heart. I shouldn't burden you with my problems. I am certain you have your own. The thing is I have no one to talk with about what troubles me. Should I fall, I wanted someone to know my thoughts and prayers.*
>
> *I am questioning everything I once believed to be true about this terrible war. General Breckinridge told me that this war is all about power, and who controls it. Some say it is a fight for independence. Others say it is a fight to preserve the Union—a noble cause, but why would anyone be willing to die for it. Surely, no one would be so foolish. There must be something more. We've been fighting for more than a year and half with no end in sight. Possibly God Almighty drives this war forward for His own purposes. I do not pretend to comprehend.*
>
> *Tonight at our prayer meeting, I preached a sermon using Romans chapter five verses one through eight as my text. I emphasized verses three through five and expressed that we can have hope in Christ. Through this terrible tribulation of war,*

He is working hope in us so that we should not be ashamed of our service to Him. I finished, as I always do when I use this passage, with verse eight and only glanced over verse seven. I believe the Lord wanted me to address verse seven but maybe it only applies to me.

I met someone today who held a different perspective. His name is Jonah Benjamin, a church pastor. He is a Negro. He claimed to be a freedman and kidnapped, forced into slavery at gunpoint. His words haunt me. If what he said is true, slavery fuels the fire of war between our people. I wonder, is slavery a national sin? If so, have we chosen rebellion over repentance, war over reconciliation? Are we so stiff-necked that God brought upon us this great calamity to liberate a captive people? How can we know? I would deeply appreciate your view on this matter.

I have wrestled with this question in the word of God. I thought I knew the answers. Every issue seemed clear. Now I am not so sure. Here is where those verses from Romans trouble me. They say, "For scarcely for a righteous man will one die: yet peradventure for a good man some would even dare to die. But God commandeth his love toward us, in that, while we were yet sinners, Christ died for us." Did Jesus die for Negroes, too? If Negroes are people who can receive God's redemption, and if it is a sin to hold one of His children in bondage, then I need to repent and seek His forgiveness. If Jonah is right, I can see how it is that he has such strong hope. If God is with him, I may have joined myself to fight for a cause that separates me from my comrades in arms, my country, my family, and Almighty God. If He shows me that slavery is the source and substance of our national tragedy, then I may find myself a traitor. If I desert the army, the penalty is death. I must seek God for His wisdom. He may ask me to help set them free because that is what my Lord would do, which is exactly what He did for *me. If I set even one slave free, it could cost me my life. Am I willing to pay that price for redemption? I fear I will fall short, be measured a coward. What would you do?*

I pray that I will have another opportunity to write to you. God's will be done.

Your servant,
Nathaniel

Nathaniel sealed the letter, and extinguished the oil lamp. He would deliver it to Captain Boyd at first light, before breakfast, and the much-anticipated march into battle. Nathaniel's mind wandered considering the possibilities. *I hope God, that You will show me what I must do.*

Dawn would break in less than two hours. With it, the world would watch a new light of liberty rise above the horizon of this young, war-torn nation.

Pleasant
Word